EXTINCTION NOTICE

Tales of a Warming Earth

EDITED BY
DAVID HARTEN WATSON

Silver Sword Press

Extinction Notice
Tales of a Warming Earth

V3.0 R1.1

Silver Sword Press

Paperback ISBN: 978-0-578-26285-7
Hardback ISBN: 978-0-578-26286-4

PRINTED IN THE UNITED STATES OF AMERICA

Praise for Extinction Notice

"Terribly entertaining... David Harten Watson has collated the work of several extremely talented authors to create *Extinction Notice*... a timely collection with just enough levity so the reader does not feel they are being preached to and just enough weight to start a reader down the road of thoughtful self-examination; both being delivered in a blend of science fiction and satire... A delicious mix that is fresh and exciting. You don't know what will come next, and that is what makes it so much fun...This book is a vacation of its own..."

~Asher Syed for Readers' Favorite (5-star review)

"The beauty of the book is in the variety of voices presented that highlight the skill and storytelling ability of its contributors, something that is not usually accomplished in a volume with a single author... This is an excellent collection that I have no doubt will warm the hearts and tickle the imaginations of its readers."

~Jamie Michele for Readers' Favorite (5-star review)

"David Harten Watson has put together an ideal collection for enthusiasts and newcomers to the genre alike, delivering a wonderful variety of entertaining and genuinely frightening realities to explore... Every single story had its own charm and style and was based on interesting and thought-provoking ideas about climate problems and, perhaps more importantly, the consequences and/or solutions that the future may bring, depending on how we act now... I would not hesitate to recommend Extinction Notice to readers from all walks of life. Get yourself a copy now."

~K.C. Finn for Readers' Favorite (5-star review)

To our children's children's children.
May you still have a livable Earth to inherit,
with a diversity of flora and fauna.

Silver Sword Press®
Avenel, New Jersey, USA

Profits from this cli-fi anthology will go to environmental charities to raise public awareness of anthropogenic climate change and help combat global warming.

All of the stories in this book are fictional. All of the characters in this anthology are fictitious except for notable public figures, including a former president of the United States, whose name, personality, and misdeeds are chronicled and parodied in accordance with the First Amendment to the United States Constitution, which protects political satire (at least as long as America remains a free country that respects the Constitution).

Contents

Part One:

The Past (250,000,000 BC to January 2021)

1

Extinction Notice

by TJ Esteves (United States)

Subgenres: Humor, science fiction

Time Period: 250 million years ago

Setting: An ocean reef off the coast of what is now Yorkshire, England

Introduction: The Permian Extinction, Permian-Triassic Extinction Event, or "Great Dying" occurred a little over 250 million years ago. It resulted in the extinction of over 70% of terrestrial species and 96% of marine species, including the famous trilobites. It is the only known mass extinction of insects. Devastation to the planet's biodiversity was so severe, it would take almost ten million years for it to recover to Permian levels.

Scientists believe the Permian Extinction happened because mass volcanism in the Siberian Traps triggered the burning of massive quantities of coal and natural gas. Through this burning of proto-fossil-fuels, the planet's carbon cycle rapidly changed, resulting in a runaway greenhouse effect. As methane was released, the oceans quickly acidified into a toxic soup, while the land of the supercontinent of Pangaea turned arid and unlivable.

While Earth has not seen this level of devastation since, the Permian Extinction serves as a grim reminder of the horrors resulting from interrupting the planet's carbon cycle.

. . .

Terry T. Trilobite was rather surprised to see a notice from his species' union pinned to the front of his reef cavern, but even more surprised by the contents.

Hello,

Please be advised that the subphylum Trilobitomorpha has been marked for extinction by the Planetary Species Commission. You will have approximately three days to vacate the premises and the planet. We thank you for your 270-million years of service and wish you the best of luck in future endeavors.

Sincerely,

Planetary Species Commission.

Terry's antennae twitched a bit as he let the words settle. In disbelief, he stared out over his kelp hedges, carefully manicured in the style so popular amongst his peers. The reef, although bleached and a shadow of its former self, still had the ghost of activity about it: cephalopods and fish swimming to and fro, seaweed shuttering in the ocean currents. Terry even thought he could spot the crazy old nautilus that sat on the edge of his outcropping, raving about the end times and holding up a sign that read, "If it happened to the Placoderms, it'll happen to us!"

Once the shock had settled, Terry felt denial settling in,

racing into his mind as he instinctively spoke, "What the bloody hell is this nonsense?" He pulled himself up and scurried across the yard to his neighbor's cavern, where he found Bill trimming his kelp hedges as if nothing were wrong.

"Morning, Bill."

"Up me duck?" Bill asked, his heavy accent from years of working and scavenging on the Yorkshire Reef as colloquially blue-collar as it had always been.

Terry wasn't quite sure what a "duck" was but gave a knowing smile and nod all the same. "You see the extinction notice today?"

"Oh, ay, right shock that was," Bill said, lowering his pincers that he'd been using to manicure the hedges. "I'd 'eard there was somethin' big goin' on up on land for some while now. But never thought it'd affect us down 'ere."

"Did you hear anything from Harry at work about it?"

"Nay, he didn't mention anythin' to me 'bout it."

"Well," Terry said, "I am going down to the union headquarters and giving Harry a piece of my mind. I've been a loyal and hardworking member of this species all my life. My father, and his father, and his father before him, and all my ancestors have worked on this reef, cleaning up the mess others leave behind. I'm not taking this lying down."

"Mind if I tag along?" Bill asked, "If we're goin' extinct, might as well collect and spend the last month's wages."

Terry and Bill set off, scurrying down the sandy bottom of the reef. As they passed the edge of the outcropping, Terry was heartened to see the crazy old nautilus was indeed there. He floated about the ground, his buoyancy a bit wobbly, his shell dissolved in places from the recent spike in ocean acidification. The nautilus' sign had changed, and now read, "When Dimetrodons Die, the End is Nigh."

"Bloody Dimetrodons," Terry said after they were out of earshot, "Develop a sail and manage to make something of the Synapsid Union and suddenly they're getting all the business."

"No point gettin' riled 'bout it," Bill said, "A couple million years from now, do ye think anybody will be talkin' 'bout Dimetrodons?"

"Bloody hope not," Terry said, "Good riddance."

They continued through the once-colorful reefs and dusty, sand-coated streets. Passing through the main square, Terry noted that nearly all the shops were shuttered. Signs hung in the cavernous holes that had once served as windows, explaining in various iterations that, due to increasing ocean acidity, they have been forced to close.

"Harry," Terry said as he used one of his several dozen legs to push over the small rock to Harry's office. Inside, Harry sat at his desk, his arced head resting on the table. While Harry had always had poor exoskeletal posture from a lifetime of exhausting and stressful disputing with Planetary Boards for union rights, he seemed particularly hunched and broken today. "What the bloody hell is this?" Terry asked, brandishing the extinction notice about his desk.

"Oh, hello gents. I see you've gotten your notices," Harry said. His voice was rather upbeat, a contrast to his ragged appearance. The sort of upbeat that came to trilobites and other marine organisms when they realized they had nothing else to lose and felt liberated by the fact.

"Aye, we got alright," Bill said, "Bit of a pisser, nay?"

"Yes, unfortunately the Trilobite Union couldn't do much to save the subphylum," Harry said, "I'm terribly sorry about it."

"You're 'sorry'?" Terry said, using a few of his several dozen legs to emphasize the sarcasm in his voice, "We're going *extinct,* Harry."

Harry's antennae twitched, and he sighed. "Terry, if there's something I could do about this, I'd have done it already. The union isn't what it used to be. I'm surprised we even managed to get a three-day grace period."

"We can file an appeal with the Planetary Species Commission," Terry suggested.

"They've made it clear that their decision is final," Harry said, "The ocean's just too acidic to support hard-shelled life. Maybe in another few million years there will be openings for descendants of trilobites..."

"Oy, we've been good workers," Bill said, "We've gone and pioneered scavengin' *and* filter feedin'. That's got to be worth somethin'."

"It's worth three days of notice," Harry said.

"Is that all?" Terry asked, "I mean...we're *trilobites*. We built this oceanic ecosystem."

"But we can't keep up with the times," Harry said, "It's all about jawed and boney organisms nowadays."

"Oh, that's what they said about the placoderms, and look what happened to them," Terry said.

Harry shrugged. "Maybe. Maybe not. The Planetary Species Commission has seen promise in some upcoming species. Crocodylomorphs and archosaurs and the like. But I just don't think trilobites will be able to compete. We've had a good run over the past 270 million years, but it looks like we've reached our end."

"...This is all because of those Siberian Traps erupting, isn't it?" Terry asked, "Couldn't we relocate to another reef? One with cooler water?"

"Gentlemen, the tropics are like saunas. There's no reef there. There's no reef anywhere. They've all died," Harry said.

Terry was silent for a long moment. "Couldn't we adapt?" He asked, despite knowing the answer.

Harry shook his front lobe. "No time. The volcanoes are spewing carbon into the air at record rates. Even if we evolved to live without hardened shells, what'd we do? Even the plankton are going extinct."

"Well...damn..."

Terry felt himself collapse back down onto a collection of shells in the shape of a chair. The cold, unfeeling realization of extinction settled on him. Bill seemed to be taking it better, removing his deerstalker hat and holding it over his thorax, a salute to a species on the way out. Harry sat behind the desk, twiddling his dozens of microscopic fingers together.

"That's it, then?" Terry asked, "Three days?"

"That's it," Harry nodded.

"Any suggestions?"

Harry shrugged. "Enjoy it," he said, "First and last time in your life you don't have the Planetary Species Commission breathing down your backs."

With that bittersweet advice, Terry rose and scurried towards the door, with Bill in tow. He heard a rumbling from Harry, as if he were about to speak. He didn't. Terry and Harry left, returning to the main square. Things were quieter now.

"Fancy a pint?" Bill asked.

"Yes, I suspect that'll do nicely," Terry said, changing their course for the pub, "Still hard to believe. A world without trilobites."

"Won't be so bad. New folks'll manage," Bill said, "Maybe those archosaurs will do somethin' good with the planet."

"I'm sure they will," Terry said, "It's just..." He sighed, staring up past the ocean canopy at the distant sun and hazy atmosphere, created from burning countless tons of carbon. In the Siberian Traps, the volcanoes were likely still burning, sealing the doom of nearly all Permian life. Terry sighed again, left at a loss of what to do.

"Extinction," He said, "I just never thought it'd happen to us..."

. . .

About the author:

TJ Esteves is a writer and editor. TJ has hundreds of hours of experience editing and writing compelling content and stories, largely in the addiction treatment industry. When he's not crafting stories for work or for hobby, he prefers to spend his free time reading, writing, or fencing at his local academy.

2

The Space Traveler's Calculus

by Benjamin S. Grossberg (United States)

Subgenres: Poetry, science fiction

Time Period: Neanderthal age (40,000 years ago) and the present day

Setting: The speaker of the poems, an alien, is traveling through space, addressing humanity.

. . .

You? Your fate was sealed the moment
you set a ring of stones around a fire:
in some Neanderthal night, the collective
tremor of northern species, and global
air circulation pausing a moment
to apprehend change. I'd like to think
the stars, too, clarified in translucent
darkness, that for a moment all
burned blue, looked down
in an earnest convocation.

. . .

What to say, human? That generally
by the time a trajectory becomes clear,
it's essentially completed? That causes
swim in conclusions? Now you know.
Now I know, too. And though
from up here I'm unable to help you,
I will say—pondering your world—
no destination seems so important, no
work trumps my attention like your
gloved hands, tenderness conducted
through latex and scrub brush toward
all those small lives you have ruined.

. . .

Perhaps a few decades from now
an interstellar cavalry will arrive—
do-gooder species watching your
accelerating bleed, moved, will pull
you back from the ledge by the x
of your crossed suspenders, will deposit
you and such Earthly life as remains
on a pristine world. Imagine
the pods launching out like bees
from a flaming hive, the furious drones
cooling with distance, and then
the landing—chrome studs among
long grasses, a field wide as Kansas.
Fanciful? Had I been there, human,

I'd have poked the Neanderthal
on the shoulder, tapped my snappish
foot until he handed me that first rock.
Then I'd have clocked him with it.

. . .

About the Author:

Benjamin S. Grossberg's books include *Space Traveler* (University of Tampa Press, 2014) and *Sweet Core Orchard*, winner of a Lambda Literary Award and the Tampa Review Prize (University of Tampa Press, 2009). His work has appeared widely, including in the *Best American Poetry* and *Pushcart Prize* anthologies. A new collection, *My Husband Would*, was published by the University of Tampa Press in 2019.

3

When We Are Ready, We Will Understand Why They Waited

by Charles Venable (United States)

WARNING: This story may be disturbing for younger readers due to Holocaust themes.

Subgenre: Historical science fiction

Time Period: World War II (1939 to 1945)

Setting: Nazi Germany

Editor's introduction: This story is perhaps the most emotionally moving story in the anthology, so even though it has less climate change content than others, I felt compelled to include it. The story describes the darkest episode in modern human history, the Holocaust, as seen through the eyes of an alien explorer from beyond the stars. The explorer's mission is to assess whether Earth is habitable and hospitable to civilized life, or if humans are so dangerous that they must be exterminated. The explorer couldn't have picked a worse time or place to judge the worthiness of humanity...

. . .

The mountains were the explorer's landing site, remote enough so no natives would notice, but close to their civilization centers. As his ship descended into the atmosphere, he saw, through the clouds, the land he'd soon explore, the cities he'd soon visit. They were marked by columns of black smoke rising from chimneys. Everything was stone and steel: the buildings, the houses, even the roads cutting through the wilderness like lines of fungus.

No, there was no wilderness in the land he'd chosen, only countryside. Humans were still primitive, territorial. They drew lines to set up their domain, and in that domain, they ravaged everything: cutting down trees, mining the earth, polluting the air and waters. They'd discovered the power of harnessing anaerobic decomposites to pronounced effect; now, they used them at a great speed, with little care for the repercussions.

To the west, a different kind of smoke rose. He almost couldn't blame them for their lack of foresight when they were distracted with a major conflict. They were territorial creatures, and they liked expanding that territory. He'd seen the cycle hundreds of times before. Some species broke it, some didn't. He was here to find out if this species could.

Snow blanketed the mountainside, caught in the crooks of black pines or piling up around their roots. Above, the peak of the mountains faded into mist; the sun was a faint glimmer through the clouds, only a whisper of light reflecting off a rippling brook running down the mountain, between the trees. Ice clung to its bank, and snowflakes found their way into the water, carried away to the sea.

Here, the conflict and the civilization seemed distant. He'd enjoyed this mission, thus far. The planet was beautiful. With proper care, it could be a great refuge. He could see it here, in the mountains, in the melting snow, in the flowing water.

Near the river, a natural spring bubbled up to become a

trickling creek, half-frozen. A gray-furred roe deer dipped its snout into the freezing water; its tongue lapped a single mouthful before it froze, muscles tense. The water rippled in an unseen wind, and the deer flitted off into the forest. The ripples cracked the ice, chunks of hoar-frosted crystal carried downstream. Soon, the puddle was dancing; water rose at the center and sprayed the snowdrifts around its banks. The thrum filled the air until snow fell from the trees.

The hollow light of the sun blotted out for a breath before the darkness drifted down through the mist, a perfect sphere of dark metal repelling both light and snow. The air around it wavered like heat off dark stones. As it descended, the water and snow fluttered away as three small holes opened at the base of the sphere, a gust of hot air evaporating the frost and slowing its fall until it floated a meter above the ground. It rotated languidly, like an apple on a branch, until finally, all at once, it fell the last step to the ground. The sphere shook the earth for meters around with a dull thud. It teetered once to the side and went still. The winter air devoured the machine's heat, and coldness returned.

Then it was gone. There was a twist to the air where the sphere lay, but weak winter light passed through it like fingers through hair or a child playing in the snow. Only a careful eye might notice it, but it was surrounded by trees. In the pond, the water dispelled the illusion, revealing the sphere's true form, a dark monolith looming above and behind, unseen. The explorer's ship struck an imposing image where it hung in the sky.

In the dark water, a pale blue light traced another circle on the side of the sphere, larger this time, large enough for the long-legged humanoid to pull himself free and stretch in the open air. Fog drifted from his thin lips. The explorer was a gaunt thing, all legs, arms, neck, and nose, his pale skin stretched over his long frame, taut as leather on the tanning rack. His lips and chin were small, pinched in, like a perpetual pucker, and his tiny eyes blinked in the dim light. Wide pupils contracted until they were black pinpricks in a yellow-white frame. He had no hair or eyebrows, and the ridge of his skull protruded from the crown of his head, an uncomfortable knot of bone. His fingers stretched out, flexed, curled into fists. A shiver ran up his body, and his arms wound around himself.

"Report: this place," he whispered with a voice like dead grass, "is cold."

The words were slow, practiced; the glottal language of the locals: Prussian? No, German.

"They were Prussian last century," he reminded himself.

One hand reached through the opening in his ship and pulled out a long coat of slick black, like leather coated with oil. He draped it over his shoulders and sighed as warmth found its weight between the wrinkles.

He warmed himself by crisscrossing the clearing, his long legs making the trip in only a few strides. Water and snow went into vials. He popped one open, wiggled it three times, and capped it, writing *Luft der Erde* on the side with a little pen. He'd arrived about a century into this species' industrial revolution. This would make a good control to test the larger environmental impact. After each sample was taken, he set it gently in the ship until finally all the tasks were done, and he stood alone in the clearing, shivering in the chill.

"Report: the planet's diverse ecosystems make an excellent intergalactic settlement. Even lower-class lifeforms will find suitable—"

The air shattered; a distant explosion echoing through the trees and up the mountainside. He turned towards the noise, staring curiously. He licked his lips once; his tongue was gray, almost black.

A second shot confirmed the direction of the explosion, and he stepped in a cautious circle around his ship before disappearing into the trees. The branches slapped at his chest and arms, needles catching on his coat. He cursed in a language that was certainly not German and yanked it free with each stride through the underbrush. His feet disappeared into the snow, missing for a moment, but returning each moment a little colder. He had no coat for his feet.

"Their word for it is... *Stiefel*," he reminded himself.

His German was poor; he could never get the vibrations right in the back of his throat, but he learned the proper way to say the word when he heard it only a few meters ahead, through the trees. He pressed forward, faster now, happy to see his first of the indigenous tribes of the planet, until all at once, he crashed out of the trees into the middle of three brown tents bearing a brilliant, black and white symbol on a red background. Near a crackling fire sat six local men in gray wool coats that fluttered to their thighs.

When he entered the clearing, all six locals jumped at the noise, grabbing long, metallic weapons resting beside them. These primitive firearms were the primary means of protection for the *Erdelings*, as they were called. All pointed their weapons at him.

"Please, don't shoot," He lifted his long arms, a sign of peace, according to his research.

The one closest to him backed two steps away, putting the fire between them; another leaned to his friend and spoke quietly.

"Who are you? State your business," one ordered.

"Hello, I am Johann." He picked a common name for ease. "I want company and warmth for the night. I am lost."

"I'll bet he is," another said, "Look at his nose; he's a Jew."

Johann's long fingers crept to his nose; like the rest of him, it was long and hooked. There were many humans with similar features, if less exaggerated.

"Hands up!" The soldier ordered.

His hand returned to the position of surrender. All the men seemed on edge; according to the last broadcasts received from the planet, prior to his arrival, the locals were going through an economic depression; their tension was understandable.

"I am not here to hurt you," Johann explained, "I am researching—"

"Quiet!"

He stopped talking, lips pressed into an almost invisible line. The man rounded the fire and approached him, the barrel of his firearm aimed directly at Johann. He did not shoot, as the visitor expected; instead, the tip of the gun found the edge of his dark cloak and flipped it aside to reveal Johann's own uniform. The soldiers behind the man gasped, and their hands tightened around their weapons. Johann glanced down: it was a plain, gray suit, mostly form-fitting, though comfortably loose around the wrists and ankles. His planet's flag, light and dark gray stripes, made up most of the suit's design.

"He must have escaped from Dachau," One whispered.

"No, I am not from—"

"I said, quiet!" The man in front of him whipped the rifle around and slammed the wooden stock into his midsection.

Johann's hands flicked down to protect his vitals, but the blow came too fast. A flash of pain ran through his body, and he reeled back. His mid-section contained the fluid-filled sac containing his brain, and he collapsed, stunned, nearly unconscious. Above him, the soldier loomed, a blurry shadow, like his own ship descending through the mist.

"Weak constitution..." the words faded out, "...him up... back to Dachau..."

He felt the frosty snow on his cheeks; the white winter turned black.

. . .

When he awoke, the ground vibrated beneath him; no, he was in a vehicle with no windows, only the dim light filtering through breaks in a canvas tarp covering a metal frame. He was not alone. The soldiers from the camp in the mountains sat around him, weapons resting on their laps, fingers never far from the triggers. His own hands were bound with lengths of thick rope. They'd stripped his cloak away, leaving him in only his gray-striped uniform while they bundled in their warm wool coats. The cold seeped in through the tarp, and their breath misted the air in front of them: a sharp hiss from flared nostrils. The rumbling automobile left the sound behind as they bounded over uneven road.

Johann glanced through a gap in the tarp, but a heavy hand grabbed the nape of his neck and pulled his head back into a stiff seated position. The soldier glared at him but said nothing. When he released his head, the soldier wiped his hands on his pants.

The rope dug into his wrists, turning his pale skin an angry red. Every movement pulled the coarse fibers against his flesh. He winced. The *Erdelings* watched him cautiously, their fingers drawing closer to their triggers each time he moved. Seeing this, Johann went still, accepting the discomfort.

"Where are you taking me?"

Nobody answered.

The truck followed a bumpy mountain road for several hours; Johann only knew it was in the mountains as he felt the change in elevation. He closed his eyes so they would not bulge: the fluid sacs behind them expanding and contracting as the air pressure changed. It always took a moment to balance. When he opened his eyes, he watched one soldier stick a finger into his ear and swallow. The man beside him swatted his hand away; they scowled at one another.

After a single, heavy bump that nearly threw the men from their seats, the road levelled, and all Johann heard was the hum of the engine and the vibration of the tires against what he assumed was one of the tar and stone roads the locals used. He leaned back against the wall, but one of the poles constituting the back of the truck's frame dug into his lower back. He sighed, and two fingers reached for their triggers. He pressed his lips into a thin line and pretended not to notice.

Explorers getting captured wasn't uncommon, but it was rare to get captured so soon after his landing. He wondered if he had set a new record; when he returned, he'd have to check the Explorers Federation's books. His eyes fell to one of their firearms; then again, he might be stuck here for a while.

Hours later, the truck trundled to a stop, and the soldiers grabbed him roughly by the shoulders, forced him out into the snow. He stumbled twice and came to rest in the middle of the road, in front of an expanse of wire fences extending left and right as far as his eyes could see through the thick mist. An iron gate loomed ahead of him. Atop the arch was the odd symbol the humans wore on their uniforms: a whirling spiral of right angles and edges, and in the local language were the words "Work Makes Free." To his right, the trees pressed close to the encampment. One tree bore a heavy rope about its trunk. His eyes followed the length up to where it twisted around a thick branch and then again around the torso of a nude man. His skin was blue with the cold, and he swung lightly in the winter wind. It turned him to face the squad of soldiers escorting the emaciated alien into the camp. The cold barrel of a rifle pressed into Johann's back, and he stumbled forward, through the gates, past the guards, into Dachau.

As Johann stepped inside, the smell of mountains and diesel hid behind the stench of unwashed bodies: sweat, blood, and sickness. The camp was mostly empty, as they entered, with only a few guards visible. They saw the approach of the squad, and quietly exchanged German with the squad leader. One disappeared inside a squad house. A moment later, a short, fat man whose uniform was too small for him stepped out into the snow; unlike the others, he wore a thick fur coat of some russet animal. He eyed Johann, eyes running up and down his body. When he approached, Johann had to look down to meet the man's gaze.

The officer grabbed his wrist and turned it over, even pulled back the sleeve. He snorted once and turned on his heel.

"This is not one of ours. He has not been processed."

"And his clothes?" the squad leader asked.

"Stolen, maybe."

"He is a Jew."

The officer turned to look Johann up and down again. A low rumble rose in his throat, the flabs of his neck vibrating. Johann's face remained flat, lips pressed into a thin line.

"So it seems. We will happily take him," The officer pointed to two of the guards, "Bring him around to be processed."

The squad leader wrung his hands, "And our reward for bringing you this escaped prisoner?"

One guard pointed his rifle at Johann and ordered him to walk forward; the officer and squad leader's dickering disappeared into the mist. The soldiers guided Johann past the guardhouse and two squat, concrete buildings, until he was at a larger structure of stone. The air around it stunk of ash and acrid smoke: some kind of gas. Johann wiped his nose on his sleeve to stifle the scent. The soldier prodded him with the barrel of the gun to prompt him forward.

Inside, the next hour and a half were a whirlwind for the poor visitor. They marred his pilot's uniform with a yellow, six-pointed star. In the middle was the word "*Jude*"—according to his research, it was the designation for the planet's financial elite, a synonym of bankers. He didn't understand why they'd imprison bankers. Next, they pulled up his sleeve and stabbed a needle into his arm over and over until a line of blue numbers stung his skin.

After that was a series of questions from a soldier with wire-frame spectacles:

"Where are you from?"

"City."

"What city?"

"The name of the city is City."

"Is that in Germany?"

"No."

The man grunted and wrote "Polish" onto the page.

"Name?"

"Johann."

"Surname?"

"None."

The man grunted again, and the questioning continued, a series of questions with only half-answers and half-truths. One of the cardinal rules of the Federation was to never reveal their origin to non-indoctrinated natives. The obfuscation earned him a few blows from the soldier, but eventually, the questioning came to an end, and they led him out of the massive building into one of the barracks. It all took less than an hour: an hour to go from a freed man to a prisoner, with no trial. Johann sighed, watching the mist rise in front of his eyes until he was inside the squat building.

It was a long, one-story structure made of stone. Inside, three-tier bunk beds lined the walls, so close together the only way to climb in was to do so from the foot. The smell of sickness and sweat permeated the air here. Most of the beds were empty, but a few were filled with bodies, still as death, only moving to shake with fits of coughing or sneezing. Their pale skin was mottled blue with cold and red with fever.

"This is your bunk."

Johann stepped towards the closest bed, but the soldier stopped him, "No. Not now. Now, you work."

. . .

They brought him out of the prison camp into an enormous block of a building leaking foul-smelling smoke into the sky. It mingled with the winter clouds until the air weighed down on him like a stinking blanket. Inside, he heard the rumble of machinery.

He sniffed the air: carbon ash. The smoke was most likely

a mixture of carbon dioxide and monoxide, along with particulates. It was common for pre-spacefaring societies to rely on combustible fuels. The Explorers Federation made a point to get to habitable planets before environmental damage occurred that might infringe on intergalactic settlements.

"The burning of anaerobic decomposites is an unsustainable means of production, long-term," he said.

For the first time in their long walk, he provoked a reaction from the guard, though it was only to turn with a look of dumb confusion. Johann did not expect the man to lean forward and sniff his breath.

"Are you drunk, Jew?"

"I am not intoxicated. I am merely stating—"

"What is..." the other guard said, "Anaerobic thing?"

"I apologize. The more common term is fossil fuels: sources of power from long dead organisms. Coal, oil, gas."

"Ah, yes, coal. It powers the factory. Be glad you do not work in the mines."

"I will keep that in mind, but it is—"

"Keep moving!"

The butt of the gun shoved into his back, forcing him forward. He decided to capitalize on their interest; perhaps, he could educate them.

"The negative impact of burning fossil fuels for power is an immediate reduction in air quality and water quality."

"No shit," the German spat in the snow. His phlegm was tinted black, like most everything in the shadow of the factory.

"Over the course of a single generation, respiratory and other diseases related to the burning of fossil fuels greatly increases. Within two generations, there is an increased risk of genetic diseases. Would you like the statistic?"

"No. Would you shut up?"

"It's kind of interesting," the other guard whispered.

"Don't encourage him."

"Within one to two centuries, there will be a noticeable

impact on the global environment: global temperature increase, changes in pressure and tidal systems, and the extinction of a wide variety of flora and fauna."

"Good," the guard said, "finally we'll have some nice, warm summers in Bavaria."

Snow crunched under his boot pointedly.

"The damage done can be catastrophic."

"Sure it is. We're here. Take him inside. Give him a job. Maybe that will shut him up."

The guard pushed open the door and motioned for Johann to enter, but before he could step away, the other guard hesitated, hand curling uncomfortably around the hilt of his rifle. He licked his lips.

"What happens after a few centuries?" the curious guard asked.

"Don't tell me you're buying into this crap," snapped the other guard.

Johann stared at the man, "The damage can become irreversible."

The guard grabbed Johann by the arm and forced him into the factory, where the stink of burning coal fell over him like a cloud: everywhere he looked, there was gray.

More prisoners wearing his gray-striped uniform—or one like it—worked on a long metal table. At the far end, a pair of prisoners used long, flat shovels to pull molds out of massive kilns and set them on the table. Inside, dozens of tiny metal cylinders glowed red hot until another prisoner sprayed them with water; the air around him filled with steam. The poor man's hair was matted to his head. Once they were cool, he slid them to the next group, who slid them down and down and down. Some men filled the shells with bits of waxy paper, others poured black powder inside, others fitted pointed bits of metal inside, and the last group hammered them into place.

Only when the soldier brought him close to the long line did he realize they were the metal slugs used in the primitives' firearms: they were making munitions. Some tables worked on munitions for much larger weapons. Johann didn't understand what such a massive slug would be used against. Metal wouldn't pierce spacecraft, and the small ones sufficed for infantry fire.

The soldier shoved him into place on the line beside another man with a pink triangle on his uniform. Johann wondered what it meant.

"Teach him," the soldier barked, and without waiting for a reply, left.

The man was shorter than Johann, but not by much, and he had a head of thick, curly hair: brown with hints of blonde sneaking through the gaps. His eyebrows and beard were just as curly and wiry, and his eyes were a warm brown, though bloodshot and shrouded in dark circles. His pale skin was stained black with soot and powder.

"Welcome to hell," the man handed Johann a hammer, "When the bullets come past, hammer them in. Then shove it to the next group."

As he finished his curt explanation, two boxes of shells slid past, and the man set to work immediately, hammering each into place with a single, practiced swing. Though he was thin and gaunt, Johann saw the muscles in his 'hammer hand' were more pronounced. The stranger wondered how long the man had been here. Mid-swing, the man paused.

"Well? Get to it."

"What is your name?"

The man sniffed once; snot dripped down to his lips. He did not wipe it off.

"Rudolf. But don't bother learning it. If your God exists, I will be dead soon."

With that, the man went quiet, and Johann followed his example, tapping bullet heads into their casings. It was simple, tedious work, and time passed slowly. The silence was one of machinery rumbling, grinding, and turning; it vibrated in Johann's ears.

Eventually, the light in the smoke-stained windows at the top of the building turned darker and darker: always gray, though. Suddenly, Rudolf stopped and stepped back. A second later, a loud whistle hissed through the air, and all the workers stopped at once. Without cleaning up their stations or finishing their tasks, they turned on their heels and filed out of the factory. Johann followed.

Outside, they lined up in two neat lines; opposite the path to the factory, more prisoners formed two lines going in. Soldiers stood watch all around, weapons at the ready. Five minutes later, the second shift disappeared into the smog, and his shift stumbled back to the barracks. Around him, he heard the quiet rumble of empty stomachs. Food was not brought. Inside the barracks, Rudolf pulled himself into one of the beds and collapsed into the sheets. This building's silence was one of coughing and sniffling, and sometimes, quiet sobbing. Johann sat on the edge of the bed, the top of his head brushing against the base of the next tier. Something shifted above him, and he looked up.

A girl peeked down at him. She was a tiny thing, tinier where her bones protruded through her skin like knots of gnarled tree roots, but her eyes were enormous. They glittered, a bright blue, like the soldiers, but her hair was a wiry brown, like Rudolf's. She blinked at him twice.

"How tall are you?"

"I am two hundred and five of your centimeters," He said.

Her eyes went wide at the number, "So big!"

At this, Johann slowly stood up. It took a moment just to stand, his long legs unfurling, lifting him up until he was standing so high that he was staring, not at the second tier, with the little girl, but at the third tier, where a petite woman lay in the throes of fever; he tried to ignore how similar she looked to the girl. He stepped back and met the girl's wide eyes and wider mouth.

"Wow!"

Her voice drew the attention of a few other prisoners, who leaned out of their bunk to look at the giant of a 'man.' Most glanced at him and returned to rest, but a few watched longer. Rudolf was among them, though the man lay on his elbow, relaxed, casual, as if he were disinterested. He chewed on a piece of splintered wood.

"Where are you from?"

"City."

"What city?"

"A city named City."

She giggled at this, "You're funny. I'm Jutta."

Her little hand reached out for his, and he accepted it, long fingers curling around her hand several times, until it was lost in his grip; this made her smile even more.

"I am Johann."

Her eyes shifted over him and his skin-tight uniform. It looked newer than hers or the other prisoners, less ratty; they didn't know it was not even made of the same material, not even from the same world. Blue eyes settled on the yellow star, and she shifted her body to reveal the star on her shoulder; her eyes sparkled, as if to say, "me too." He did not return her smile; he lacked facial muscles for such things, but he nodded once to her, as if they shared a secret.

Eventually, most of the prisoners fell asleep, and Johann laid in his bunk in silence, listening to the sounds of the camp; this was not how he intended to learn about the planet's environment. Native research was always the last step.

But silence never lasted forever; he heard the prisoners awaken, one by one: the girl above fidgeting in her blankets, Rudolf chewing on his piece of gnawed wood, one man stumbling out of bed and out the door—when he returned, he smelled of piss.

After a meager meal of greasy, gritty sausages and stale bread, they marched back to the factory. Johann fell into step beside Rudolf, who said nothing to the tall stranger. He looked around but did not see Jutta.

"Where is the girl?"

"Kids have different jobs," Rudolf explained tersely, "Don't get too attached. She won't last long. Nobody does."

"You have."

Rudolf paused, mid-step, and raised a brow at the stranger.

"You are used to your task."

The man's hand touched his pocket, where the piece of wood he chewed on waited, and he glanced at the guards on the edge of the line. Most were facing away from him.

"Come with me."

They slipped out of the line and disappeared between two barracks. Rudolf paused there, watched the road for a moment, then led Johann out, away from the line and the factory, towards the fence. Johann followed dutifully; this was the kind of information he was supposed to gather.

Through the mist, he saw the fence rising from the ground ahead. Rudolf led him to the edge of the fence and pointed out, through the snow and trees, to a distant pile of dirt.

"See that?"

Johann squinted, eyes adjusting to the ever-changing light of this world, until he saw: what he'd assumed was dirt was a pile of bodies lying, half-frozen, in gray-striped uniforms. Their arms and legs were bent at unnatural angles, and their eyes were open, eyes frozen solid, misty and gray. In the winter, no bugs or carrion ate the corpses. They would stay like that until spring.

Johann reached into his pocket and pulled out his wood. He nibbled on the tip.

"They cremate most, but sometimes, if they do a bunch at the same time, they will throw them out there."

"Burying corpses is a much more sustainable alternative. It returns nitrogen to the ground and provides nutrients for other organic materials."

"Nobody gets a burial here unless it's a mass grave. A lot of death trains come here. The crematoriums are busy."

"Death trains?"

Rudolf pulled the wood from his mouth and stared at the end. He had gnawed the tip to a sharp point, a tiny knife in his hands, wet with saliva.

"I'm sick of this place," Rudolf said, "I'm going to make sure I don't have to stay any longer."

"How?" Johann asked.

He held up the sharpened piece of wood, "I will not go without taking one with me. Let them kill me."

Suddenly, he tucked the wood into his pocket. Behind them, a voice barked at them in German, and they turned to see a soldier staring angrily at them. His eyes flitted from them to the distant pile of corpses, and his shoulders relaxed.

"Get to your station."

Rudolf did not argue or complain; he obeyed, and Johann followed. They made their way through the snow, frost, and barracks until they arrived at the factory again.

That night, laying in his bunk, Johann felt a small finger prod his foot; he was so tall, his feet and legs hung off the end of the bed. He craned his neck to see Jutta poking him. She smiled at him.

"Hi."

"Hello, Jutta."

"What do they have you doing?"

"I make bullets. What is your task?"

"Shovel ashes."

. . .

The next week was the same: sausages for breakfast—since he did not need to eat every day, he shared the food with Jutta, her mother, or Rudolf, who all happily accepted the extra rations—making bullets, and talking with Rudolf or Jutta. The other prisoners were unwilling to speak; they shuffled around the camp and their jobs with dead eyes, only livening for a brief moment when they ate each day. Everyone grew thinner and thinner with only one meal a day. Jutta spoke less. Rudolf chewed on his wood more.

Then one day, when he returned from the factory, there was no Jutta. She did not return that night, or the next day. In her place, Johann dutifully brought an extra ration back to the barracks for her sick mother.

On the third day, on their way to the factory, Johann touched the sleeve of Rudolf's arm, near the pink triangle.

"Take me to the pile."

It was a clear day—less mist than usual, and when they arrived at the fence, the soldier was already waiting. He did not stop them. They peered through the slats in the fence, into the distance, where corpses lay in the cold. Atop the pile, Johann saw the bright blue eyes of Jutta staring back at him. He stared in silence for a long time. Rudolf's hand rested on his pocket.

The guard took a cigarette out of his pocket and lit it, "She could not lift the shovel," he explained, "And was no longer needed. Work makes free. If you cannot work—"

He never finished. Rudolf's wooden knife found his throat, and the man sputtered, stumbled back, lifted his rifle. The air boomed three times, and Rudolf collapsed in a pile on the ground. His striped uniform turned red. The German collapsed.

Rudolf laughed; it was the first time Johann heard a human's laughter in person. His species did not have such a sound. On either side of him, Johann watched two humans bleed out.

The prisoner crawled to the German corpse, a trail of blood following. First, he spat on the man's face, then, he took his cigarette and breathed in deep. The tang of smoke and burning paper and leaves filled the air. Johann did not understand the cultural practice. The chemicals in cigarettes were poisonous to both the natives and the environment. It was unsustainable.

"You should run," Rudolf said, "Climb the fence. Hide in the mountains."

"And you, Rudolf?"

He looked down at his chest. Blood pooled in his stomach, his chest, and his arm. The wounds were fatal, if slowly so.

"I got what I wanted. If your God exists, I will tell Jutta you said hello before he sends me to hell."

"What is hell?" Johann asked.

"Dachau is hell."

The man smiled and laid his head back, but he did not die. He laid in his own blood, slowly freezing to death, enjoying his final cigarette. The pink triangle disappeared as his clothes stained pink-red. In the distance, German shouts echoed through the camp, and behind him, Johann stared into Jutta's lifeless eyes.

The baying of hounds and German shouts echoed behind him, but he was not worried. Long legs carried him past the pile of corpses, past Jutta, and into the woods, where he pinched the edge of his sleeve. A moment later, the air vibrated as his ship returned to retrieve him. The door opened, and he disappeared inside. As the Germans and dogs entered the clearing, they saw the prisoner's footsteps through the snow suddenly end, lost without a trace.

He guided his ship slowly back along his path until it hovered between the pile of corpses and the fence, where he could see the soldiers returning from the woods giving Jutta's corpse a wide berth. Inside the fence, another soldier put a gun to Rudolf's face. Johann closed his eyes and guided the sphere away. He did not want to see the end.

Slowly, quietly, the sphere rose back up into the air, invisible; it flitted through the mist and snow, until the gray sky turned blue, for a single moment. Johann stared through the translucent wall of the sphere at the soft sky and the bank of dark clouds below, stained black with soot from the factory's columns.

At the console of his ship, a voice echoed from the communicator, "Explorer 3113, report."

He sat down at the console and pressed the button, "This is Explorer 3113, apologies for the delay. I faced difficulty with the natives."

"Report?"

"Planet MW-Sol-004, colloquially known as Earth, Terra, or Gaia, by the natives, is habitable for all Class-B and above organic sentient life. However, the natives are highly violent and present a serious threat to non-*Erdelings*."

"Explorer 3113, are you recommending military action to make Earth habitable for intergalactic settlement?"

His ship's revolution around the earth brought him into the shade of the planet. Below, a sea of lights glowed to rival the stars themselves. On the subcontinent he'd abandoned, the clouds tinted black, and the light flickered like red fire. So far away, he could feel the ripple of explosions and flames as the human war waged.

"No," he said, "Unnecessary. The *Erdelings* will wipe themselves out within a single galactic cycle, if not through territorial disputes and conflict then through their unsustainable rush to win such wars."

"That bad?"

"They are a greedy species," he whispered, "They want what they cannot have, and they are willing to die for it." He thought of Rudolf, bleeding out on the ground with a smile on his lips. His thoughts inevitably turned to the pile of corpses, to Jutta and the ashes she shoveled, "They are a cruel species. I have no doubt, if it meant fueling their machines, they would burn even themselves."

"I see..." His handler went quiet. Johann wasn't known for hyperbole. His species was incapable of it, "Understood, Explorer 3133 Please continue to MW-Sol-005 for assessment."

He rotated his ship away from the planet below, facing the darkness of space, and in the distance, a brilliant, red star.

As he piloted his way through the void, the darkness brought calm.

"Thank the stars the *Erdelings* will not escape their world."

. . .

About the author:

Charles Venable is a storyteller from the Southeastern United States with a love of nature and a passion for writing. He believes stories and poems are about getting there, not being there, and he enjoys those tales that take their time getting to the point.

4

Love and Vibrio Cholerae

by Shari K. Ladd (United States)

WARNING: This story may not be suitable for younger readers due to language.

Subgenres: Historical science fiction, pandemic science fiction, young adult

Time Period: 1970 to 1991

Setting: Unites States and Peru

Author's Introduction:

While the characters portrayed in this story are fictional, all other facts and science are portrayed as accurately as possible. The research conducted by the characters is based on the work of microbiologist Rita Colwell, the first female director of the National Science Foundation. The consequences of climate change are often discussed in futuristic summer-blockbuster scenarios, but we must beware setting our focus exclusively on disaster movie cataclysm. The quieter, less sexy calamities often get passed by and forgotten.

. . .

The first time my mother described the process of collecting plankton with silk, I imagined ribbons and fancy dresses. She said they set up silk to trail behind boats for hundreds and thousands of miles. I would picture dolphins playing in decorated slipstreams and sharks swimming past sunken tea parties. The truth was far less fanciful. The ship tows a device holding two rollers, one slowly unspooling silk onto the other. Water rushes through the silk, capturing the plankton and preserving it perfectly. They would then divide the silks into ten-nautical-mile sections and analyze the plankton from the samples. It was a filter, nothing more.

Still, I loved that they used silk. It seemed such a delicate luxury in the lives of scientists like my mother and her research partner, Anita. Even as a child, I knew it was rare for science to engage with anything feminine and delicate. It was the 1970s. Women were allowed to have a seat at the table in academia but were often met with the air of a child trying to give a serious suggestion where the family should go on vacation. You can give your opinion, but don't expect to be taken as seriously as the *real scientists*. Many years later, Anita confided in me that when she was applying for fellowships, one rejection came from a professor who proudly said he didn't "waste fellowships on women." I bought us another round of whiskeys, doubles, and we drank in the name of "fuck 'em."

. . .

My early memories of my mother pale in comparison to the bright spot that was Anita. She was the sun around which all things revolved. She'd bring her rotating cast of boyfriends onto the research boats, and my mother would bring me. Even then, I remember being jealous of the boyfriends. I loved the way Anita's dark hair stuck out in a little nubby ponytail and how she'd carry around her massive stack of research notebooks. I always thought it made her look so important, like she knew something we didn't. During back-to-school shopping, I made my mother buy me extra notebooks to play scientist with, and she had to ground me in third grade for trying to recreate the ponytail with kitchen scissors. Mom was furious, but Anita laughed.

In the early 1970s, Anita found the *Vibrio cholerae* bacteria in waters off Chesapeake Bay. At the time, cholera was thought to be a disease transmitted only by contaminated drinking water. It was a problem of poor sanitation. One of those *over there* problems. Finding cholera clinging to plankton in the sea raised a lot of questions, most of which were swiftly shouted down by their scientific peers. "That just isn't how cholera works," they said. They said she was even wrong about the plankton, which doesn't really move; it's more like cling wrap on a bowl of jello. However, that did not change one simple fact: Anita knew the cholera was out there, and so, the microbiologist teamed up with my oceanographer mother. That's where the silk came in.

The problem was the rising ocean temperature. The excess carbon in the atmosphere warms the air, which begins to heat the water, creating a whole ripple effect of damage. I remember eating at a Rhode Island pub with Mom and Anita sometime in middle school. An Anita-visit was always a special occasion. I would count the days and chat about her endlessly to the teachers at school. By that point, I had slowly become involved in their work too. We had just returned from collecting cassettes of silk samples from merchant ships in the Providence River. I always worried about what to wear, whether I should strive to look more pretty or scientific. My very thirteen-year-old decision that day involved a baby-pink peasant top that I "scienced-up" by painting my fingernails with little bacteria patterns. I anguished over which color to paint the nucleus of the cells and whether I should use a glitter topcoat. However, I always knew that learning something was the best way to earn her affection. My moment came after ordering burgers at the Providence dive bar when Anita decided I needed to understand about the ocean temperatures.

"It's not just the top of the water, you know. We're sampling the top, but it's just the beginning of the damage."

I was picking at my macramé bracelet, knee bouncing up and down, trying to focus. "So, it isn't just the top?" I asked, committing everything to memory.

Her dark eyes narrowed, and I stopped my knee mid-bounce. My heart started racing, but a smile began to play at the corners of her lips. Anita hopped off her stool and strode over to the bar. I glanced at my mom, who was only half watching from behind her book. Anita returned a moment later with one pint glass and one shot glass. The pint glass was about two thirds full of something dark. The shot looked light and creamy.

"This is the ocean," she waved the pint glass. "Now, that's how it's supposed to be. Right temperature. It's stable. If you change the surface temperature, the heat doesn't just stay at the top. It impacts the entire system. Currents start moving, patterns start shifting, water starts rising. Once you disrupt the system—"

She plunked the shot glass into the pint glass. At first, I thought the disrupture of the liquid was due to the splash of the shot glass, but it was more than that. It was fizzing and bubbling up, looking like it was about to foam over the top of the glass. I looked around for napkins, sure that the drink would pour over everything, but then Anita began to chug the drink, racing to the bottom. It was gone in a second.

"What was that?" I asked. I couldn't resist, even if she thought I had missed the point of her lesson. She was laughing though, tossing the van keys to my mom.

"A magician never reveals her secret." I remember she wiped the foam from her rosy, sunburnt lips with a smirk.

"It's an Irish Car Bomb," my mother said. "It's just a cocktail."

"Hey," Anita said in mock hurt. "It's a science experiment!"

"Irish Car Bomb?" I asked.

"Yes, but don't call it that in Ireland. Don't think they like that much."

I looked out the window down on hilly Providence, and I started picking at a scab on my knee. I looked at my mother's gloomy face, then over at Anita's. She was up at the bar again, charming the bartenders while they poured her another drink and made a kiddie cocktail for me. I thought how funny it was. I wanted nothing more than to be a scientist. A great scientist. My mother happened to be one, and yet, I often forgot. It was this other woman I aspired after while my mother faded into the background.

. . .

Doctors used to think that malaria was spread by foul air which would blow in and sicken its victims. It even got its name from the Italian *mal* and *aria,* meaning "bad air." Dr. Robert Ross proved that malaria was actually a parasite transmitted by the bite of a mosquito. However, he wasn't too popular with the "bad air" crowd.

"They all thought he was batshit crazy," Anita ranted to me one night.

I was in high school then, taking an AP biology course. I called her with the smartest-sounding fake question I could come up with about the Krebs Cycle, and she began explaining to me about malaria. I didn't mind. In fact, it was half the reason I made these homework help calls. I learned more interesting things about science from those conversations than I ever did in class. On one phone call, she told me that bats are so biodiverse, one in every four mammals is a bat. The night of the mosquito rant, she explained the reason people of African descent are more prone to sickle cell disease is because it comes with an immunity to a type of malaria endemic in Africa. I was constantly dazzled. I tried to get her to tell me more, but Anita was fixated on the malaria mosquitoes that night.

She identified with Dr. Ross. For her, ocean plankton was the mosquito of cholera. It was the disease vector that people were ignoring. She could prove that the *Vibrio cholerae* could go dormant attached to plankton in the sea. When the water is just warm enough, it comes alive again to begin producing deadly cholera toxin. However, to their peers, Anita and my mother were crazy to suggest it. The open ocean, like mosquitoes, is too far-fetched a place to carry a disease.

"Ross got a Nobel, though," Anita told me. "Maybe they'll listen someday. Crazier things have happened."

. . .

Slowly though, I watched as piece by piece, the world started to realize that Anita and Mom had been onto something. The possibility that the ocean may be a source of new cholera outbreaks was beginning to make sense to some of their peers. People were listening. It was the late eighties, and I was working on a microbiology degree of my own. We rang in New Year's 1989 toasting their latest paper. This one actually seemed to be garnering some positive attention. Anita appeared incredulously happy, and even my mother seemed to peek out from her usual darkness.

I graduated undergrad a semester early in December 1990. By the time I had settled back into my mother's apartment to start the arduous grad school application process, cholera had hit South America for the first time in almost a hundred years. It was all playing out exactly as their research predicted. The disease was spreading from Peru's coastal beaches inland to the mountains. This disturbed my mother, but in ways that I had not expected. She would sit, fretting on the couch, angry that Americans didn't know what cholera was or where to find Peru on a map.

"None of these people know anything that's happened

outside this country since the Berlin Wall came down. Nothing we're doing matters at all," she'd say before falling into listless silence, picking at her mother's crocheted afghan for the rest of night.

Then something incredible happened.

Anita asked me to join her research trip to Peru. It was the best thing I have ever felt. Better than Christmas. Better than sex. Better than proving you are right. I felt like I had finally won. Anita wasn't bringing my mother. She was bringing me. I knew deep down that this arrangement had more to do with my mother's decline than my virtues. Not to mention that I conveniently had several months unhindered by work or school. But was it too much to hope that Anita saw me for my virtues too? My value? All I wanted then was for her to take me seriously. My mother was fading and had been for many years. Even as child, I sometimes wondered what Anita still saw in my mother. A desperate, irrational something hoped that it was me.

. . .

The travel agent booked our flight to Jorge Chávez International Airport in Lima, the only way in or out of Peru from the United States. I had never used my passport before. It was still crisp and new. Anita's was full of beautiful, smudged stamps of countries most people would never dream of visiting. I saw Cyprus, the Czech Republic, Egypt, and Myanmar all on one page. I wanted to ask to see more, but I hesitated. I didn't want to look too overeager. I realized a moment later that she probably would like showing it to me, but by the time I thought to ask, the passport was back in her money belt. I was left feeling dumb and childish, wondering why this was so much harder than asking her about the Krebs cycle. By the time we boarded the plane, I was feeling nervous. This trip was a chance for Anita to prove her research right after all these years, but I knew I was proving myself, too.

. . .

Lima was much cooler than I expected. The skies were overcast the way they never are on the travel brochures. Our interpreter, a sharp little woman named Luz, told me that a smoggy sea mist comes in winter, hanging over the whole miserable city from June to November.

"We call it *la garúa*. It means more than a fog, but less than rain," she said. "Americans come here in your summer expecting beach paradise, but they get air so wet you can choke."

Lima appeared to be the epicenter, but Anita wanted to get a sense for how far the cholera had spread up the coast. Luz arranged for us to rent her father-in-law's boxy red Hillman. We drove north up the coast, intending to take samples as we made our way back south to Lima. Then we would do the same to the south, working our way back up to Lima again.

The car had no air conditioning, but Anita seemed invigorated as we drove north out of the city. Luz drove jerkily, darting around large trucks, shouting about Lima's infrastructure problems over the noise of the honking cars and open windows. Then the women started chatting animatedly about how shocking it was that Alberto Fujimori won the election. I was sitting in the backseat with no context for their conversation. Somehow, I felt like I was back in my mother's van, struggling to follow along with the grownups.

. . .

Chimbote was a fishing town. I've learned in the years since that it has become the largest fishing port in the world, but it wasn't back when we visited it. Luz told me that more people were coming to the town every year. They were mostly families from struggling mountain towns seeking fishing industry jobs. It was a pinpoint on Anita's map. Luz sped down a dirt beach-access road, scattering a flock of seabirds. She cursed at the birds casually like a greeting, then turned back to us.

"There's a river over that ridge," she said, indicating the direction with her neck. Luz took a sharp turn that sent me hard into the door panel. "The beach is ahead that way. I'll drop one of you there, and the other can drive up the river with me. Unless you want to do it all together?"

"I'll take the beach, you take the river," I said, forcefully as I dared.

I knew that the river would mean Luz as babysitter. I wanted a chance to shine on my own, even if it was just collecting samples. Anita looked at me curiously for a moment, but she agreed.

"Whatever floats your boat, buttercup," she said as Luz pulled up, parking the car as close to the sand as possible. I tossed the sample collection bag over my shoulder, and we agreed to meet back at this spot in one hour. The car door slammed harder than I'd meant, but the sound was satisfying. As they drove away, I finally started to feel myself relax.

I had the beach to myself. Black rocks jutted out against the hot sand, and I saw a scrawny beach cat slinking between them. It was strange to see so many beautiful beaches empty. They should have been packed with spring breakers and cabana boys. But I wouldn't have to share today.

I hiked down to the shore in my little rain boots. I'd brought them at Anita's instruction, a precaution against the warm cholera tides. They were bright yellow rubber with black on the bottoms, the kind that little kids wear to jump in puddles. I felt the sun beating down on me. The skin was peeling on my sunburnt ears, but I didn't care. I wanted to enjoy this heat. I dug the hard black toes of my boots into the wet sand, trying to sink in. The sand was powder fine, and my toes wanted so desperately to wriggle into its cooling softness. I began wondering if removing the boots would be worth the risk, then reminded myself that Anita would kill me if she found out. The sample case was growing heavy on my shoulder, but I needed to take just another moment in the sun.

I didn't see the woman approaching me at first. She appeared in my periphery, like a car in my blind spot. I jumped so badly that I dropped my bag. It splashed into the water, and my stomach dropped thinking of the samples inside. When I snapped up the dripping bag and looked up, my stomach leapt up into my throat instead. The woman looked perfect. She was walking across the beach toward me, like she was in a commercial for a travel agency. Except she was too serious, too somber. In a commercial, she would have laughter in her eyes and a drink in her hand. She was serious, like the most tropical mourner at a funeral.

She raised her hand a few yards from me in greeting, shouting, "This beach is not safe! It is dangerous. It is making people very sick. You need to leave here." Her voice was soft and higher than I expected, and she spoke in fluent English.

"Thanks," I said, "I'm okay though, I'm actually a scientist."

The woman's eyes lit up, breaking her somber expression. "You're a scientist! Are you here to help?"

"Yes, I'm here to help!" I said, my voice cracking with excitement. I implored myself to stay cool.

I could not stop looking at this woman. She had to be around my age, twenty-two or twenty-three at the most. Her skin was smooth and tan, with big eyes set in her serious face. Her hair fell in big curls naturally, the kind of hair that the WASPy, thin girls at school spent all their time and energy trying to recreate, but their attempts were just a pathetic imitation of this. No amount of perming and teasing could ever compare to her. This girl's bangs caught the beachy breeze and frizzed, blowing across her eyes, dark and light at the same time.

"Thank you though, for coming to warn me. And for letting people know about the beaches. That's really nice of you," I said, trying to appear casual while closing some of the distance between us. I was sweating now, and not just from the heat.

I wanted to make her stay.

She looked down, a serious, thoughtful look on her face. "The beaches should all be closed, but they will not do it. Not here at least, because it will look bad for the fish. Most of us know better, but not all of us. The president made a big show on TV eating raw fish to convince everyone that our fish is safe, but even his own government is telling people that it wasn't true. That fish wasn't even from our coast. It was deep sea fish. He just lies."

"That's awful."

"Even after they say it was not true, people want the fish to be okay," she sighs, looking out at the ocean for a moment, then looking back at me with a grim smile. "I will keep warning people or scaring them off if they should know better. But I could tell that you are not from here."

"Oh, was it that obvious?" I tried to joke. I flipped a piece of my violently ginger hair over one freckled, sunburnt shoulder for comedic emphasis, hating myself and regretting it immediately.

But she laughed. I made her laugh.

There was one thought in my mind. *Don't fuck this up.*

"It was a safe guess," she said.

"You didn't even try to talk to me in Spanish. You skipped right to English."

"Well... that seemed like the place to start. And I like to practice."

"You're very good."

She looked down, smiling. "So," she asked, "You're a doctor?

"No," I wished I were. I wanted to impress her. "I'm studying to be one. Not a medical kind that treats patients. But the other kind, that I look at diseases when they happen like this, and I figure out why it happened."

"Oh," her face looked puzzled. I was sure I had disappointed her, but then she said, "So, why has it happened? All of this. Tell me everything you know. Please. I want to know everything."

I remember thinking, *This is it. I might not be the best scientist in the world. I might not be Anita. Fuck, I might not even be my mother. But I know this science, and I can tell her.* "You want to know everything?"

"Everything." She looked at me, hungrily.

And so, I told her. I told her everything, beginning with the coal emissions and greenhouse gasses, then to the rising water temperatures, and how all of this plays into the water currents and the plankton. Then how the cholera bacteria and the plankton can travel together and end up in new places. I explained how the El Niño Southern Oscillation weather pattern brought the plankton and warm water to the coast of Peru, and that when the coastal surface waters began to warm further, the *Vibrio cholerae bacteria* began producing the cholera toxin, and that's what made it all happen.

I was giddy, racing to finish telling her. This person, who is kind and cares about the world, wants to know what I know. I wanted to hold her, to kiss her. I remembered that I was in Peru, and I wondered if they put women in jail for that kind of thing. I wondered if I cared.

I finally took a breath, exhilarated. Then I realized that she was frowning, and I began to worry that I had gone too fast. But she looked me directly in the eyes, and I smiled at her.

"You really enjoy this," she said.

"I really do," I said.

She looked away from me, crossing her arms. *Something was wrong.*

"My sisters died. Both of them. They were nine."

My heart dropped.

"They were playing in the water. I told them not to. They were telling us that it was safe, but I still told them no. But they thought that just a little bit, just in the shallow wouldn't hurt."

I noticed a stray, emaciated dog sniffing around by the rocks. I didn't want to look at her. I had to.

"Jasmina went first, then Lousia a few hours later. Do you know how fast it happens? Your body opens up and lets go of everything inside. Have you seen it up close? Have you? Or do you just look at it under a microscope?"

I'd fucked up.

"If you had seen it up close you wouldn't talk about it with so much glee in your voice. You look at this place and see a pretty beach. I look at it and see my dead sisters' bodies. I see a dead village. I see my people.

"Did you know this city's hospital is so full, they had to put tents outside? And that's for the people lucky enough for a tent. The rest die at home. And their shit runs off into the gutter, into the street, into the clothes, and the rugs, and the sheets, into the laundry to get recycled into the water to get passed around. And the rest are so poor and desperate to feed the family that is left that we still fish from the same poison water, because the same thing that is killing us is keeping us alive. That is why we are dying."

I thought she would walk away, but she didn't. She stayed. She took a breath. It was like she had finished, but she wasn't leaving.

I had another moment with her. I was grateful for one more moment. Because she was right, of course.

She was right.

I spent my life working with cholera on a boat, looking at silk and bacteria under a microscope. I was a fake. I wasn't a real scientist. I wasn't even a real researcher. I was a fraud with a bag of dirty water. I was only there because I knew a real scientist. I was a child playing make believe with bacteria fingernails with a glitter topcoat. I thought this field trip was a test. I had failed.

If I were a real scientist, I would have known better.

"I'm sorry," I said. It wasn't enough.

She wasn't crying. I thought that she might, but she didn't. She looked at me with her soft eyes that were both light and dark. I wanted to be lost in them.

"Thank you for explaining," her voice was steady.

"Thank you," my voice broke. "For explaining too."

She looked at me, then I could tell she was about to go. I wanted to stop her. "I'm sorry. Is there anything I can do?"

"No." She looked away from me, "Just remember. When you talk about the coal killing us, remember the little girls shitting themselves to death and dying because their organs have no water left in them. Because that is both."

I felt sick watching her disappear. Like she had shamed me, like she had pointed out something so fucking obvious I should have known it all along.

She was gone before I realized I'd never asked her name.

. . .

I was never quite sure how I managed to finish collecting the water samples from that beach in Chimbote. I remember walking down the shore in the opposite direction from the girl, frequently checking over my shoulder. The emaciated street dog I saw before ran up behind me and into the water, splashing the surf up my body. I felt the water trickle down my leg into my yellow boot. I thought of the *Vibrio cholerae* bacteria sliding down my leg and wanted to be sick. I kicked the water back at the dog and immediately felt intense guilt. I thought I might cry. I didn't want to contract cholera, but I also did. I wanted to feel it.

It felt like it took an age to walk the distance back to the place where Anita and Luz would be waiting for me. I wasn't sure if I hoped the girl would be there when I returned, but the beach was empty. The red boxy car was waiting for me, and I wordlessly climbed in.

. . .

Luz and Anita chattered again on the drive back to Lima, but for once, I did not mind being left out of the conversation.

I thought about the girl on the beach, with her dead sisters and her pretty hair. I wondered if I would be able to keep her perfectly in my mind, or if she would begin to fade away. I hated myself already for knowing that I would begin to lose some of the details. I knew this was important. I wanted to keep it.

I was seeing something different in Peru on the return trip to Lima. I wasn't noticing the beauty of the beaches anymore, just the water full of deadly toxins. Beautiful sailboats were vessels catching poisoned fish to feed to the children I saw playing by the side of the roads, who would surely be dead by morning. The skies became hazy and wet as Lima loomed. I remembered *la garúa,* the fog you can choke on, and imagined being able to contract cholera from the water in the air. An entire city, exposed to death by breathing.

Anita was staring at me again from the front seat. I hadn't noticed at first, but when I did, she smiled at me. I didn't smile back.

I began to wonder if Anita suspected something was wrong shortly after leaving Chimbote. At first, my mind was so wrapped up in the beautiful girl, I didn't spare much of a thought for Anita. Slowly though, I realized, the overwhelming thing I was feeling wasn't just about the girl. It was about Anita too, and I didn't want to talk about it. Of course, she forced my hand.

"Are you alright, *chica?*" Anita asked.

It was the evening. On our halfway point in Lima before heading south, we were spending the night at Luz's home. She was inside with her husband and father-in-law, and the smell of dinner wafted out the windows. I was standing in the garden, looking out at the setting sun when Anita walked up behind me, a lit cigarette in her hand.

"Why?" I snapped. A mistake.

Anita paused for a moment, taking me in. "You look like you've seen a ghost."

That was when the blind rage took over. "This whole place is full of ghosts. That's the damn problem," I said, forcefully.

I waited. I wanted her to say something, but she just looked at me. But she wanted me to explain. She wouldn't respond. I hated it. I hated that she knew me that well, and I hated that I let her tactic work anyway. "I met this local girl down on the beach while I was collecting samples—You didn't tell me. After everything you taught me," my voice cracked. "You always needed me to understand every little thing, but this is a pretty fucked oversight. I liked cholera better when it was in a damned petri dish."

I was no longer afraid I would cry. Now, I was just angry. "Was this why you brought me here? Take off the blinders, show me the real world? If so, congratulations. It worked." I turned to stride away from her toward the house.

"I'm sorry," she said.

It was a testament to the hold Anita still held over me that that was enough to make me stop and turn back. She still held the cigarette in her right hand, but she was not smoking it now. It dangled limply between the fingers of her right hand, forgotten. There was a shimmer in her eyes that may have been the beginning of tears but might too have been setting sunlight.

"Do you know you remind me of your mother sometimes?" Anita asked.

A flutter of panic rose in my chest. Something of this must have crossed my face.

"Don't look at me like that. It's not a bad thing," she said. "Well, it doesn't have to be, but you know what I mean."

I didn't.

"You told me the world was fantastic, and it isn't," I said, the next words catching in my throat. "I tried so hard to be like you and not her."

I had never said it out loud.

"Do you think I don't see the bad shit? It's terrible. But I choose to see the good shit too. That is the difference between your mother and me. She is like a sister, but she gets lost in the bad. I try to help her see the good, but it sometimes makes her so depressed she can't leave the couch for weeks. You know that better than I do. That's why I always wanted to show you the sense of wonder. So when you had this moment, you, my darling girl, would have something to hold on to," Anita said. There were tears in her eyes, but I knew they would not fall.

Anita pulled me in to face her, one hand on each shoulder. "I never lied to you," she said.

Something clicked for me then; there was a choice to be made. It wasn't a choice between seeing the world as beautiful or ugly, life or death. It was between hope or despair. "Okay," I said, and that was enough.

Her mostly unsmoked cigarette had burnt out, and we walked together back to the house. Something had changed between us. Our relationship no longer resembled that of child and teacher. We had become two adults who understood each other. My desire to become like Anita was no longer a silly crush. It wasn't even just professional admiration anymore. I knew for me, it was a means of survival. To be like Anita was to retain essential hope.

Her face was illuminated then quickly cloaked again by shadow as she lit another cigarette, the cherry of it still hanging in the dusk between us. I was surprised when she handed it to me. She lit another for herself, taking a long, slow drag and exhaling. She had never offered me one before, but on that night, we stood together, our little lights, staring out into the darkness.

5

Donald the Crooked President

by David Harten Watson (United States)

Subgenres: Political satire, humor, song

Time Period: January 2017 to January 2021

Setting: United States

Synopsis: Most of this song was composed December 19, 2019, the day after Donald Trump became the third United States president ever impeached and the first to have anyone from his own party vote to convict him. I added four more stanzas in 2021 after he became the only United States president ever to be impeached twice. This time, it was the most bipartisan impeachment in history, with seventeen Republicans voting to impeach or convict a member of their own party.

. . .

Sing to the tune of "Rudolph the Red-Nosed Reindeer"

Donald the crooked president
Had a very tiny brain,
And if you ever saw him,
You would say that he's insane.

Donald the crooked president
Was a climate-change denier,
Even while global warming
Set the western states on fire.

All of the world's leaders
Used to laugh and call him names,
Except for poor Zelensky,
President of the Ukraine.

Then one treasonous July,
Donald told Ukraine,
"If you want our aid, you know,
Please do me a favor, though."

Then the Democrats impeached him,
And they shouted out with glee,
"Donald the crooked president
You'll go down in history!"

Then he lost the next election,
And launched a terrorist attack
A January insurrection
To steal the Presidency back.

He held back the National Guard
Three hours while blood was spilled
By terrorists at the Capitol
Where five Americans were killed.

Most of the House and Senate
Voted to impeach this time,
Ten short of the two-thirds needed
To convict Donald for his crime.

This bipartisan impeachment
Meant Donald was impeached twice,
A stain upon his legacy,
History will not be nice!

. . .

Permission is hereby granted for this song to be freely copied, shared, sung, and distributed, provided credit is given to the author.

. . .

About the Author:

David Harten Watson, editor of this cli-fi anthology, authored the young-adult fantasy series *Magicians Gold*, including the award-winning novel *Magic Teacher's Son* and its sequel *Fortress of Gold*. David has worked in a dizzying array of jobs including US Army Armor officer at Fort Knox, experience that came in handy for his second novel, *Fortress of Gold*. Raised in snowy Buffalo, New York, he has degrees from Princeton, Canisius College, and Buffalo State College. He's the Organizer of the Woodbridge Science Fiction & Fantasy Writers Meetup, which he founded in 2008. He lives in New Jersey. Author's website: www.davidhartenwatson.com

Part Two:

Today, Tomorrow, or the Day After Tomorrow

6

Boiling Alive

by Ross West (United States)

WARNING: This story may not be suitable for younger readers due to language and violence.

Subgenres: Political, thriller, suspense, eco-terrorism

Time Period: Present/near future

Setting: Oregon, United States of America

Synopsis:

A high school boy lives through an eco-calamity similar to the conflagration in Paradise, California, and, as he sees it, loses everything. When he discovers the cause of the fire to be global warming, he gets involved with mainstream political efforts to save the planet. Soon disillusioned with the movement's lack of urgency and effectiveness, he's swept up with militant eco-terrorists. But even their radical and destructive acts are not enough to appease his anger and avenge what he has suffered. He decides to take matters into his own hands.

. . .

Why? Because a hundred million people are going to die. A billion people. Ten billion. How's that for a reason?

—Fight for Earth

I'm sitting in a window booth at an all-night coffee shop with a perfect view of a huge warehouse just half a block up the street. The Target Corporation uses the warehouse to stock the shelves of its Oregon, Washington, and Idaho stores with plastic shit from China. In two minutes, it's going to burst into flames. That should be pretty cool.

The waitress is carrying a coffee pot around to her customers. One of them is hunched over at the counter, scruffy looking, wearing an old army jacket. The other two are eating 3:00 a.m. eggs and pancakes. Could be lunch on their graveyard shift.

She asks—Refill, hon?

I put down the pen on the pad of paper where I'm doodling and pretending to be an eighteen-year-old Shakespeare or whatever and give her a drowsy night owl smile—Yeah sure.

She fills my cup. Gray-blue eyes, light, like Jillian's, but without the gold flecks that made J's eyes look like opals. I dump a bunch of sugar and cream into my coffee and think about Jillian for a while, then try not to.

One minute.

I pick up the pen and stare out the window like I've been staring for half an hour, looking for inspiration, I guess.

Thirty seconds.

I check my phone, making sure for the third time it's set up to shoot video. I don't want to miss anything good. They told me they wanted it all.

Over the middle of the block-long building comes a wisp of smoke that looks like a ghost in the light of the giant red and white Target sign on the warehouse roof. Nobody else in the diner has noticed. I keep my hand away from the phone.

Then *BANG*, an explosion and a bright flash.

Everybody in the coffee shop turns to see. There's noise and hubbub, and the cook sticks his head out from the back and says—What happened?

The waitress yells—Somebody call 911.

I grab my phone and start shooting. The little screen is filled with a rolling billow of smoke, then the first fingertips of flame wiggle up over the rooftop. I zoom in. The fire is spreading fast. In just a couple of minutes the whole side of the building is going up, flames roaring higher and higher in a tall orange triangle. I stare at it, hypnotized.

Sirens start up and get louder, and soon two fire engines come screaming up the street, their jittery lights flickering everywhere, blue, red, and white. A bunch of other emergency vehicles show up, so many colored lights strobing on and off it's like some nightmare disco. The firefighters hustle around with oxygen tanks on their backs, the reflective bands on their jackets and pants give off a weird silvery glow. A big extension ladder is silhouetted against the flames, a heavy stream spraying from its top. More trucks show up and more and more. Arcs of water are pouring in from all sides.

They don't have a chance.

. . .

Your moral duty is to quit servicing and enabling the Death Machine—resist, destroy, freeze up the gears, sabotage the apparatus. Until YOU act, the boxcars will keep rolling to Auschwitz.

—Fight for Earth

It's after six, and I'm pedaling fast, the chilly early-fall wind in my face, my fingers cold on the handlebars. Everything is tuned up, brighter and sharper and more colorful than usual. A bakery has its morning loaves in the oven, and the smell is so intense it's like I'm chewing the bread. I lock my bike to a parking meter a block from where I'm to meet up with the NDF guys.

I find an alley and dig out a cigarette and my lighter. The little flame reminds me of Mom telling me I should quit. A hundred times she told me, and I'm never gonna.

She says—I gotta go, sweetie. When I get settled, you can come visit.

I need to circle the block, on the opposite side of the street from where the NDF hangs out. They told me to act like I'm out for a leisurely stroll, looking in shop windows, killing time. The cops or the feds might be watching. Anything or anybody that seems even a little out of place.

They kept telling me and telling me—This isn't playing around.

And even though they said that, it still felt like we were all in a movie or something. Until this morning, watching that warehouse burn.

I toss the cigarette and pull my knit cap down low on my forehead, cover it with the hood of my sweatshirt and start walking. The street looks like any other shitty gray downtown block this early in the morning—papers blowing down the sidewalk, parked cars and delivery vans, a trash truck rumbling its way from dumpster to dumpster. Nothing unusual.

I was part of it, The Great NDF Target Action of 2021. Maybe I wasn't exactly in the thick of it, but I played my part, shot video like a motherfucker.

I turn the corner and up ahead there's a beat-up white van. Right across the street from where it shouldn't be, the old brick building with the rooms sign. I get closer and kneel down, pretending to tie my kick. The back windows are papered over, just like a cop van might be. It rocks just a little. I stand up and get closer, walking along its side. As I'm passing the driver's window something big and angry lunges at me—*BARK BARK BARK*—a crazy-eyed pit bull, teeth snapping, slobber on the window. I jump back like three feet and hear a voice inside yelling—Bucky, Bucky. Shut the fuck up.

I turn in front of the van and look in through the windshield.

The dog's jumping around and a bushy-haired guy is sitting up in a sleeping bag.

I take some breaths, try to get my heart to slow down, light another cigarette and take one pull after another.

That coulda been a cop van. They coulda stopped me for questioning, coulda found the video I took.

I flick the butt and duck in the door under the rooms sign and climb up the four flights of creaky stairs.

When they asked me to shoot the video of the fire, Denver said some guys are cut out for this kind of resistance, some guys aren't. Like he wasn't sure about me. But now he'll know who he's dealing with, know I'm ready.

And he's gonna say—We got another plan, another NDF action all set up.

And we'll do it, all of us together. I'll be the one with the bolt cutters snipping the lock on the chain link fence. I'll lead the way in, a five-gallon can of gas in each hand. I'll be the one lighting the match.

From the fourth floor I look back down the stairs to make sure nobody's following me, then give the door five sharp raps—*BOP-BOP BOP-BOP BOP*.

The door cracks, and there's Denver, big and bulging with muscles like some superhero. He peeks his shaved head out into the hallway and looks both ways, then waves me in and locks the door.

The place is a shithole, just like the other times I was here. Crap all over, mattresses on the floor and empties and wadded up cigarette packs and books and magazines and stacks of *Fight for Earth*. Except for a halfway decent big-screen TV, the furniture looks like junk you couldn't give away to Goodwill. Five guys are sitting around, mostly in their late twenties and looking about as wrung out as you'd expect after the night they've had. Five guys with vision, commitment, and guts. I know four of them.

Chattanooga is sitting on a mattress barefoot and leaning

against the wall smoking. He raises his cigarette at me and in his heavy southern accent says—If it ain't our combat photographer.

Denver—Did you get it?

I wave my phone around and hear cheers from SeaTac and Homer slumped on the pukey-looking couch. Homer looks like a pudgy, red-cheeked gnome, but Denver called him a crazy-ass bomb-maker. Pretty cool. The guy I don't know is sitting farthest away on a metal folding chair, his arms crossed on his chest. He's got a bushy beard and is sizing me up from behind little wire-rimmed glasses.

Denver—That's Boise. Boise, Phoenix.

I bob my chin and Boise cracks a little bullshit smile like he isn't so sure he's happy to see me. Whatever.

I move a couple of old pizza boxes off a milk crate and sit down.

SeaTac, laptop on his knees—The fire's trending big.

He reads a news report from his screen, diddles with his keyboard, starts reading social media posts. Next to me SeaTac's the youngest and kind of a geekpimple, but a hacker and a really brilliant computer guy.

I try to look like I'm listening to him, but *I was there, genius*. I'm the one who saw it.

Another track in my brain is thinking my name is as good as SeaTac's. Or any of the rest of them. Maybe better. Denver asked where I'm from, and I sure as shit wasn't about to tell him Tinkle Valley in the middle of bumfuck nowhere, so I said—Arizona. And he said—Phoenix?

He told me the dorky fake names are for security, which these guys are super paranoid about. Maybe that's why Boise is being such a dickweed iceberg.

SeaTac finally finishes up with the Mr. Newsman routine and pushes his long hair behind his ear.

Homer, who'd been listening, says—Burned that sumbitch...*to...the...ground*.

He's slurring his words pretty good and has a half-empty tequila bottle pinned between his muddy boots.

Boise, pushing his glasses higher up on his nose—You gonna show us what you got?

I hit the play button on my phone and hand it to Chattanooga.

SeaTac is craning his neck—Is it going? Is it burning?

Chattanooga—Just smoke.

—There was a big-ass explosion that got it going.

Homer, a proud grin on his face—Goddam right there was.

SeaTac—I wanna see.

Denver is standing and leaning against the wall with his tattooed arms folded over his black T-shirt. He says—Can we put it on the screen?

SeaTac takes the phone and diddles with it.

—When should I post the video?

Denver's hand shoots out, palm facing me—*No!*

Chattanooga shakes his head like posting is the worst idea ever.

—Well what the fuck did I get it for?

Chattanooga—The cops would be all over it with a fine-tooth fuckin'...y'know?

Denver sees the look on my face and tells me—What you took'll help us, a lot, with planning, other actions...the next one.

Chattanooga—They'll know who did it when we post our manifesto.

—You didn't post it yet?

A lot of squirmy looks go around the room.

SeaTac—Got it. Check this out.

The fire is starting to get going really well, and it looks even more ferocious on the big TV screen than it did on the phone. Boise moves his chair around so he can see. All we need is popcorn.

Homer—Whoa, look at that.

He takes a slug of tequila and passes it to Chattanooga, who drinks and passes it to me. The shit burns, and I take a second swig. The bottle goes around and around, and we drain it while watching the fire grow.

But what Chattanooga said keeps eating at me.

I can't hold back—What do you mean *when* you post the manifesto? What's wrong with *now*? Wasn't that the plan? You said you were gonna—

Denver—Yeah, we said that, but shit changes.

—You told me this like three days ago. What shit has changed in three days?

Denver, looking away—We didn't quite finish it yet.

—What?

Chattanooga—We thought we'd get it done before last night, but we had a few other things on our mind, okay? Don't you worry, we'll take care of it. The longer we wait the more—

—Wait? What are you talking about, wait? We're not writing the fucking Declaration of Independence. Can't we just copy something out of *Fight for Earth,* sign it NDF and call it good?

Homer—How 'bout if we just watch this, huh? Look at them flames.

He rolls a joint, lights it, stares at it while he's letting smoke curl out of his nostrils, hits it again, and passes it to me. I get a lungful, hold it, and can't believe these guys.

Denver—We need our *own* manifesto. Articulate our *own* identity. We agreed on that.

Exhaling—I didn't.

Chattanooga—You weren't around when we decided.

—What's the hold up? We all know what we gotta say. They're killing the planet. We're doing something because if we don't, they'll keep doing exactly what they've been doing for a hundred years, driving the car over the fucking cliff.

Chattanooga, like he hasn't heard anything I said—What if we leave it a big mystery? Give the media stooges something to speculate about. Save the manifesto for next time.

On the screen the fire's become a hell-roaring monster. We can't take our eyes off it.

SeaTac—But if we don't say something nobody's gonna know it was us who did it.

Everybody starts arguing. Yack, yack, yack. Jesus Christ.

—Look, it's the actions that matter. Let's do another warehouse. How about tomorrow? That'll get their attention.

Denver sneers at me—It took us three weeks to plan this one.

Fuck you, Denver.

Snotty and sarcastic as I can be—Well maybe we oughta speed things up a little, huh?

They look at me like, who is this guy?

Boise—You got a problem, Phoenix?

Denver—Hey, let's all take it down a notch. It's been a long night. We can talk about it later.

Like he's the big boss, and that's the end of it. Bullshit.

—How much time do you think we have? *Millions of people are dying*. Sitting around with our thumbs up our asses isn't gonna get it done.

That sounded good. And it felt good too, having something to say. Them looking at me, listening, like they're expecting something more. Out of nowhere I have a thought and blurt it.

—I can get a gun.

Nobody moves a muscle.

Boise—A gun...like for doing what?

I have no idea. But getting it would at least be doing something, you lazy-ass bitches.

—No comment. Security first, right? You'll hear all about it after it's over.

Denver—Hey, settle down. We gotta stick together.

Chattanooga—You can't—

The hell I can't. I stand up and get my phone, and I'm at the door, and just because it feels right, I give it a hard slam.

Clomping down the staircase two steps at a time, it hits me, this shit just got real.

. . .

Breaking things is far easier than building them or protecting them once they're built. Attack the infrastructure, the institutions, the pipelines, the trucks. Watch the flowers of destruction bloom.

—Fight for Earth

Outside, the sun is bright, the air has warmed up. I know exactly what I need to do.

Pedaling east through the downtown area I go past the turn I used to take to Joey's apartment, my only real friend since I left Arizona. I'm remembering the time the two of us drove to San Francisco to hear Tillie "One Degree Fahrenheit" McBivens give a speech. All the way down we talked about how she was like Martin Luther King, but for the whole planet. The huge auditorium was packed, and she was on the stage going all fire-and-brimstone about how bad things are and how much worse they're getting and how fast. All those people cheering at everything she said, it was like a pep rally I could actually give a shit about.

Then she told us her best shot for how we're going to stop planetary incineration...and what was it? Sign the petitions out in the lobby, write our representatives, read her book and her blog, join her organization, and send her a bunch of money so she can keep up the fight.

Joey and I looked at each other like WTF?

As she wrapped up her talk, McBivens bragged about how she's given more than three thousand speeches on six continents, at a UN conference in Japan, to villagers on a beach in Sri Lanka, before a gathering of CEOs in Switzerland. And she swore that nothing could stop her from giving thousands more.

I tilted my head toward Joey and whispered—That's a lot of fuckin' jet fuel.

Afterwards, just outside the auditorium a woman in long blond dreadlocks was yelling—McBivens is a sell out! Resist or die!

She handed me a little newspaper, the first copy I ever saw of *Fight for Earth*.

The drive home sucked. We were tired and totally let down by McBivens and her hypocritical bullshit. At around three in the morning, we passed Mount Shasta, huge, covered in snow and glowing bluish white in the light of the full moon. Joey sparked a joint to enhance the view, and we handed it back and forth. That's when the trouble started. We talked about what we could do to make a better world. Joey said that for him it was writing songs about animals going extinct.

I started laughing at his dumb-shit idea and said—Yeah, right, let's all strum along, like that's really gonna make a difference.

This got him pissed, pissed like I'd never seen him. When we stopped for gas. I stayed in the car while Joey scrubbed bugs off the windshield, glaring through the glass at me, shaking his head, giving me the stink-eye. We didn't say one word for the rest of the long drive home.

Once I hooked up with the NDF, Denver told me that guys like Joey are called reactionary gradualists. And that was the end of Joey.

The road cuts through trees and farm fields. I pedal up a little rise into a ritzy residential area, and there's Uncle Carl's house, in all its mock-Tudor glory, with his big shiny Winnebago, my former home, parked in the driveway. His BMW is gone. Maybe he's on one of his business trips to Hong Kong or maybe just down at the supermarket.

I park my bike in the side yard, get the spare key, and let myself in the back door. The keypad for the home security system starts blinking. It's been a couple of months since I moved out, and I freeze up, then the alarm code pops into my head, and I punch it in. Nobody's home, but I'm still creeping like a burglar, walking on tiptoe and listening at every corner. Down the hallway and up the stairs to Uncle Carl's office. As soon as I'm inside, I feel eyes staring at me and look up at the mounted head of the rhino he shot in Africa. Right below the rhino is the big metal safe where he keeps his guns.

From the top drawer in his desk, I get the key, unlock the safe, and swing open its heavy doors. I look through the rifles until I find the one Carl taught me to shoot, the Remington. It's heavy and solid, and I put it to my shoulder, whip around, take up cool firing positions. Above the leather sofa is the head of an antelope with long corkscrew horns. Yeah, got you, sucker. *Pow.*

I take a box of cartridges from the safe then close the doors and turn the key. Carl probably won't realize anything's missing for months. I set the rifle and ammunition on the desk and am putting the key back in the drawer when I notice an envelope propped against the telephone. It's torn open, sticking out is a fancy invitation.

Golf tournament

Fair Oaks Country Club

fundraiser for Friends of Kelso County LNG

opening remarks by

Opportunity Oil CEO Gerald X. O'Toole

There's a small photo of O'Toole, the piece of crap who wants to build a pipeline and shipping terminal so he can make money exporting tankers full of death. He looks just like Clint Eastwood, a squinty-eyed relic from another time.

The invitation says O'Toole will speak at noon today.

The clock on the desk reads 10:51.

Fair Oaks is just a couple of miles from here.

As I shove the invitation into my pocket there's a mob yelling in my head, and everybody has ten different ideas for what to do and how to do it. One of the voices outshouts the rest: I can't ride my bike down the street holding a damn deer rifle.

With a blanket from the sofa I wrap up the gun and take it to the kitchen where there's a hook holding the keys for the Winnebago.

I work the key into the RV's door lock with a shaking hand then climb behind the steering wheel. That's when the smell hits me, the unmistakable stuffy Winnebago smell of plywood and new carpet. The dashboard has knobs and dials and switches like a jet plane's cockpit. I've watched Uncle Carl drive it plenty; how hard could it be? I get the big bus rolling, and it bucks and weaves a little until the controls start to make sense.

If Carl's in Asia, great, but what if he's not? He comes home, sees the Winnie gone, and maybe notices about the gun. He calls the cops, and I'm driving around in a thirty-eight-foot-long billboard that screams—I'M THE GUY YOU'RE LOOKING FOR.

. . .

Stopping any one of us is stopping one molecule in a tsunami, for we are vast and rising and soon we will tumble forth with the power of a redemptive flood. We will come at you, wave after wave, a storm surge, a hard rain, the deluge.

—Fight for Earth

I drive carefully, keeping an eye out for cops, and just before the bridge that leads to the country club over on the north side of the river, I turn west on a country lane. It meanders through the dense woods that run along the south bank and up and over the ridge. While living with Uncle Carl I spent a lot of time alone out here, smoking weed, roaming around, and imagining I was in Jurassic Park hiding from a T. rex.

I spot the trailhead that leads down to the river across from Fair Oaks and park the RV. In the closet I grab the jacket from Carl's camo hunting suit, put it on, and shove the cartridge box in the pocket. Rifle in hand, I descend the zigzagging path to the riverbank.

I keep back in the trees and see the country club buildings a hundred yards upstream. Working my way through the dense brush parallel to the bank, I come to a place as close as I can get.

Across the river, everything is happening on a big grassy lawn between the main clubhouse and the water. To the right an outdoor stage, an elevated platform with a podium and flags and big arrangements of flowers and stands holding a couple of good-sized PA speakers. Facing the stage are rows and rows of chairs, and behind the chairs, way over to the right, are big white tents where some of the early arrivers are loading up on drinks.

I find a little clearing that's sheltered from the river by some low, gray boulders. A log is laying on the ground, and I lug it a couple of feet to make a better place to sit.

From here to the podium is about seventy-five yards, give or take. Unobstructed. With a scoped rifle. Piece of cake.

It's turned into a warm sunny day, and I'm hot in the camo jacket, but I don't want to be seen. I wipe sweat off my forehead on the sleeve, and it fills my nose with the Winnebago smell. I remember how that smell got stronger and stronger as the summer temperatures got hotter and hotter. And how after the fire, after there was no more apartment or town or Tinkle Valley High School or much of anything else, Uncle Carl gave us a place to stay. Mom in the guest room, me in the Winnie. The hours I spent lying on that bed talking on the phone with Jillian in fucking Florida, trying to cheer each other up about our stolen senior year, talking shit about how we could be together again. A couple of weeks later, she told me about the fuck she met playing tennis. After that, I didn't have much reason for getting out of bed. That was my life, laid out in the heat and that plywood and new carpet stink, reading everything I could find about the Tinkle Valley Fire, the 726 homes burned, the three people and six smoke jumpers who died, and the thousand fingers pointing to one cause, global warming.

If the judge asks me why I shot Gerald X. O'Toole I'll say—Because I'm part of something bigger than you and your laws, more important than anything that has ever happened before. I'm just one guy, and look what I accomplished. And there are lots of others just like me all over the world. Maybe they'll follow my trial. Maybe for them, I'll be some kind of hero. Or maybe they won't give a shit because they're too busy doing their own actions. What do you think of that, Mr. Judge Man?

People have arrived and filled all the seats. A fat bald guy in a dark suit waddles up to the podium.

I shoulder the rifle and look through the scope. Definitely not Clint Eastwood. Probably some jerkoff introducer. I check the magnification indicator on the scope. The power ring is set at ten, and I dial it up to eighteen and look back into the eyepiece. Oh yeah. Mr. Introducer's blurry image now fills the view, and I adjust the focus and sharpen him up to where I can see the colors in the little American flag on his lapel. He's saying something into the microphone, but at this distance, drifting on the wind, the amplified words don't make any sense, just bits and pieces, distorted mumbles like in some weird underwater dream.

My boy G.X. O'Toole must be on deck. I dig a cartridge out of the box and cup it in my palm. Long, cold, and heavy. For some reason, this makes me happy. No, not just happy, a jolt of electricity crackles up and down my chest. I kiss the bullet then slide it into the magazine. Then two more, not sure why, one's more than enough. Uncle Carl used this rifle to drop a seven-hundred-pound bull elk. I open the breech and shove the bolt forward to chamber the round.

Mr. Introducer finishes talking and...*fuck*.

Some white-haired lady is now blabbing at the mike. Get out of there grandma, nobody wants to listen to you. I try to hear what she's saying but her words are faint and garbled, *America...economy...jobs...greatest in the world.*

A bead of sweat rolls down my forehead, and I wipe it on my sleeve. Another whiff of plywood and new carpet. I wish I had some water.

The memories come streaming back in a rush, and I pinch my eyes shut.

Mom is yelling at me—Come on, come on! We gotta go. *Right now!*

I'm standing in the living room looking at my aquarium—But what about my fish? We have to save them.

Mom yanks me out the door, and we get into the car and drive through a tornado of smoke, ash, embers, and fire.

We leave behind our apartment and my fish. But I can't get the picture out of my head, the inferno blasting through our front door and into the living room, lighting the drapes and table and the sofa. The fire gets higher and higher, closing in on my aquarium and Pinky and Elmer and Speckles and Fat Charlie and Skidmarks and Brainiac. They see the shimmering flames, feel the water getting hotter. They're scared, swimming faster and faster, but there's no place to hide. They're boiling alive.

I hear what sounds like applause. At the podium, grandma sweeps her hand toward the clubhouse, and out he comes. Yeah, that's him. Here comes the birthday boy. He bounces up the little staircase onto the stage with a springy step, and the old lady presents him with a trophy. Probably an Academy Award in the category of biggest earth-killing douchebag. He's tall and bends the microphone holder upwards and starts giving his speech.

The great O'Toole is centered in my scope, crosshairs on his forehead. I thumb the switch on the safety, *click*, ready to fire. A few deep breaths, and I move my finger to the trigger.

He's mouthing away, face all stern. Now he's smiling, his eyes all twinkle-twinkle, and he's looking around the audience like he just got off a good joke.

The breeze carries a murmuring *ha-ha-ha*.

You're so funny. Let's put in an LNG terminal. Why not just strangle the whole fucking planet? You're evil, you pig. Pure fucking evil. And I'm gonna do this. I'm really gonna. I'm gonna put a bullet right in your ugly fucking pig fucking head. I'm gonna—

Wait. Something's happening.

The fat bald guy, cell phone jammed to his ear, is at O'Toole's side, grabbing him by the upper arm, pulling him close and saying something. Then bug-eyed fatso leans too close to the mike, and the word *EVACUATE* explodes like a clap of thunder. I take my eye away from the scope to see everybody in the audience walking, jogging, running toward the clubhouse.

The sound of a faraway siren drifts across the river.

Fucking Uncle Carl.

I whip the scope back over to O'Toole just as he takes a look this way, scanning the tree line through his squinty eyes, like he's wondering if I'm out here, some crazy fuck with a rifle, ready to drop him where he stands.

My last chance. Aim. Breathe. Feel the trigger.

The fat guy jerks O'Toole from the podium and hustles him off the stage.

Two or three sirens are now whining and getting closer.

Everyone is inside the clubhouse ballroom, but I can't find O'Toole among them. They're milling around like they're safe. *Hey dumbasses, the whole wall along the river is windows.*

I could shoot up the glass and give the TV news a couple of bullet holes to gawk at.

But I didn't come to assassinate a window.

I stand up and start to go but pause to look back across the river. Chairs, stage, flags, flowers, podium, and microphone. Deserted. Empty. All set up for something that never happened. But something could have happened. Something important. I could have fired the first shot in the war.

Crouching low, I trot along the bank and back up the zigzag trail to the Winnebago. I turn it around and tear off, a straightaway then around a bend and—*shit*! A cop car is stopping traffic at the intersection by the bridge. I brake hard, shift into reverse. The road isn't wide, and I back up into the bushes, and *CRASH,* the rear bumper rams into something that shakes me in my seat. I crank the wheel fast and complete the 180 and stomp on the gas pedal. The Winnie flies through a couple of turns and groans up an incline, and at the top I slam on the brakes. Another cop car, parked diagonally across the intersection below, its lights flashing.

They won't find anybody. Then probably search parties, helicopters, and dogs.

To my left, the forest goes all the way up and over the ridge and down to the north side of town. It's my only way out. I turn the rig around and backtrack until I see a gravel road leading up a hollow. I cut the sharp turn too tight and slam into a row of posts holding mailboxes that tear into the siding. The lane twists and turns, the RV bounces over potholes, branches rake along the roof screeching.

At the dead end an overgrown trail takes off into the forest. It's a hell of a long way up the steep ridge. I grab the rifle and start running. The trail is good for about a hundred yards then narrows and becomes harder to follow. Soon it's gone altogether, and I'm busting through bushes, ferns, and branches, climbing over fallen limbs and trees. The rifle gets tangled in a vine, and I yank hard to get it free. A thorny stem slices across the back of my hand like a red-hot knife, and I'm bleeding pretty good. I lick at the deep cut and have never tasted so much blood. I start to gag and spit and wipe my tongue on the sleeve of the jacket.

The slope eases up for a while, and I try to cover it quickly. My foot lands in a hole, the ankle folds sharply to the side, and I fall to the ground, clutching it. When I can get back on my feet, there's a jolt of pain with every other step. I use the rifle as a cane, clutching the barrel, and limp on. No time to stop.

A half hour of this, and I'm bent over and panting, still nowhere near the top. My ankle is swollen over the top of my shoe, and I'm dying for some water.

Just ahead there's a huge tree, and I hobble over and lean against its thick dark trunk. Dripping with sweat, I try to control my gasping so I can listen. Nothing.

Two minutes of rest, that's all. Breathe. Breathe.

I stare at the gash across my hand, the dried cake of blood, the dark steel of the rifle barrel.

I feel it all washing away, everything, my whole life. It's gone. Everything and everybody I've known, gone. There's nowhere to go back to.

My gut feels sick and watery. The ferns and bushes and trees around me don't look real. They don't know I exist, don't care. I want to lay down, just lay down right here and think.

No time for that. I've got to get my ass over that ridge. I push off from the tree, and my ankle screams with the first few steps. Keep going. No other option.

Another quarter mile, and I come to a clearing, pause, look at the terrain, and try to see my best path forward. A bird hidden high in a nearby tree shrieks. It shrieks again and flies out from cover, and with a few powerful strokes of its big black wings flies straight up the slope, weightless, soaring above the very highest of the trees, to the top of the ridge, and over. I stare at the jagged line where the black forest rips into the blazing afternoon sky. I am floating. I am at peace. I am protected. I have nothing to fear. Everything in the past is gone, peeled away, meaningless. I know exactly what is going to happen. It is all inevitable now, gears in motion, *click click click.*

I will hide the rifle out here.

I will make it back to town, to my comrades, the NDF.

They'll help me.

They need me.

I'm ready to pull the trigger.

And next time I will.

. . .

About the Author:

Ross West has placed fiction, essays, journalism, and poetry in publications from *Orion* to the *Journal of Recreational Linguistics*. His work has been anthologized in *Best Essays Northwest, Best of Dark Horse Presents*, and elsewhere. He edited the University of Oregon's research magazine, *Inquiry;* was senior managing editor at *Oregon Quarterly*; and served as text editor for the *Atlas of Oregon* and the *Atlas of Yellowstone*. A collection of his short stories, *The Fragile Blue Dot*, is due out in spring 2024.

7

Sunburn

by Fabiyas M V (India)

Subgenre: Poetry

Time Period: Present day

Setting: India

Author's Notes: For those of us not living in India, the author explains "These red wild blossoms" from the third stanza: "They are the deep-red blossoms appearing on the rain tree here in my homeland (Kerala, India) in the parching sunlight. The leaves have almost fallen. Men harm nature in different ways, so these red flowers are like the red angry face of nature."

. . .

Sunburn

They muted us with
a poisonous smile
and political power.
Then they beheaded

our hills, massacred
trees, buried ponds...
We mistook their new
concrete buildings
for development.

They sit in the chill
of a/c rooms with
prostitutes. Venom
from their deeds'
fangs affects the
earth's organs.
Climate malfunctions.
Embryo of rain dies
in the womb of cloud.

Sand suffers from
dehydration. These
red wild blossoms
are nature's fury,
burning bright on
the branches. This
isn't sunlight, but a
pyre. Life's wings
are being burnt.

Butterflies don't
decorate plants.
Flowers are like
breasts of silent
starving women.
Even a tough crow
doesn't dare to fly.

A poor peasant
falls down, thrust
with sun's arrows,
in his field of parched
dreams. Sunburn is
our annihilation's
developmental stage.

. . .

About the Author: Fabiyas M V is a writer from Orumanayur village in Kerala, India. He is the author of *Monsoon Turbulence* (Poetry Nook, US), *Shelter within the Peanut Shells* (Red Cherry Books, India), *Kanoli Kaleidoscope* (PunksWritePoemsPress, US), *Eternal Fragments* (erbacce press, UK), and *Moonlight and Solitude* (Raspberry Books, India). Fabiyas has won many international accolades, including Merseyside at War Poetry Award from Liverpool University; Poetry Soup International Award; and Animal Poetry Prize 2012 from RSPCA (Royal Society for Prevention of Cruelties against Animals, UK). He was the finalist for Global Poetry Prize 2015 by the United Poets Laureate International (UPLI) in Vienna. His poems have been broadcast on All India Radio. Poetry Nook, US, has nominated him for the 2019 Pushcart Prize. He has been working as a teacher in English at Gov. Higher Secondary School, Maranchery, in Kerala.

8

Extremism in Defense of Mother Earth

by David Harten Watson (United States)

Subgenres: Dark humor, political satire, horror

Time period: Present day

Setting: The Black Thunder coal mine, Wyoming, United States of America

Author's introduction: This story came to me in a dream. Combining dark humor with political satire, it parodies the deep political divide in America today. This story has no heroes and pulls no punches, mocking both right-wing news media and environmental activists who risk their lives in attention-seeking publicity stunts—which don't always result in the desired outcome.

Disclaimer: The environmental group EFASHT is fictional. The other organizations in this story, however, are all too real, including Fox News, Peabody Energy, Arch Coal, and the American Coal Council, whose ungrammatical slogan is indeed "Economic [sic], Abundant/Secure, and Environmentally Sound Coal."

. . .

Fox News reporter Lindsay Rogers waited until she heard the anchorman's voice in her earpiece say, *"We go live now to our very own Lindsay Rogers, who's at the Black Thunder coal mine in Wyoming covering the protest by the environmental extremist cult 'Earth First, Animals Second, Humans Third,' or EFASHT. Lindsay, have you spoken to the cult's leader?"*

"Not yet, Jim, but the leader, who insists we call him by his 'tree name,' Forest Lake, issued a press release promising us an 'unprecedented and unforgettable demonstration today, something that no environmental group has ever done before.'"

"Are you expecting today's protest to turn violent? I see that in addition to corporate security from the joint owners of the Black Thunder mine, Arch Coal and Peabody Energy, there are Wyoming state police behind you in riot gear. Does this mean Fox News viewers can expect to see some violence today?"

Lindsay could hear the eagerness in Jim's voice. She, too, felt excited at the prospect of violence, despite the risk to her own safety. *If my camera crew can film footage of liberal protesters acting violently—smashing, burning, looting, or rioting—Fox News viewers will eat it up! Ratings will rise, and with them, so will my chances of promotion.* "Nobody knows quite what to expect when dealing with EFASHT," she said. "Some people call the group eco-terrorists, although the cult's leader denies that label. Wait, I think I see him now."

Lindsay led her camera crew over to the man she'd been searching for, a tall, gray-haired, bearded man in his fifties. Like everyone in his environmental cult, he was dressed entirely in forest green, but he was twice the age of most of the protesters. The majority were either Millennials or younger. Lindsay scrutinized the crowd—*probably rich liberal college kids who've been brainwashed by socialist "Green New Deal" propaganda.* Glad to be the first reporter on scene to recognize the cult leader, she said, "Lindsay Rogers, Fox News. Are you Forest Lake?"

The man nodded. "That is what they call me."

"Can you tell our viewers exactly what sort of demonstration your group has planned for today?"

"I can't tell you, but you'll soon see. The whole *world* will see!" Forest Lake said, his voice breaking into a mad cackle.

He's a nutcase, Lindsay thought. *But that's good because interviewing nutcases always boosts ratings.* "Is your group planning something violent today?"

"An interesting question," Forest Lake said, stroking his beard thoughtfully, appearing saner now. *Too bad.* "It all depends on your perspective. Some might call today's actions violent, but to rephrase anarchist Karl Hess, 'Extremism in defense of Mother Earth is no vice. Moderation in pursuit of environmental justice is no virtue.'"

Lindsay corrected, smiling smugly, "It was conservative Barry Goldwater who said that, and he was talking about liberty, not the environment."

Forest Lake shook his head. "No, you're the one who has it wrong. It was Goldwater's anarchist *speechwriter*, Karl Hess, who penned those famous words."

Lindsay's smile faded. She changed the subject. "Can you tell me why you're protesting here today?"

"*That*, I can answer," Forest Lake said. "We chose the Black Thunder Coal Mine as the site of our climate change protest because coal is the dirtiest form of energy, emitting more carbon dioxide pollution than any other energy source. As everyone knows, carbon dioxide is the chief greenhouse gas that causes global warming."

"Allegedly," Lindsay added.

"The science is undeniable," Forest Lake said, "even if your corporate sponsor polluters won't allow your TV station to *admit* it. Anthropogenic global warming caused by greenhouse gas emissions is the greatest threat to humanity today.

"But humans aren't the species most impacted by global warming. Mankind will find ways to survive no matter what the climate, but climate change means *extinction* for mammals, birds, reptiles, fish, amphibians, insects, trees, and other plant life. Extinction is forever. As you might guess by our group's name, Earth First, Animals Second, Humans Third, or EFASHT, we care about all species on Earth, not only humans."

Lindsay asked, "Doesn't your group's name indicate you care *more* about animals than about humans?"

"Well, yes, but—"

Point scored, Lindsay continued on the offensive, hoping to goad him into revealing that he was a Luddite. "What do you propose humans do to prevent this *alleged* global warming? Stop using coal? Stop using electricity? Stop using fossil fuels entirely? That would *destroy the American economy"*—her producers at Fox had insisted she use those four words—"and leave citizens freezing in the dark, with no means of transportation. Is that what EFASHT wants?"

"No, even if mankind stopped burning coal, the dirtiest form of energy, it still wouldn't be enough to stop global warming. The biggest culprit for anthropogenic global warming, even worse than coal, is human overpopulation. Two hundred years ago, Earth's population was only one billion people, but global population is projected to reach *nine* billion people by 2042.

"The trouble is, Mother Earth can only sustainably support *one* billion humans at most, even less if they all lived at the American level of overconsumption. The only way to prevent mass extinction of animals and plants is for humans to decrease our population to a sustainable level of one billion."

Lindsay asked, "So, are you proposing to decrease the population through birth control combined with abortion-on-demand? Some people consider birth control to be a sin, and abortion is murder." Her Fox News producer required her to say that, even though he'd paid for his assistant's abortion after getting her pregnant in an extramarital affair.

Forest Lake said, "Birth control alone can't lower the population," ignoring the controversial topic of abortion. *Too bad,* Lindsay thought, *because Fox relies on stirring up controversy about hot-button, culture-war topics like abortion to boost ratings.* "Birth control can only slow the rate of increase, or at best, stabilize the population at the current level. We believe Earth's human population needs to be reduced rapidly by nearly 90 percent, which means a much more radical plan is necessary."

"What exactly *is* your group's 'radical plan' for rapidly lowering the Earth's population? Bioterrorism, perhaps, releasing a virus to kill 90 percent of the world's population?"

I sure hope I didn't just put an idea into this crazy man's head.

"No, of course not," Forest Lake snapped. "As I've told you media people time and time again, EFASHT is *not* a terrorist group. We don't set off bombs, we don't burn down buildings, we don't kill people, and we certainly don't commit bioterrorism."

"Then how," Lindsay asked, arching her eyebrows, "do you propose to decrease Earth's population by almost 90 percent?"

"We will lead by example," Forest Lake said, smiling. "One thousand members of my environmental group have traveled here today, from all over the United States and Canada, to show the world what must be done." He unzipped his green jacket and pulled on a cord hanging around his neck.

He's triggering a suicide vest! Lindsay jumped back, nearly jostling her cameraman.

Forest Lake chuckled at her reaction, holding up the cord for her to see it was harmless. The brown leather cord held only a whistle, carved out of wood. He blew three long toots on the whistle, so loud that Lindsay had to cover her ears, followed by three shorter toots. The crowd of demonstrators grew so quiet that one could've heard a leaf drop—if there had been any leaves remaining in the vast, bulldozed, strip-mined, desolate wasteland that was the Black Thunder coal mine.

Forest Lake pulled a silver flask from his hip pocket, held it above his head for all to see, and shouted, "To Mother Earth!"

"To Mother Earth!" the crowd echoed in a thunderous voice, as a thousand protesters each raised their flask high.

Forest Lake raised his flask a second time and shouted, "*For* Mother Earth!"

"*For* Mother Earth!" the crowd roared as one, and then along with Forest Lake, they chugged the contents of their flasks. After drinking the toast, all one thousand protesters put the flasks back in their pockets, then quietly, peacefully, lay down on the ground. The only people still standing were media members, mine security, and police in riot gear.

Lindsay turned to the camera and explained, "Jim, it appears the protesters are acting out what's known as a 'die-in' to make their political point. This is a very old, tired technique that liberal activists have used for decades. Frankly, I'd been expecting something more creative and original, but perhaps they have something else planned for later in the day."

She lowered the microphone to the supine form of Forest Lake and said, "Mr. Lake, how long is the *die-in* portion of the protest going to last, and what other forms of protest are you planning today? You'd promised us something 'unprecedented' in your press release, but there's nothing original about a die-in."

The environmental cult leader did not respond.

"Mr. Lake? Can you hear me?" Lindsay knelt next to Forest Lake and felt his neck. Gasping, she said into the microphone, "He's dead, Jim. I think they're *all* dead!" So flustered that she was at a loss for words, she stood up and stammered her closing line, "Back to you, Jim."

As the anchorman in New York took over for her, Lindsay signaled her camera crew to stop filming, then let her microphone arm drop to her side. The deaths of one thousand tree-hugging liberals didn't bother her, but she was frustrated that her exclusive interview had been cut so short. *I bleached my roots blonde again this morning just for this*?

Her soundman turned on a speaker so the remote crew could hear the rest of the news broadcast from headquarters. Having prematurely given her closing line, Lindsay had nothing else to do but listen to the insipid voice of the overpaid, over-coiffed, underworked male anchorman in New York as he took over her news segment.

"*That was an unexpected turn of events.*" Jim's voice erupted from her soundman's speaker and simultaneously over the airwaves to millions of Fox News viewers. "*Tonight, the CEOs of Peabody Energy, Arch Coal, and fossil fuel companies all over America will sleep soundly, knowing there are one thousand fewer environmental extremists today than there were yesterday. As my friend Bob jokes about suicide bombers, 'If we had more men like these, we'd have less men like these!'*

"*This is a definite win for the energy industry. They'd feared acts of violence against a coal mine today, but instead, environmental extremists chose to commit mass suicide, ending a threat to America's leading coal companies. And now, as the crisis at the coal mine was averted with absolutely no property damage,*" Jim's voice gloated, "*it's time to cut to a message from our sponsor, the American Coal Council, about the virtues of 'Economic, Abundant/Secure, and Environmentally Sound' coal.*"

. . .

About the Author:

David Harten Watson, editor of this cli-fi anthology, authored the young-adult fantasy series *Magicians Gold*, including the award-winning novel *Magic Teacher's Son* and its sequel *Fortress of Gold*. David has worked in a dizzying array of jobs including US Army Armor officer at Fort Knox, experience that came in handy for his second novel, *Fortress of Gold*. Raised in snowy Buffalo, New York, he has degrees from Princeton, Canisius College, and Buffalo State College. He's the Organizer of the Woodbridge Science Fiction & Fantasy Writers Meetup, which he founded in 2008. He lives in New Jersey. Author's website: www.davidhartenwatson.com

9

Elemental Crisis

by Dawn Vogel (United States)

Subgenres: Poetry, literary cli-fi

Time Period: Present day

Setting: Earth

. . .

Water, earth, fire, and air,
surge and quake and burn and gust.
All out of control, these days.
This is the way the world ends.

Despite our need for each one,
They also offer danger.
We balance trust and fear of
water, earth, fire, and air.

Our planet is as stable
as the ever-shifting sands,
so we watch the elements
surge and quake and burn and gust.

Our impacts exponential,
the forefront of climate change,
little is done to halt it,
all out of control, these days.

Pollution in cities, the
Amazon is burning, land
crumbles, water can't be drunk.
This is the way the world ends.

. . .

About the author: Dawn Vogel's academic background is in history, so it's not surprising that much of her fiction is set in earlier times. By day, she edits reports for historians and archaeologists. In her alleged spare time, she runs a craft business, co-runs a small press, and tries to find time for writing. Her steampunk adventure series, *Brass and Glass*, is available from DefCon One Publishing. She is a member of Broad Universe, SFWA, and Codex Writers. She lives in Seattle with her husband, author Jeremy Zimmerman, and their herd of cats. Visit her at http://historythatneverwas.com.

10

A Ray of Hope

by Frank Roger (Belgium)

Subgenre: Science fiction

Time Period: Near future

Setting: England and the rest of planet Earth

Synopsis: Alien ships appear all over earth and start transforming the planet according to their wishes. Mankind tries desperately to resist their efforts. Despite the upbeat title, this story paints a picture of a grim, dark future.

. . .

**** The planet we discovered seems perfect for our purposes. It is for a large part covered by water, with land masses spread all across. The two poles are crowned with ice caps. Both the oceans and the continents appear to be teeming with a wide variety of life-forms. These are all likely to be harmless and should in no way interfere with our plans. Preliminary tests will be run, and if these prove successful, we will proceed with our project.* ***

. . .

The fleet of alien spacecraft took the world by surprise, appearing out of nowhere and descending majestically through the atmosphere. None of them landed anywhere. They all ended up hovering somewhere above the ocean, at various places around the world.

I watched the special news bulletins on TV with my wife, Marsha, and my daughter, Jessica. The images merely showed gigantic spacecraft, hanging unmoving in the air. Many people were interviewed. Politicians, scientists, army generals, representatives of the church and other religions all offered their views and theories.

Some were excited and claimed we were on the threshold of a new dawn. Others were wary and warned we might be under attack, even threatened with extinction. There were those who said the arrival of these spaceships was a sign from God and that we should mend our ways. Everybody had an opinion, including those who seemed to have little knowledge of the issue at hand.

At one point, Jessica turned to me and asked, "Did the aliens come to help us?"

I nodded and said, "Yes, they came to help. There's no need to worry. They'll solve all our problems."

Jessica accepted my reply. It seemed like the logical thing for a kid to ask, and for a father to answer.

Everyone wondered what would happen next. Would extraterrestrial creatures emerge from the spacecraft? Would they be friendly? Would they try to establish contact with us?

I got lots of questions like that at school. Naturally, kids turned to their science teacher with such issues. I tried to satisfy their curiosity as best I could.

Time went by, and nothing happened. No contact could be established with the visitors from beyond the solar system. Many people began to lose interest, as if these spacecraft had already become part of the scenery. There were still news bulletins, but they just offered images of ships hanging there motionless and interviews of people who had less and less to say.

Jessica grew disappointed. "You said they came to help us. What are they waiting for?"

This time, I didn't have a reply ready.

All we could do was wait. So, we waited.

. . .

**** All preliminary tests proved successful. This planet is definitely useful. There are two minor problems: the average temperature of the oceans is too low, and the water's chemical balance is a bit off. We should be able to fix this. The techniques have been applied before on several occasions. The general feeling is that this will be an uneventful procedure.* ***

. . .

About a week later, Jessica told me, pointing at the image of an alien spacecraft on TV, "I don't think there's anyone in there. I'm sure there are just machines and computers on board."

"You may be right," I said. Some leading scientists had opined that these might be unmanned spacecraft. Teams of scientists and the army had monitored and examined the gigantic vessels and had failed to detect any signs of life aboard.

Nothing was known about our visitors; nobody had a clue where these ships came from, what they were doing here, for how long they would stay, who had sent them, or why. Nothing seemed to happen; the ships just hung there.

Mankind's first contact with alien life-forms was an anticlimax. The invasion began to fade from the news, as there was little new to report. Only the scientists kept working, and the generals still weren't convinced military intervention would be unnecessary.

We went on with our lives. The kids at school hardly ever raised the issue of alien spacecraft anymore. Jessica suddenly announced her plans to become a ballet dancer, no doubt after watching a ballet on TV. I made a note of it, fully realizing that another TV show next week might cause a drastic shift in career choice. It had happened before.

Then there was a mildly interesting item on a news bulletin: a team of scientists had discovered that the temperature of the water under one of the spacecraft had risen by a few degrees. The water was also slightly polluted. They would now try to find out if this was the case everywhere, and if there was a connection between this phenomenon and the presence of the spacecraft.

Perhaps the ships produced a kind of radiation that raised the water's temperature and spilled some waste material. Or it could be a planned action, in which case thorough research would be carried out. It looked as though the special bulletins would become interesting again. Even Jessica was back at my side for the TV news.

I just wasn't sure whether that was a positive sign or a bad one.

. . .

**** We are proceeding with our operations as planned. Everything is running perfectly. It is expected that the melting of the two ice caps will accelerate the process considerably. There might be an added benefit: if the water level rises, the lower parts of the land masses will be flooded, thus increasing the planet's water surface. No problems are anticipated.* ***

. . .

Four weeks after the aliens appeared, the ships still hadn't moved an inch. There was still no sign of life on board. And we still didn't have a clue as to what was going on.

Scientists discovered that the temperature of the water under every spacecraft was rising markedly, and the pollution was increasing. This could not be a coincidence. Although there was no evidence that the aliens were responsible, there appeared to be no other explanation. The shift in temperature was too sudden and too generalized to be caused by natural phenomena. The pollutants appeared to be quite toxic, although their exact composition remained unclear. I reckoned that if any alien technology were involved, we would be unable to grasp what was happening.

There were some who said this was a dangerous evolution, and that we might have to take action—although it wasn't clear what we could do about it. And there were military types who said it would be a mistake to wait until the situation deteriorated, and that it would be wiser to attack the alien spacecraft right then. As we couldn't take for granted that they were friendly, we had to assume they were hostile and should act accordingly. A surprisingly high number of people shared this point of view.

One question I asked myself: if the aliens—whether or not they were physically present in those vessels—were indeed superior to us, wouldn't they have ways to counter any offensive we launched? Of course, I wasn't a military man. I thought differently.

In the meantime, Jessica's career choice for ballet dancing appeared to be final. Marsha suggested we check whether there were any ballet courses for children her age. I remarked that Jessica was still a kid and likely to change course a few times, considering how easily she was influenced by what she saw on TV.

Yet Marsha stood firm with Jessica's decision; ballet dancing it would be then. I managed to resist proposing an alternative career in high-tech combat of alien invaders. I was convinced my well-meant advice would have been thrown to the winds.

. . .

**** Considering the ease with which the first phase progressed, it was decided to speed up the operation. The sooner* *we manage to prepare the oceans for our project, the better. We are likely to cause a major disruption in the planet's ecosystem, but that should have no influence on our plans. A full-scale disinfection of the planet is not required for our purposes but might avoid interference from local life-forms.* ***

. . .

The world was in turmoil.

It was clear to everyone that the ocean's temperature was rising spectacularly and that the ice caps were melting fast. The pollution was spreading quickly as well.

These facts could not be attributed to anthropogenic global warming or any other "traditional" explanation. Obviously, the aliens—or whoever was aboard those ships—were responsible.

More and more political leaders adopted the idea of military action, which the generals applauded. The problem was that no one knew which weapons would be effective against this invisible enemy. It was understood an offensive was imminent: a joint effort by the world's most powerful nations.

In the meantime, the sea level was rising drastically as the ice caps disappeared. Archipelagos in the Pacific and low-lying countries including the Netherlands and Bangladesh prepared for major evacuation. Traditional flood-control methods such as raising and strengthening dikes were useless, considering the rapid sea level rise.

Every night, we watched the news on TV, and Jessica often reached for Marsha's hand. Our daughter was not the only one who was upset by what she saw on the screen. We were all in the grip of fear. Our world was changing. *What exactly was going on, and what could we do about it? Who were these aliens? What brought them here, and how did we fit into their plans, if we did at all? Why did they poison the oceans? Were they out to destroy all marine life?* There were many questions, and all remained unanswered.

The president addressed the nation on TV, saying, "The government will not remain idle but will take decisive action to protect the country and its citizens." He did not go into too much detail. I couldn't wait to see how he would solve this problem.

At school, the kids pressed me with questions. It was clear they were afraid of what was going on. Their rose-colored view of a life without major disruptions had been shattered painfully. It was awfully hard to ease their minds. They seemed to understand very well that I was merely trying to reassure them, rather than supplying solid answers. It was one of the hazards of the trade for a science teacher. Fortunately, Marsha wasn't facing this problem—travel agency customers tended to head elsewhere with such questions.

Neither Jessica nor Marsha brought up the subject of ballet dancing anymore. Apparently, their minds were focused on other things. I didn't think this boded well for our future.

. . .

**** The operation is running smoothly. We estimate that a sufficient expanse of the oceans will reach the required temperature and chemical balance within a short range of time. Tests will be run at regular intervals. No major problems are expected. This planet may prove ideal for our purposes.* ***

. . .

We were in front of our TV, on the edge of our seats, like most people all over the country, and probably all over the world. Nobody wanted to miss the first images of the "War against the aliens," officially called "Operation Blue Planet."

"We have waited long enough," the president of the United Nations, flanked by his counterparts of the world's leading countries, stated in a live TV broadcast. "It's time to give a signal to the aliens, to tell them we do not appreciate their meddling with our planet's marine ecosystem, which is causing irreparable damage. We have no hard evidence that they're responsible, but scientists say there can be no other explanation. So we have decided to take action, hoping to elicit a response which will ultimately lead to negotiations and possibly a deal. Five spacecraft have been selected as targets. Warning shots will be fired first. If these are ignored, high-precision bombings will follow. All necessary precautions will be taken. The armed forces of the world's leading nations are prepared for every scenario."

And so we were privileged spectators of the first intergalactic war, as Jessica called it. I wondered if she realized this was not another science fiction movie, but harsh reality. I also asked myself if there would be a happy ending as in most of those movies.

The warning shots weren't very spectacular, at least not from our vantage point in the safety of our house, far from the battlefield. The spacecraft were huge, and the explosions off their sides seemed insignificant. After this first phase, the operation was suspended. If there were no reaction within "a reasonable amount of time," then the real action would begin.

In the meantime, we got lots of background information. Images were shown of dead whales and dolphins washed ashore in various parts of the world. In an interview, a marine biologist said, "Literally tons of dead fish were discovered floating in the water. The oceans are being turned into a hot, poisonous soup in which no life is possible. We're facing a planet-wide tragedy here. Urgent and drastic measures are called for before it's too late."

"Do the aliens realize what they're doing to us?" Jessica asked me. "Do they care? How can we know they're aware of us? And if they're not, how can we make them listen and change their plans?"

These were excellent questions, but I didn't have any replies ready. I merely said: "We'll find out any moment now if we can get their attention. And if we don't, we'll hit them where it hurts."

Jessica didn't look too convinced. I wasn't too convinced myself.

Later that night, bombers were sent to drop their lethal cargoes. Explosions flared up where the bombs struck. We all watched and waited anxiously. *Would the aliens launch a counterattack? Would they blow us to smithereens with superior military technology? Was mankind on a suicide mission?*

The five selected spacecraft were showered with bombs at regular intervals. There was no reaction. Either the aliens were quietly preparing their counteroffensive, or our shock-and-awe tactic didn't impress them.

After a while, the bombers returned to their bases. The generals and politicians, along with everyone else on the planet, waited for a reaction. It soon became clear no response was forthcoming. Was this an indication that the spacecraft were unmanned indeed? Or were they simply so well-protected, by force fields invisible to us, for instance, that they could easily withstand any attack?

Would we ever find out?

. . .

*** *Several minor discharges were reported near some of the workstations. There was no damage. The operations were not disturbed or interrupted, but a routine investigation of the phenomenon is planned. In the meantime, everything is running on schedule. The first test runs are being prepared.* ***

. . .

The general feeling was, *My God, who were we up against?* Three days of heavy bombing didn't make a dent in any of the spacecraft and didn't even elicit a response. There were some who cried out for a nuclear strike, and others who realized all our efforts were pointless. The spacecraft appeared perfectly protected against our "primitive" military technology.

So where did that leave us? We had to face it: Earth was occupied territory. The aliens—we assumed there were aliens involved, although we'd never seen them, and no contact could ever be established—landed, took control, and were transforming the oceans into something that would suit their purposes.

The teams monitoring the situation on a twenty-four-hour-a-day basis reported that all marine life was dying because of the water's rising temperature and the highly toxic pollutants. We were heading for a worldwide catastrophe on an unprecedented scale, the consequences of which could not be fathomed at that point.

But there was another unsettling discovery: under some of the spacecraft (not the ones that were under attack), organic material was found, of unknown origin but likely to be alien.

Some scientists claimed that the material was food, and that our visitors were turning our oceans into the alien equivalent of a fish farm. Others thought it was a breeding ground for the aliens' eggs, and yet others gave free rein to their imagination, leading to a wide variety of crackpot theories.

Of course, none of these claims carried any weight, for lack of hard evidence. Yet, this discovery might have held the clue to the mystery: this organic material, whatever its nature, must have been the reason the oceans were "adjusted" to suit its requirements.

Both Jessica and the kids at school fired round after round of questions at me, and I tried to come up with answers that were comforting, but it wasn't easy. *Why were the aliens doing this? What were they really planning? Preparing a nice hot place to hatch their eggs? Had their home planet dried up, which was why they had to look for a world with lots of water? Did we figure somewhere in their plans?*

There was more bad news, too much to list. With the

rapidly rising sea level, many cities and coastal regions would soon be flooded or might disappear completely under the waves. Large-scale evacuations were planned, but it was clear there would be all sorts of social and economic consequences. Flooding might impact poor third-world countries even worse than industrialized western nations. It was obvious this would hurt. We just didn't know exactly how much, or how long the pain was going to last.

With marine life in its death throes, the fishing industry was a thing of the past. Many people had lost their jobs and wondered what the future had in store for them. It would be interesting to see how our society would cope with the sudden and drastic changes forced upon it.

. . .

*** *The first test runs show we're not ready yet. This planet's water mass is huge, and it'll take some time before a sufficiently large volume of it reaches the right temperature and balance. Our operations are speeded up now that the oceans are virtually disinfected. There is still life on the continents, unlikely to cause any interference. We are optimistic that this project will prove a success.* ***

. . .

The images on TV sent shivers down our spines. I exchanged glances with Marsha, and we seemed to have the same reaction: the world was falling apart at the seams.

Regardless of where the images were from (Louisiana, the Netherlands, Bangladesh, Vietnam...), it was clear the mass evacuations of flooded areas were poorly organized and carried out in a great hurry. Nobody seemed to know where all those hundreds of thousands of refugees had to go. Many of them didn't even want to leave their homes and declared they would stand their ground, come hell or high water.

The authorities just couldn't cope with the situation. Social unrest was brewing, and in some places riots and looting ensued. The police did what they could to restore law and order, but chaos was looming on the horizon.

One inhabitant of New Orleans, Louisiana, summed it all up in an interview: “This is a lot worse than Katrina. And this time there won’t be any reconstruction. The water flooding the town will never go away again. We’ll drown unless we manage to adapt. And the worst thing is that we’ve only seen the beginning.”

In the meantime, the teams that tried to catch some of the alien eggs (that’s what everyone called them, whatever they really were) for analysis failed to get close. The organic material, stored in an underwater grid, turned out to be protected by an invisible barrier or force field. Alien technology was clearly superior to our primitive resources, so we wouldn’t be able to study the eggs, after all. The clues to unlock this mystery would remain beyond our reach.

To make matters worse, it was discovered that the pollutants the aliens added to the oceans must have gone up with evaporated water and came down again onto land with the rain. This meant the soil and ground water were getting contaminated with this toxic stuff as well. I hoped the results for plants and animals (not to mention mankind) wouldn’t be as disastrous as for marine life.

It was hoped that the particles coming down from the clouds would be diluted to the point where their effect would be negligible. So far, there was no scientific basis for this hope, though. Recent analyses confirmed this material had an unknown composition and was thus clearly of an alien nature.

Before we retired, Marsha and I had a short discussion. *Were the aliens out to destroy all life on earth, or were they simply not aware of the havoc they were wreaking? Or were they aware of the damage but considered it irrelevant?* Marsha compared it to people building a garden shed and destroying an ants' nest in the process. Even if they knew, they wouldn't care. Ants were of no importance.

We were worried about Jessica. *Would she have a future? In what kind of world would she grow up? Would there be a place for her generation in an alien-occupied world?* There was no way to know, but the news bulletins had chilled us to the bone.

And as that man from Louisiana had said on TV: "We've only seen the beginning."

. . .

*** *We're getting there! A large expanse of water now has the right temperature and chemical balance for our purposes. If the final tests prove successful, this planet will be extremely useful. Thanks to the rapidly melting ice caps, the volume of water is increasing, an added benefit. It's clear we stumbled onto a perfect world here. Too bad these water-covered planets are so rare.* ***

. . .

Jessica was scared, like most kids those days. We were trying to comfort her and hoped she didn't see we were scared as well. The schools were closed. Most parents would have deemed it safer to keep their children at home, anyway. It meant I was home as well, just like Marsha—no one was booking vacations right now. If this went on, the economy would collapse like a house of cards.

It was clear politicians were losing their grip on the situation. Nations were no longer cooperating, as each government resorted to desperate measures to save what it could.

There were rumors that China (or India, or Pakistan, according to other sources) used a nuclear weapon against a spacecraft off its shores, only to discover that it had as little effect as traditional bombings. *So much for the military approach.*

The massive evacuations of coastal regions resulted in sheer chaos. Driven to despair, people started rioting and looting supermarkets, realizing that supplies of food and water would become scarce. In areas threatened less directly, people bought as many supplies as they could. So did we. We told Jessica it was wise to be prepared.

In a TV interview, a biologist summed it all up: "The toxic pollutants the aliens introduced into the oceans are now also hitting the ecosystems on the continents, even if the doses coming down are relatively small. We're witnessing the first signs of a breakdown of the food chain. This will have dramatic consequences for us. As agriculture and cattle breeding become problematical, famine will inevitably result. There's no way to tell how fast this will go, but once the breakdown has set in, it will be extremely difficult to revert, stop, or even slow down the process."

Politicians, not used to thinking beyond the next election, were clearly unable to cope with a problem of this magnitude. They limited themselves to dealing with the symptoms of the problem, without trying to eliminate its cause—they didn't have a clue how, of course, didn't even think about trying. There was little that gave us hope for any constructive countermeasures.

I had a discussion with Marsha one night, when Jessica was already off to bed. If things turn sour, we won't be able to stay in London, I told her. Life in the big cities will become impossible as the battle for survival reaches its boiling point. Once supplies start running out, people will be at each other's throats. It would be a jungle, with the last remaining supplies going to those who had the most firepower.

She stared at me and asked me what we were supposed to do then.

I told her about my plan. We should find kindred spirits, people we can trust, because as a group we would stand a better chance at making it. Then we should leave the city, taking all our supplies with us, and look for a safe haven, somewhere in the countryside. There we should try to start a new life and adapt to changing circumstances. It would not be easy, but there was no other choice.

Marsha shook her head, said that this was not an expedition for children like Jessica, and that there was no way we could survive out there, left to our own devices.

I understood her criticism but repeated that we didn't really have a choice.

. . .

*** *Disinfection of the oceans is now complete; the continents were only partly cleared of life-forms, but this is of minor importance as the land masses are of no use to us. The latest tests show that conditions are now perfect, and underwater breeding structures are being deployed on a massive scale. If all goes according to plan, the first harvest should be reaped before long. If the quality proves satisfactory, a non-stop cycle of breeding and harvesting will be started.* ***

. . .

It was amazing how quickly society could disintegrate. One moment we were living in a world of peace and quiet, then before we knew it, the veneer of civilization stripped away, and everything fell apart.

I had already discussed my plans with friends and neighbors, and many seemed to agree. We prepared ourselves for the expedition, buying supplies (some euphemistically declared they had "laid hands" on supplies—I did not push for details) and everything else we might need—including weapons. We realized we were facing tough times, especially for the children joining us.

When the last in a series of power failures seemed to be the definitive one, and we fell without running water, we knew there was no point in staying in the city anymore.

The final reports we'd heard on the radio (TV and the internet had been down for a while already) stated that frantic activity was observed around all the spacecraft hovering above the seas, although the exact nature of that activity remained a mystery. The evacuation in Britain—there was no more news from the rest of the world because of the total communication breakdown—had ended in sheer chaos. Refugees flocked inland in vast numbers, only to find villages and cities on the verge of collapse, with their arrival only making matters worse.

The toxic pollutants were quickly pushing all life on earth to the brink of extinction, and it didn't look as if they'd make an exception for mankind. Crops and livestock were doomed, and people were dying already, especially the weakest—children, old folks, and those in poor health. Society was disintegrating fast. Once supplies ran low and structures began to fail, the descent into barbarism would be inevitable for those still left. We had reached the end of the line.

The members of our group, optimistically calling ourselves the Survivalists, got together and prepared for our imminent departure from the city. We knew where we were heading, how to get there, and which problems we might face. What we didn't know was how long we would be able to stand our ground. What would we do when our supplies ran out, and no more food was available? How could we possibly survive in a dying world? On the other hand, what other options did we have?

. . .

*** *More than a hundred breeding stations have now been set up, and so far, everything is running perfectly. If the first harvest proves successful—and that appears highly likely—yet more stations will be added. This world covered by vast oceans, slightly adapted to suit our purposes, is a welcome addition to our home breeding grounds that no longer allow* *full expansion, and a rare treasure we will no doubt benefit from for a long time.* ***

. . .

It took us several days to reach the mansion in Hitchin, north of London, that we had agreed upon to use as our hideout. It belonged to a friend of one of my neighbors, and he said it would be perfect.

Our journey was dreadful.

The landscape we passed through was in a state of decay. All the vegetation—trees, shrubs, grass, everything—was either dead or dying. Hardly any animals could be seen. The world was being transformed into a lifeless wasteland, through which a handful of stragglers moved on their way to a mirage. It was hard not to yield to despair when faced with such bleak surroundings. Out here in the open, the extent of the damage was much more evident than in the city. It was incredible how fast life on earth was wiped out. *Would we ever find out if it were done on purpose, or if it were a mere side effect of a greater plan? Did it matter?*

As we travelled north, we passed through a city in its death throes. Traces of violence were omnipresent: charred houses, abandoned cars, looted shops and supermarkets. Bodies of people who hadn't survived the clashes littered the streets. At times, we were under attack, as armed gangs noticed the supplies we were carrying and wanted to get hold of them. We defended ourselves, but sadly, more than half of our party didn't make it to the finish. We lost, among others, both Marsha and Jessica. I cursed myself for having taken them on this perilous journey, but then again, leaving them in London would have been equally disastrous. I reached the mansion a broken man—like most of the others. I just cannot bring myself to recount the details of our losses here.

To our relief, we found the mansion unoccupied and in decent condition. That first night, we took stock of our situation.

As our party had been decimated, we had supplies for more than a week. We could only hope there would be no uninvited guests eager to share our meals, and we preferred not to think yet of what would happen when we ran out of food and water.

We didn't talk a lot. We had seen too much and lost too many people. We were exhausted, both physically and emotionally, and retired for the night after a frugal meal, fearful of what tomorrow would bring.

Tired though I was, I couldn't sleep. We were, of course, cut off from any news, and I wondered what had happened to all those big cities along the world's coastlines: New York, Barcelona, Hong Kong, and so many more. Had the rising seas swallowed them all? How many inhabitants had managed to escape to higher land, and how many were still alive? The world as we knew it had come crashing down with such suddenness that it seemed unreal.

Had those alien pollutants ravaged the entire world, or had certain regions escaped the onslaught? Were there places on earth where life was still possible, where mankind yet had a chance to survive?

Of course, there were no answers to these questions. There might never be any.

. . .

**** The planet is now virtually cleansed of native life. There were a few minor disruptions at some workstations where embryos turned out to be contaminated. The problem was easily contained and the losses negligible. The execution of our plan will by no means be affected by this incident. In fact, the success the first run achieved was bigger than expected. We have high hopes. ****

. . .

We'd been at the mansion in Hitchin for five days. The landscape was drained of color now that all vegetation was gone.

No birds flew in the air; no insects or spiders were crawling around. A deadly silence reigned supreme.

Although we rationed food and water, our supplies were dwindling fast. Most of us were yielding to despair. There was no way to know whether our little pocket of resistance was the final stronghold of mankind, or if others had been more successful. Perhaps nomads in the desert or tribes in the Amazon basin, accustomed to extreme hardship conditions, were better equipped to deal with such a worldwide catastrophe and still struggled on. It was equally possible that they were the first to go...

There was one bizarre incident. One member of our group, a man called Martin, did a tour of the area, hoping to find supplies and possibly other survivors. He failed to find anything useful and came back with an ugly insect bite on his upper right arm. He claimed he had been attacked by a big flying bug he had never seen before. In a sense, this was good news: it was evidence there were still insects around, and maybe other animals. On the other hand, aggressive creatures inflicting serious injuries were not exactly what we needed.

We could only give basic first aid, but we did what we could. The following morning, the bite was infected, though, and Martin said it was throbbing with pain. There was little we could do about it—the small amount of medication we had didn't have any effect. Things were looking bad indeed for Martin.

Later that day, we saw two of the creatures with our own eyes. They must have discovered us and decided to check if we were an interesting food supply. The insects were large and extremely aggressive, as Martin had claimed. It took several men to chase one of them and catch the other one. Well, we didn't quite catch it; we managed to smash it to the ground, where it remained motionless, probably dazed rather than crushed.

Upon closer inspection, it proved to be an insect unlike any we had ever seen, a monster straight out of a horror movie. It was the size of a mouse and sported claws and jaws that could tear apart a small animal. It was no wonder Martin had suffered such a serious injury.

We studied the creature and concluded it had to be a mutated new species of insect. Could it be that it had developed an immunity against alien pollutants and evolved into this horrific thing? Or had it feasted on some alien eggs that had strayed from the underwater grids to become, a few generations later, this hybrid, half-alien monstrosity?

All we knew for sure was that we'd have to protect ourselves against this fearsome enemy, as if our situation weren't bad enough already.

. . .

*** *The first harvest has been reaped. The quality is higher than expected: more than 90 percent of the embryos have matured. They will be transferred to breeding docks, where they should develop into larvae. This planet is perfect for our purposes. More workstations will be deployed, and embryos will be planted on a massive scale. There are no problems or glitches of any significance. It was observed that native life-forms fed on a small number of failed and discarded embryos, miraculously survived, and even thrived. This is of no importance. Further disinfection of the planet is not required. The operation will proceed as scheduled.* ***

. . .

Martin died today. The infection had grown massive, and a high fever had driven him beyond the limits of endurance. We buried him, wondering who would bury the last ones to go.

The rest of us aren't much better off. Our supplies have virtually run out. We have no idea what we'll do next. It's clear the game is over.

We've seen a few more of the killer insects. So far, we have managed to chase them, but as we grow weaker, we will become more vulnerable.

I wonder what these creatures eat. Apart from a handful of humans like us, there doesn't seem to be any food around—strange to think of ourselves as a food supply for insects. Do they prey on something else we're not aware of? Maybe they nibble at alien eggs whenever they can, but in that case, what drove them so far inland?

Bleak and desperate though our situation is, it offers a ray of hope. I know this sounds paradoxical. An analogy may clarify what I mean: after the gigantic asteroid struck that wiped out the dinosaurs and so many other creatures millions of years ago, mammals arrived on the scene, some evolving into man and leading to civilization. So in the final analysis, the cataclysm paved the way for new successes.

Now these aliens have struck a similar blow, perhaps consciously, perhaps inadvertently, and again some resilient species was, against all the odds, given a new lease on life. Maybe this planet-wide genocide will one day lead to the dawn of a new age on earth, with various species evolving from these insects that adapted to the new circumstances.

Maybe one day in the far future, a new civilization will arise, able to live alongside the aliens if they're still here, or perhaps able to exterminate them.

I don't know if anyone will ever read these lines, but it's nice for me to end on a positive note, strangely enough, as I may be among the last men left on earth.

All is not lost. Some will carry on.

I'll go with that idea in mind.

. . .

About the author: Frank Roger was born in 1957 in Ghent, Belgium. His first story appeared in 1975. By now he has a few hundred short stories to his credit, published in more than forty languages. Apart from fiction, he also produces collages and visual art in a surrealist and satirical tradition.

11

The Burning

by Jay Caselberg (Germany)

Subgenre: Poetry

Time Period: The present

Setting: Australia

. . .

Blood-bruised sky
Once where blue
Blood-bruised sky
Raining ash
Once where blue
Now splashed with ochre
Crow silhouetted on spindly branch
Feathers singed
Gasping against muddied palette
No birdcall

Red sky at night they said
Shepherd's delight
Red sky in the morning

Noon and night
A warning
Already gone
Too late

. . .

About the author:

Jay Caselberg is an Australian author and poet whose work has appeared around the world and been translated into several languages. From time to time, it gets shortlisted for awards. He currently resides in Germany.

12

My Personal Space

by Tom Jolly (United States)

Subgenre: Science fiction

Time Period: Present day

Setting: United States, on an altered Earth

Synopsis: What happens when every human on Earth is allocated their fair share of atmosphere and land to treat as they wish? It's unlikely that any government on Earth has the desire, will, or power to do this. But aliens whose technology is millions of years advanced beyond our own? They might have some lessons to teach. How does one man deal with his eighteen acres of air, land, and ocean when he can't "share" his waste with the rest of the world?

. . .

The last normal thing I remembered was sitting at the Western Steak-Out eating a tri-tip sandwich. Then I woke up in my bed. There was no gap in time between these disparate events. One moment: eating. The next: waking up. I assumed some catastrophe had ensued. Maybe I passed out or had a heart attack, although I think I'd remember the second case. I'd only been drinking lightly, so passing out seemed unlikely, too.

I got out of bed and dressed, not worried about work since I'd retired three years ago. After starting a pot of coffee and making some oatmeal and toast, I looked at the latest news on my iPad, not bothering with the TV.

None of it made sense. Aliens had sort-of invaded, but there were no pictures of any invasion. There were pictures of small fields of crops and work buildings crowded together as always, but nothing that implied we were being attacked. No walking tripods with death rays.

A friend emailed me with the cryptic words, "Have you gone outside yet? This is nuts."

I went outside.

I was in an enclosure of sorts. It was big. My house had somehow been relocated inside this glass enclosure without my being aware of it. The house sat on the edge of a small bit of farmland, already in crops of some sort. South of that was a lake, a few acres at least, trees near the shoreline which rose up toward some hills and mountains, still only a few acres, and a large sandy section that could have been a desert. It was like someone took small samples of the world and slapped them all together in a mosaic.

All this blended topography was enclosed by glass walls, through which I could see similar parcels bordering my own. I leaned back, gazing upwards, trying to follow the corners of the glass walls, trying to see the top, but it just kept going up and up and up.

A disembodied voice said, "Good morning, Mr. Cole." I jumped. The voice was soft and melodious, but it was impossible to determine where it came from.

"Who's that?" I demanded.

The voice explained to me that it was an artificial intelligence representing a coalition of alien species that were intervening in human development. It also described to me the basic characteristics of my new home.

When the aliens arrived, they split Earth up evenly between every human, reorganizing it as needed. Every single human was allotted eighteen acres. In a case like mine, where I lived alone, my eighteen acres were bounded by what may as well have been infinitely tall walls: clear as glass, thin as paper, and a perfect thermal insulator. Alien tech. The AI assured me that the wall was only (roughly) a hundred kilometers high, the tops open to space, but as far as I was concerned, it may as well have been infinite, though I could see that the vertical lines of the corners of my glass cage converged above to a small rectangle of sky a few degrees wide.

Families, the AI said, were kept together with land allocations based on the family size, so a family of three would have three times as much space as I did: a whopping fifty-four acres to their name. It was very egalitarian. The rich and poor equalized in one fell swoop.

The thing about those eighteen acres, calculated so simply by dividing up the world's total acreage by the total population, is that most of it was saltwater. Ocean. A large fraction was desert and mountains and ice. We all got a piece of what was essentially unusable territory. What was left was potential farmland, about one acre per human, minus the size of the house one owned that occupied part of that acre.

So, one might be curious why the aliens suddenly decided to do this. It was an interesting question, and as it turned out, it was quite easy to ask the aliens, or at least their representatives, for a direct answer.

"So am I likely to *see* one of these aliens-in-charge?" I asked the AI.

"Oh, no, they're far too busy with other tasks. But I can answer any question you have. And I can communicate with ten billion data streams simultaneously, so I can talk to all humans at once if needed."

"What's going on here, then?" I waved my hands at the clear walls surrounding my allocated area. "Are we in a zoo?"

"No, Mr. Cole. That would be unethical, to say nothing of boring for the observers. Your species has shown the ability to travel to other planets and settle them, without first resolving your tendency to pollute and destroy your own surroundings. Think of this as an educational process."

I stared up at the endless vertical walls, then down at my acre. It was full of crops of various fruits, nuts, and vegetables that I, apparently, was supposed to nurture if I wanted to stay alive. "I suppose since you created all this on a whim, you could just put it all back the way it was, right?"

"Yes."

"But I suppose it's useless to ask you to do so?"

"At this point, that is correct."

I explored my eighteen acres. Assuming the aliens kept other animals alive on Earth, I wondered who got possession of things like whales on their twelve acres of water, and how deep it went. A lot of the ocean areas were butted up against each other to make it appear as a larger body of water, but I was fairly certain that it would be futile to try to "swim under the wall" to get to an adjacent property.

To the north was a Kenyan, to the east a Chinese couple with no kids, to the south was an Englishman, and to the west was a Costa Rican. I could make no sense of the "why" behind the random distribution. The Chinese family was the only one that didn't speak some English. We could hear one another through the thin walls separating us. Like me, they were living their lives performing some random activity just before finding themselves on this changed Earth: going to work, hiking, eating dinner, whatever, and they suddenly woke up at home as though from a dream. After that, they walked outside and found themselves in these tall glass cages.

Our phones still worked, which I found surprising. My bank account still had my money in it. Amazon was still up, even eBay. How did that work? How could I ship something if I couldn't leave?

"Hey, alien?"

"A reminder that I am an artificial intelligence, not an alien. You may give me a name if you wish."

"Alien is fine, alien. How does Amazon work? If I order a book, how does it get here?"

"It will be delivered to your doorstep as normal, though no delivery vehicle will be evident. However, you will be allotted a greenhouse gas cost as though it had, plus the cost of making the book."

"Greenhouse gas cost?" I asked, confused.

"Yes. There is a pipe on the north end of your lot that will deliver CO_2 to your unit's atmosphere equivalent to the energy cost required to manufacture and deliver any product you desire in the future. We recommend e-books if you read a lot, which eliminate most production and delivery greenhouse penalties."

Wandering on the property, I found myself standing next to an apple tree. I pulled off a ripe apple and bit into it. It was surprisingly good. "What if I feel like going to a restaurant?" I asked.

"You must get in your car and your car will be transported to an artificial restaurant. You will accrue a CO_2 penalty equal to the cost required to produce the food you eat, clean the dishes, heat and light a fraction of the restaurant, wash the dishes, maintain the fraction of the staff time you use for your meal, clean the linens, and drive your car as if you had used normal roads."

I must have been staring blankly at the sky for a minute because the artificial intelligence asked me, "Are you all right, Mr. Cole?"

It took me a moment to answer. "Um, if I wasn't and I needed an ambulance..."

"You will acquire CO_2 equal to..."

"Never mind," I said, cutting the AI off. "So this is all about humans using too much energy?"

"Yes. You are destroying your own planet."

It did seem warm in there, inside my eighteen-acre glass cage, but I'm sure that was my imagination. There wasn't much of a breeze. "Can I get a natural breeze for free?"

"Certainly, Mr. Cole."

A light breeze arose, cooling my forehead. I relaxed a little. "So what are the end conditions of this little experiment of yours?"

"The test goes for two years. Some fraction of humans will be unable to control consumption and will receive copious quantities of carbon dioxide and methane within their enclosures. We expect their enclosure temperatures to rise above 150 degrees Fahrenheit within that period. They will die. Those who live will be allowed to return to their original lives."

"You're going to cook them?"

"No, they will cook themselves, instead of doing the same to the entire planet, which is not their possession to abuse."

"Then all I have to do is reduce my CO_2 for two years, and then go back to normal life."

"Ideally, yes."

Easy-peasy. I walked around the property until I found a big red spigot sticking up out of the ground, venting out a port ten feet above the ground. I started getting a headache as I approached, and I could feel a breeze coming from it. "Is that..."

"Those are the greenhouse gases, primarily carbon dioxide and methane, that you are nominally producing. It includes the average cost for the annual heating and cooling you have used in your house for the last five years. It is premixed with your containment's atmosphere to avoid immediate asphyxiation."

"This is all from my house?" I asked.

"No, it includes your average daily transportation costs, commercial consumption, infrastructure development in your country, public buildings, and significant military expenditures. Tax and deficit related expenditures for government goods and manufacturing."

That didn't seem fair. "But I don't get to choose how government money is spent," I whined.

"You vote for them. The carbon cost is distributed equally between the people in your nation, the US."

I gaped. This might be easy to fix by the next election. With the understanding that aliens with god-like powers were looking over our shoulders, reducing the military budget by half or more should be a no-brainer. I considered myself a conservative energy user, so I should at least last out the year. America was a leader in alternative energy, wasn't it? "So if I last out two years..." I began.

The AI interrupted, "You will not. You will be dead within the next four months at your current use levels."

"*What?*"

"The world per-capita average carbon dioxide production is equivalent to burning three tons per person per year. Americans, of which you are one, use sixteen tons per person. Before we appeared, your greenhouse gas production was spread throughout the world's atmosphere. The present experiment limits your personal pollution to the volume of air and land allocated to each individual."

"So if I stop driving my car anywhere..."

"That would reduce your carbon penalty considerably."

"I'd live?"

"For an extra four months."

I sat down on the grass and put my head in my hands.

"Do you require an ambulance, Mr. Cole?"

"Dear God, no. How do I live through this?"

"Reduce your carbon footprint."

"Yeah, I got that part. But I have no control over most of it."

"You could move."

I looked up at where I imagined the disembodied AI voice might be. "Move?"

"Declare allegiance to a lower-usage country."

"I'm allowed to do that?"

"Yes. "

"What countries?"

"Currently the five lowest usage countries are Burundi, Liberia, Comoros, the Democratic Republic of the Congo, Rwanda..."

"Ah. Poor countries."

"There is a strong correlation between wealth and energy usage, Mr. Cole."

"Keep going up the list of countries until I say 'stop,' please."

I settled on the Philippines. Per-capita greenhouse gas emissions were well below the world average, and most of the population spoke English. I could survive there. I was allocated a smaller house and would have to find a new job or learn to live off my garden. The fruits and veggies there had all changed for the local environment, and it was much warmer and more humid than my old place. I'd miss apples, unless I wanted to have them shipped in. I worked out in my garden for a few days, trying out the new foods, before I started worrying again.

"Hey, Alien."

"Yes, Mr. Cole."

"What happens to the land I'm on when your experiment ends?"

"The land will be reallocated to the country you have adopted. That country's land mass will increase in size, while your country of origin will decrease. Your previous greenhouse gas load for industrial, government and military use will have been distributed to anyone remaining in your original country."

"So they will heat up faster than before?"

"That is correct. The US has lost 11 percent of its land mass and population since the beginning of this correction, with subsequent increases in greenhouse gases for the remaining people."

"That's...surprisingly fast."

"Based on prior experience with other defective worlds, there will be a cascade effect as people shift to new countries. The US will probably not exist as a land mass longer than a month, and any stragglers will be dead by then anyway, freeing the vacant landmass for redistribution."

"Ah." I spent a few hours on the phone that day, telling my few friends the news. Most of them had figured it out already and were spread across a number of third-world countries.

When I was finished, I asked the AI, "What of China? They use more energy than the US. Are they going to die, too?"

"On an individual basis, the Chinese used approximately half the energy that each person in the US used, Mr. Cole, equivalent to burning eight tons of coal per year. They will last longer and be affected more slowly, but most are expected to die within fourteen months unless they relocate as you did. China, along with many other countries with a strong oil or coal dependency, will also cease to exist within the year."

"Don't you feel even the least guilty about killing so many people? Destroying entire countries?"

"We do not. We are merely subjecting individuals to their own pollution, rather than distributing that pollution into a shared resource to areas that receive no benefit from it."

My own pollution. I eyed a small pile of trash that I'd accumulated in the last three days; a black plastic bag set outside next to the house. Another pile of debris was growing next to the garden: weeds, sticks, stems, and edgy fruit. These piles were going to keep getting bigger. "So, at the end of two years, all this trash..."

"Will keep accumulating as you produce it."

"But when we're let out..."

"Did I imply that you would be released after two years? I said the current test would last two years. The second test, the resolution of solid waste production, will require ten years. We recommend composting and procuring some chickens to control your organic waste. Your neighbor to the east has some for sale."

"Um..."

"We also recommend an electronic dating service if you are feeling lonely. You are allowed to combine lots with a suitable mate. Though this may be counterproductive for the third test period: population control."

I sighed and sat down on the grass, tilted my straw hat back and wiped sweat from my forehead, reluctant to ask the AI why there weren't any flies.

. . .

About the author: Tom Jolly is a retired astronautical/electrical engineer who spends his time writing SF and fantasy, designing board games, and creating obnoxious puzzles. His stories have appeared in *Analog SF, Daily Science Fiction, Amazing Stories, MYTHIC*, and a few anthologies, including *As Told by Things*, and *Tales from the Pirate's Cove*. His fantasy and SF novels, *An Unusual Practice, A Game of Broken Minds*, and *Touched*, are available on Amazon. He lives in Santa Maria, California, with his wife, Penny, in a place where mountain lions and black bears still visit, especially if you own any chickens. You can discover more of his stories at www.silcom.com/~tomjolly/tomjolly2.htm and follow him on Twitter (@tomjolly19) or Facebook (@TJWriter).

13

CH4 is 28 Times More!

by Kirby Biggs (United States)

Subgenres: Song/poem, political, humor

Time period: Present and near future.

Setting: Planet Earth.

Synopsis: Anthropogenically-induced climate change is currently accelerating on today's Planet Earth. Methane, while shorter-lived than CO2 as a heat-forcing gas, is approximately twenty-eight times more potent. The addition of methane to the atmosphere is increasing, especially from ruminants (cattle, sheep, goats, bison) we grow to eat, fracking process leakage, and more importantly, from the climate-change-induced melting and decomposition of the tundra. As planetary temperatures increase, this release accelerates the effect of the planetary warming feedback loop. This song/poem explores some causes and effects of methane's effects in a parody that intends to educate through dark humor and historical reflection, set to a tune that many will recognize, "A Bicycle Built for Two," in the scary style of Arthur C. Clarke's Hal in the Stanley Kubrick movie *2001: A Space Odyssey*.

. . .

Sung to the tune of "A bicycle built for two"—try it!
(Parentheticals) are spoken as asides.

Me-thane, Me-thane,
That's what the British say.
It's a gas, that,
comes from our swamps today.
(And a whole bunch of other places)
As long as it's under cover,
It will not make us smother,
but when it's out, we twist and shout,
and the planet gets fried, it's true.

Meth-ane, Meth-ane,
that's the American way.
Frack it, Frack it, till it all bleeds away.
Maybe the wells are leaky,
the grout is getting creaky,
but we won't weep, 'cause gas is cheap,
so we don't care if we are screwed.

Warming, Warming,
that's what the scientists said.

(A long time ago. Fourier: CO2 forcing effect—1826, Foote: operating experimental model—1856, Arrhenius: full model—1896... I mean... puleeze?)

Some strange people
think it's all in their heads.
They say, "How can one puny man screw,
around with things the gods do...?"
They'll be upset, and they'll get wet,
when they find out it's really true.

De-Nile, De-Nile,
we know it's a river too.
It keeps flooding, in ways it shouldn't do.
They say that the seas are risin',
the storms are super-sizin',
(Fingers in ears)
but...La-la-la, la-la-la-la
La-la-la-la-la-la-la-la.

Tundra, Tundra,
it's usually frozen through.
Now it's melting,
goodness what should we do?

(Ummh, sticking with the Paris Accords and moving immediately to sustainables to replace fossils would be a small start).

It's getting hot as an oven,
and we are tins of muffins.
I guess we'll bake, I'm sure we'll ache,
as the Sun keeps on shining through,
as the Sun keeps on shining through,
As the Sun...
Keeps on...
Shiiiiiiiining...
Throoooooooough...!
Dah-Dumb

. . .

About the Author:

Kirby has loved our planet for seven decades, still finding delight in nature's mysteries. His concern for the health of the planet and his long exploration of how humans and natural systems can coexist, reinforce daily how fragile is the balance that maintains our Earth as a welcoming habitat for all the things we love. By sharing poetry, songs, and stories, Kirby joins his voice with other voices of warning about the state of our planet and the need for immediate action, if we are to survive ourselves. For forty-five years, Kirby has protected air, land, and water as an environmental professional.

Part Three:

The Near Future (Between Now and 2040 AD)

14

The First Man

by Christopher Walker (Poland)

Subgenres: Political satire, with attempts at humor

Time Period: Near future

Setting: United States of America

Synopsis: We are in the mind of Jared Kushner, the First Man; his wife, Ivanka, is president. Jared is about to travel around the world on a diplomatic mission—to deny climate change and its effects. But denial has a habit of catching up with people...

. . .

Even though it's early enough for the sun only to be creeping in under the blinds, when I reach over to the other side of the bed there's nobody there, just a declivity suggestive of a presence now gone. *No rest for the wicked*, or so they say. I rise and shower, then dress.

"Is everything ready," I call through to the next room as I adjust my slim red tie in the mirror. The knot is too tight, and I know it gives me the look of a hanged criminal, but that's what the people have grown used to, and so it's what I must unfailingly give them.

"Yes, sir," comes the response.

"Enough filters for the masks," I say. I never ask, I state, an old trick I picked up at my *alma mater*. If you state, others must accede to your wishes or go against them, and in that heightening negative space you can grasp control of the discourse. Or so goes the logic. Maybe I'm so used to speaking in a flat tone that I don't even know to use a rising inclination anymore. Like when I say, "You love me," to my wife, and she smiles vapidly, as if at a Twitter notification. She doesn't deny or accept what I say, and so we both move on.

Speaking of... I must remember to tweet more frequently, and more furiously. The success of the next two weeks depends on it.

"Enough, sir, yes, though I wouldn't recommend..." he says, though he lacks the gumption to finish the sentence. No, I wouldn't recommend it either, but I'm not about to say.

"Have the car brought around."

"Very good, sir," he says. The car's already in the drive. I know that, he knows that, but it's good to be giving the orders.

The car is a Humvee, and as I approach, the engine roars. The driver is anxious to get away, to beat a line through the serried ranks of protestors beyond the gate. Hence the Humvee, with another behind and one in front. The one in front has a cowcatcher across its front, the sort of thing they used to put on the front of a train to clear the snow from the line.

Inside the car, sitting next to me is my man. I forget his name, I use it so rarely, but he's there with his chest armor on, or at least it looks that way. I think I sometimes call him Puffy, but he doesn't like it much. He doesn't like much of anything. I wonder if he'd ever take a bullet for me, and sometimes I wonder about asking. For the president, sure, anybody'd take a bullet for *her*. But not for the First Man. Across from Puffy, there's another member of the security detail, with a shotgun lying across his lap pointing at the door I entered by. Hope nobody tries to force entry through the other side.

There's one more person with us in the Humvee. I wait until we've accelerated past the crowds before I even contemplate addressing him. Out of the corner of my eye, I observe him. I've seen his picture before, been given a complete briefing that I didn't bother reading. I know his type. Still in love with Foster Wallace. He's got shaggy brown hair and an overgrowth of stubble, but thankfully no bandana. The bandana would have been too much. Only one guy in the world could get away with a bandana, and that's Hulk Hogan, thank you very much.

Leaning forward, I snatch a glimpse at the protestors with their placards and homemade signs. "If they cared so much about the planet, you'd think they'd use less wood and paper," I mumble. Puffy dutifully laughs, but not much. His gurgling laugh could just have been an attack of reflux. The shotgun guy smirks. I can tell from the glint in his eyes that he wishes, he really wishes, that one or another of the protestors might try to block the convoy like they did a year ago. Goodness, that took a while to die down in the papers, and yet after all, it did boost our numbers with the core demographic, so I guess that's all fine.

The guest, a reporter with, I don't know, *The Atlantic* maybe or *Rolling Stone*, clears his throat. "Mr. Kushner," he says, stretching a hand forward to me. I take it, give it a quick pump and then the old wrap around on the forearm with my free hand, and I try not to grimace. He must have had some greasy breakfast, or he's never been in a Humvee before with someone as famous as me, because that's one damp squib of a handshake.

"Welcome," I say, smiling that toothy grin that I believe accounted for the vast majority of the female vote that put Ivanka in the White House. It's wasted on this guy, of course; I knew it would be, but that's fine. I'm just practicing smiling now so that I'm ready for the big smile when my muscular, dominating frame exits the Humvee on our arrival at the airport.

He's already talking to me. My thoughts having drifted, as they are wont to do when I am the subject of them, means that I have no idea what he's going on about. I smile again, wanly this time, as that usually does the trick.

"So, you have nothing to say on the matter?"

"There's really nothing to say."

"I see. Well, in that case, do you at least have a comment on why the satellite imagery over the area has been blocked? The latest pictures we can access through Google Earth are about five years old. Here, look."

He's taking out his phone, and the shotgun guy is on him like a, well, shot. Grabs the phone and pockets it.

"Sorry," I say. "He's a little worried about electronic devices in the car with us. Thought you would have been told not to bring your phone with you. You *were* told."

The man shrugs. I nod my head when the shotgun guy looks at me, and with a grumble he gives the phone back.

"I was just going to show you how the aerial photos are all out of date, and nobody can get a drone anywhere near the place."

Ah, it makes sense to me now. He must be talking about Mar-a-Lago, or as I prefer to call it since it collapsed into that giant sinkhole, Submar-a-Lago. The recollection of my great wit makes me smile again.

"We're nearly at the airport," I say to Puffy, and he whispers into his lapel mike and gets the response back that we're still twenty minutes away. Strange. The traffic's light, as well it might be, given the price of gas in D.C.

"Perhaps then we can talk a little about the election? Your wife's victory came as a surprise, did it not?"

"It did not," I respond coolly. I know I'm the genius behind my wife's ascendancy, but part of the deal we have with each other is that this fact must go unrecognized, at least until her two terms are up and it's my turn to run. *Dynastic*, that's the word my mind is groping for. "We had a target demographic in mind, and we played our election in their favor. It was an entirely natural, some might even say predictable, turn of events."

"I see," the reporter says. "Your father-in-law won his first election by demonizing immigrants, and the second one by demonizing Congress. And your wife?"

"By demonizing climate change protestors. You can thank Greta if you like. She put Ivanka into the White House, almost single-handedly."

"I'm sorry?"

"Of course you are." I raise my eyebrows suggestively. I love being shown to possess more intelligence than those around me. This guy hasn't got a clue. "The American people don't want to think about climate change. It doesn't sell. So, if you deny, deny, deny, enough people will come round to your side of the argument—or they'll be there before you, in fact—to ensure that victory comes easily."

"The flaw of democracy," he mumbles. Puffy snorts. I don't like that. It wasn't as funny as half the things I say.

As punishment for showing me up, I don't say another word until we arrive at the airport. The Humvee rolls up at our private terminal and is waved through straight onto the tarmac. The Learjet is waiting, though there's no red carpet. Such niceties they reserve for the president, I suppose. I am the first out of the Humvee, danger be damned. I need to put on a strong front for all those women supporters who think I'm the real power in the country. That's the impression we feed them. The focus groups showed that they would never have voted for a woman, even though she was the daughter of their hero. They needed to see me up there winking down at them, my right hand placed boldly on Ivanka's shoulder; to one side of the demographic, it meant that I supported her, and to the other it showed who the real boss was. Ah, politics, what a noble sport!

The usual paparazzi aren't here today. Only one or two have turned out. The protestors have been kept far back, out of sight. It's a balmy December day, a lovely eighty degrees. Eighty degrees in the week before Christmas, in Washington D.C., and they have the temerity to protest that! They should be thankful. You can enjoy life so much more when it's warm.

"You want a photograph with me," I say to the reporter. His name has slipped from my memory. It'll come back later. He'll probably have tweeted great things about me if he isn't a complete and utter loser, and I'll find his name in the inevitable retweets and cross-taggings. He lumbers up to me all bashful, and I stand posing with him, my hand resting on *his* shoulder this time.

"Who are we smiling at?" he says between his teeth. There isn't a proper photographer waiting to take our photo. Puffy comes ambling up, pulls out his phone, and gets a photo of the two of us.

"Make it a selfie," I tell him. "More authentic that way." Actually, what I'm thinking is that this will strike a chord with our African-American demographic, though there are only two or three of them numbered among our supporters. I checked. Hardly any of *them* voted Republican, but is it any surprise? Second-term Donald came up with so many ways to block the blacks from voting, I'm astonished that any of them were left to attend the ballot box in the first place. Oh, well. Life is for winners like me.

We climb into the jet. On my desk, by the leatherette sofa, I see a clipboard with my itinerary on. "Want a copy," I say to the reporter. He pulls a wad of paper out of his jacket pocket to show he's already got one. Why didn't I have one already, if he has? Maybe I do. Maybe it's back in my study in the White House, but that makes no sense. I'd never have looked for anything important there.

The first stop on our whistle-round-the-globe tour is the United Republic of Ireland. Two days in Dublin to meet with the Taoiseach. He'll want to talk about how the north of his country is falling into the sea, and how the wind in the south is blowing away the roofs faster than they can be rebuilt. What a bore.

After that, it's the United Kingdom of England and Wales. London's fine, a grand city, though prone to the occasional spot of flooding. Boris will be happy to see me, a welcome distraction for him from the massive flooding that has left hundreds of thousands in the north homeless, but as Boris says, *they've* turned back to the Left after the 2019 election victory, and technically can't vote if they're homeless, so that's a problem that takes care of itself.

It surprises me to learn that I've been narrating my thoughts to the reporter all this while, and he's making assiduous notes. Well, throw the fool a bone, why not? If he writes any of this up in his article, I'll just declaim it as "fake news," as Father would have done. I mean Father-in-law. I often call him Father, seems so natural.

Since I've started telling the reporter everything, I might as well give him the whole scoop. "After London, we thought about a visit to Brussels, but since the trade war started in the middle of Donald's second term, we haven't been as friendly as before. Besides, they keep going on in Brussels about the climate, and that's such a drag."

"An understandable drag, surely," he says, licking the tip of his pencil in anticipation of my juicy response.

"Not in my book," I say. "Climate change is a hoax, that's all plain to see. We're just going through a warm period. Variations in the sun's intensity. That sort of thing."

He raises an eyebrow at this.

"Is that truly what you believe?" he says, pocketing his pencil and his notebook.

"I've talked myself into that position," I say. Then,

throwing caution to the wind, and assuming that I'm off the record here, "Listen, you don't get voted into power by telling the people bad news. You saw the protestors. They didn't vote for me—for Ivanka, I mean—they voted *against* us, but not in any significant number. The power is all with inertia and denial; you must be aware of that."

"I suppose I am," the reporter says glumly. He takes out the pencil and notebook again. Our moment of brutal honesty has passed. The Learjet hums to life, we accelerate down the tarmac, and as we head into the sky, I find myself talking through the rest of the itinerary.

"Moscow, obviously," I say with a wink, but I don't get so much as a smile in return. Puffy stands up and heads to the back, hopefully to get the drinks started. It's a long flight, I'm thirsty, and since I'm not flying with Donald, we've stocked up on a lot more than just Diet Coke. "And after Moscow, we're going to drop in on my pals in India. That's where I need the filters for my mask," I say, patting the bag that's sitting on the floor next to the sofa. "It gets so polluted that you can't see across the road. Last year, I paid the Indians a visit and never actually left the car, just had a lookalike go out and press the flesh in my stead, and the air was so dirty nobody could tell it wasn't me, no matter how close they got. Sadly, I haven't brought the doppelganger along this time."

"May I ask why not?"

"Dead, lung cancer. Can't think how that happened. Must have been a smoker on the sly."

Puffy returns with the drinks. Mine is a double martini, but the olive's missing, so I send Puffy back with it. What does he think he's playing at, bringing me a martini without a stuffed green olive. Seriously.

"I have you down as visiting the Emirates before India—did you miss that one?"

I check the paperwork, and much to my chagrin find he's right. Puffy's back with the martini. He sees me looking at the itinerary, whispers in my ear, and then I remember the news stories.

"Too hot this time of year," I mutter.

"But it's December."

"Too hot."

"All right," the reporter says, turning the page in his notebook. "And then to Australia?"

"Possibly," I reply. "Depends if there's anything left to visit. But they're good friends of ours over there, and if the fires aren't too close to the city, we'll set down at least long enough for a chat."

"You do seem to have a few friends scattered here and there," the reporter says. It sounds almost like a compliment, and that's what puts me on edge. It's not like reporters to compliment, unless they're hardcore Fox.

"Thank you," I say guardedly.

Again, the reporter puts his pencil away, now leans back in his seat. He's not drinking, I notice, and Puffy hasn't made a move to offer one. *What's going on here?*

"Have you ever heard the Turkish proverb about the forest and the axe?"

"I doubt it. I haven't thought much about Turkey since Erdogan lost his grip. Good ally, he was. Knew when to listen to us and when not to, if you remember the Kurds."

"I'll always remember the Kurds," the reporter says, but he's not looking at me, he's looking at the other guy, not Puffy, not me. I look at him too and see him nod sympathetically, as if he too remembers the Kurds. Swarthy man, hadn't noticed that about him before. Very odd.

"So, what's this proverb, then," I say. This is the weirdest interview I've ever given. So few questions, no challenges, and now this oblique game that I don't totally get.

"The forest was shrinking, yet the trees still voted for the axe because its wooden handle convinced them it was one of the trees."

"Huh," I say. "That's *trees* for you."

If this is all the reporter has to say for himself, and since there aren't any more questions, I decide I may as well get forty winks. I kick off my shoes and make myself comfortable on the sofa, focusing on two things and two things only as I recline backwards: my drink, and the clever things I intend to say when we land.

All is quiet in the Learjet.

Ivanka is ignoring me. I turn her around by the shoulder, but suddenly it's not her but Donald grimacing back at me, calling me a loser. My legs twitch. I realize I've been sleeping. I wonder if I snored.

Surely, we must be making our final approach. I peer out of the window. Strange—the sun is on the wrong side of the plane.

"What's going on," I say to Puffy. He doesn't make a move. Just smiles at me wanly, showing off his bright white teeth. The other guy is sitting across from me, looking sternly at me as if I were nothing to him. The reporter's there too, and I don't like that expression very much, either. I know that expression, because it's the one I wear when I'm about to do something my handlers will have to clean up for me afterwards.

"Answer me. What's going on. Why is the sun on the wrong side of the plane. We are going to Dublin." I try to mask the panic I'm feeling, but it sneaks in around the edges of my voice. I don't know why I fell asleep before—it's still early in the day; there's no reason for me to feel so groggy.

"Have you heard the Turkish proverb about the forest?" the reporter asks.

"We've done that one already."

"The problem for the axe is that he grew complacent. He stopped fearing. He thought he was the apex predator. But what you must remember is this: the burning fire burns the axe too, not just the trees."

"What is this nonsense."

"You have to learn, Mr. Kushner; you have to learn what it is like out there."

"I don't get it."

"You will," says the reporter, leaning in close. Suddenly, I think I must still be dreaming, only now I can't wake up, because the reporter lifts his hand, pulls away his nose, rips it from his face, and the whole face tears away like a mask, yes, it *is* a mask! A disguise!

"You!" I shout. I look beseechingly at Puffy and the other guy, but they're immobile; they just sit watching me. They're enjoying this!

"Yes, it's me," says Greta, as she finally reveals herself. "You always said, Mr. Kushner, that I was too much talk and too little action. I've taken you at your word. Welcome to the forest."

I slump back in defeat. What can I do now? I've been betrayed by those closest to me, bearing in mind of course that I know neither of their names, but that shouldn't matter! I'm the First Man! *When Ivanka hears about this...*

"What are you planning to do to me," I say. I realize I'm getting hot, sweaty even, so I slip off my jacket. It's too light on the right side; my phone must have been taken from me as I slept; there really is no escape it seems. It is horrendous to be so much under someone else's power.

"You will find out in a few minutes. Buckle up, Mr. Kushner, we're coming in to land."

I do as I'm told. That surprises me: have I been following Ivanka's lead for so long that it is now natural for me to follow the instructions of a woman? I thought I was the one in charge in the White House, but now I am assailed by doubts; they overwhelm me; I don't know which way to turn in my thoughts. Mechanically, I slip the safety belt around my waist. My ears pop. We're coming down fast—too fast. Is that the plan? Is this a suicide mission? I heard rumors that Greta was linked to ISIS... no, wait, *I* was the one who started spreading the rumors, so they can't be true.

With a bounce, we come back down to earth. I look out the window and see a glorious landscape, the sun gleaming over everything its light touches, and there's barely a cloud in the sky. This definitely isn't Dublin.

"Come on down, Mr. Kushner," says Greta. She's gotten changed, I don't know when, but she looks more her usual self, like in the pictures when she collected that ridiculous Nobel Prize—she deserves it as little as Obama did, or Gore for that glorified PowerPoint presentation. I deserve... well, I deserve a lot more than I'm currently getting. I don't even look at Puffy or the other guy, though I notice out of the corner of my eye that neither of them seem armed, neither of them seem to care what I do as long as I keep my calm, which is all very strange. What's to stop me from yelling for help?

I take a few tentative steps on the tarmac. It's warm out. I don't need my jacket, and I roll up my sleeves. D.C. wasn't like this. I stand still and try to compose myself. This is all real, this is really happening, so I'm not still dreaming. But I still can't figure out where I am. We've landed at some provincial airstrip, and the terminal building is more like an outhouse. I try to calculate how far we could have flown, but my brain is still trying to catch up with the time shift from falling asleep. I'm beginning to think there was more to that martini than I was expecting.

"Follow me," Greta says. Puffy walks behind me, and the other guy stays behind with the plane. I wonder if they had to threaten the pilot to make him do what they wanted. I wish I knew. If it was just a question of money...

"Where are we," I say. Greta tells me that I need to figure that out for myself. There's something otherworldly about the place, though. It's so green and full of life that I would have thought this America's garden, which most certainly is not the Garden State, but where? Florida is constantly inundated, so it can't be there, and there's no humidity. There isn't that fiery crackle to the air you get in California. And we're definitely not in New York. I wasn't paying attention to the scenery when I was stuck on the campaign trail with Ivanka, and besides, we put our focus on the swing states and on Twitter. This looks like neither.

We get in a car and drive off a way. The road is deserted. There aren't many trees growing around here, I notice. Is that why Greta is so obsessed with that stupid Turkish proverb?

After ten minutes, we come to a halt, the car pulling off on the side of the road.

"Get out," Greta says.

I do as I'm told. "Are you leaving me here?"

"No," Greta says. She climbs out too, and there's Puffy leaning his massive frame against the car, dwarfing it. But he doesn't look ready for action. He just looks curious, as if he wants to know, too, what the plan is and what's going to happen next.

"Come with me for a walk," Greta says.

"Fine," I say. We head away from the road. The ground is weird, though, soggy, as if it's just been raining here, but the cloudless sky suggests there hasn't been any rain for a while. I find my steps take an unusual bounce, and water—not mud—actual water seems to be springing up to fill the space left by each of my footsteps.

"What is all this," I say.

"Have you figured out where we are yet?"

I cast my eyes towards the horizon. We can see for miles in every direction across this gently undulating landscape, glorious but so desolate, as if it were new, and nothing had the time to grow here yet. Is it weird that the land is so flat and yet not flat? It looks almost like the sea has come in to land, as if there were waves stretching out in every direction. In the far distance, there is a bluish smudge that I take to be mountains, tall, looming mountains, but they're not snow-capped, which is especially odd given the season. Have we come to the southern hemisphere? Are the seasons reversed? I still don't get it.

"I give up," I tell Greta. I hardly recognize my voice; it's become so soft. I feel as if I'm sinking into the ground. Greta takes my arm; she's almost friendly now, and we keep walking. If we were to stop walking for more than a minute or two, would I be swallowed up by the land? I don't trust what's under my feet.

"You'd recognize this place easily enough if you'd visited a decade ago," Greta says. "Back then it looked more as it should: white everywhere, a blanket of snow and ice locking the earth in stasis and keeping trapped what was meant to be trapped for all of human history. But climate change is real, Mr. Kushner, as you know well, and it has wrought its havoc on this landscape too. We are close to a tipping point, a point from which there is no return, and life on this planet is completely doomed. Forget the predictions, forget the forecasts of how much land will be lost to the rising sea, because what you see before you, what you are standing on right now... Very soon, massive quantities of carbon, sequestered by the permafrost, will escape into the atmosphere, and nothing we do will have meaning anymore. It will be too late for us."

"Permafrost," I repeat. A veil is being lifted from my mind. I look around with fresh eyes, and when I realize what it is that Greta is showing me, I crumble, a big part of me dissolves, and there I am collapsing onto the ground, pounding the mushy land with my fist, decrying all of our stupidities.

"Alaska! Alaska! Alaska!" I cry out loud.

Greta places her hand soothingly on my shoulder as I begin to sob.

"Welcome back to the forest, Mr. Kushner," she says.

. . .

About the Author: Christopher Walker has a BSc in Physics from the University of Leicester (a university with a long history in space science and technology, including Earth Observation Science that is critical in measuring the effects of man-made climate change). He is also a published author, with several journal publications and anthologies to his name (full details available at www.closelyobserved.com).

15

The Rights of Nature

by Patrick Ritter (United States)

Subgenres: Political, legal, science fiction

Time Period: Near future (after 2029)

Setting: California, United States of America

Synopsis: This story, while fiction, addresses an actual and growing new field in environmental law: the rights attributable to natural systems. The story is a variation of David vs Goliath, in this case Climate Activists vs Big Oil, but recent rights of nature laws have leveled the playing field.

. . .

"The International Court of Climate Justice is now in session. All rise for the Honorable Judge Ashton B. Crofton."

Those who didn't know Judge Crofton would say he looked quite scholarly as he walked in, but to the attorneys who knew him, his slight scowl was unmistakable.

Crofton didn't like the new International Rights of Nature law. He liked adjudicating it in his courtroom even less. He was old school, nearing retirement, and longed for the days when his court dealt with predictable law of the sea cases. Now these natural rights cases. *Animals with rights*? Hard to see. *Watersheds bringing lawsuits*? Even crazier, but their rights had been upheld recently by the Supreme Court, which had unleashed a torrent of cases waiting to be heard. He had taken an oath to uphold the law, even quirky ones. *Well, only a few more years before retirement*, he thought.

He looked at the jury, then around the courtroom packed with journalists, industry lobbyists, and environmental activists. *The whole carnival.* "In the matter of *Santa Barbara Channel Marine Ecosystem versus Extraction Energy*, is the counsel for the plaintiff ready to proceed?"

Standing quickly, Sean Purtell said, "We are, Your Honor." Purtell was forty, tall, lean with the weathered tan of a surfer. Because he was one.

"And for the defense?"

"Ready, Your Honor," said Calder Blackstone, gray suit, grayer hair, and a practiced look of indignant annoyance. As if he shouldn't really have to be here at all defending Extraction Energy. Which is what Judge Crofton was thinking. *But the law is the law*.

Jury selection took the entire morning, and the court recessed for lunch. The parade filed out of the International Climate Justice courthouse, an historic former Army building in the San Francisco Presidio with a million-dollar view of the Golden Gate Bridge. Driven by the rapid melting of Antarctica's glaciers and the immediate two feet of sea level rise, the Rights of Nature International Treaty became law in 2029. It gave the Paris Agreement claws and fangs. Many said it was too late. Nevertheless, an international climate change court was established.

Many nations wanted to host. Polluting countries lined up to "offer" their cities, hoping to stifle and delay climate change lawsuits. Didn't fool anybody. Fiji argued that, because it had the most at stake, it should host. Nice vacation spot, despite the dead coral reefs, but not cosmopolitan enough to lure the high-level legal professionals needed. In the end, the original site of the United Nations—San Francisco—was selected. California's leadership in cap-and-trade legislation for climate change was the swing factor. A recycled building in the former Army Presidio was outfitted with solar panels and heat pumps, and a sustainable courthouse was born.

That afternoon, Judge Crofton said, "Mr. Purtell, you may proceed with your opening statement."

"Thank you, Your Honor. Ladies and Gentlemen, my name is Sean Purtell, and I represent the Santa Barbara Channel Marine Ecosystem. My client is currently being harmed by the activities of the defendant, Extraction Energy. We therefore seek to bring an end to these destructive practices that not only harm the marine ecosystem, but also result in greater production of oil. And as I am sure you are all aware, oil is one of the biggest contributors to greenhouse gasses that are so imperiling our planet."

Judge Crofton rubbed his eyes. *The global argument again.* It hadn't been global when the rights of nature movement started in Ecuador, followed by New Zealand, and then the Great Barrier Reef. In the United States it was only an interesting law school topic until counties in Pennsylvania and California enacted rights of nature ordinances. While impassioned, they had no legal teeth. Corporations fought them back based on "individual" property rights, meaning individual humans. It took a rise of two feet in sea levels to put the power of international law behind it.

The first class-action lawsuits represented unwieldy groups: all ocean mammals, then the entire Phylum Coelenterata, which included corals. The suits were dismissed because the classes couldn't be certified. So, the plaintiffs regrouped and were back with new, more focused clients. This plaintiff was a 350-square mile marine ecosystem off the Southern California coast.

Who would have thought, Crofton mused, that an ecosystem would someday have the right to bring suit? But then, no one thought the planet would be in this much trouble. Maybe a radical solution for a radical problem was needed. *Just hard to adjudicate.*

Purtell continued. "This trial is about hydraulic fracturing, commonly known as fracking. Extraction Energy has developed a new method of fracking beneath the ocean, called SEAFRAC. They are using this powerful new method to squeeze the last bit of oil from offshore shale deposits in the Santa Barbara Channel. I will prove, with a preponderance of the evidence, that this practice is causing irreparable harm to the entire marine ecosystem, from zooplankton to whales. The natural rights of an ecosystem, acknowledged by the United States Supreme Court, must be given precedence over industrial profiteering to produce more petroleum."

It wasn't a pretty picture as Purtell told it—threatened and endangered species under attack, biodiversity impairment, loss of aquatic habitat—the full scientific menu that supported a Rights of Nature case. He made an ardent close. "The defense is likely to tell you that Extraction Energy is delivering essential fuels while providing jobs and economic growth. This is really a double insult to your intelligence. Extraction Energy is not only depriving my client of its natural rights, it is producing petroleum products that generate greenhouse gasses that we know are already at catastrophic levels. During this trial, I would like you all to contemplate the effects of climate change in your own lives. We all know someone who's lost a home or business as a result of climate-induced wildfires. We're all paying the heavy tax burden to build seawalls, raise roads, and relocate infrastructure. Our state treasury is in debt. These are real economic burdens to all of us." He paused for effect.

"The age of oil is over for our planet. It has to be. It's damaging our climate, and as you will see, could further damage one of the most magnificent ocean ecosystems anywhere. Is squeezing the last bit of oil from some rock really worth that?"

For the defense, Blackstone presented a forceful, although predictable, opening statement that included the points Purtell said he would raise. He challenged the notion that an ecosystem had any rights at all. He downplayed the environmental effects and up-played the safety policies of Extraction Energy.

Blackstone also ended strong. "If Extraction Energy is denied its right to employ a technology it has invested considerable effort and money to develop, it will stifle technological innovation throughout California. It will be a first step towards eliminating other essential property rights. Ladies and gentlemen of the jury, you have the opportunity, you have the privilege, to say no to this overreach. If you value freedom, you will say no to this lawsuit."

The next day, Purtell said, "We call our first witness, Dr. Ara Sanderson."

The African-American PhD walked confidently to the witness chair and was sworn in. With Yale and Stanford pedigrees, and a deep briefcase of papers in hydrological modeling, she seemed unassailable as an expert witness. The jury didn't really understand her recent paper on "Hydromechanical Modeling of the Monterey Shale Formation," but it sounded impressive.

Purtell led her through a series of questions starting with the hydrogeology of the Santa Barbara Channel. She then described the fracking process, how chemicals are transported to the platforms, stored, and mixed with massive amounts of seawater to make injection fluids. The injection fluids were sent down boreholes and injected under high pressure into shale rock to fracture the rock and free up residual oil.

Purtell asked, "And these fluids remain in the rock?"

She leaned her head back. "Indeed no, these fluids do not remain in the rock. Fracking fluids, called *flowback,* come back out of the rock and may then migrate upward, into the ocean sedimentary layer, and into the water column. Additionally, many of the wells in the Channel are old and were drilled under less stringent regulations than today. Some have degraded since installation. So, some of these wells may not withstand the high pressures used in hydraulic fracturing and will essentially be conduits for contamination to reach the ocean."

"And flowback from the shale is the only way contamination could reach the ocean?"

"No. In addition, when the wells are pumped to remove oil, the vast majority of the withdrawn fluid, about 90 percent, is produced water, which is essentially wastewater."

"And this wastewater is pumped back into the shale formation?"

"*Objection.* Leading the witness."

"*Withdrawn.* How is this wastewater disposed, Dr. Sanderson?"

"The wastewater is partially treated at the platform, or sometimes not treated at all." She looked directly at the jury. "Then it is discharged into the ocean."

"Thank you. No further questions. Your witness."

The defense poked at the testimony of the accomplished African-American woman, cautiously, but they made little headway.

After lunch, Purtell called a toxicology expert named Clifford Valance.

Valance looked confident, almost bored, wearing a three-piece suit he reserved for court appearances. With just the right amount of silver in his hair and a voice some compared to Walter Cronkite, he made an outstanding expert witness.

"Dr. Valance, does the fracking process use any chemicals?"

"Yes, several chemicals are added to the injection fluids in order to break open the shale. They're essential to the process."

"What chemicals are used?"

Purtell watched the jury closely. Valance got through biocides and corrosion inhibitors pretty well. They had at least heard of those. As he launched into quaternary ammonium compounds, eyes started glazing, and when he started on phenol formaldehyde resins, Purtell interrupted.

"To summarize, Dr. Valance, could these chemicals be toxic?"

"*Objection*. Calls for speculation."

"*Overruled*," Crofton said. "The witness is an expert in toxicology. That is a branch of science, Mr. Blackstone, pertaining to the effects of toxins. Proceed."

"Individually, they are strong chemicals with demonstrated toxic characteristics. In combination, they are a very toxic batch, possibly lethal."

"Dr. Valance, in addition to the chemicals added to the injection fluids, are there any other potentially toxic chemicals involved?"

It was a fat pitch, and Valance ripped it. He described how the injected fluids can pick up materials present in oil shales, including dissolved salts, heavy metals, petroleum derivatives like benzene, and, he ended dramatically, "even toxic radioactive materials from deep within the earth," as if being deep underground was, in itself, an issue.

On cross-examination, the defense was able to get Valance to agree that the "massive amount" of seawater used would greatly dilute the chemicals. However, they couldn't effectively counter the argument that the fluids could pick up radioactive materials from the shale, albeit in small concentrations. "Given the variable and unknown long-term effects of these radioactive compounds," Valance said, "any concentration must be considered potentially toxic."

The defense had to retreat. "No further questions."

Looking at his watch, Purtell said, "Your Honor, in view of the time, we request a recess until tomorrow morning." He wanted the jury to dwell overnight with the thought of radioactive contamination, and he didn't want to give the defense time that night to respond to his last witness.

"Nonsense, Counselor," Crofton said. "It's only three forty-five. Proceed." He did enjoy keeping attorneys in line.

"Of course, Your Honor," Purtell said. "We call Dr. Adrian Foley."

Observers along the aisle could hear Foley's footsteps before they saw him, as he lumbered toward the witness chair. At six feet five and two hundred ninety pounds, he could have been a linebacker. Actually, he had played football in college, but as a tight end.

Crofton watched him approach. *Good thing he wasn't a hostile witness.* At that size, with balding head and thick neck, he looked like, what? Staring at Foley's thick, drooping mustache it came to him. *A walrus.*

Dr. Foley's credentials were anything but shaggy. Degrees in marine biology and environmental risk assessment. Chairman of the department at UC San Diego, and Adjunct Professor at Scripts. Foley squeezed into the witness chair and was sworn in.

"Dr. Foley, can you describe why the Santa Barbara Channel is important from a biological perspective?"

Foley spoke in a deep and confident voice, not aggressive but powerful. And friendly. Just what an expert witness should be, authoritative, but charming. He cast a huge shadow but didn't intimidate. *Sort of like a walrus.*

"Simply put, it's one of the most biologically productive ecosystems on Earth."

He paused to let that sink in. The jury stared intently as Foley continued. "Congress designated the Santa Barbara Channel a National Marine Sanctuary for good reasons." He described the upwelling that provided unusually high concentrations of nutrients to the zooplankton, a primary driving force behind the incredible biological productivity and biodiversity. He outlined the rare meeting place of both southern and northern currents that formed a transition zone bringing enormous concentrations of species. "Home to acres of giant kelp beds that provide habitat, the Santa Barbara Channel hosts unparalleled species density and diversity, including numerous endangered, threatened, and sensitive marine species such as blue, gray, and humpback whales, southern sea otter, and marbled murrelet."

Dr. Foley paused. "The blue whale, the largest mammal to ever live on Earth, has the highest recorded concentration near the Santa Barbara Channel."

Purtell asked, "And what does your research indicate about these blue whale populations?"

Foley's voice became lower and a bit emotional. "They are being harmed by offshore fracking." He catalogued the adverse effects, citing species counts and biopsies he had conducted near the platforms, and citing statistics by memory. It was almost too easy. Foley had the jury spellbound.

Purtell upped the ante. "Why is the Channel vulnerable to pollutants associated with fracking. Don't they just flush out?"

Foley explained how the eight Channel Islands create a natural barrier to the colliding warm and cold currents, creating a huge rotating gyre. "Pollutants can't flush out into the rest of the Pacific Ocean, but instead they remain essentially trapped."

"And what is the biological effect of this, this entrapment?"

"*Objection.* Lacks foundation. Entrapment has a pejorative legal meaning."

"*Withdrawn.* Let me rephrase. Because these pollutants can't disperse, are there any adverse biological effects?"

Should have stuck with entrapment, Crofton thought. *I would've allowed it.*

Foley described adverse effects to leatherback sea turtles and the only breeding population of brown pelicans in the United States. "Potential impacts to threatened and endangered species, including the Southern sea otter and Western snowy plover, are of particular concern," he said, looking at the jury.

Don't know about the snowy plover, but everyone loves sea otters.

Purtell had the jury's attention so decided to go in for the clincher. "Dr. Foley, based on your experience and expertise, could you please tell us, from a marine ecosystem's point of view, what is the overall effect of Extraction Energy's fracking operations?"

"*Objection*! What is the relevance of such a fanciful exercise, Your Honor?"

Judge Crofton knew what was coming. The plaintiff was an ecosystem, and its counsel had the right to use their expert to present the ecosystem's perspective, since the ecosystem could not speak for itself, whale songs notwithstanding. The Natural Rights Law made it admissible. Crofton didn't like allowing it, but he disliked being overturned on appeal even more.

"*Overruled.* The witness may answer the question."

"From the ecosystem's point of view," Foley said, "it is highly stressed. It exists in an injured state, progressively dying, akin to slow poisoning. The ecosystem's right to exist and thrive is eventually lost."

"Thank you, Dr. Foley. No further questions."

After Blackstone's cross-examination, Crofton recessed for the day.

At dinner that night, the defense team and Extraction Energy management dined at one of San Francisco's finest restaurants, commandeering a private room where they could strategize. Blackstone looked around the table at somber faces. The Extraction Energy management didn't look pleased, even while sipping three-hundred-dollar wine.

Blackstone said, "I think we need to push the envelope."

"Meaning what?" the Extraction Energy CEO asked.

"Look, they lined up some pretty decent experts, and they

did quite well, to be honest. We've done a deep search and couldn't find dirt on any of them, so they're in play. They've had great press coverage, and all the ocean groups are behind them. But most importantly, they've got the 'rights of nature' argument in their favor. We aren't going to overturn that legal precedent, at least not in this venue. So, we have to roll the dice and try to use it ourselves, to our own advantage."

The CEO looked puzzled.

"Let me explain."

The next day, Blackstone began the defense. He trotted out their industry experts—engineers, chemists, and safety managers—who cited the sterling safety record of Extraction Energy and referenced their "environmental stewardship ethic, incorporated into every aspect of operations."

An environmental engineer stated, with great certainty, that they treated all fluids "to render them harmless." Avoiding the term wastewater, he informed the jury, "We've been safely disposing *production water* into the ocean for more than forty years," as if the passage of time alone made it safe. He emphasized that they had been discharging "at over two hundred platforms worldwide."

Suggesting that more discharges meant more safety? Crofton wondered.

Purtell didn't object. That was intentional, as he used that very argument to his advantage on cross.

Another expert tried to disprove biological degradation in the Channel using her own studies. After Purtell got her to admit that her work was funded by the petroleum industry, she sounded a little less fervent.

Juries may not understand environmental science, but they know bias when they see it.

They ended the day with the standard "we are really regulated" argument. Their operations manager explained how Extraction Energy was under the strictest environmental rules anywhere, regulated in Southern California by "the toughest agencies in the world." On cross-examination, he acknowledged that, due to climate change spending on infrastructure, the budget for California environmental agencies had been cut by over 30 percent. His response, "I can tell you they are still hard on us," didn't seem to impress anyone, and the court recessed.

The next day, Blackstone said, "The defense calls psychologist Dr. Robert Morton. Dr. Morton, the plaintiff's expert provided testimony from an ecosystem's perspective. In your opinion, is this even possible?"

Purtell stood up quickly. "*Objection.* Argumentative. It *is* possible, because the court heard it."

"*Sustained.*"

"Let me rephrase; do you have an opinion regarding an ecosystem's *point of view*?" Blackman asked, with a subtle and well-practiced hint of sarcasm.

"Well, an ecosystem lacks consciousness, intelligence, or awareness. Furthermore, it cannot communicate, appear in court, or testify. Therefore—"

"*Objection.* Relevance. This matter of law has been settled by the Supreme Court, Your Honor. For example, a corporation lacks consciousness, some would say lacks intelligence, and cannot communicate or appear itself in court. The same is true for states, municipalities, and other entities. They can and do appear in court through their legal representatives, as I am doing today as counsel for the ecosystem."

"*Sustained.* The jury will disregard that answer."

Blackstone knew full well that argument wouldn't succeed, but he had to at least to get the jury to hear it, even if it was to be "disregarded." And he had to show some muscle in front of the Extraction Energy bigwigs. "No further questions. Your witness."

Since he had clearly won the point, Purtell said, "No questions, Your Honor."

"Does the defense have additional witnesses to present?" Crofton asked.

"Yes, Your Honor. We have one last witness, Dr. Russell K. Burson."

With the help of a cane, Russell Burson shuffled forward slowly. He was in his late eighties, a professor emeritus in geological sciences at UCLA. Although now over fifty years old, his breakthrough treatise on California geological processes was still in use. Burson may have been short and stooped, but he was huge in reputation. He settled slowly into the witness chair, adjusted his thick glasses, and peered at the jury. Russell K. Burson, PhD, expert in millions of years of California geology, looked as ancient as his expertise.

"Dr. Burson, could you please describe how petroleum products were formed in the shale underlying the Santa Barbara Channel?"

Burson cleared his throat. Then he cleared it again. He seemed to be gazing absentmindedly into the distance. The defense team fidgeted. Purtell repressed a smile, but Burson recovered and spoke with a clear, professorial voice, remarkably crisp coming from a face so wizened. "During the Mid-Miocene, diatomaceous sediments were deposited following a major alteration in marine thermohaline circulation."

"Dr. Burson, let me interrupt you there, if I may. For the benefit of non-geologists, which is most of us, could you please explain that in simpler terms?"

"Certainly. About ten to fifteen million years ago, during a period known as the Miocene, oceans covered much of California. Tiny, single-celled plants called diatoms flourished in the ocean. When they died, these diatoms fell to the bottom of the sea, where they became trapped under multiple layers of sand and silt. Over millions of years, thousands of feet of sediments built up, and pressure and heat transformed the organic compounds into shale oil."

Burson was doing pretty well. Then he had to cough and clear his throat again. When he had recovered, he said, "The complex array of lithofacies within the Monterey Formation is the product of the interplay between biogenous as well as terrigenous sedimentation."

"Dr. Burson, in plain English please?"

"The sediment layers within the shale were built up from remnants of marine diatoms, as well as organic matter from land."

"So, the natural evolution of these diatoms was responsible for the oil within—"

"*Objection.* Leading the witness."

"*Sustained.*"

"Dr. Burson, these diatoms—"

"*Objection.* Relevance, Your Honor. We are talking about fracking here, not diatoms."

Blackstone was ready for that. "The Rights of Nature law is clear on this matter, Your Honor. Under 2.1.1—Definitions and Applicability—it specifies that the rights so described in the law shall apply to plants and animals of the Earth, without limitation as to size, location, or metabolic function. As Dr. Burson has testified, the formation of shale oil was caused as a result of marine diatoms, which are single-celled plants. Unless the plaintiff has evidence to the contrary, all marine phytoplankton, including diatoms, must be given equal protection under the law and are relevant in any discussion of shale oil."

"I will allow it. But move it along, Mr. Blackstone."

"Thank you, Your Honor. Dr. Burson, would you agree that the decomposition of plants such as diatoms into oil is one of Earth's natural systems?"

"The formation of petroleum is a process that has naturally evolved over millions of years, and without human intervention. So yes, it is a natural system."

Picking up a thick book, Blackstone said, "Dr. Burson, the Merriam Webster Dictionary defines the word *thrive* as to grow vigorously. Do you agree with that definition?"

"Yes."

"*Objection!* Purtell stood up indignantly. "What is the possible relevance of this line of questioning?"

"*Overruled.* I am going to let it go, but you need to bring this in for a landing, and quickly, Mr. Blackstone."

"Yes, Your Honor. Dr. Burson, in what way could petroleum hydrocarbon be able to *grow vigorously*?"

"Well, heating any material results in its expansion. The process of combustion results in the rapid expansion, growth if you will, of liquid petroleum into gas."

"So, the only way a hydrocarbon can complete its natural progression, its evolution as you say, is through combustion?

"Yes, it's similar to other energy cycles in nature. The natural progression, from plants to shale deposits to fuel to combustion, releases the elements back into nature, completing the cycle."

Did I just hear that?

"Dr. Burson, could you please read Section 1.1: Intent, of the Rights of Nature law?"

No one else in the courtroom understood what Blackstone was driving towards, but Purtell did, and he had no objection to counter it.

"The intent of this law is to acknowledge and protect the inherent rights of plants and animals of the Earth to exist, thrive, and naturally evolve."

"And how is this related to shale oil?"

"The final phase of the diatom cycle is the release of energy. These petroleum reserves contain energy built up over millions of years. They have the right to release that energy, in order to thrive and evolve."

Seriously?

"*Objection!* Lacks foundation."

"*Sustained.*" *The Defense is throwing everything at the wall to see what will stick.* "This is a matter of case law that has already been decided by the courts. If you have nothing further..."

"I do, Your Honor," Blackstone said.

"Dr. Burson, could you please read Section 2.1.2 of the Natural Rights Law."

"Natural rights shall accrue to all plants and animals on Earth. Ecosystems representing holders of natural rights shall, by extension, also attain natural rights."

"So, an ecosystem such as the Santa Barbara Channel has natural rights?"

Burson looked surprised. "Yes, isn't this what this trial is about?"

"I move to introduce this exhibit as evidence," Blackstone said, handing the court reporter a thin report. "This is a paper titled 'Essential Components of an Ecosystem,' written by the plaintiff's own expert witness, Dr. Foley. Could you please read this sentence, Dr. Burson?"

"There are four essential components to an ecosystem: producers, which are living organisms like plants that convert sunlight to food; consumers, such as animals; decomposers; and nonliving elements, such as water, air, rocks, and minerals."

"So, by Dr. Foley's definition, does the Santa Barbara Channel ecosystem include rocks, such as the Monterey shale?"

"Yes," Dr. Burson said, "that would meet his definition."

"No further questions."

Purtell's head was spinning. *Oil has the right to combust? The jury won't buy that, and it wouldn't hold up on appeal. Doubtful that Blackstone will even use it on closing. But the ecosystem angle...* He considered countering with a chemical trespass argument but decided against it. There was a better way.

"Your Honor, we request the court's permission to recall Dr. Foley."

"Under what grounds, counselor?"

"The defense introduced as evidence a single sentence from one of Dr. Foley's publications. We believe that additional information from that paper needs to be presented."

"Alright, I'm going to allow the recall of Dr. Foley, but his testimony needs to be focused solely on the issues raised by the defense."

"Understood, Your Honor."

It took an hour to locate Foley, as he was at the airport eating a plate of fish tacos. As he walked in, he didn't seem happy being interrupted during his lunch. He conferred for a few minutes with Purtell and his team, then took the stand.

"Dr. Foley, the defense presented an argument that shale, and the oil contained within it, is included within the Santa Barbara Channel ecosystem? Do you agree?"

"Yes, shale is part of the ecosystem, even if it's non-living."

"Then shale oil is covered under the Rights of Nature law?"

"No," Dr. Foley said, "absolutely not."

"Why is that?"

"Well, as my paper pointed out, an ecosystem is a *self-sustaining* entity, a principal also incorporated into the Rights of Nature law."

Purtell handed him the volume. "Section 3.1 reads: To qualify for natural rights protection, plants, animals, or entire ecosystems cannot be destructive to themselves, other protected classes, or to humans. Could you explain that?"

"It means that destructive beetles that kill forests don't have protected rights. Same for mosquitoes, since they transmit malaria and encephalitis that are harmful to humans and animals. Size doesn't matter, either. Parasitic mites that kill foxes and wolves aren't protected."

Purtell asked, "What about harm to an ecosystem?"

"Well, gypsy moths pose a considerable threat to the oak and aspen ecosystems in the northeast and therefore don't have natural rights."

"So, returning to the question about shale oil, why doesn't it have natural rights?"

Dr, Foley said, "Shale oil does provide fuel, asphalt, and feedstock to make other compounds. But its negative effects to plants, animals, and ecosystems far outweigh any benefits, especially since we now have other fuel and energy sources and alternative components."

"What are these negative effects?"

"Petroleum and other hydrocarbons are the principal generators of greenhouse gasses, which in turn are causing the climate change that is wreaking such pain and havoc on humans and nature alike. Continued use of shale oil will also result in air pollution from the refining process, as well as from its combustion. Spills and releases of oil cause enormous damage to marine ecosystems. So, on balance, from both a human and ecosystem point of view, it is destructive. Therefore, it does not qualify for protection under the Rights of Nature law."

Purtell made an impassioned closing. Blackstone gave it his best, but several jurors looked skeptical. Jury deliberation began.

The next day, Judge Crofton entered the courtroom thinking, *Maybe it's not such a crazy law after all.* He watched the jury file in.

Something that had been gnawing on him surfaced. *I really need to get rid of my gas guzzler and get an electric car,* he thought.

The courtroom was buzzing. "Order," he said, rapping his gavel. "Has the jury reached a decision?"

"We have, Your Honor. We find in favor of the plaintiff."

The courtroom erupted in applause. Purtell stood and high-fived his entire team. Crofton let the celebration continue for only a minute before calling for order.

"As specified in the complaint, the defendant shall cease all hydraulic fracturing activities in the Santa Barbara Channel within thirty days."

Judge Crofton raised his gavel. *Maybe I'll look into solar, too.*

"This court is now adjourned."

. . .

About the author:

After getting his master's degree in civil engineering at Stanford, Patrick Ritter pursued a career in environmental engineering and consulting. He has worked on hundreds of projects throughout California and the United States, including hazardous waste cleanups, renewable energy development, environmental impact analyses, and most recently, climate change modeling. His story draws on these experiences. He has previously published short stories in *The Cold Creek Review, Fiction on the Web*, and *Freedom Fiction*, and poetry in *Defenestration*.

16

Vacation Time

by James Lipson (United States)

Subgenres: Humor, flash fiction

Time Period: Near future

Setting: North Pole, Alaska

Synopsis: The EPA discovers the smoking gun of climate change.

. . .

The EPA Confirmed Today the Smoking Gun of Global Warming Has Been Discovered.

Over two thousand acres of noxious, spewing factories were found operating at North Pole, Alaska. The snow and ice surrounding the area's workshops melted years ago. What remains closely resembles a pockmarked moon under a never-ending rain of acid. Wildlife in the area vanished long ago; the only reminders are the sun-bleached skeletons of land-locked seals, lost polar bears, and what appear to be gigantic reindeer bones.

When asked what happened, a cherubic, red-clad caretaker

was quoted as saying, "Looks like someone is getting a permanent vacation."

. . .

About the Author: James Lipson's books, including *The Fairie King: A New Adventure Begins, Fallen and Other Stories, The Girl with Hands in Her Hair*, and *Game Over and Other Stories*, can be found on Amazon.com. Additionally, his short stories have been featured in various publications such as Black Hare Press Anthologies, Zombie Pirate Publishing, Clarendon Publishing Anthologies, Teleport Magazine, and others. With a background in art, James has naturally turned to illustrating as he writes, bringing many of his short stories to life not only with descriptive detail, but also detailed visual imagery. You can find his illustrations and other artwork at www.jameslipson.com, www.thefairieking.com
www.instagram.com/jameslipsonart/ or www.facebook.com/james.lipson.1654

17

A New Year in the Same Old World

by Willow Croft (United States)

Subgenres: Science fiction, pandemic fiction

Time Period: 2038 AD

Setting: The Red Zone in a floating pod city somewhere above the former nation of Japan.

Synopsis: Former Olympic swimmer Umi now lives in her quarantine pod in the Red Zone that is part of a floating Pod City. The virus evolves each year into a new (and stronger) form that requires the citizens of Earth to remain in ever more stringent social isolation and physical isolation from the exterior natural world, which is healing itself with the help of AI-driven machines. Humans hope animals will also bounce back from the brink of extinction.

. . .

Another new year. And another new pandemic. Each passing year brought a new and more resistant virus strain. Umi was glad they stopped naming the viruses after the year, but she wasn't sure if naming them like they did earthquakes and hurricanes was any better. She kicked off her cooling sheet and checked the external temperature.

Only 110 degrees. Practically spring-like, this close to the equator. With the fall of the United States, the more stringent global warming restrictions imposed by the new-and-improved Paris Agreement seemed to be making a difference. She brushed her teeth as the newscaster continued: "It's now known as the Hercules virus. So, again, stay indoors, stay cool, stay safe, and stay healthy. Love to all, your comrade in hardship, Airi."

Umi placed her brush back in the sanitizer. *Like they had any choice but to stay indoors.* Sometimes she wondered if the Americans hadn't the right idea when they had resisted the government and insisted on going back to business as usual. Of course, the whole country had been wiped out within a decade, but at least they got to see the sun. The real sun. She changed the news station for a live streaming video of a polar bear family in the Arctic. Those cameras were the only thing that made her rote, confined, dull life seem worth it. The animals were bouncing back, without humans running around polluting and destroying everything.

The screen just showed white. If she stood really close, she knew she could see snow flying across the screen. Another Arctic storm. She'd have to wait to check in on the polar bear family later. Today was Red Zone's exercise day. Her garden walk was in five minutes. She left her pod and entered into the sanitizing *genkan*. The room darkened to a near black, and she held as still as possible while a dim blue light clicked on. The blue light began scanning her. It beeped and froze at her midsection. She took some deep breaths, but her hands started to shake. She braced herself for the words "Bio-hostile organism detected," but they never came. The blue light continued its downward scan.

She knew she didn't have to be nervous anymore. The world had gotten a lot more civilized, and those infected with the virus were no longer instantly terminated. Terminated and incinerated. So many in the first few decades of the pandemics that the sky had turned black with ash as if Mount Fuji had finally erupted. She jumped when the blue light clicked off, and a panel emerged from the wall. She put on the biodegradable swimsuit and covered herself with her workout clothes. A blast of cool air hit her as the door slid open, and she quickly stepped out into the warmth of the artificial sun. She did her required twenty laps under the artificial trees, then sunk to the fake grass.

"Twenty laps completed in the year 2038. Four—"

"I don't need to know." Despite her Thursday remedial language classes, followed by her weekly social interactions to help keep her conversational skills up, her voice still sounded strange to her ears. She was rewarded for her exercise efforts by the appearance of a squirrel; automated, of course, carrying her lunch to her in a little basket. She unwrapped the cloth, almost daring to hope it would be something different, but it was still the same old nutritional block and the same tube of vitamin-infused liquid. She nibbled at the block. Fake sushi, again.

She pushed it aside, and the automated squirrel removed it. She stood up and stripped off her workout clothes, stuffing them in the disposal panel by a pink flowering bush. She waited for the blue scanning light to allow her to enter into the aquatic pod. She knew the pool was a small one, and that it merely rotated as the swimmer swam—she'd helped design it after she earned her engineering degree from the online university—but the virtual background could be whatever the swimmer wanted.

She could have chosen the competitive swimming loop, but she still couldn't bear to experience the sights, sounds, and smells of the Aquatics Center, even though it had been over seventeen years since she'd had to give up her passion. She'd just made it onto the Japanese team for the 2020 Olympics;

held in her home country. Her familiar training ground. And it had been postponed to the following year. And then the year after that. And again, and again, until it was decided that the Olympics were to be canceled for good.

She picked the virtual background that reminded her of the small lake near her childhood home. Only this one went on forever, all the way to the horizon. She swam out under the artificial sky that was just turning twilight. Mist swirled around her like ghosts, and she heard the loon, crying for its lost world. Though in actuality, it was the world that should have been crying for its loss. It was extinct, for now, while the scientists made their way down the laundry list of known extinct species to be recreated from stored DNA samples. A gentle chime sounded from the shore, reminding her that her time in the pool was drawing to a close. She swam back to shore and plopped onto the warm, fake earth. A louder chime sounded right overhead, and she stripped off her suit and put it in another recycling chute next to a tree.

Another blue-light sanitizing wash, and she was in the sauna, swirling steam massaging the soreness out of her muscles. She closed her eyes until the chime sounded. Within a few minutes, she was freshly steamed and dried, waiting for the dim blue light to complete its scan. It beeped at the same spot around her midsection and began the scan all over again. Umi frowned. *Must be a glitch in the system, or a malfunction in the AI's program.* Tomorrow was her work day, so she'd schedule time to inspect Red Zone's monitoring systems.

She ate dinner back in her room; another sushi-flavored block, followed by some screen-watching until she felt tired. She chose not to artificially dream, and instead slipped into a black, still void that mimicked the darkened room around her. But something, deep in that void, was awake. The darkness itself was the factor, the code that activated dozens of minuscule organisms.

Organisms that had evolved past mere biologically

determined evolution. Organisms that had an intelligence that went beyond the confines of Earth-based life forms. They relied on synthetic proteins kept in their internal storehouse, and on knowledge transmitted synthetically from elsewhere in the universe. The natural pandemics were more than just the perfect cover for these organisms. The constantly mutating viruses were the waste products from their consumption of synthetic proteins, left behind as the organisms moved onto a new human host. A healthy host, while the old one writhed and died.

Because, as the organisms' creators found out, nature's "survival of the fittest" law needed a little extra help when it came to the human race. And they celebrated the new year, right alongside the humans, as another species returned from the brink of extinction. As one of the young polar bear cubs successfully caught its first fish on the live streaming video.

. . .

About the author: Willow Croft has had short stories published in *Mad Scientist Journal*, *Rock N' Roll Horror Zine*, *Speculative 66*, *Sirens Call eZine*, *EconoClash Review*, and in several anthologies, including the Olympic-themed *The Phantom Games: Dimensions Unknown 2020*. She is a former wildlife rehabber and is dedicated to animal rescue and animal welfare causes (#AdoptDontShop), most currently volunteering on a campaign to have chimps that are being held at a laboratory released into the care of a licensed sanctuary (https://apnm.org/). Find her on her blog at https://willowcroft.blog.

18

Terraforming Earth

by David Harten Watson (United States)

Subgenres: Science fiction, political satire, humor, and alternate history

Time Period: 2020 to 2040 AD

Setting: Washington, D.C., United States of America

Synopsis: What if Donald Trump had won re-election in 2020 by colluding with another hostile foreign power—not Russia this time, but aliens?

. . .

July 24, 2020: Donald Trump sat down for his Presidential Daily Briefing (PDB) reluctantly, as always. These daily intelligence briefings consumed valuable time that he could have used tweeting to his Twitter followers, listening to Fox and One America News flatter him, or chatting with his friend Putin on the phone. While his Director of National Intelligence (DNI) droned on about distant countries Donald had never even *heard* of, he looked around the room and noticed an unfamiliar face, a bald man in an Air Force uniform. Interrupting his DNI, he pointed his finger at the stranger and said, "Hey, Baldy, what's your name?"

"General John Raymond, Chief of Space Operations for the US Space Force. You appointed me, Mister President, remember?"

Annoyed at being reminded of his poor memory, Donald nevertheless forced a smile. "Oh yes, my space commander! *Space Force*, I love that phrase, *Space Force*. General, did anyone ever tell you that you look like Captain Picard from *Star Trek*?"

"No, Mister President," General Raymond said, stone-faced.

Donald hated it when people didn't laugh at his jokes. As payback, he told the general, "Well, from now on, Baldy, I'm going to call you 'Picard.' What brings you to my PDB, Picard? None of the other Joint Chiefs are here today, and I don't remember inviting you."

The DNI sighed. "Go ahead, General; I was almost ready to call on you anyway."

General Raymond said, "Sir, NASA recently detected a non-terrestrial object orbiting the Earth at one of the Lagrange points, the L4 Earth-Moon Lagrange point."

Donald didn't understand the technobabble, so he seized on the one word he *had* understood, NASA. "If NASA discovered this object, why are *you* here telling me this, rather than the NASA Director?" Then he remembered the 2020 election bumper sticker he'd seen that read "**Giant Asteroid 2020—JUST END IT ALREADY!**" Worried that one might hit Trump Tower or one of his golf resorts, he asked before the general could answer, "Is this an asteroid that's going to hit Earth, destroying a city or something?"

"No sir," General Raymond replied. "The non-terrestrial object isn't an asteroid. It's not any kind of natural object. It's an artificial satellite."

"Russian or Chinese?" Donald asked.

The general shook his head.

"Don't tell me it's the North *Koreans,*" Donald whined, feeling betrayed. "Kim Jong-un promised me he wouldn't launch any more satellites without letting me know first. He wrote me such *beautiful* love letters, and Putin told me I could trust him."

"No, sir. We believe this satellite was built by aliens."

"Illegal aliens? Why do they keep crossing our border if they have enough money to put satellites into space?"

"Sir, I'm talking about non-human aliens. Space aliens," General Raymond clarified.

"Are you sure?"

General Raymond nodded. "Yes, sir. The aliens established communication with us yesterday. It seems they learned English by monitoring our television broadcasts."

Hey, if they caught episodes of The Apprentice, *maybe I'm famous on other planets, too!* Donald brightened. "What have they told you so far?"

"Not much, sir. They said they wanted to speak directly with you, and only with you."

"That's great news!" Donald said, "*tremendous* news!"

"It is?" asked General Raymond.

"Yes, absolutely! It means they recognize that I'm the leader of the entire planet Earth."

"Sir, we have no way of knowing whether they've also contacted *other* world leaders—"

Donald waved a hand dismissively, "Why *would* they? If they've been watching TV, then they know I'm the most important person on Earth, the smartest leader on Earth, and the one with the highest TV ratings. Wow, this means my TV ratings are so high that even aliens from other planets watch me on TV, and now they want to talk to me. Can you set up a direct line in the Oval Office for me to talk to the aliens?"

"Yes, sir, but—"

"No buts, Picard, just *make it so!*" This time, his *Star Trek* reference was rewarded by laughter. Deciding to quit while he was ahead, Donald stood up and left the briefing room with a new spring in his step. *Even aliens recognize me as the leader of the world!*

. . .

July 25, 2020: The communications link to the alien spacecraft was installed in the Oval Office overnight. Donald arrived in the Oval Office in the late morning to find a shiny new microphone on his desk. Wires from the mic led to a black metal box on the floor that looked like one of those "tower" gaming PCs that had multiple hard drives, CD drives, and DVD players. He summoned General Raymond to the Oval Office. When the general arrived, Donald said, "Okay, Captain Picard, show me how to work this thing."

General Raymond frowned. "Sir, I'm a general, not a captain."

"Okay, *General* Picard. How do I use this thing to dial the aliens?"

The general reached down, flipped a few switches on the black metal box, and twisted a dial. An LED panel showed a series of numbers, which Donald assumed was a radio frequency. Then the General flipped a few more switches and said, "It's ready now, sir. Do you want me to make the call?"

"Of course. The president of the United States doesn't dial his own phone."

General Raymond grimaced, and Donald guessed that a four-star general rarely dialed his own phone, either. "It's not exactly dialing a phone," Raymond said, as he reached down and flipped three more switches on the box, then leaned over to the shiny microphone on the desk, pushed a button on the side of it, and said, "Aliens, this is General Raymond, Chief of Space Operations for the United States Space Force. Are you there?"

A monotone voice boomed from the speaker on the box. "We are listening."

"Please hold for the president of the United States, Donald J. Trump," General Raymond said. He released the button on the microphone and told Donald, "Push the transmit button to talk, and release the button to listen."

"I know how radio transmitters work," Donald snapped, although having never served in the military, he'd only seen them in movies.

General Raymond stepped away from the desk and said, "It's all yours, sir. Do you wish me to remain here?"

"Yes, but don't discuss the contents of my conversation with the aliens with anyone. You *do* know how to keep your mouth shut, don't you?"

The general said, stone-faced, "Yes, sir."

"Good." Donald sat down at the Resolute Desk, leaned in toward the microphone, pushed the transmit button, and said, "Aliens, you are speaking with the president of the United States, Donald J. Trump. I heard that you asked to speak directly to me. That was a very smart choice. Can I ask what made you choose me?"

The monotone voice from the speaker said, "We know from your TV broadcasts that you are the most powerful man on Earth. We have also heard that you are the wisest, the most handsome, and the most virile."

"Yes, that's true," Donald said proudly. It was the same thing his friends Putin and Kim Jong-un often told him. "Well, you're obviously friendly, so what can I—"

The general flipped a switch on the black box and pleaded, "Sir, please don't offer to *do* anything for them! We know nothing about these aliens, and we can't trust them."

Donald fumed. "Did you just disconnect us, Picard?"

"No, but I flipped a switch to disconnect the transmitter and speaker. Basically, I hit the mute switch on the call."

"Well, *un*mute it, Picard, or I'll bust you down to captain, like your namesake!"

The general sighed, but he flipped the switch back on.

Donald pushed the button on the microphone and said, "What can I do for you, my alien friends?"

The alien voice said, "You have already done so much for us, Donald Trump. More than you can possibly imagine. We just want you to continue doing what you have been doing."

"What have I done for you, and what do you want me to continue doing?"

"You pulled out of the Paris Agreement of the United Nations Framework Convention on Climate Change. You revoked the Clean Power Plan that limited carbon dioxide emissions from coal and natural gas plants. You revoked California's waiver to set its own vehicle emissions standards under the Clean Air Act. You restricted how government agencies can conduct climate science, limiting them from assessing the future consequences and worst-possible outcomes of climate change. You rolled back automotive fuel economy standards."

"How did this help you?"

"That is not important," the alien voice from the speaker said, in its monotone. "What is important is that you continue your work of rolling back efforts to fight climate change, or what you call global warming."

Trump laughed, "*I* call global warming a hoax invented by the Chinese!"

"Yes, we know," the voice said. "It is important that you continue calling it a hoax, and that you continue rolling back environmental protections and blocking any and all efforts to stop global warming."

"Of course, I will continue my work," Donald said. "I like rolling back everything Obama did, including his environmental protections. But I would like you to do me a favor, though. To continue my anti-environmental work, I'll need to be re-elected, and to get re-elected, I need dirt on my opponents. I'll tell you the same thing I told the Russians in July 2016. Aliens, if you're listening, I hope you're able to find incriminating emails about my opponent, Joe Biden, and give them to me. You'll be rewarded mightily."

General Raymond flipped the mute switch again and said, "Sir, that is highly inappropriate! Asking for help from foreign nations like Russia and Ukraine was bad enough, but asking for campaign help from *aliens*, creatures who aren't even human—"

Donald snapped, "General, do I have to remind you what happened to Lieutenant Colonel Vindman after he testified against me in the impeachment hearings?"

The general grimaced. "You fired him, sir."

"I didn't just fire *him*; I fired his twin *brother*, too. I told the nation that I fired those two for 'doing a lot of bad things,' but I really fired him and his twin brother for disloyalty, for making me look bad.

"Now that I've been *totally exonerated* by the Senate impeachment trial, I can do anything I want. Not only can I fire you, but I can also have you thrown in prison. I can even have you killed. I can have your whole *family* killed, your wife and kids, your grandchildren, anybody I want, just like my friend Putin does to his enemies! As I've said many times, 'I could shoot someone on Fifth Avenue and not lose any support.'"

Donald opened a drawer in the Resolute Desk and pulled out his .45 pistol, a gold-plated 1911. "I could shoot you right now, then go and kill your entire family, and I *still* wouldn't be impeached by the Senate, because Mitch McConnell has my back. Not only Mitch, but Putin too. My friend Putin has agents who can assassinate anyone he wants, anywhere in the world! Get the picture, Picard?"

The general's face darkened. Nevertheless, he said, "Yes, sir."

"Then unmute that damn microphone and put me back on the radio with the aliens right now!"

The general flipped the switch on again.

Donald said, "I'm sorry, but we were briefly disconnected.

Did you hear my request? Aliens, if you're listening, I would like you to do me a favor, though. I need dirt on my political opponent, Joe Biden."

"Yes, we heard, and we understand. Contact us again in thirty days, and we will have the information that you desire."

"Good, glad to hear it," Donald said gleefully. "I'll talk to you again in thirty days." He turned to the general and said, "How do I hang up the radio?"

The general flipped the switches on the black metal box.

Donald said, "If the aliens want to contact me again before I call them, how will I know they're trying to reach me?"

"A buzzer will sound," the general said, "and then you simply turn these switches on."

"Picard, before you return to the Pentagon, NASA, or *wherever* it is that you work, I want you to show my Chief of Staff, my secretary, my lawyer Rudy Giuliani, *and* me exactly how to use that radio to talk to the aliens."

Donald summoned his secretary, his chief of staff, and Rudy Giuliani, his personal lawyer. Grudgingly, but dutifully, General Raymond showed the four of them how to work the radio to communicate with the aliens. After they'd all been trained, Donald dismissed the general with a smile, thinking, *Now I no longer need him, so it's time for him to have a little accident before he can become a whistleblower like Lieutenant Colonel Vindman. Before he can tell anyone what I discussed with the aliens.* He buzzed his secretary again and said, "Get me General Raymond's schedule for the next couple weeks."

. . .

Two weeks later, General Raymond and his family were traveling to Europe on vacation. Their private jet suffered sudden, catastrophic engine failure and cabin decompression over the Atlantic and crashed into the ocean. A Russian Navy spy ship, disguised as a fishing trawler, searched the crash site to ensure that there were no survivors.

. . .

August 24, 2020: Thirty days after his first conversation with the aliens, Donald called them again on the radio. "Aliens, if you're listening, it's the president of the United States, Donald J. Trump, the most important man on Earth calling. A month ago, you asked me to call you again in thirty days."

The alien voice came from the speaker, "Yes, Donald, we remember. Do you promise to continue blocking all attempts to fight global warming?"

"Yes," Donald said. "I will. I need you to do me a favor, though. I need the information that you promised me on my political opponent, Joe Biden, so I can get re-elected in November."

. . .

November 3, 2020: Thanks to the dirt that the aliens gave him on Joe Biden and his son Hunter, Donald won re-election with only 48 percent of the popular vote, but a majority of the Electoral College vote, which was all that mattered. Donald called his victory a "landslide," just as he'd called it a "landslide" in 2016 when he'd won with only 46.1 percent of the popular vote.

. . .

In his second term, Donald kept his word to his alien benefactors by continuing to roll back environmental regulations. *He would have done it anyway, because he hated environmentalists almost as much as he loved the coal, oil, and gas industries which had donated millions to his political campaign. Thank the Supreme Court for their* Citizens United *ruling, which made it legal for corporations to give unlimited amounts of money to political campaigns!*

In 2023, when the aliens informed Donald that they wanted to also help his son, Donald Trump Junior, become the forty-sixth president of the United States, Donald readily agreed. He showed his son how to work the radio to communicate with the aliens and warned him not to let *anyone*, other than the Trump family and their lawyers, know the contents of their conversations.

Throughout Donald's second term, hurricane season got worse each year. As long as hurricanes didn't hit any property Donald owned, he didn't care. When a major hurricane hit Puerto Rico in 2023, he actually celebrated, rejoicing at the deaths of hundreds of brown-skinned, Spanish-speaking people who had the audacity to call themselves "Americans" even though they stubbornly refused to speak English.

Donald's response to Puerto Rico's pleas for help in 2023 was the same one he'd given after Hurricane Maria struck Puerto Rico in 2017: "Puerto Rico is an island. An island surrounded by water. Big water. Ocean water," he said, as if ships and planes hadn't been invented yet. He didn't care how many Puerto Ricans died; in fact, the more the better. *They* hadn't voted for him. When his advisors insisted he visit the island, he repeated his 2017 performance there. That is, he did another TV photo-op throwing paper towels at hurricane victims, pretending he was shooting hoops on a basketball court. *Paper towels were all the Puerto Ricans deserved*, he figured, *so it's all they would get*.

Donald's final year in office, 2024, had the worst hurricane season in modern history. This time, the hurricanes *did* bother him, because they hit places that he actually *cared* about. In July of 2024, Hurricane Irene struck Mar-a-Lago in Florida, as a Category 5. It utterly destroyed Donald's golf resort there, the place he'd dubbed "The Winter White House" because he'd spent hundreds of days golfing there while he was supposed to be running the country.

Just because Donald continued to claim global warming was "a hoax invented by the Chinese," reporters from the fake news media gleefully mispronounced Hurricane Irene as "Hurricane Irony." They thought global warming was responsible for the hurricane that had wiped out his own Mar-a-Lago golf resort, but Donald knew global warming was another Democrat hoax.

Hurricane Irene—or "Irony"—wasn't the last major hurricane to strike the United States in 2024.

Donald didn't believe in karma. He considered karma a religious concept, and he didn't believe in religion, but in 2024, Donald found out that Karma was also a first name when the National Hurricane Center called the eleventh named storm of the year Hurricane Karma.

While crossing the Atlantic from Africa—*yet another export from the shithole continent Donald hated*—Karma became a hurricane, grew in strength to Category 5, and hurtled toward the US East Coast near Maryland. Hurricane Karma was the first Category 5 hurricane ever to score a direct hit on Washington, D.C.

Karma destroyed the White House, demolished the Capitol Building, and flattened the Smithsonian Institution museums. *Karma* flooded the Washington National Zoo, blew down its walls and fences, and sent dangerous animals including polar bears, alligators, hippos, and crocodiles rampaging through the flooded streets.

Donald was evacuated to Camp David before Hurricane Karma hit, so he didn't see any of the damage personally until after the storm was over. When he flew over the ruins of Washington, D.C. in Marine One to survey the damage, he was awestruck at the devastation caused by Hurricane Karma. For a brief moment, he wondered whether there really was such a thing as karma, the religious concept. Could he possibly have done something to deserve the destruction of the White House? Was he wrong to have agreed with space aliens to roll back environmental regulations and block all attempts to stop global warming? *No, my radio conversations with the aliens were perfect, just like my July 2019 phone call with the president of Ukraine was perfect!*

He wondered why the aliens had wanted him to block any efforts to confront global warming, though. Why did *they* care how humans treated our planet? It was *our* planet, after all, so we could do whatever we wanted with it. Mankind had chosen, on its own, to burn fossil fuels, regardless of the consequences. If aliens wanted to aid the Trump family just for doing what they'd been planning to do *anyway*, why should he turn down their aid?

In November 2024, the Electoral College made Donald Trump Junior the forty-sixth president of the United States, with help from the aliens who gave him dirt on his opponents, just as they'd done for his father. Because *Karma* had destroyed the White House, Don Junior had it rebuilt as "Trump Tower Washington," with the ground floors for the president and vice president, and the upper floors to rent out for profit to billionaires and visiting foreign dignitaries. All profits from renting out the upper floors of the White House—now Trump Tower Washington—would go to the Trump family.

In 2028, alien computer hackers helped Don Junior win re-election. By his second term, Earth's temperature had increased so much that it became hard to deny that global warming was happening. The aliens instructed Don Junior to switch to a different story: telling Americans that global warming, although real, was caused by *natural and temporary* fluctuations in the sun's energy output, not by any pollutants from industrial civilization.

Don Junior, building on the tactics of his father, made sure that any scientists or reporters who dared to go against the Republican Party's new line on global warming were either fired, imprisoned, or died under suspicious circumstances. Scientists and the news media quickly fell in line. American democracy had been replaced by Trumpocracy.

In 2030, aliens helped Don Junior abolish term limits so he could run for a third term in 2032, and then a fourth term in 2036, rigging each election so there was no chance he would lose.

During the sixteen years of Don Junior's reign, from 2025 to 2040, Earth's warming trend accelerated. Glaciers in Greenland and Antarctica were rapidly melting, and the Earth grew uncomfortably hot, with snowless winters in North America, and frequent heat waves over 110 degrees in forty-nine of the fifty states—all except Alaska, whose heat waves only hit one hundred.

Looking back, when historians performed an autopsy on the corpse of American democracy, they placed the date of its demise as January 31, 2020. That was the day that the US Senate, under the iron fist of "Moscow Mitch" McConnell, voted against allowing *any* witnesses or evidence in the impeachment "trial" of Donald J. Trump, turning the proceedings into a cover-up, not a real trial.

. . .

In Don Junior's sixteenth and final year in office, 2040, he finally discovered why the aliens had helped the Trump family control the White House for twenty-four years. On December 25, 2040, with the temperature 115 degrees in Washington D.C. on Christmas Day, a flying saucer the size of three tennis courts approached Trump Tower Washington. It landed on the Astroturf front lawn, near what had once been the White House Rose Garden before roses had succumbed to the extreme heat.

A bevy of Secret Service agents cautiously approached the saucer. None of them drew their weapons, not only because they didn't want to create an interstellar incident, but also because the president had told them that the aliens were on his side, and therefore, *America's*.

One hour passed, then two, without any movement from the saucer, and the media's initial excitement turned to impatience. Network news crews had been denied approach to the site of the alien landing, and they grew tired of showing the same scene from the same angle, *outside* the Trump Tower Washington fence. Every news organization with a presence at Trump Tower Washington demanded to know why their correspondents weren't being allowed to approach the saucer to film it from close up.

After three hours, the Secret Service grudgingly allowed one reporter from each major news organization to bring a cameraman with him past the cordon of agents surrounding the saucer. Soon, a gaggle of news reporters surrounded the saucer, none of them sure which side of it was the front.

Finally, the smooth surface of the flying saucer was broken by an opening, and a ramp lowered. An eight-foot tall, green, reptilian alien waddled down the ramp, its long tail swaying behind it. It was wearing a thick, red coat, possibly a uniform. Addressing the bevy of reporters and Secret Service agents surrounding the saucer, the alien lizard demanded, "Take me to your leader."

The reporter lucky enough to be facing the front of the flying saucer shoved his microphone toward the alien and said, "Mister Alien, isn't that kind of *cliché?* I mean, you probably came halfway across the galaxy to visit Earth, and the best line you could come up with upon landing is, 'Take me to your leader,' like a low-budget sci-fi movie?"

The alien growled and said, "Are you Donald Trump Junior, the leader of this planet?"

"No, but I work for *Fox News*," the reporter said proudly, "the organization responsible for putting the Trump family in office and keeping them in office for the past twenty-four years."

The alien said, "My species and I are the ones responsible for keeping the Trump family in office for the past twenty-four years. Take me to your leader, Donald Trump Junior, *now*."

Secret Service agents escorted their alien guest to the front door of Trump Tower Washington, then opened the door for the visitor to enter. A gust of refrigerated air escaped from the doorway, and the alien jumped back as if in pain. "Close that door!" the alien lizard demanded. "Were you trying to *kill* me with that icy blast of wind?"

"Sorry," the lead Secret Service agent said.

"Tell your President Trump to come and meet me here, outside," the alien said, backing farther away from the door.

One of the Secret Service agents went inside, closing the door quickly behind him. A few minutes later, President Donald Trump Junior came out. He took off his suitcoat and tie on the way out of the door and handed them to the nearest Secret Service agent, but he was already sweating in the 115-degree heat. Don Junior said, "They told me a gust of cool air from inside bothered you. I apologize for that, but the interior of the building is air-conditioned for my comfort."

"Cold air may be comfortable to you *humans*," the alien lizard hissed, "but it is painful for my species. Sorry for my three-hour delay in exiting my ship, but as an advance scout, it was my job to take atmospheric samples and readings to make sure you had terraformed Earth sufficiently for our comfort."

Don Junior's jaw dropped. "You had us terraform *our* planet for you?"

"Of course," the alien said. "We kept your family in power for the past twenty-four years because any other president would have tried to stop global warming, to save the human species. You and your father, however, were corrupt enough to collude with *anyone* if it would help you personally—Russians, Ukrainians, even aliens. You and your father were also sufficiently stupid and easy to manipulate through flattery into terraforming Earth for our species."

The alien turned and looked up to the sky, which was now filled with hundreds—no, thousands—of flying saucers, all descending to the steaming surface of streets, parking lots, and Astroturf parks of Washington, D.C. "I see our fleet is arriving. As I said, I was their advance scout, making sure you had terraformed Earth sufficiently for us before our invasion fleet arrived."

Dozens of flying saucers landed on the National Mall in Washington. They lowered their ramps, and hundreds of lizard soldiers poured out, each wearing an identical red coat. Some Secret Service uniformed guards and US Marines moved forward to challenge the invaders, but the alien soldiers fired silent death-rays that vaporized them instantly.

The alien scout said, "Now, President Donald Trump Junior, your term of office is over, and your family's long reign of power has ended. It is not just the end of your family's rule, either. The time of humans being the dominant species on this planet has ended.

"Thank you, Donald Trump Junior, and your father, for terraforming Earth for us, your new alien overlords. You saved us many years of effort! Now, the human species will be our slaves. If any humans resist our rule, we will simply turn off their electricity, depriving them of the precious air conditioning that keeps your species from dying in this heat."

Don Junior's shoulders slumped. "Can I get out of this heat now and go back inside?"

"Sure," the alien scout said. "Go inside and rest comfortably, Donald Trump Junior. You've earned yourself a rest by your loyal and dedicated service to our species! We will make sure *everyone* on Earth knows what you and your family have done for us. You and your father will forever be known, to all humanity, as the humans who betrayed their species to alien invaders."

Don Junior walked inside to the Oval Office, which had been reconstructed on the first floor in Trump Tower Washington after *Karma* had destroyed the White House. He opened the drawer of the Resolute Desk, where he kept the gold-plated 1911 pistol he'd inherited from his father.

Moments later, a single gunshot rang out.

. . .

About the Author:

David Harten Watson, editor of this cli-fi anthology, authored the young-adult fantasy series *Magicians Gold*, including the award-winning novel *Magic Teacher's Son* and its sequel *Fortress of Gold*. David has worked in a dizzying array of jobs including US Army Armor officer at Fort Knox, experience that came in handy for his second novel, *Fortress of Gold*. Raised in snowy Buffalo, New York, he has degrees from Princeton, Canisius College, and Buffalo State College. He's the Organizer of the Woodbridge Science Fiction & Fantasy Writers Meetup, which he founded in 2008. He lives in New Jersey. Author's website: www.davidhartenwatson.com

Part Four:

The Mid-Twenty-First Century (2041 to 2060 AD)

19

Birthing in Place

by Kimberly Christensen (United States)

WARNING: This story may not be suitable for younger readers due to language.

Subgenres: Realistic science fiction, pandemic fiction

Time Period: Circa 2045 AD

Setting: Seattle, Washington, United States of America

Synopsis: As Seattle, Washington, braces for a viral pandemic, midwife Sonja works with her obstetrician colleague to plan for the safe care of mothers and babies during the viral outbreak. When her client develops a pregnancy complication that may land her in the hospital, it becomes obvious that the hospital's Pandemic Protocol hasn't been properly implemented. Sonja struggles to ensure the well-being of her clients in a situation where safety is anything but guaranteed.

. . .

"Can we listen to the baby's heartbeat?" my client Mari asks as she settles onto the couch in my midwifery office.

"Stressful week?" I ask.

She nods and sighs deeply, gesturing at the surgical mask she's wearing with a sense of resignation that says more than words. Then she stretches out on the couch that serves as my improvisational exam table. At thirty-nine weeks pregnant, Mari knows the drill.

Mari's bangs lie damp across her forehead, and her face looks puffy, though it's hard to tell around the edges of the mask. I make a futile wish that the electricity will come back on, but without rain to fuel Seattle's hydropower, the rolling brownouts will go on all summer. It's only June—I can't justify running the generator for the sake of a little air conditioning, even though wearing masks makes the sticky heat worse. Still, sweating beneath a face mask is better than passing a virus to a pregnant woman. So far, this novel virus has only reached Northern Europe, but we can't be too careful, so we're following the Stage One Pandemic Protocols carefully.

"Your baby looks like he is growing well." I always start with something to reassure the mother, even when I see things that worry me. Like a puffy face. Fluid retention can be an indicator of pregnancy-induced hypertension—a serious pregnancy complication. It also could be the heat.

I press on Mari's belly to feel the baby's position. "Baby's head down and well engaged in your pelvis. His back is on your left. You have just the right amount of fluid, from the feel of it. Is he moving lots?"

"Yeah, especially at night." Mari shifts. I'm sure she's uncomfortable on her back. I tuck a throw pillow behind her head and shoulders, so she doesn't get lightheaded. It's hard enough to breathe when you're nine months pregnant without a mask separating you from fresh air. My own mask makes me panicky sometimes, even though I'm practiced at wearing it.

"You're growing a strong, healthy baby. Let's listen to his heart." I squirt room-temperature gel on Mari's belly and press the doppler stethoscope against it. It projects the steady sound of the baby's heartbeat into the room.

Mari closes her eyes and takes a deep breath. "Soon," she whispers. She looks over the swell of her belly at me. "Sonja, do you ever wonder if we're foolish for bringing a new life into the world right now?"

"Every day for the past fifteen years—since Anya was born." Anya herself chides me for bringing her into a world of rising seas and rationed electricity.

"Do you ever wish you'd made a different choice?" Mari's voice quavers.

"At least twice a day," I say with a smile, hoping that she can hear my humor through her worries. "Mostly because teenagers are impossible. But I know what you mean—there's a lot to worry about right now." Potential pandemics are troubling enough without this drought in the background. "Tell me more about what's bothering you, Mari."

"So many things." She raises her hands in a gesture that speaks of being overwhelmed. "Pandemic, drought, yes. But also something bigger... more existential. I can't stop thinking about how different his childhood might be from mine. Food shortages, unstable weather, beaches closed because of red tides. Everything I read is bad news." She sniffles. "I wanted a baby so badly, but now I think I was just being selfish."

The word hangs in the air like an accusation, and I wonder if someone has said this to her, or if she's wielding it at herself. Either way, the choice has been made.

"Maybe you were being hopeful," I say gently.

Mari rests her hand on her belly and rubs it. The baby stretches in response, the lump of his foot pushing against Mari's palm. Tears stream from the corners of Mari's eyes. I let her cry for a minute, offering a silent prayer for her and the new life that she grows within her. Then I offer her my hand and a tissue. She accepts both, and I help pull her back into a sitting position.

"I've seen mothers and babies find their way through all kinds of catastrophes. You will too." I offer her my best reassuring-yet-sympathetic smile, the one that every midwife learns to perfect. Of course, she can't see it through my mask, but I hope she can feel it.

She sighs. "Yes, I suppose we will. Life finds a way, doesn't it?"

That phrase—from the old *Jurassic Park* movies that have an almost cultish devotion these days—is a favorite of Anya's too. But it's true, at its core. Life does seem to find a way, even when the odds are oppressively bad. Mothers and babies are resilient. That resilience is one of the joys of being a midwife.

"Life does find a way, Mari. And you and your baby will find yours. I know it."

. . .

After Mari leaves, I put to rest my unease about her puffiness by double-checking her urine sample for protein. The results are normal, again, but I can't loosen the small knot of worry that's formed in my gut. I pay attention to this feeling. Intuition is a central part of midwifery care. After hundreds of births, you start to pick up on warning signs well before lab results confirm your hunch. Sometimes nothing comes of it except that you spend a little bit of extra time checking on a mother-to-be. Sometimes, you employ a few midwifery tricks that you hope will help her go into labor before things get worse.

Between Mari's fluid retention and the Stage One Pandemic Alert, there's a lot that could get worse.

My pager vibrates in my pocket, startling me so much that I nearly drop the urine sample. Pagers—those nearly obsolete relics—have made a comeback in these times of unreliable electricity, along with their counterpart—the landline. I glance at the number, and the knot of tension in my stomach tightens. It's Eleanor, my obstetrician-consultant. She never calls first.

"Good afternoon, Sonja." Her voice is even. Professional.

"I wanted to alert you to a statement that's going to be issued by the Department of Health in the morning. Our clients are going to be in a panic, so I thought I would give you a head start on making plans."

Department of Health? This can't be good. "They're upgrading the virus threat, aren't they?"

There's a brief silence from Eleanor. *Shit.* "Worse. Contact tracing indicates that the virus is probably already loose in the metro-Seattle area, brought here by one of those cruise ships that goes up to the Arctic Circle. Why they haven't shut those things down yet is beyond me."

My mind races ahead of Eleanor's words. A disease brought back from the Arctic Circle could be a novel virus released by thawing permafrost. A novel virus that's been contact-traced to Seattle will lead to a state-of-emergency declaration by the governor, and with it, progressively restrictive shutdowns, school cancellations...and babies being born in the middle of all of it.

Eleanor's next words add a chill to the already bad news. "Sonja, in Norway the early data is showing a respiratory virus with a 25 percent mortality rate in symptomatic persons. But the virus also appears to be transmitted from mother to fetus. Three pregnant women on a Swedish cruise ship had late miscarriages or preterm births. If this truly has jumped to the general population... well, I wanted to suggest that you contact all your clients to advise strict self-quarantine measures—even if the governor doesn't mandate them yet. And NO babymoon vacations."

"Absolutely. I'll get right on it." After I call my midwifery partners so we can triple check that our office's pandemic kits are up-to-date, order extra face shields, prepare home-monitoring kits, drop them off at clients' houses...

"Stay healthy, Sonja. I'll be in touch if I hear any news before it's released to the public."

Eleanor's connected to decision-makers. But there's a

glaring hole in what she's told me. "Eleanor, shouldn't we talk about the *Joint Pandemic Response Playbook for Respiratory Viruses...*"

She cuts me off. "We're not there yet. After all, there haven't been any documented cases in Seattle—just contact tracing. Besides, I don't think transferring our patients to the home setting is a good idea. You wouldn't want a newborn with potential respiratory issues being born at home, would you?"

This again. Eleanor and her hospital-based obstetric colleagues agreed on paper to the Joint Pandemic Task Force recommendations: In event of a highly contagious disease, women with normal pregnancies would be transferred out of the hospital setting to reduce the chance of otherwise healthy mothers and newborns being exposed to contagion. I've always suspected there was no buy-in. Obstetricians are used to accepting *our* midwifery clients into care if they develop an obstetric complication, but few would sign over care of *their* patients to *midwives* if it weren't mandated.

"Of course not, but neither would I want healthy moms and babies sent into a hospital that's potentially a hotbed of germs." I keep my tone even, fighting my desire to shout.

"Oh Sonja, you and your fellow midwives need to have some faith in our protocols. We won't be admitting healthy laboring mothers through the ER with the sick patients." Eleanor laughs like my fears are unfounded, but we both know stuff like this happened in the past. That's why we have a task force—to prevent such obvious stupidity the next time. I resist pointing that out though. I need her as my consultant, and overall, she's supportive of midwifery care—for an OB.

I finish the call with a pit in my stomach and fire in my chest. I should be focusing on my clients—and my daughter—and here I am having to play politics about an issue that we have a whole playbook for. Ugh. I pull out my copy of the *Pandemic Playbook* and start reviewing it. This midwifery office, at least, is going to do things by the book.

. . .

I open the front door of my house to an explosion of craft supplies. At their epicenter is my daughter, Anya, wielding a hot glue gun like a girl who means business.

"Hi, hon. Looks like you've had a busy afternoon of not studying."

"You don't know the half. I've got twenty special orders that I have to fill—STAT." She inserts a fresh glue stick into her gun.

"Masks?" The hodgepodge of sequins, paint, feathers, and other materials covering the surface of the living room could mean anything, but I hedge my bets, knowing Anya. She's got an entrepreneurial spirit and a hand-me-down sewing machine.

Anya holds up a piece of black cloth with sparkly elastic loops on each side and silver cording trimming its perimeter. In the center, she has hand-painted some kind of spacecraft. "Nicer than the Chinese tourist look, am I right?"

"Anya!"

She rolls her eyes at me. "What? It's true."

"Just because in China they care about the welfare of their neighbor..." I thought we'd gotten past this stereotype. I'd felt so proud when Anya had put on a mask without any arguing after the governor announced the Stage One Protocol last week. I should have figured there would be backlash.

"Yeah, yeah. Anyway, since 'surgical mask' doesn't go with my aesthetic, I made one that does, which I wore to school today." She shakes her long hair—black on the top layer and dyed like a rainbow waterfall beneath it—to prove her point about aesthetics. "Other kids liked it, so now I have more work than I can manage."

"That's awesome, but remember that homemade masks are only somewhat helpful in slowing down a respiratory virus." The last thing anyone needs is a group of teens thinking they're even more invincible with masks on.

"I know, I know. Stay home when you're sick, wash your hands, blah, blah." Anya puts down her glue gun so she can use her hand to talk to me, an accurate representation of a nagging mother.

"You sound like a midwife's daughter."

"Maybe just a little."

. . .

I make a point of eating dinner with Anya—my Sisyphean need to maintain normalcy is kicking in already. We chat over the hum of the sewing machine until it's time for the virtual sync-up meeting with my midwifery partners Fran and Rojani. Fran launches in the minute our connection light goes green.

"Girls, I am tired just thinking about what's ahead of us. Thank God we have an action plan. I wouldn't know where to start otherwise." Fran is our "airy fairy" midwife—amazing with clients and clinically competent, but not paperwork-oriented. Her chart notes—often vague and incomplete—give our office staff fits. "Can I take first call while you two sort out the clinic stuff?"

First call means Fran will attend the births and do the bulk of the postpartum visits, leaving me and Rojani to tackle the clinic and our pandemic response.

"Works for me," Rojani says. She's probably already knee-deep in research. "I'll start calling clients first thing tomorrow."

That leaves me to deliver home-monitoring kits with blood pressure cuffs, urine test strips, and fetal heartbeat monitors to all our third trimester clients. I'd like to see everyone in person anyway—even if it is from six feet away. "Ro, I'd like to tell Mari. She was pretty stressed already at her appointment this afternoon."

"Sure thing, Sonja. You two let me know if there's anyone else you'd like to contact personally. Otherwise, I'll brief the office staff to start moving all the appointments to telehealth, and I'll field the million questions we all know are coming." I'm so relieved Rojani volunteered for that job—she's just the right mix of reassuring and able to translate complicated issues into layperson's terms.

"Speaking of Mari, her blood pressure was slightly elevated today, and she looked a little puffy." I don't finish my thought, wondering what conclusions they will come to on their own.

"Oh geez. Do you think she's pre-eclamptic? This would be a bad time to send someone to the hospital." Rojani sighs loudly enough for the mic to pick it up.

"There was no protein in her urine, and she had plenty of fluid around the baby, so I want to say no, but..."

"What about castor oil?" Fran asks. It's an age-old trick for bringing on contractions, but not one we usually use before the due date.

Silence stretches as we each contemplate Fran's suggestion. "Why don't you assess her again when you drop off the monitoring kit tomorrow?" suggests Rojani. "Maybe it was just stress."

"Either way, I'd better get some sleep," Fran yawns. "You know that as soon as Mari goes into labor, three other moms will go into labor."

We all laugh our goodnights. Midwifery is exactly like that. Predictably unpredictable.

. . .

I sleep in small fits between anxiety dreams. First thing in the morning, I scan the latest bulletins from the DOH and the CDC. The message that Eleanor warned me about yesterday has been officially delivered.

However, there's no school closure yet. I breathe a sigh of relief that Anya can have another day—maybe even a week—with her friends while we wait for a confirmed case to materialize in Seattle. For now, vulnerable populations are advised to stay home, and everyone else should continue wearing masks and washing their hands.

It doesn't feel like enough.

Anya's halfway out the door by the time I emerge from my room, but she stops for a hug—a rare gift from a busy fifteen-year-old. She always seems to know when I need it. She probably also wants me to admire her handiwork. The mask she made for herself gives her a larger-than-life pouty smile with a little glittery star tattoo on the cheek.

"Wow, honey. Way to make a necessary evil into *haute couture*. Promise me you'll actually wear it all day? We just got a new advisory from the Department of Health. They've contact-traced the disease to Seattle."

"Of course, Mom. Maybe I should skip school?" Her voice is full of hope, and I'm tempted to let her. But my intuition says she's going to be stuck at home a lot over the next months—while I work long hours—and she's going to be desperately lonely, so I should encourage her to soak up all the time with friends she can get. My intuition also says that I'm an idiot for sending her into the petri dish environment of high school. I reassure myself by deciding that high school kids and teachers are unlikely to have gone on an Arctic cruise in the middle of the school year.

"Let's talk about it tonight. We're going to need to make some plans—and some backup plans." During my sleepless bouts last night, I decided on my sister as a backup plan. She has a nice, safe desk job and two amazing dogs that would keep Anya from getting too lonely—or from being exposed to the germs I could bring home from work. I blink back tears, missing Anya already.

She doesn't notice. She's off, a spring in her step despite the mask on her face, like she's headed to a cosplay convention instead of to school at the start of a pandemic. If only I could make it so.

. . .

When I arrive at Mari's house, I set a telehealth kit on her doorstep, knock, and step back a safe distance. She's pulling on her mask as she opens the door. Today she has on shorts, so I can see how swollen her ankles are. Her face still looks puffy around her mask.

My pulse elevates, but I don't want to alarm her. "Do you think you could test the kit for me, to make sure you know how to use everything? You'll need a chair for testing your blood pressure."

Mari drags a stool to the front door. "Do I just put it on my arm and press the button?"

"Left arm, and if you're wearing a shirt with sleeves, push them up." I mimic the action on my own arm.

Mari slides her hand through the cuff, which she pushes onto her upper arm. "Like this?"

"Yes, perfect. Be as still as you can while it squeezes your arm." We listen to the sound of the cuff as a motor inflates it. "I'm so glad you're having a home birth, Mari. You and Qinqin can just cuddle up at home with your babe and enjoy a quiet beginning as a family. It will be almost like there's no quarantine, just a new baby." The monitor beeps, and the cuff begins to release. It's too far away for me to see. "What's it say?"

"One-forty over eighty-eight. Is that normal?" Mari slides the cuff off, resting it on her lap. Her pupils are large like a frightened rabbit's. I wish I could hug her tight and help her feel in her bones that she is going to be fine, but I can't. I have to stay at least six feet away.

"It's higher than your usual, but it could be a lot of things: the cuff, the heat, the stress. Take it again this afternoon when you're feeling calm and test your urine with one of the strips in the kit. Then page us. Fran's on call this week—she'll get back to you." And to me. We try not to have pet clients, but I have a special fondness for Mari and her wife, Qinqin. If something's up, I want to know about it. In some ways, it's comforting to worry about the more typical pregnancy complications like elevated blood pressure. It takes my mind off this pandemic.

"Mari, I'm also going to call my consulting obstetrician, just so that you are on her radar in case we need her help. Rising blood pressure sometimes means a transfer to the hospital."

Mari's face pales. "Is it that serious?"

"Sometimes, yes. Drink lots of water. Spend as much time as you can reclining with your feet up and then recheck yourself. You're really close to giving birth, and probably everything is going to work out fine for a homebirth. But I don't want to take chances." I work hard to project a confidence that I don't feel.

"Going to the hospital feels risky. I don't want to give birth there." Mari rubs her arms like she's got a chill, despite the heat.

"I know you don't. Tell your babe it's time to come out. Maybe you can get labor started." If it were that easy, every mother I know would have her baby before the due date. But getting Mari to think labor thoughts can't hurt.

Mari rubs her belly. I get the distinct feeling that she doesn't think it's time for him to come out—or safe for him to come out. I can't blame her. But if she develops pregnancy-induced hypertension, it's not going to be safe for him to stay inside, either.

. . .

"I'd like to bring her in for a fetal stress test," Eleanor says.

It's not a bad idea to check on a baby's ability to tolerate labor, but misgivings crowd my brain. "At your office?" I ask. "Or the maternity ward?"

"Office. And I'll need the code to access her medical chart." Someone talks to Eleanor in the background. "Anderson says they admitted a feverish mother with a stillborn to delivery this morning."

They admitted her to *delivery*? Where other healthy mothers are? "Tell me they isolated her, Eleanor."

"We always sequester the mothers with stillborns, for their own privacy. But no, she was on the main ward." Again, she talks to someone in the room with her, presumably Anderson.

"Eleanor, you're the one who called me about the DOH advisory. Why hasn't that ward been locked down?" My voice is shrill with frustration. *Dial it down, Sonja.*

"We don't make those decisions until there's a confirmed positive case, Sonja. You know that." Her smugness carries through the phone line, loud and clear. *Doctors.*

"What I know is that it could be weeks before we have a reliable test for a novel virus. How many mothers and babies will die before you act out of precaution?" I shouldn't have said that, but the words are out there now.

Eleanor clears her throat. "We are following the *Pandemic Handbook*, Sonja. Until the data tells us to act differently, we are not changing our protocols. The directive from the DOH says that vulnerable people should self-quarantine. The mother who was admitted today will be quarantined in her room. All of our delivery rooms are very private, with bathrooms and showers, you know. Just like home."

Not "just like home" when you look at how many foreign germs you're likely to encounter, but I stop myself from continuing to argue. We need to be on the same team right now. There are mothers and babies who are counting on us. Like Mari, who I am *not* sending to the hospital for her birth. "I know we both want what's best for our patients, Eleanor."

"Absolutely. Have your client call my office to schedule the stress test." She hangs up before I have the chance to ask whether the feverish mother had visited her office recently, and what measures they are taking to ensure that the office is safe for clients. But I already know that I'm not sending Mari to that office. Handbooks be damned.

I page Fran to call me back as soon as she can. There's an at-home fetal stress test followed by a castor oil milkshake in Mari's future, as long as she and Qinqin are willing. And I suspect all our intuitions will be in sync about not having this baby at the hospital.

. . .

"Yo, Mom. Why are you wearing a mask at home?"

"Just trying to get in the habit." Anya tips her head and crosses her arms, waiting for more of an explanation. I lift my copy of the *Pandemic Playbook*, hoping that will suffice.

"You going to be like this for the foreseeable future? Are we going to social distance in our house?" She crooks one eyebrow at me in disbelief. Sarcastic-teenager face is not a good look on her.

I shrug. "I honestly don't know, hon. During COVID-19, healthcare workers slept in tents in their garages to avoid exposing their families." Her lower lip juts out, just a tiny bit, a change that only a mother would notice. "But there haven't been any confirmed cases in Seattle yet, so hopefully we will avoid the worst of it." How many times have I said that today?

Anya nods as she scrolls through things on her phone. Stress behavior.

"What are you looking at, hon. Anything good?"

She shrugs without looking at me. "Mom, do you think the Four Horsemen of the Apocalypse are actually a thing?"

"No, I think they're a metaphor. Why?"

She holds up a grainy image of Pike Place Market on her phone. "Oh, people are sharing this video of a white ghost-knight-dude riding a horse through the middle of Seattle. It's really convincing."

I reach for her hand, make her look me in the eye. "People are scared, honey. It's easier to believe in a CGI horseman than to think about another pandemic. Especially since it looks like this virus is like something out of a bad science fiction film." I put on my bad "movie narrator" voice. "Frozen in tundra for thousands of years, the virus lurked, biding its time until it could show the world which species was *really* at the top of the food chain."

Anya gives me the smile I was hoping for. "Haha, Mom. You missed your calling."

I shake my head and squeeze her hand. "No, I found it. The day I had you."

. . .

After a reassuring message from Fran that the stress test was fine, and Mari and Qinqin agreed to induce labor, I fall into a deep sleep. Predictably, this is interrupted by a 3:00 a.m. page.

"What's wrong?" I ask as soon as Fran answers my return call.

"Nothing big, girlfriend. Take a breath." I do, but my stomach still clenches as I wait for the news. "The good news is that Mari's in labor. Her blood pressure is on the high side, but stable, and baby is doing great. But—I think Mari wants *you* here, not me. She's stalled out in second phase."

Lots of first-time moms stall in the second phase of labor—pushing. Sometimes we have to take them to the hospital for an epidural and some sleep. Sometimes they stay for a C-section. That's not an option today. "I'll be there in a few."

I enter Mari and Qinqin's house as quietly as I can in the crinkly paper of my hazmat suit. It's so uncomfortable—and different from the comfortable clothes that I usually wear. Sweat plasters Mari's hair to her forehead, and her legs tremble with the exertion of giving birth. Thank goodness it's the middle of the night and not so brutally hot. A masked and face-shielded Fran listens to the baby's strong heartbeat as Mari rests between her contractions.

"Hey, mama," I say, speaking louder than I'd like, to compensate for my own personal protective equipment. "You've progressed so quickly! You're so strong."

"I'm so tired."

"I'm sure you are. This is hard work."

She closes her eyes and takes a deep breath. The next contraction must be on the way. She pushes for a few seconds—I can see her belly tense with the effort, but then she arches her back and screams a bit. It sounds more like frustration and fatigue than pain, but whatever the source, it's not helping her baby move down.

"Let's pick up the energy," I suggest once the contraction ends. "How about a little dancing?"

Mari looks at me uncertainly, but her wife, Qinqin, is ready.

"Play Mix Three," she instructs the computer.

In the Mood starts up, and Mari smiles. "Alright, alright. I'll dance with you."

She stretches her hands out to her wife, who hoists her off the bed. The two of them start up an easy sway, and I feel Mari's energy lifting. Fran and I exchange an appreciative glance as we observe the swinging of her hips, opening a pathway for the baby. A couple of minutes into the song, the next contraction arrives in force.

"Heee!" shouts Mari as it catches her off-guard.

"You've got this, Mari," I coach her from across the room, trying to give her and Qinqin a little space to cocoon together. Mari leans her weight into Qinqin, resting her head on Qinqin's chest and spreading her legs in a wide squat. She continues to sway her hips in time to the music, even as she grunts with her pushing efforts. Now we're making progress.

"How did that feel?" I ask as the contraction eases.

"Different. More pressure in my bum."

"That's good. That's your baby moving down."

She stops swaying her hips and looks at me with panic in her eyes.

"Mari? Is the feeling in your bum too intense?"

She shakes her head against Qinqin's chest, moistening her wife's skin with her tears. Her cries turn into a wail as the next contraction arrives. Rather than working with the contraction, she arches her back again and shakes her head "no," ending the contraction with a high-pitched shriek that sounds for certain like pain.

"Mari, look at me." I use what Anya calls "teacher voice," and it gets Mari's attention. She opens her eyes, focusing on me as I talk.

"I'm so scared, Sonja. So scared for him." She rubs her belly as she tucks her head onto Qinqin's chest, her shoulders shaking as she cries.

I've felt like this a thousand times since becoming a mother. I see Anya in my mind's eye. Strong. Smart. Facing an uncertain world headfirst. "Mari, your baby might be just who this world needs to heal it."

"You think so?" Mari's voice is small.

"I would not be surprised if the children of this generation are a tribe of healers."

Mari closes her eyes suddenly and gasps. Then she sinks down into Qinqin's arms and groans with the deep, beautiful full-throated sound that midwives around the world love to hear. This baby is coming.

"It burns," she says, once the contraction lets up.

"Your body is stretching to let your baby out." Progress. Praise the gods.

"I want to kneel."

Qinqin shuffles with her over to the couch. Mari kneels at its edge, grabbing onto the seat as another contraction overtakes her. Fran moves the birth kit to this new location, tucking a Chux pad between Mari's knees.

"That's it, Mari, push into that sensation," I coach. "A few more like that, and the baby's head will be born."

The contraction passes, and Mari is panting hard. Qinqin kneels on the floor next to her, rubbing her back and whispering encouragement. The next contraction comes, and Mari bears down with everything she's got. The whole top of the baby's head comes into view.

Mari barely gets a break before she yells loudly with the next contraction. The widest diameter of the baby's head passes through her vaginal opening. "Fuuuuuuck! Oooooow, fuck, fuck, fuck!"

"Stick with it, Mari," I coach her. "Move that head all the way out."

She grabs onto the couch pillow and pushes hard once more.

"Head's born," Fran calls out, for Mari's benefit and so I can note the time in her chart.

Fran gently slides her fingers along the base of the baby's head, checking to make sure that his umbilical cord isn't wrapped around his neck. The baby shifts his head, reorienting himself for the final push.

"Ooooooooout!" Mari shouts as the next contraction arrives. "Out, out! Fuck!"

The baby's shoulders clear the pubic bone, and out he slides into Fran's waiting hands. He's pink and wailing, just the signs of health that I look for in this first minute of life. Fran has a blanket at the ready and rubs him dry.

Qinqin helps Mari turn over without getting tangled in the umbilical cord that still connects her to her babe. Mari shifts into a reclining position against the base of the couch and opens her arms to the pink and mewling newborn. She and Qinqin look at each other and begin to cry.

"Welcome to the world, little one," says Qinqin, stroking her child's cheek.

It doesn't matter how many times I witness this moment; I cry. I cry remembering the birth of my own daughter, and the hope and awe that filled me as she was placed in my arms. I cry remembering the surge of protective love that filled my heart as I learned to care for her. I cry remembering all the sleepless nights, wondering if I was doing this right or if I was ruining the baby. I cry because I had no idea who she would become—or who she would cause me to become.

"Do you have a name for him?" Fran asks, as she presses a stethoscope to his back.

"Malcolm," Mari and Qinqin say together, as they look at this new little person.

"Like Jurassic Park?" I ask.

They nod, laughing and crying mixed together.

My pager vibrates. It's Eleanor. I text her a picture of Malcolm and his mothers and let her know that Mari won't need that stress test, after all. She messages me to call her back when I can—the hospital has a presumed positive case.

Today is going to be a long day, filled with tense negotiations as we roll out the Joint Pandemic Response Plan. My practice's client load is going to increase, quickly, and we'll be besieged with questions, not just about the novel virus, but the safety of homebirth. A mantle of fatigue settles on my shoulders.

Then Mari cheers softly as baby Malcolm latches on to her breast in an instinctive movement that has propelled generations of the human race forward. Just like this new baby, I know we'll figure it out.

After all, life finds a way.

. . .

About the author: Kimberly Christensen has worked as both a midwife and a climate activist. Most recently, she was employed by CoolMom, a non-profit organization which sought to engage families in climate activism and to educate families about personal changes they could make to reduce their carbon footprint. She writes short stories and novels. Her website is www.KimberlyChristensenAuthor.com.

20

Of Machines and Monsters

by Thomas P. Tiernan (United States)

Subgenres: Science fiction, horror

Time Period: Mid-twenty-first century

Setting: United States of America

Synopsis: Aliens had been watching Earth from a distance, happy that humans had been doing their terraforming work for them by making the Earth a hotter place, more suitable for the aliens. When it began to look like mankind was finally going to clean up its act and stop overheating the Earth, aliens decided it was time to come down and finish the job of turning the Earth into a high-temperature wasteland...

. . .

In the coolness of the evening, Simon Ross took out the folder he had taken off the dead man. The man had been stepped on, and his top half was flattened into the ground. It reminded Simon of an old cartoon, where the coyote tried to use a big boulder to squash his intended prey. The boulder always rolled back and smashed the coyote. No coyotes could do this much damage, however.

His day had been spent evading the newest creature that emerged from the Machines. The Machines had landed on Earth sixteen months ago, setting down in the exact center of each continent. All communication stopped within one hundred miles of these Machines. Anyone within twenty miles of them was killed by a combination of seismic forces and poison gases that spewed from them.

They, whoever They were, had been monitoring the Earth for centuries. They'd looked for a shortcoming in the progress of the human race. That shortcoming came in the form of our penchant for not cleaning up our own mess. Pollutants of all kinds had been allowed to amass on the ground and in the seas without check. The Industrial Revolution had pushed mankind into the next level of civilization, but the price for the future was dire.

Hundreds of years of unchecked neglect began to take its toll on the Earth. The temperature began to rise due to the unprecedented increase of CO^2 and other greenhouse gasses in the atmosphere. Big Industry and Big Military pushed on, informing us that their efforts were for the good of all. Too late, they realized that the Earth could only cleanse so much putrefaction before she choked on it.

Shortly after the third decade of the twenty-first century, mankind took its collective head out from between its legs and began to take a serious look at the incredible being it had been torturing over the generations, Mother Earth. After its forty-plus centuries as "rulers" of the globe, it found the view unattractive and, periodically, smelling of flatulence and excessive waste from good times.

Fortunately, the Earth had not reached the final tipping point. Mankind got its act together and, in a worldwide effort, began to clean up after itself. They, watching from up above, saw this and decided that it was time for Them to act. They now had their opportunity to push a bad situation beyond the point of the Earth's capacity to repair itself.

Apparently, They needed a much warmer climate than we had enjoyed for the past several centuries. During their observations of us, they had noticed that we had begun to do their work for them. The Machines could have warmed up the Earth, and that may have been their original plan. But that would have taken another fifty years, and we would have fought against the Machines for that entire time. When they saw that we were already doing the warming, they must have been very happy. We couldn't fight two wars at the same time, one for the environment and one against the Machines.

That was the time for the arrival of the Machines. The Machines began to speed up change to the environment far beyond Man's abilities to fix it. The ground burned as the temperature of the globe began to rise in a dramatic fashion. Like an asteroid strike, this was an extinction event, but much faster than Nature could have ever produced.

But that was not enough for Them. They had found ways to keep the world distracted from doing anything about the environmental crisis. Propaganda smothered the facts in every facet of our communications, from the internet to television entertainment. This propaganda was so pervasive that the population spent much of their waking hours arguing over which "fact" was real. It was a horrible situation.

Perhaps worse were the monsters that came from the Machines at set intervals. Periodically, a new Monster would emerge, larger and more dangerous than the previous one. They spread across the land in waves, wiping out every living thing in their wake. The latest one was dubbed Leviathan by what was left of the US government, the only surviving member of the United Nations Security Council. They were decidedly reptilian, with six legs and a whip-like tail. To say it resembled a toad would be like comparing a canoe with an aircraft carrier. Both floated on water, but that was about all they had in common. Leviathans were swift and deadly. To catch sight of one was usually the last thing you ever did.

Simon had been lucky. His Leviathan sighting had been when he was walking with a crowd of a thousand refugees heading for a shelter in downtown Atlanta. He had been at the back, making some notes on his digital recorder. The creature had risen out of the airport, taking almost everyone by surprise. Simon had fallen off the small bridge he was crossing. He slid down the embankment and hid under the bridge until he was fairly certain the Leviathan had moved on. With some luck, he made his way into a suburban area and tried doors until one of them opened.

He picked up the stapled papers that had "TOP SECRET" stamped on them. One edge was burned, and a boot print ran across the top page. The stem of his favorite pipe provided some comfort, clamped between his teeth. Beside him was his backpack filled with several days' food and water. The house was sound enough, and all the doors and windows were sealed. He would do a complete inspection in the morning, if he lived through the night. For now, there was no other living thing in the house.

Two cushions from a big easy chair were under his sore buttocks. He leaned back against a heavy dining room table on its side. He began to read, ignoring the sounds outside of the house he had broken into an hour before.

"P. 9 *—Excerpt from the Green Manual of the Bureau of Non-Human Resources:*

Re: Bulletin 629-49, regarding item 6700, in respect to extract 75,131/monarch/v=kd7/dontgetkilled-483-331/siynid/J9k/fp.booi==l/guire9[jurga]6/encounters

"In the wake of the ongoing Crisis, the Federal Government has taken steps to help citizens get through the early stages of this situation. These standards have been partitioned into seven stages. It is strongly advisable that the guidelines be followed as written. Unforeseen consequences and death may result if deviations occur.

"The following is Stage Six:

"Monster Encounters, And What to Do When an Encounter Occurs. Extra Large Monsters.

"Monsters have become a regular part of our everyday life, now that everything has broken down, and we are making every effort to rebuild the governments, both national and statewide. Local authorities are keenly aware of the situation and advise that families and individuals ascertain the type and quantities of Monsters in their area before making any organized crusade against them, or it.

"The following are the size comparisons for the known Monsters in our midst. Take every caution when comparing these descriptions, and any accompanying photos, to the actual Monsters in your vicinity. It is vital that you indicate the correct size on any correspondence you send to the Bureau of Non-Human Resources. Precise information is vital when determining the actions that may be required by the Military for the situation in your area.

Elephantine. The size of a garbage truck.
Gray Whale. The size of a public bus.
Dunwich. The size of a two-family house.
Leviathan. The size of an apartment building.
Classified. Something this size will be dealt with by the Military. Get away from the area before any high explosives are deployed. There may only be minutes between an Encounter and Military response to it.

"The New Guidelines in dealing with Unknown Monsters. (Revised 4/02/7C, pending monthly revisions)

"While these guidelines won't account for all circumstances, it should prove to be reasonably successful in assessing what exactly we are dealing with on a day-to-day basis. It is advised to record any data concerning any Monster(s) for future use. Civilian data in such circumstances could prove to be very useful.

"When a creature that is unknown to you comes into view, get out of its sight. You must not have the creature looking for you while you are making plans to get away from it. Evading something fifty feet tall and very hungry can be difficult.

"When the Monster is simply too large, or there are too many of them, the best thing to do is to get out of the area. Monitoring and recording any data concerning the Monster(s) can be implemented once you have situated yourself in a safer place for doing so.

"Some Monsters emit dangerous, often fatal, fumes when consumed by fire. The current list of Monsters this applies to has sadly not been updated since 09/2052 at the onset of the arrival of the Monsters to Earth. A safe distance of at least one hundred yards is advisable when a Monster is burning.

"Once you have escaped from whichever Monster you have encountered, the next thing you are strongly advised to do is to get a good visual assessment of it. Eyewitness accounts are valuable in and of themselves, but it is recommended that a mechanical, electrical, or digital device be used for documentation if possible.

"If you are a person who still owns a functional camera or similar device, it is imperative that you make every effort to safely document the encounter with said creature and any details as to height, width, color, hide-type, method of locomotion, dietary predilections, mating habits, sleep cycle, weaknesses, day or night sleeping preference, body temperature, etc. Do not put yourself or anyone you are with in danger. Safety comes first. Any data accumulated would serve as a bonus.

"Once you have moved to a safe place and have taken the time to document the Monster in as detailed an amount as possible, your best option is to get away from it. Getting away will mean different things depending on the size, disposition, quantity, and appetite of the Monster involved. Taking a good head count of your opposition will go a long way toward your potential survival.

"The most efficient way to get away from a Monster is on foot. Don't run. Running creates a lot of noise, and that is not something you want to do. Walking in a brisk manner away from the Monster is the best course of action.

DISCLAIMER

"The Bureau of Non-Human Resources does not, nor will it ever, condone approaching a Monster for the purpose of recording data on it. While such recordings can and often are very lucrative, it is not advisable to get within a mile of any Monster, regardless of how large or small they are.

"The one thing that a person or persons could do to ensure their survival is to..."

That was where the pages ended. Simon was despondent. When he'd seen that the folder held the reports issued by the government on how to deal with creatures, he'd been hopeful, but to his utter disappointment, the report ended at the point where he needed it most. He sighed and put the folder down near his backpack. His phone blinked green. Fully charged.

Simon crept to the picture window of the house. He moved his head like it was made of clay, one inch at a time. The streetlights still worked in the area, by some miracle, illuminating the front yard. He could see the smashed cars along the curb. The house across the street had a gaping hole where the two-car garage used to be. An Elephantine creature lay on the front lawn, scanning the neighborhood for food. While it looked nothing like an elephant, there was no one around to argue with.

His camera phone was set on video, less likely to make any noise or light that would bring the thing into the house to eat him. To make sure that there was no light flash as it started, Simon turned the video recorder on with the phone near the floor. He breathed calmly as he raised the phone to the window. With a smile, Simon filmed the creature for several minutes.

He didn't know what to make of the dinosaur-thing. To him, it looked like an Ankylosaurus, with sharp spikes along its waist and on its head. Wasn't Ankylosaurus a herbivore? Simon was confused. Perhaps it was just angry when it chased him down the street. As he watched, the creature stood and began to growl. Another creature came into view. It was much larger, and not at all like a dinosaur. The report called it a Dunwich. This one seemed to be composed of black cables and eyes in a dozen places. The Elephantine hissed at it and swung its heavy tail. The tail struck the black thing and plunged into it.

With a howl, the dinosaur-thing tried to pull away from its attacker. The Dunwich seemed not to be bothered by the commotion as it sucked the spiny dinosaur into its mass. Simon wet himself as the black ropy creature slid toward the house where he sat. All he could do was sit still, breathe, and hope it didn't smell him or see him. The thing stopped at the edge of the porch, swaying back and forth. Tentacles slithered out and probed the windowsills and outer door. Pieces of the door and a window box were torn free and dropped to the ground.

The Dunwich backed up on its hideous pseudopod footing like some enormous slug. The lawn was slicked down and shone in the streetlight. Simon couldn't move for several minutes. The street was clear, and he heard nothing outside. He allowed himself to back away from the window and across the floor. Simon heard the Dunwich slither away with a slurping sound that made him wretch. He heard a roar from down the street and then a great metal-tearing crash.

Shaking, Simon crawled into the hallway and upstairs. The first room was a bedroom. It was clean and smelled fairly fresh. The shutters were bolted shut and the door locked behind him. He sank onto the bed and let himself fall into a foggy slumber.

"Welcome to the New World," he said as he drifted off to sleep.

. . .

About the author: Born in Rahway, New Jersey.
Early childhood in Colonia, New Jersey.
Later childhood in Menlo Park Terrace, New Jersey.
Graduated College with an AA degree.
Married a beautiful and intelligent young woman.
Moved to Edison, New Jersey.
Graduated College with a degree in Computer Technology.
Fathered a beautiful and intelligent daughter.
Moved to Iselin, New Jersey.
Graduated College with a Bachelor's degree in History and English.
He writes for seventy-five minutes every day, seven days a week.
Creative Director- Joe's Writers Club

@ www.joeswriters.club
He is a Game Designer, Author, Avid Gamer, Trekker, Movie Buff.
So Far, So Good.

21

Survival in the Age of Nonsense

by Paul Freedman (United States)

Subgenres: Science fiction

Time Period: Mid-twenty-first century

Setting: Northern arctic Russia

Synopsis: In a melting arctic, nomads discuss a mysterious asteroid, then make their final migration with the family's herd of reindeer.

. . .

For thousands of years, the untold tribes of the steppe roamed Central Asia from the North Pacific to the Caucasus, from the Arctic Ocean to the Himalayas. Some invaded India, China, and eastern Europe. We only know the names of the most destructive: Vandals, Huns, Tatars, Khimar, Samars.

The Nenet are now restricted to peninsulas extending into the polar sea. Each year, the land shrinks visibly. In the face of rising sea levels, the peninsulas are shorter and narrower. Freshwater lakes spread above the water table, wider and shallower than ever.

Baihu had spent four days with the herd. The time to move was at hand, and she needed to make sure the animals were fit to travel. Now she set out for home.

Tundra is waterlogged prairie. Now, even in frozen winter, the land gives like a mattress beneath walking feet over bogs of unfathomable depth. Grasses, dead and dry, fuel prairie fires that run fifty klicks across the land. Smoke obscures the sky, and cinders fly into the eyes of humans and reindeer alike.

As she crested a slight rise, she glanced behind her. She thought she saw a flicker of light perhaps a klick away. At the next bump, she stood still and looked again. Yes, there it was.

Along with her father, Boris, and her mother, Khioniya, her family now included Grigory Tchilkovsky, her husband. They had married two years ago. Grigory had been an astronomer at the University of St Petersburg. Since the sun barely dips below the horizon in the Summer Solstice, the University Observatory is closed May through August. Grigory had spent that vacation three summers ago camping alone on the steppe. One morning, he awoke to find his tent surrounded by the Nenet's herd.

Their paths kept crossing. At trading stations and river crossings he found himself again subsumed by the herd. Often, Baihu was with them. She was easy to talk to. By September, he was looking forward to finding her popping up amidst the animals. Surprisingly, he had become fond of the beasts, too, and they seemed comfortable with him, so he simply never went back to his job.

Grigory felt more at ease with Baihu and her family than he'd ever been in his life, and that winter, he married her. She married him, she said, because he rarely spoke, and she valued the silence. Without any explanation, she endorsed everything he did. When he did talk, she understood only four words out of ten, but what she understood she agreed with completely.

Hoping to find her mother finishing dinner's preparation,

Baihu entered the tent (choom). Her father was bent at the table, engrossed in assembling a cuckoo clock kit. By the choom wall, Grigory was repairing a cargo harness. The stove, alas, was cold. Baihu built a fire in it. She opened a plastic bin, extracting the last cabbage and four potatoes. She brought two large reindeer steaks in from the meat locker, defrosted, diced, and browned them in the bottom of a pot. Filling the pot from the water jug, she cut up the vegetables, put them in along with seasonings, and set it on to stew.

"Did Lemoya calve?" Her father, Boris, held the clock's escape gear in his needle-nosed pliers and did not look up so as to not lose his place.

"Not yet."

"We will see to her in the morning. Maybe we will stay an extra day or two."

"Any word from Mama?"

Boris smiled. Baihu did not see it, but she heard it in his voice. "Oh yes. She took a short side trip on the way home, is all." Baihu's brother Aleksandr, four years her junior, was in government school in a village a hundred or so klicks off the direct line home from the market.

"And how is my younger brother?"

"She reported nothing out of the ordinary, neither extraordinary nor ... the other thing."

By the tent wall, Grigory finished what he was doing, stood up, and stretched. He took his work out to the sleds to test.

"Papa, there was someone on the steppe when I was coming home."

Boris took a second to position the escape gear on its pin, and another second besides.

"Oh really? Tell me about him."

"I didn't meet him. He was quite a ways off, easily a kilometer. But he had a lantern and a beard, and he walked with a limp."

"A limp. Was he an old man?"

"I don't think he was even as old as you."

"Were you carrying a lantern? Was it lit?"

"I was carrying it, but it wasn't lit. The moon is almost full. I didn't need it."

"Well, then there's some chance he didn't see you."

She said nothing.

The wind had risen. Boris carefully lined up his tools and put a cloth over the unfinished clock, apparently done with it for the night. He got up and walked the perimeter of the choom. Wherever he noticed something flapping, he tucked it in or laced it down. The wind shook the heavy tent, but nothing else sprang out of its bundle.

With a gust of cold, the door flap opened. Khioniya stepped in. She was greeted with happy burbling from her family. Setting down what she had brought, she kissed and hugged them both before unwrapping herself from layers of scarves and poncho-like garments. She looked in the stewpot, stirred it, tasted it, apparently approved, and then opened a package of beans and emptied it into the pot.

About ten minutes later, the wind still in an uproar, someone outside called, "Hello the tent!"

Khioniya, busy with Baihu putting away what she had bought, looked up at the door and then at the girl. Baihu kept her face toward her work.

"Is anyone there? I need to be inside."

Boris crossed to the door. He raised the flap and saw a man of mid height, less than two meters. The man held his lamp beside his face, showing his light brown beard. Shaggy hair the same color peeked out from under his parka hood. His moustache was fringed with frost.

"I have spent the last week out here and am frozen to my marrow."

Boris held the flap slightly wider, stepped back out of the doorway, and the stranger came in. Walking determinedly toward the stove, he looked first at Baihu, who had still not looked up, then at Khioniya. "The warmth compels me."

"Of course," said Khioniya, smiling. "We will eat soon. And you will join us, I hope."

"Thank you."

He opened his parka when he sat down but would not take it off until he had eaten most of his dinner.

"What is your name, sir?" asked Boris.

"Adrian Advuschenko."

"And what brings you onto the tundra in the black of winter?"

At that moment, Grigory came in. "Did I hear the name Adrian Advuschenko?" He seemed more astonished than happy, but not unhappy all the same. He filled a bowl at the stove.

"You did, Grigory Tchilkovsky." Advuschenko's face was filled with smiling delight. They hugged.

Grigory brought his bowl and sat at the table. "Adrian is also an astronomer," he explained. "He started at the Observatory four months after I did. As Junior Assistant, he had no experiments of his own but assisted on all those of the Chief Astronomer and, occasionally, mine. By the way, did Kirill ever complete those calculations on the mysterious chromium-carborundum collisions in the Colander Constellation?"

"Yes, he did." Grigory ate while Adrian touched on the highlights of the previous three years.

Presently, Khioniya and Baihu cleared the table. Grigory and Adrian went outside.

"When I left, Kirill and I were both looking for asteroids likely to collide with Earth. I know Kirill had compiled a list. Did he eliminate any?"

"Almost all, in fact. His calculations were, uh, premature. With more data, he found a larger mechanism that corrected itself. Over and over, it presented threats that were then swept away just as readily."

"The three-body problem."

"Exactly." Whereas the movements of two celestial objects could be laid out completely, once a third object was added to the system, it became impossible to calculate their future paths. What's more, nobody could formulate a general rule as to why not.

"Now he's involved with this eternal mystery," said Adrian. "His observations have resolved to predictions of when the problem will affect whatever asteroid he discovers. So far, he's cataloged over three thousand objects."

"And what is the rate of recalculation?"

"Sixty per cent, more or less."

"Well, I'd say he's likely found his life's work."

Adrian silently looked straight up. The air was extremely cold, about -29°C (-20°F) but was not completely clear. No water vapor remained, but some fine haze, perhaps smoke from prairie fires over two hundred klicks away, blurred the view very slightly. Even so, the canopy of stars was dazzling, awe-inspiring.

The wind that had swept the area a couple of hours ago had fallen off to an occasional mild breeze. At the current temperature, this was bracing enough. The men never noticed it.

Adrian said, "Tell me about the Green Asteroid."

Tschilkovaky hadn't thought of the Green Asteroid since he'd come to the steppe. At first, his impulse was to deny any knowledge of it. Then his brain cleared, and he realized he was having a professional conversation with a colleague, and he was stuck with it.

"Didn't you read about it in my log? That was all there was."

"The way you acted whenever it came up—"

"I don't remember anything strange—"

"I do. I remember you walking out of Soyuz Bar when Mariya Gusev asked you about evolved organics—"

"Such a question!"

"She asked you if there was any telescopic evidence of photosynthesis. Not even if anyone admitted finding any—"

"Preposterous. An unprofessional approach—"

"Not at all. She wanted confirmation or denial of a rumor, is all. I thought it was entirely proper."

"She was trying to—"

"She wasn't doing anything outside her job."

"Mmm..."

"But there was evidence, wasn't there? A lot of green."

"Aah..."

"Not only the green surface growth."

"Rrr..."

"Also the green in the spectral analysis. Not only did the asteroid have an atmosphere—highly irregular on so small a body—but a heavily oxygenated one. So, between the chlorophyll in the growth and the green glowing in the spectrum, she had a lot of reason to ask the question. Didn't she?"

"Uh huh."

"So why did you run out on her?"

"Well, it's a very controversial subject just now. Panspermia. Life transferred throughout the galaxy. We're so scrupulously careful *not* to leave traces of biology on any of the bone-clean, bone-dry, life-hostile surfaces of the planets around us for fear we'd be creating monsters. Meanwhile we live on this planet, in this center of teeming life. And here's this furry little green speck that could conceivably puke its guts right on us. What sort of monster could *that* evoke? I didn't want to be responsible for any worldwide panic."

"So as long as she left your name out of it, you'd be all right with whatever she wrote?"

He looked at the back of his left hand. "Why?"

"I think I know where the green thing came from."

"Really?" said Grigory. "What gives you that idea?"

Through his parka, Adrian patted an inside pocket. "When we go back inside, I'll show you."

. . .

Boris and Khioniya were already on their pallet, wrapped in

each other's arms beneath furs. Baihu was also curled in bed. Grigory sadly contemplated the space beside her, wishing he were there.

At one end of the table, Adrian opened his tablet. Grigory, still outside, rummaged through plastic tubs filled with metal, cloth, and reindeer-sourced things. Presently, he came in carrying a screen, a frame, a miniature projector, a battery pack, and several cables. Quietly he assembled this impromptu theater, then joined Adrian.

A quadrant of sky appeared on the screen. Grigory recognized it. "It comes from somewhere in here?"

"Beyond this, actually. I want you to orient yourself easily." A sequence of four enlargements focused on a tiny area to the left and above the center of the sector. Two more enlargements expanded spaces between the stars. The stars behind them ranged deeper into the galaxy than anyone had mapped.

"I hate to demystify the suspense, but—how old is The Green One? How many more enlargements yet?"

"Oh, it's not so mysterious. We're here, actually. About 140 light-years from Earth, there's a G2 yellow star just like the Sun."

Orbiting this star, Adrian said, he had identified an exoplanet with a thick atmosphere and a "very green" spectrum. Not only the planet, but also two of its moons had this same signature. That wasn't what had ultimately held his attention, though. Obviously, there had previously been four moons.

With atmosphere similar to the planet's, it would have taken a collision with something almost the size of itself to decimate one of these moons, Adrian had thought at the time. Almost a year later, after several unrelated coincidences, he'd stumbled upon the idea that maybe one of those moons had been retrograde and had been captured passing the planet in the opposite direction from the natural orbit.

The star, the planet, and the Green Asteroid were all the facts he had. From that thin store, Adrian concocted a sequence of dramatic guesses. What if the green growth covering the asteroid was a hardy, quick-growing cyanobacteria? What if it could survive baths of liquid oxygen and centuries of crossing interstellar space, then reanimate in the presence of sunlight, or reenergize once it had any warmth? What if, tiny as it was, it had a thermonuclear core?

He traced several possible paths between this star, which he called Verda, and Earth, paths that passed other stars. Was it possible that periodic awakening could help sustain cyanobacteria and maintain it for the perhaps millions of years this crossing would take?

He showed Grigory the calculations of the paths. He readied images of known cyanobacteria that could possibly have survived the conditions. He started to show them, but Grigory, well familiar with them, didn't bother with them.

"The Green Asteroid is still approaching the Sun, is it not? And will for some years yet?"

Adrian nodded. "Of course. You know that."

"You know all this is just an idea, your imagination, don't you? Not even a hypothesis, much less a theory?"

"Of course." Adrian gathered himself. "Look. I wanted to know if you wanted to announce it or not. After all, it was your discovery."

"What does Kirill think of it?"

"Did you mention it to him?" Adrian asked.

"I? No, not at all."

"Then, nothing. He's busy. Barely looks at the sky, and never at this sector or at the Green Asteroid."

"Well, I suppose the news must be all over the press by now," Grigory said. "Ms. Gusev knew about it, what, three years ago?"

"She hasn't said a word," Adrian said. "She's a personal friend of mine, too, as she is yours. We're both from the same neighborhood in St Petersburg. She told me because she knew I worked with you."

Grigory didn't hesitate. "Then you announce it. Take all my notes and copy them into your journal. You'll verify all the observations, of course. That'll catch you up, and you'll be able to face the press. You'll do fine," he said.

"That won't do."

"What would?"

"I won't lie on a worldwide stage," Adrian said.

"Not even if you could get away with it?"

"I might if it was fun. But I won't tell people I made history when I didn't."

"Then don't," Grigory said. "Do not copy my journal. Verify my observations if you would. Then announce that I discovered this Green Asteroid before vanishing."

"Evaporating."

"Disappearing. You don't have any idea where. 'He left his journal and his socks'—I'll have to remember to give you a pair of my socks—'and, of an instance, evanesced.' You think maybe I'm in Ukraine, Kazakhstan, or maybe South America. I mentioned all of them..."

"You did."

"I did. Right now. When you last saw me." Grigory stood and looked down at the younger man. "I'm really tired. I'm sorry. Astronomy exhausts me more than any other activity. Your bed's right over there." He indicated a pallet separate from the others with a short pile of deerskins on it. "I'll get you the socks and the journal in the morning. Good night."

Grigory went to his pallet. Taking several skins, he tied them with rawhide strips hanging from tent poles and from the choom itself and soon made a curtain around his sleeping wife. He entered the curtain and soon was curled with her.

"That is you, isn't it?" Baihu muttered.

"Who else?" said Grigory.

"Mmmm. What was that all about with the stranger?"

"Oh, just some leftover astronomy stuff."

"What was green?"

He took a deep breath, then let it out. They had created their own tradition of always answering each other's questions with summaries of all available information, no matter how unfamiliar the other was with the subject matter. That way, if anything needed clarification or more information, it could be asked for specifically.

"Just before I retired, I discovered an extremely rare asteroid that was green. It needed more study before I could talk about it, even to other scientists. That study was left undone. Now Adrian wants to talk about it. He will have to study the asteroid first, so he needs my records in order to learn everything he can."

"Your words sounded like the end of everything."

"Well, there are some who believe it will be. But they're wrong."

"They think so?"

"They believe this could be the end."

The Nenet language draws a strong distinction between "thinking" something may be true and "believing." The verb "to think" is a synonym of "to imagine." "To believe" is a synonym of "to experience."

"Teenagers?" asked Baihu.

"Mostly. But some grown men and women, too."

"People with no real problems."

"Not enough real problems, sure," Grigory said.

. . .

Boris and Baihu were both with the herd when Grigory awoke. Khioniya scooped him out a bowl of kasha and a cup of tea, and he ate. The two of them then set to repacking the bins. Usually, they tried to empty as many as they could, paring down the load against the next migration. However, this could well be the last migration. Grigory wanted to keep as much as he could.

Adrian, having served himself from the porridge pot,

emerged from the choom in his parka. "I've arranged to meet Ludmilla in Kyrnie Obirisk in two days," he said, naming a friend and a town twenty klicks to the west. They all shook hands, he and Grigory hugged, and he set off.

Boris returned.

"How is the ewe?" said Grigory.

"Tired but fine. She had her fawn maybe two hours ago. The fawn's also very healthy. We can move as soon as we're ready."

Grigory continued loading a sled. The surface of the grass was frosted. He knew not all the surface of the land was fit for sleds. They would have to pick their way around the soft spots.

They would have to deal with numerous recently created obstacles. In just the three years he had been on the steppe, he had seen railroads and pipelines spread, clutching the open prairie like a falling tall man grasping a tablecloth, insanely hoping it will hold him upright. The fenced-off parcels could no longer sustain themselves, as they couldn't support those living adjacent.

The herd arrived two hours later. Ana-Alla was the lead reindeer, and Baihu rode him. His bell preceded them, a single sleigh bell, soft but penetrating amid the hoof rumble. Immediately behind her, four reindeer carried loads of hay.

They were heading to a meadow they had used two years before. No one knew in what state they would find that meadow. Everyone knew the frequent detours would add hours to their journey. No one knew how many.

Late in the afternoon, they came to a lake nobody'd ever seen before. Boris was at a loss. "Too much has changed," he said. "Which way is the town, you suppose?" He named a village they had used before.

"Well, we're still so far north, I'd guess south."

"Which way's that?"

Grigory looked up. He didn't need a second. "There." He gestured. They went right.

Grigory had discussed the future with Boris only twice. After he'd asked for Baihu's hand but before the wedding, Boris had said, "You know our time here is very short. What do you see yourself doing in five years?"

"I can't see that far," Grigory said.

"Do you think you might regret giving up a career that extends far beyond the paths we walk?"

Grigory did not smile. "The one and only thing I knew about the stars was that they weren't where I saw them. All the rest was stuff I believed I knew."

Another time, Boris had said, "I think, after our last crossing, I will go to a city. St Petersburg, probably. I haven't been in a city in close to thirty years. Surely, they've changed. Then there were still Communists in the cities, in high positions. But they've all died off by now. And there is jazz! Jazz, and no Communists!"

"You'll be on vacation. How many days do you think you'll stay?"

"Days?"

"Yeah," Grigory said. "You figure, five days? Seven?"

"I wouldn't spend the night in the city."

"It's days of travel to St Petersburg."

"Even so," Boris said, "I wouldn't spend the night there. Too much light, too much noise. I don't know how they can stand it."

"How will you deal with the herd?"

"We shall see," Boris said. "Possibly tonight, possibly tomorrow, the solution will present itself. After all, I remain part of the world. I'm certain it's time for all this."

They came to a tavern. Boris and Khioniya went in. Two vehicles were parked by the door, a twenty-year-old Mercedes and a homemade small flatbed truck formed from a Saab sedan.

"Doesn't look good," Grigory murmured. Only Baihu heard him. Grigory watched her out of the corners of his eyes.

A secret smile seemed to flicker across her face. Or maybe it was merely his private hope.

Grigory turned to Ana-Alla. "What will you do next, Ana-Alla? Ever hear the name, 'Santy Claus'?"

The reindeer snorted.

While Grigory and Baihu put out bales of hay for the herd, Boris and Khioniya went inside.

Boris noticed three guys standing at the bar. The guys noticed them, too, but then turned silently back to their drinks. Near the door, an old couple sat at a table. In a far corner, a middle-aged man in an expensive leather coat sat at another table, nursing a brown liquid in a highball glass. No music was playing. A small fire burned silently. Nevertheless, the room was comfortably warm. Khioniya went to the only empty table while Boris went to the bar.

The bartender wasn't behind the bar, so Boris took four glasses and the bottle of vodka off the backbar and brought them to the table. He sat with his back to the door. Setting the empty glasses before the empty chairs, he poured for Khioniya and himself. They raised their glasses to each other and knocked back the shots. Grigory and Baihu came up to the table, and Boris poured for all.

"*Nasdrovia!*"

All the while, Boris was watching the guy in the leather coat, who was watching them. "Will you come, drink vodka with us? Or do you prefer your own?"

The man stood up. He picked up his glass, drained it, put it down on his table, and crossed to theirs. "Of course I will drink vodka with you."

Grigory fetched a glass from the bar and grabbed a chair from the old couple's table. Boris poured. They all clinked. "Genri Mikhalikov," said the gentleman in introduction. "And you are Boris and Khioniya. I've been waiting for you. I want to buy your herd."

22

Slow Burn

by Dustin Walker (Canada)

WARNING: This story may not be suitable for younger readers.

Subgenres: Horror, military fiction

Time Period: Near future to mid-twenty-first century

Setting: United States of America

Synopsis: As a destructive heat wave spreads across the planet, rookie soldier Dan Ellis must choose between saving himself or giving others a shot at survival.

. . .

A few minutes ago, my uniform was soaked in sweat. It streamed down my face and onto my lips like salty tears. It stung my eyes and blurred my vision. But now, I'm bone dry.

And that scares the shit out of me.

Because it means I'm either dehydrated and on the verge of heat stroke, or it's now so damn hot that every drop of moisture evaporates as soon as it forms.

And it will only get hotter.

I just spent way too long searching through a big house for anyone who hadn't evacuated yet. When I finally emerge, the desolate streets of Perry Heights shimmer like desert sand, blurring distant objects. I look around for any sign of my fellow reservists or the military truck we were supposed to bring evacuees to. Movement down the road catches my eye: another soldier, just passing a bright-white house less than a block away. I shout and wave before slow-jogging over to her.

"Hey, where is everyone?" I ask.

"Gone already, it looks like. I'd be with them, but I got hung up dealing with a couple of looters." She's pretty, but not in a soft or delicate kind of way. More like fierce-pretty, with sharp eyes and carved shoulders. I feel like I've met her before. But her confident, straight-back posture makes me think she isn't a newbie reservist like me.

"Yeah, I spent too long at a place up the road," I say. My heart's still pounding, but just running into someone else makes me feel a bit safer. "Hey, is your radio working? Mine's dead."

"Mine's dead too. No signal on my phone either."

"Shit." My stomach tightens as I run my fingers through my hair. "So what the hell are we going to do then?"

"Stay calm," she says, her voice cool and steady. She stares at me for a few moments, like I'm a kid who needs scolding. Like I have no business carrying an M4 rifle. And maybe she's right. "There's a checkpoint a couple miles from here at the elementary school. If we move quick, we can get out from there."

"Yeah, I remember the one you're talking about," I say, although I'm only vaguely familiar with where the elementary school is.

She sees the name tag on my uniform and asks, "Corporal Ellis, what's your first name?"

"Dan."

"Okay, Dan, call me Jenn, since we're both the same rank."

We head up the road and, fortunately, Jenn is just fine with the slow-jog pace.

Maybe it's her confident demeanor or simply the relief of not being alone out here. But traveling with Jenn makes me feel much more confident. And less afraid.

Before today, the biggest crisis I ever faced was realizing that third-year biology was way over my head. And I guess that really speaks to my motivation for joining the reserves in the first place—the need to do something beyond the safety of a lecture hall. Something a little risky. Something that would prove I'm not soft and weak. But I sure as hell didn't expect to have to deal with this sort of thing. Although, with all the warning signs, none of us should be surprised.

After a couple of blocks, we hear a bang. It sounds like a bird hit a glass door. But then I hear it again. And again. I look around.

Across the street, an old lady with fluffy white hair is slapping a bay window with her hands to get our attention.

"Oh shit, over there," I say, pointing.

Jenn jogs over without saying a word. I follow.

She opens the door of the townhouse and walks in. By the time I catch up, she's already in the living room.

The woman is sitting on a couch peppered with faded-yellow flower prints. Across from her, an equally old man in overalls sits in a duct-taped lounger. Both their eyes are wide.

"We called a taxi, but they never came," the woman says, her voice shaking with each word. "And I—I didn't know who else to call. I tried the police, but..."

Her once-white-blouse is now moist and yellowed. But the old man looks much worse, with sickly pale skin and trembling hands. There's an oxygen tank at his feet.

They both have to know what's coming. Pretty much everyone with a TV or a smartphone must know by now.

"Okay, ma'am. We'll get you both out of here," I say and

turn to Jenn, lowering my voice. "We'll each help one along. I can take the old guy."

Jenn scratches her neck and looks at the floor. "No, we can't. The school is at least two miles away, and we have maybe thirty minutes to get there. I don't see them making it."

Her cold matter-of-fact tone surprises me, even though she does have a point: it is unlikely they'll be able to walk that far. But what's the alternative? Just leave them to die?

I say, "We can't just abandon them. You know what'll happen."

"They're not going to make it to the checkpoint. And if we don't leave ASAP, we won't make it either."

"We can't just leave them here."

I don't realize I'm almost shouting until the old lady starts to cry. It's so hard to think in this heat, like my skull is filling with hot lead. I'm thirsty as hell too and wish I hadn't forgotten my canteen at the last house.

"Wha—what are you talking about?" The old woman furrows her brow. Then she and her husband exchange a quick, nervous glance. "Shouldn't we be leaving?"

"We will, just hold tight," I tell them.

Jenn seems to be in her own little world, just staring out the bay window. Then she lowers her voice before saying: "So we end it for them. What else can we do?"

I try to act shocked by what she said, but the idea has crossed my mind as well. It sounds horrible, but after seeing the video of what happens when The Heat catches you... I know I'd prefer a quick death.

My fingers tighten over the butt of the M4. Then I shake my head.

"No, we can't just kill them like that." I'm whispering, but the couple can probably still hear us. "That's not what we do."

"So what do we do, Danny?" My dad used to call me Danny years ago, and it's unsettling hearing Jenn say it now. "You want to try and carry two frail seniors to the checkpoint in half an hour? Are you going to be the one hauling that guy's oxygen tank with us too? In this heat?"

I open my mouth to speak, but Jenn raises her hand in a "stop" motion, cutting off my words.

"Or do we leave them both here alive. Knowing that in an hour or so, their skin is going to blister, and their guts are going to boil. They're going to sit and suffer and scream as they slowly burn to death. That's assuming they don't figure out a way to kill themselves beforehand. So which one is it, Danny? What do we do?"

The old woman is bawling now.

"Who are we to say whether they live or die? We don't kill people."

"They're already fucking dead." Jenn gets right in my face. "The only questions are how will they die and will we die with them."

I shake my head and clench my teeth, not yet sure what to say back. That's when the old man blurts out: "I'm ready!"

Everyone looks at him. He continues, teary-eyed: "I'm ready to go. Please."

"Charles?" The old woman reaches across the couch and takes her husband's hand. "What do you mean, Charles?"

"I love you, Mary, but I don't want to die like that. And we can't get away in time. I can barely stand the heat already."

"No, Charles!" Mary shakes her head and takes her husband's hand in both of hers. "No. No. No."

"I love you, Mary. And I hope you make the same choice I am." And then he turns to us and says: "I want you to end it now, please."

Everything seems to stop. No sound. No movement. But the heat is still there, weighing me down like a wet wool trench coat.

Jenn raises her gun and fires.

The old man's head snaps back and Mary screams. Charles slumps against the arm of his recliner, blood dripping down his face and onto his plaid shirt.

My ears ring from the shot and my stomach lurches. I turn and throw up behind an antique end table as Mary's screams devolve into wet, bubbling sobs.

Wiping my mouth, I look over at Jenn. She's aiming her rifle at Mary now.

"Don't!" I call out. "Wait!"

She lowers the gun and looks at me. "For what?"

Her voice is stone. Unwavering. And I don't say anything at first, because I'm scared that what I say next could determine whether this woman lives or dies, so I choose my words as carefully as possible.

"We need to ask her first."

Jenn gives me that fuck-you're-dumb look again for a moment. Then she shrugs. "Fine."

She turns to Mary. "Would you like me to kill you quickly like I did your husband? Or would you like to sit here for another hour or two and wait for your head to swell and your skin to blister and your insides to boil?"

"I want to live!" Mary yells. Tears and mucus run down her face. "Please! Help me!"

Jenn puts her hands on her hips and lets out a big sigh. Then she pulls her phone out of her pocket, taps it a few times and points the screen at Mary.

Within a few seconds of hearing the rapid panting and hollow moans, I knew it was the video they released this morning—the one of the couple in the log cabin.

It starts out with the twenty-somethings lying on the couch, their heads slack against the back of the sofa. Eyes half-open. Fast-forward thirty minutes and they're moaning with their once-limp bodies now rigid and twisted. Their faces a deep red.

In the next cut, things get really bad. I force myself not to think about those images as the video plays, but hearing the audio is just as disturbing. First crying. Then screaming. And then a final high-pitched wail that sounds more mechanical than human.

Followed by silence.

The old woman gawks at the screen, mouth open, until Jenn puts the phone back in her pocket.

I feel faint. Everything goes hazy for a second, and I stumble against the wall. White light creeps in at the edge of my eyes.

"Dan, you okay?" Jenn's voice is distant.

I will myself back to full consciousness. "Yeah, I'm fine."

"Let's go, the old woman wants to ride it out, I guess."

"Help me! Please!" Mary slowly rises to her feet. "Take me with you."

"Sorry, that's not happening." Jenn says.

I straighten up and take a few deep breaths. "We could try. Try to take her along."

Jenn shakes her head. "C'mon Danny, you know not everyone can make it. That's the hard truth."

"At least give me a chance." Her big, emerald eyes shine with tears.

"We will, Mary, come on." I say and grab her gently by the arm. It feels like a broomstick covered in mushroom flesh. Mary takes a few shuffling steps, and my heart sinks as I realize just how slowly she's moving.

"This is pointless!" Jenn says. "It'll take her two hours to walk to the checkpoint, and by then we'll all be dead."

"You don't know that. We just need to help her."

Mary furrows her brow again and shoots me this strange look, like she's confused about who I am. Maybe the searing temperature is messing with her head. Then she starts moving a little faster.

The two of us trudge up the street, slowly passing by once-coveted condos and townhomes that now sit empty. Her thin fingers grip my forearm, and she looks down at her feet as we shuffle up a small hill toward the intersection.

Jenn lingers on the sidelines with this pissed-off look on her face. But she's not sprinting toward the checkpoint without us, so I take that to mean she actually cares whether Mary and I live or die. Or at least, I hope that's what it means.

By the time we get to the top of the hill, both of us are panting. Mary a lot more than me. The air feels like hot ash as it's sucked into my lungs. We stop for a moment.

"We can't rest, we need to keep moving," Jenn says.

Mary gives me that weird look again and shakes her head. I go to help her, but she shrugs me off and starts walking. Her pace is even slower now. And her labored breathing seems to get louder with every quivering step.

"Dan, we can't keep this up." Jenn's face is granite.

Mary stops again and puts her hands on her knees. Her breathing is louder, and her legs are shaking.

"We need to move faster," I tell her. "A lot faster."

She looks at me with those massive jade eyes, like little emerald fires. "I know."

"I'm going to carry you, okay? It's the only way we can cover enough ground in time."

Tears stream down Mary's face. And for a moment, I think she's going to push me away again. But instead, she nods.

"Oh, for Christ's sake," Jenn mutters behind me.

"Throw your arms around my neck and I'll pick you up."

I slip my hands under her back and then, channeling all my strength, I lift her off the ground.

Or at least, I try to lift her.

Everything starts spinning. My vision fades. And I feel myself slipping into darkness.

I'm not hot anymore.

Everything is silent and black.

Until my dad's smoke-scarred voice creeps in. Just above a whisper.

"It's time to man-up, Danny Boy."

I'm crouching in the woods just a few miles from my childhood home. Dad's next to me, clad in dark camo and wearing that tattered Army hat of his. A few hundred yards in front of us, a buck is grazing in a small clearing. A big five-pointer.

"What are you waiting for? Take the shot. He won't stand there forever." His cigarette breath is warm against my cheek.

I pull the rifle tight against my shoulder, put the deer's head in my crosshairs, and exhale slowly. Just how dad showed me.

But I can't pull the trigger. I keep picturing what the deer will look like when the bullet rips into its chest. I think about how much blood will spill out. And how the animal will twitch and jerk before finally laying still. Just the idea of destroying another living creature like that makes me sick, so I just keep aiming and keep watching that buck as he eats the grass.

"For fuck's sake, Danny, take the shot. This is why we're here." His voice turns harsh, like static. In my peripheral vision, I see him glance at my uncle and my older cousin, Cindy, behind us. My face turns hot.

But I still can't bring myself to kill the deer. All I can do is sit there and try not to inhale my dad's stale, acrid breath as he barks at me.

"I got this," says Cindy. I look over and see her aiming her rifle at the deer. Eyes sharp and focused. Confident, straight-back posture.

I watch the ground as the gun fires.

My uncle lets out a bellowing cheer, but my dad stays quiet. For a moment.

Then he snatches the rifle from my hands.

"That's real disappointing, Danny. You need to start manning up, boy. You need to learn how to do hard things."

Mary's scream snaps me back to reality.

She's laying on the sidewalk, gripping her left hip. Blood trickles down the side of her face as she's shrieking—a shrill, moist sound that digs into my skull. Then I realize I'm also on the ground.

I try to crawl over to her, but I'm sapped of energy and my vision is still fuzzy.

"For fuck's sake, that's it." Jenn aims her rifle at Mary. "I'm sorry, but this is enough."

Mary stops screaming and looks over at me. Those green eyes wide with fear. "Please, I don't want—"

Bang! Her head jerks back and her face hits the pavement. Dark fluid flows over the bright-gray concrete, swelling out from the edges of her skull like a blooming flower.

"It's done. Now let's get moving," Jenn says and shoulders her rifle before walking up the street.

I sit there for a moment longer, still dazed, with my ears ringing from the shot. Then I haul myself up to my feet and amble after Jenn.

I try to focus just on keeping up with her, but seeing Mary die so suddenly like that shocks me to the core. Part of me feels like I failed her. Like I should have done more to stop Jenn from pulling the trigger.

But another part of me, as much as I hate to admit it, is relieved that Mary is dead. Maybe there really was a chance that all three of us could get out of here alive. But deep down, I knew Jenn was right all along.

My mouth is sandpaper-dry, and everything around me is becoming soft and unfocused, like looking into a fishbowl. The walls of homes waver, and dark-green trees twist with blue sky in a spinning vacuum of color.

My heart hammers faster in my chest, and my legs go wobbly. I stumble off the sidewalk and onto the road.

Jenn grabs my shoulder and pulls me near. "Focus, Danny. We're close, but we're not there just yet."

"Yeah, yeah, okay." The words pour out of my mouth like sand. I manage to stay upright for the next few blocks, but I'm staggering like a drunk.

"If we had left earlier, we could have avoided all of this." Jenn's voice is steady and cool. For a second, I wonder how she's acting so normal in this heat. But my brain doesn't have enough juice left to work through those sort of complex thoughts right now.

"Okay," I say between heaving breaths. Her pace is a few steps faster than mine, and it's tough to keep up.

"That old woman never had a chance, but you didn't have the balls to leave it at that. You really need to start manning up, Danny."

"What?" My brain is buzzing so fiercely, and my thoughts are so jumbled, that I'm not even sure I said that out loud.

"You think just joining the Army and playing the hero makes you tough? Makes you a man? Not a chance. Because you still can't do the hard things. The things that you need to do to survive now."

It takes me a moment to process those words: what they mean, who they originally came from. And even in my heat-soaked stupor, I realize that it's impossible for this woman to know such personal things about me.

"How do you—who are you?" It's all I can think to ask.

Jenn looks like she's about to speak when we round a corner and see the elementary school. There's a tent and a pair of military jeeps parked out front. One of the soldiers waves at us.

"Looks like you made it." Jenn smiles for the first time since we met. "Maybe I'll see you again. Hopefully not, though."

She turns and starts walking back the way we came. I'm confused at first. Help is literally around the corner.

Then she starts to fade away, like soap dissolving in boiling water.

. . .

Just forty-eight hours later, the world has gone to shit.

The Heat kept moving, and by the time it covered the entire Western Seaboard, throngs of people fled either east or north. Highways became clogged. Riots broke out in every major city.

Before the radio went dead, I heard that the taps were still running up in Winnipeg. I managed to find a Honda with a full tank of gas and headed north. Sticking to rural highways and avoiding the cities. Syphoning gas from abandoned cars and breaking into empty country stores to dig for food and water.

By the time I get halfway up South Dakota, I'm down to just two twelve-ounce bottles of water. I've hardly eaten or slept, which makes the one-hundred-degree heat even tougher to bear. My lips feel like they've been hit with a sandblaster, and the headaches are getting so bad I can barely focus on driving.

Route 83 is lined with abandoned vehicles and the occasional body rotting along the shoulder. By five o'clock, I still haven't seen another living being all day. Then I notice a cardboard sign anchored on the roof of an old Buick. It reads:

"Help. Stranded.
6-Year-Old Needs Water."

For all I know, whoever put that sign up was long dead, but I still slow down as I pass by. A young woman frantically waves at me with both her arms from the back window.

Leaving anyone out here would be a death sentence, so I pull over and park the car. The woman is already out of the Buick by the time I slam my door shut.

"Please, we need help. We ran out of gas this morning and don't have any water." Her legs wobble as she walks up to me. Dual lines of dried mascara stain her bright-red cheeks, and her long, blonde hair is tangled and matted. "My daughter is sleeping in the back. Do you have any water?"

I get lightheaded the moment those words leave her lips. It's almost like I'm waking from a dream, stuck in that murky place between sleep and consciousness. At first, I think it's just a side-effect of The Heat.

But then I feel her.

I know she's just in my mind. Just a feverish delusion.

But it's like I can sense Jenn lingering somewhere among the abandoned cars that clog the shoulder of the highway. Just watching and waiting.

I shake my head and force myself to focus. "Yeah, I have some."

I grab a bottle from the car and hand it to her. The woman thanks me, walks back to the Buick and opens the back door.

"Beth, baby, wake up," she says, leaning inside. "Take small sips, don't chug it back."

The little girl has messy blonde hair like her mom and eyes that shine brilliant green. They remind me of Mary.

"Thank the nice man for the water."

"Thank you." The girl says, as she clutches the bottle in one hand and a stuffed toy sloth in the other. "Mom, I want to stand up now."

Beth grabs a pair of metal crutches lying next to her in the backseat. That's when I notice the white plastic braces on her legs.

Not everyone can make it, Danny.

Jenn's voice slithers into my head. Cold and whispering.

I spin around and try to spot her, but she's nowhere to be seen. That doesn't mean anything, though. She's here now. And I guess, she always has been.

"What's the matter?" The woman asks.

I turn and walk back to the Honda without answering. My heart is revving and my gut's turning sour. A foul, metallic taste sits at the back of my throat.

"Hey, where are you going?" The woman cries out. "Can you give us a ride, please?"

I ignore her.

My hand wraps around the door handle of the Honda. I stop for a few seconds and just stand there, staring at the slick-black steering wheel. And I think about what my options are; about what *their* options are.

What are you waiting for? You have a seven-hour drive

to Winnipeg ahead of you and just one bottle of water. Get going.

Her voice scurries through my head like a foraging beetle. I grip the chrome door handle harder and the hot metal stings my hand. The pain helps me focus.

"Excuse me, mister?"

Behind me is the little girl. She somehow manages to hang onto the toy sloth even while using the crutches.

"My mom told me to say 'hi' to you."

I just look at her for a few moments, hypnotized by those oddly familiar green eyes. And then I finally say: "Okay, hello there."

"My name's Beth."

"I know. I heard your mom call you that."

"Are you going to leave us?"

I pull in a deep breath of hot air and then crouch down. "No, I'm not going to leave. But I need you to go back to your mom. Okay, Beth?"

She nods and heads back to the Buick. Her mother is sitting on the hood of the car, watching us.

My legs are weak and rubbery, so I sit on the hot pavement and close my eyes. Somehow, the darkness makes the world feel just a little cooler.

"Don't even think of it, Danny. That little bottle of water won't be enough for all three of you."

I open my eyes and expect to see Jenn's granite face staring back at me. But she's still just in my head.

"We could find more along the way."

Okay, let's say you do. Let's say all of you actually arrive in Winnipeg. The Heat will catch up eventually. And then you know what happens to people like Beth and Mary. The people who can't make it.

I don't say anything back to her. Across the road, Beth smiles from the backseat as she dangles her toy sloth between her hands. Like she's putting on a puppet show.

If you really want to help them, you know what you need to do.

I close my eyes again, only this time there's no darkness. Instead, I see Mary. Her face twisted in pain as she crawls along the sidewalk. Blood trickles down the side of her head.

You tormented that poor woman, Danny. All because you couldn't do the hard thing. So I did it for you. If I have to, I'll do it again.

"I know you will."

I get up, head to the back of the car and pop the hatchback. The sun glistens off the black metal of my M4. I pick up the rifle and sling it over my shoulder, its weight feeling strangely reassuring. Then I walk over to the Buick.

Something in my face must look different. Beth's mom frowns and tells her daughter to get into the car.

"Is everything okay?" She calls out.

I don't answer and keep walking. When I get to their vehicle, I'm breathing hard. My skin itches and I realize I'm not sweating anymore.

The woman greets me with a forced, awkward kind of smile. Her gaze slips over to my rifle and then back at my face. Just a quick glance that she probably thought I wouldn't notice.

"Beth told me you're not going to leave us?" Her voice is thin and shaky.

"She's right." Everything seems to spin a little. "Because you guys will be leaving instead."

The woman stiffens and her smile falls away.

I take a deep breath.

Exhale.

Reach into my pocket.

"Here." I hold out the keys to the Honda. "Take my car and go. There's another bottle of water in the car."

The woman stares, her face twists in puzzlement. "But, why? Why can't we just go together?"

Jenn appears. She's sitting on the hood of the Buick,

wearing that tattered Army hat my dad always wore. Her eyes are hard and narrow. And it reminds me of how Cindy looked just before killing that deer.

"You'll never make it if you're with me." I tell the woman. "Take the keys and leave now. Don't ask questions, just do it."

She does. The two of them gather up a few bags and toss them into the backseat of the Honda. And then they drive north along the sun-scarred highway.

"Well, that's very disappointing, Danny."

Jenn is next to me now, in her full Army uniform, watching with me as the car disappears into the horizon beyond the hazy heat waves rising from asphalt.

I smile, look up at the cloudless sky, and thumb the selector switch on my M4 rifle from **SAFE** to **SEMI**. "Like you said, not everyone can make it."

Jenn doesn't speak. I'm not even sure she's there anymore. And it doesn't matter anyway.

Because I finally did the hard thing.

. . .

About the author: Dustin Walker is a Canadian writer of crime, horror, and comedy. His work has recently appeared in *Shotgun Honey*, *Rock and a Hard Place*, and Mystery Weekly's *Die Laughing* anthology. He also took first place in *Flash Fiction Magazine's* writing contest in 2021. You can find him on Twitter at @dustinjaywalker.

23

Tomorrow's Ghost

by Mike Fiorito (United States)

Subgenre: Science fiction

Time Period: Near future to mid-twenty-first century

Setting: United States of America

Synopsis: Tomorrow's Ghost is about the near-future United States facing the consequences of neglecting climate change. The story revolves around one boy's inspiration to save his family and the world.

Editor's comments: "Tomorrow's Ghost" somehow reminds me of Ray Bradbury's story in *The Martian Chronicles* about another family with young children facing a crisis, "The Million-Year Picnic."

. . .

Lucas awoke that morning drenched in sweat. He could still smell the scent of his wife, Kate, on the warm sheets. She'd left to go to Canada for the International Climate Change Conference the night before.

While still in bed, he mulled over his recurring dream of being followed by an alien being. In his dreams, the alien's presence was protective. Sometimes his dreams were violently interrupted by another force. The other force was demonic in nature. It seemed intent on suffocating him. Nailing him shut into a coffin where he couldn't breathe.

Shaking his head, Lucas rubbed his eyes. *What's wrong with me? I have to get Torrin ready for school by myself today and then head to work.*

He waved his hand near the sensor to turn on the solar-powered light in Torrin's bedroom. "Come on, kid. Rise and shine."

Torrin began to stir.

"Get yourself ready, come have breakfast, and I'll drop you off."

They got dressed and ate.

Opening the door to the house, the flaming sunlight burst in like water breaking through a dam.

Lucas and Torrin ran to the electric car to escape the scorching winds. As they rushed toward the car, Torrin dropped one of his books.

"Go, go," said Lucas, motioning for Torrin to get into the car. Lucas reached down to pick up the book. It felt like a piece of hot iron. He pulled the book up by its pages, his fingertips burning just touching them. There were puddles of sunshine on the ground, the light blasting his eyes, blinding him.

Opening the car door, Lucas jumped into the front seat, then slammed the door shut and sighed, resting his hands on the dash. His eyes were watery and his chest heaving as he looked at Torrin. "Are you ok?" he asked.

Torrin nodded affirmatively. "Daddy, they're saying we won't have school soon. That we'll attend school virtually," he said, his voice cracking with worry.

"That might not be for a while," replied Lucas, still huffing, knowing it was going to happen sooner. This just couldn't go on, people running around, children scampering out of the sun, like the earth was on fire.

As a college professor, Lucas gave his lectures remotely. They could be recorded and cataloged. But kids needed socialization. His couldn't have been the last generation to socialize, make friends in school, play basketball on an outdoor court. *What will tomorrow's world be like? Will people be trapped in their homes, caged in their rooms?*

After school, later that day, Lucas picked up Torrin. They came home, did homework.

"Are all stars as powerful as our sun?" asked Torrin, after they finished.

"Our sun is a normal star. It's not what you would consider a powerful star. Though, of course, it is powerful."

"Will the sun exist forever?"

"No, the sun will one day implode, scientists say, pulling the planets apart when it does."

"When will that happen?"

"Not for millions of years," said Lucas. Though millions of years was far away, it still seemed final and dreadful.

"What will we do on the Earth when the sun explodes?"

"We don't have to worry about that now," replied Lucas, knowing that Torrin was asking the right questions.

"I want to be a climate scientist like Mom when I grow up," said Torrin.

"That's a good goal," said Lucas, moved by his son's earnestness. Only eight, and Torrin already showed great empathy for people, for the world.

"How long will I live?" asked Torrin, out of the blue.

Questions, always asking questions. "Well, normal lifespan is about a hundred years," answered Lucas. "How long do you want to live? Do you want to live forever?"

"I only want to live forever if you and Mommy are with me," said Torrin, innocently.

Lucas wiped the tear that welled in his eye.

That night, Lucas dreamed again about the alien. He didn't know what else to call it. The being's presence was comforting in the midst of his nightmares. Perhaps he was so addled from worry that his dreams became disturbed and turbulent. In his dream, the alien spoke to him, but the words were garbled and distorted, like you'd hear on a shortwave radio that was just out of reach.

"I can bring you here," said a light-blue vaporous form. It looked more like a wrinkle in the air than a being.

"But where are you?"

"I am far away; I want to help you, to help others, escape," it said, its voice like ribbons of notes.

"How will you help me, or us?"

"There is a way. There are paths opened."

"I don't know what that means," said Lucas.

"You will know," said the voice, and then the dream ended.

The next day, Lucas and Torrin watched the news on the video screen while eating breakfast in the kitchen nook. The screen showed images of gigantic glaciers melting in Greenland, their waters spilling into coastal cities, destroying everything in their wake. The video then zeroed in on the faces of some of the people. Because of the demolished houses, trees ripped down, and streets turned upside down, some people's faces ran with tears. One man spoke to a reporter, saying that the glaciers melting was God's way of punishing humanity for its greed. The man's eyebrows were tinged with frost.

Kate arrived back from Canada the next day, just as Lucas and Torrin were preparing to have dinner.

"We missed you so much," said Lucas, after embracing his wife. Torrin rushed to his mother, hugging her by the waist.

They all sat down together, Kate's knapsack and luggage still piled on the kitchen floor.

Lucas could tell by the look on her face not to discuss the details of the conference. It might be too unsettling for Torrin to hear. With the daily images from the news video and lessons at school, it was already too much.

"How was Canada?" asked Lucas, trying to focus on something positive.

"Canada was beautiful," said Kate. "The air was cooler and fresher in the Northern Rockies. We went on a number of excavations in the mountains, testing the soil and collecting tree samples," she added, as her bright blue eyes sparkled.

"How are they treating their American peers?" asked Lucas, knowing that there was growing tension between the United States and Canada and other international democracies. There had been an increasing number of American refugees fleeing to Canada. Some people even pleaded with the Canadian government to take their children, even if they couldn't stay in Canada. With climate change running amok in the United States, on top of an increasingly authoritarian government, the rest of the world had begun to look at the United States suspiciously.

"Well, they know that climate scientists certainly don't side with the current administration," said Kate. She asked Torrin, "What did you learn about in school these last few days, honey?"

"We've been learning about the sun, about climate change, about how big the universe is," said Torrin.

"Those are tall subjects for a little man," said Kate, smiling, now holding Torrin's chin in the cup of her hands.

"I want to be like you when I grow up, Mommy."

"That's so sweet, honey. You don't want to be like your dad?" asked Kate, now rolling her eyes at Lucas.

"I want to save the world, Mommy, like you."

"Daddy's saving the world in his way, honey."

That night, Lucas again dreamt about the alien. First the blue-ribboned form, then the garbled voice.

"You are back," said Lucas.

"Yes, I came for you."

"You came for me?"

"To take you to our world." Its voice whirred and whizzed,

the syllables sometimes separated in time, but sometimes doubling, like two voices speaking at once.

This was the first time the alien said the word "our."

"Where is your world?"

"It is very far away."

"How far away?"

"We are so far away; you could never fly to us in a machine of any kind."

"How long would it take us to get to you?"

"It would take sixty thousand years by conventional travel methods."

Suddenly, Lucas felt like he'd had this conversation before.

"Sixty thousand years by conventional methods?" asked Lucas.

"Remember, just like we had talked about before," said the alien.

"We've had this conversation?" asked Lucas.

Now, ignoring his question, the alien reached out his hand. "I need you to take my hand," said the alien.

"What will happen?"

"When you take my hand, I will pull you into my world. You see, this is how we travel. In dreams."

"I'm dreaming, that's right," said Lucas. He'd had a few lucid dreams before.

"Yes, you're dreaming. Remember how you used to say that you have to live your dreams."

"I used to say that to Torrin when he was a little boy."

Now a radio whir roared, as if from inside a gigantic subway station.

The alien held out his hand. Lucas reached toward the hand. Their touching set off a series of electrical sparks. Lucas found himself in a spinning tunnel; a cyclone of swirling color swarmed around him, rotating and turning. He held the alien's hand tightly. Whatever was happening, whether he was dreaming or not, he felt at peace. Somehow, the presence of this being seemed to fill his heart with love. It reminded him of how he felt holding his son's hand.

After tumbling, his body shuddered and pulled, he was set free, then floated gently, his body slowly descending to the ground, like a bird that landed. Lucas looked around at the sky in this world. It was magnificent. There were so many stars, but these stars seemed closer and brighter. There were gigantic swatches of color across the sky, like the yoke of the galaxy had oozed out of its membranous enclosure.

Now, looking down from the sky, he noticed that he was still holding the hand of the alien.

They looked into each other's eyes.

"You look just as I remembered," said the alien. Its voice was no longer travelling over great distances. It was right in front of him.

Lucas knew the face in front of him. "Who are you?" he asked, confused about who it was he was looking at.

"We travel through dreams to cover the expanse of space."

"I'm not sure I understand," said Lucas. "Am I dreaming? Is this real?"

"I am who you think I am," said the alien.

Lucas's eyes filled with water. They joined both hands now, gazing into each other's eyes.

"And now, we have to go get Mother," said the alien.

. . .

About the author: Mike Fiorito is an Associate Editor for *Mad Swirl Magazine* and a regular contributor to the *Red Hook Star Revue*. His latest book, *Falling from Trees* (Loyola University), was released in 2021. His other books are *Call Me Guido* (Ovunque Siamo Press), *Freud's Haberdashery Habits*, and *Hallucinating Huxley* (Alien Buddha Press).

He is currently working on a novel.

24

I Dream of Earth

by Rann Murray (United States)

Subgenres: Science fiction, young adult

Time Period: Near future (mid-twenty-first century)

Setting: Mars

Synopsis: Abby was too young to worry about the alien invasion until her family was forced to leave their home. Everything she depended on was torn away, and she had to grow up fast. In the years since the invasion, she discovered that the aliens weren't her enemy. Her true enemy came from within, and there was no guarantee she would be able to defeat it. Even if she and others like her could, it might not be enough to save a species hell-bent on its own extermination.

. . .

Me: gotta go
homework

Britt: not yet
need talk bout Ronny

Oh boy, here we go, I think. *Britt's current obsession when we're texting.*

Me: ok
let's hear all bout luv of yr-life

Britt: hes such a good kisser
he-is-so-hot

Me: true dat but I prefer fantasy to real deal

Britt: its time u dangled ur feetsies in water again

Me: no tanks
still getting over last 1

Britt: not like u dont have ur pick
entourage of guys follow u round between classes

Me: i know
just not ready

Britt: poor witless thang

Me: village idiot lol
gotta go
mr Siebert will b on my case big-time
if dont turn in paper friday

Britt: what horror he thought up this time?

Me: not too bad
going to chew chunk of time
bout what we remember of far peoples arrival
how affected our lives
what learned from it

Britt: far ppl
old nws eh

Me: 10 yrs now
mr siebert thnks was yesterday
lucky though

Britt: ru?

Me: when little
dad told me to keep journal bout all of it
thought waste of time but glad now
less work to wrt paper

Britt: i'll bet
gr8 dad
my dad thinks aliens worst thing ever
too bossy wrecked economy
blah blah

Me: dat crazy
economy better than ever out here
self-awares r better off

Britt: what?
they took everything we wanted away
self-awares just animals
cant compare humans 2 animals
cant treat same way as us

Me: u didnt just say that
theyre as important as us if not more so

Britt: there u go
little angel Abby
better than rest of us

Me: truth and u know it

Britt: not
just ur truth

Me: stop it
have 2 go
lu

Britt: bye
lu2

. . .

Hard to love her when she gets this way. It's like she hasn't learned a damn thing from the Far People. Not the first time my best friend Britt and I have argued about this. We don't see each other much anymore. She's a year behind me in school because I got promoted to a higher grade, which I hate. We were close friends before that and refuse to give each other up because of a stupid school admin thing.

That's a good thing, considering that I have zero friends in school. That's not all their fault. I'm pretty shy and don't feel comfortable around people.

But damn it, why does Britt have to talk like that? Maybe her dad's rants about the Far People are starting to have an effect. And there's no denying he has a lot of company. But it seems like she's moving to the dark side and becoming a parrot for the resistance movement—*The Far People are invaders, the Great Filter isn't real, they took away capitalism, freedom*, etc., etc.

But I've got to admit, my own dad isn't too far from that way of thinking. Sure, he doesn't think the Far People are invaders, but he is having a hard time giving up the lifestyle he was used to, like most adults. I've had a lot of talks with him about my feelings regarding the whole thing, but I only drew him partway to my side. He would say, "Why should we give up all that we've accomplished because some aliens want to do our thinking for us? It should be our decision about how we manage our own planet. Earth is ours, not theirs to do with as they wish."

He just doesn't get it, and Mom pretty much goes along with him.

Maybe Mr. Siebert's assignment came at a good time. I can get a few things off my chest and get my head on straight about all this.

I throw my cell on the bed and bury my face in my real best friend—my zebra pillow. The one that doesn't talk back and is never a smart ass.

Screw it. I'll deal with the paper tomorrow, or maybe never.

But I know better. Britt was right—I am a little angel. When I'm *supposed* to do certain things, I'll nag and torture myself until I give in and get them done. It's a curse.

I grab my journal on the nightstand, open it up, and start another entry.

I hear a noise downstairs.

"Is that you, Mom?"

"I said, dinner's ready."

"Oh, Mom, I'm in the middle of something; can't it wait?"

"You gave me that line yesterday. Hurry up, your food's getting cold."

"Oh, all right." *Perfect timing, as usual.*

I roll off the bed and take the stairs two-at-a-time. The sooner I get this over with, the sooner I can get back to my journal and homework.

. . .

Back in my room.

I take out the copies of Dad's journal entries he said I could use and give them a second read-through.

My dad's pretty smart. He teaches physics at New Western. He said, "Now Abigale..." He always calls me Abigale when he gets serious. "You can use my journal entries, but no plagiarizing. Paraphrasing is okay, though."

I told him, "No problem. Mr. Siebert said it all has to be in our own words." *Anything to make it more difficult.*

How to start this report? The Far People. We call them the Far People because their actual name is too hard to pronounce. No, that's lame. Best to start with some of Dad's stuff.

. . .

The Far People's Arrival and What I Learned
by Abigale Stewart

I'm sixteen now, but when I was much younger my dad, who kept a journal for most of his life, taught me to do the same, and I've been making regular entries ever since. I'm glad I have them, not just because of this class assignment, but also because it's a way for me to relive those early times in my life before the world turned upside down. To say we've all changed since then doesn't even come close to describing what happened.

They arrived in the fall without warning. Astronomers spotted an asteroid that displayed an anomalous (Dad's word) orbit indicating that its point of origin was outside the solar system. That was later confirmed, but what we couldn't see from such a vast distance was that the asteroid preceded a ship a fraction of its size. We assumed the asteroid was towing the ship but soon found out that it was being pushed by the ship using some kind of powerful force field. Later observations revealed the ship was as tall as a twenty-story building with a diameter close to a kilometer. Not so small after all. It had a strange warped, elongated shape like an egg stretched lengthwise. It was blueish white with no ports or markings on the surface. Scientists assumed the asteroid was used for mineral resources and/or fuel. In any case, it was obvious that their technology was centuries in advance of ours.

It was only one ship, so we assumed the beings piloting it were emissaries, here to greet us in peace. And for the most part, they were, except for a few conditions that were completely unexpected and didn't sit too well with a lot of people.

Soon after taking up position at Lagrange Point 1, between the Earth and Moon, a port opened in the egg, and smaller ships emerged. From that point on, it was pretty scary, because they came in so fast we couldn't even track them. Next thing we knew, they started landing in open areas such as parks and stadiums in major cities.

They began communicating with us over PC monitors and TVs across the world, in all our languages, like something out of a sci-fi movie. I was five at the time so had only a limited understanding of what was going on.

When the aliens announced they were here in peace and wanted to offer their help, people started to calm down. Things remained that way until the Far People's next communication. They said they were prepared to offer their assistance to help reverse humanity's impending mass extinction due to climate change and the rapid depletion of planetary resources. Left unchecked, the Earth would soon become completely uninhabitable for all life forms.

Our response was immediate and furious. "We don't need your help. We didn't ask for it. We're managing our planet quite well, thank you." This came from heads of governments, political groups, and corporations who felt threatened and didn't want any radical changes to the status quo. But that was just the start of the troubled times.

Some people still thought it was an

invasion, but my dad said the aliens had given no such indication in any of their communications. He said invading forces don't have such an intense, friendly back-and-forth dialog with those they intend to conquer.

But of course, some countries cordoned off the ships and surrounded them with military hardware. A few attempted to fire at the ships but soon found that the Far People had managed to nullify the weapons in their vicinity. As soon as an explosive shell made contact with one of their ships, it would shatter into a mist of fine particles that fell harmlessly to the ground. There was no retaliation from the Far People. No need, really.

After things settled down, some of the Far People exited their ships. We were shocked by their appearance. They were every bit as strange looking as anything seen in the old pulp monster magazines. Large bulbous heads sat atop even larger collars that flared out on either side like great leaves on an exotic flower. When they left the ramp of their ship, their heads expanded to an even larger size, and they glided along in midair as they approached the human delegations they requested we assemble.

Later, we discovered that what we'd thought was their head was merely their method of conveyance and contained a lighter-than-air gaseous substance. We speculated that their brains resided within the collar's flowery twin leaves. The rest of their bodies trailed off below in a series of tightly bundled tentacles. At intervals, they would float toward open ground and plant their tentacles in the soil. This peculiar activity led some to conjecture that they were half-plant, half-animal, and the tentacles were a root system used to obtain nourishment from the soil. That explained what the asteroid was for. The Far People were most likely using the asteroid for food! Its regolith must contain the right mixture of specific minerals their bodies required for sustenance.

They didn't seem to have an external breathing apparatus, so either they had no difficulty breathing our atmosphere, or the apparatus was hidden internally. The only thing they had in common with us was bilateral symmetry. The closest comparison we could come up with was an octopus, but even that wasn't an adequate parallel.

Communication with them was an odd, unnerving experience. Unlike their earlier appearance on TV, they never uttered a sound but had no difficulty communicating their ideas and words to us. When they spoke, it was as if our minds had initiated an internal dialog of our own, and it took some time before we realized what was happening. They were using a subtle form of telepathy that employed our own unique life experiences to convey their intent and meaning. That capability alone eliminated all language barriers. How they achieved this feat with no apparent limitation on the number of people they could communicate with at one time was a complete mystery.

In turn, we learned to communicate with them by either thinking the spoken word or using sub-vocal speech. An astonishing method of communication, but we quickly adapted.

. . .

Not long after the Far People's arrival, my parents were excited about what they called The Offer. They talked about it in hushed conversation as if it were something they had waited for their whole lives.

That excitement only lasted for a short time, then they seemed very sad, as if they had lost something or someone important to them. I couldn't tell what was wrong, and they wouldn't discuss it with me. They would only say, "Don't worry honey, everything will be fine." Then they would bring home a new toy just to keep me distracted.

But things weren't fine. I could hear them downstairs from my bedroom talking in low, worried tones. Sometimes I would get out of bed and quietly sit on the stairs, high enough up so they couldn't see me but close enough to catch most of what they said.

Mom, "My God, we really blew it. They were here to educate us, to get us to the point where we weren't throwing the planet away. It shouldn't have been that hard to comprehend. But we looked at them as if they were an abomination."

Dad, "Well, what did you expect? We see the worst, get paranoid, we fight, that's who we are. Men with guns. Isn't that inevitably our go-to solution for everything? Maybe they're asking too much of us."

Mom, "Too much? They're not asking enough, as far as I'm concerned. All we had to do was come to an agreement on one idea, significant enough to change the self-destructive path we're on. Just one single idea."

Dad, "That's exactly what I mean. We can't do it because we want too much. We've become a species of greed. A long time ago, we lost sight of what our real priorities should be. It may be too late for us to change. But look—let's give it more time. Maybe things will get better."

Sometimes I'd hear Mom crying and Dad trying to console her. I got less sleep and started having stomach aches. Things didn't get better; they got a lot worse.

The majority of the world's people didn't want to give up what they thought was a perfectly reasonable lifestyle just to meet the needs of other lifeforms on Earth whom they considered inferior and not worth saving. The Far People had no business dictating their moral imperatives to us as if we were the inferior ones.

Protests broke out at all the Far People's ships. Troops and weapons mobilized around the ships. In some locations, terrorists made futile attempts at setting off explosives.

Political factions formed on each side—pro-Far People and against, pro-species preservation and against. Religious sects began to form, most of which claimed the Far People were more sinister than they seemed and were forerunners of the end times. Some foretold dates when the world would end. Numerous countries were forced to declare martial law. In many areas of the US, the National Guard was called out to control rioting, and curfews were set.

Several countries looked at the situation as an opportunity for preemptive strikes against their enemies. Iran sponsored missile attacks against Israel. The US intervened, sending warships off the coast of Iran and support troops into Israel. They soon found themselves in air-to-air battles with the new Russian unmanned Su-57s. Russia invaded Ukraine again and Latvia. Too much was happening for anyone to stop them. Troops began massing along borders. All-out world war was imminent.

Suddenly, the entire world stood still. The lights went out everywhere, all power gone. It wasn't just the power plants that no longer functioned—cars wouldn't run, aircraft wouldn't fly, trains, computers, factories, schools, everything went down. The Far People issued warnings, but some ignored them. Planes fell out of the sky, for the most part military planes and Predator drones. Many died. Worldwide, economies ground to a halt. All military activity ceased.

The Far People certainly got our attention. And, although all this chaos added to the furor against them, we had no choice but to listen.

They told us they had been observing us for some time, and not just us, but also other species that had gotten to a similar point in their evolution. The Great Filter, which humans theorized is a massive and common challenge that ends alien life before it becomes intelligent enough and widespread enough for us to see, is highly accurate. In fact, self-annihilation through war or disregard for limited planetary resources are the primary reasons intelligent lifeforms are rare within our local group of galaxies that the Far People have managed to survey.

"You are a young species," they said, "with only two hundred generations of recorded history. What a shame for it to end now, so soon, when you have just begun."

The Far People view the loss of any

intelligent civilization as a calamitous event. The problem is so prevalent that there is a very real danger intelligent organic species could die out altogether, leaving robotic AI's to inherit the universe. They said intelligent species' diversity must be maintained at all costs.

They warned us that if the human species continues its current unsustainable practices, it is inevitable that they will die out in a short period of time.

But not everyone was convinced that our demise was imminent. In fact, all of this just spurred most of us on to form an underground resistance movement. Even if their technology is vastly superior to ours, they reasoned, we might be able to resist them long enough to learn more about their technology, to defend ourselves against them or, given enough time, they will tire of trying to intervene and leave us to ourselves.

A few governments and private enterprises talked of migrating from Earth to form colonies in the asteroid belt, or perhaps joining and expanding the small colonies on the Moon and Mars.

The resistance to and denial of what the Far People were saying was very strong and eventually convinced the Far People that perhaps their efforts with humans were futile. We were just too entrenched and seduced by our current economic prosperity to see the reality of our own self-destructiveness.

So, the Far People decided to change course and try a different approach.

. . .

Several months later, I noticed a change in my parents—in the way they looked at me, the way they behaved around me. I thought maybe I'd done something wrong and might get punished. I finally worked up the courage to ask what I did wrong.

Mom, "Not a darn thing, Sweetie. But this would be a good time for a talk." Mom turned to Dad.

Dad, "Abby, do you remember when we talked about the people who came to visit us a while back?"

"Yes, Daddy, I remember. They're the people from really far away. You said from so far that you can't even imagine it."

"That's right, Abby. That's why we call them the Far People. They came to see us because they thought we needed their help."

"What kind of help?"

"They told us they've been observing us for quite some time, and not just us but a few other people from far away who don't look like us but are smart like we are. The ship that's between Earth and the Moon is one of many they've sent out to warn us and other intelligent beings that we are all in serious trouble. Someday soon we might... I'm not sure how to put this..."

Mom cut in, "We might not be able to live on Earth much longer if we don't change how we do things. Do you understand what we're saying, Sweetheart?"

"Yes, I think so."

Dad gave Mom a look of thanks and continued, "Anyway, they said the number of intelligent beings spanning the galaxies they've surveyed is at a dangerously low level. There are so few like us that if we humans were all to go away, it would be a terrible loss. That's why it's so important to make sure we're protected, and a certain level of species diversity is maintained. We have to make sure all intelligent beings don't completely die out."

Mom, "Do you understand what diversity means?"

"Sure, it means different kinds. Like all the different kinds of smart people."

Dad looked pleased, "That's my girl. So, that's why they made the trip to see us. Now, this may be a lot to take in all at once, Abigale. Just let us know if you have any questions. Promise?"

"Promise, Daddy."

"The Far People asked us to bring representatives of all the people in the world together for a big meeting to decide what things we need to do to survive. They don't want to decide for us, because we might not have the will to follow through on ideas that aren't our own. Whatever we settle on, they promised to help us see it through."

"Did we have the big meeting?"

"Yes, we did, Abigale. We all tried really hard to agree on what our most important needs were. But I'm afraid we didn't succeed. There were protests, some representatives felt they didn't get a fair hearing, fights broke out. Lots of ideas were proposed, but we weren't able to agree on a single thing.

"A lot of people thought the idea of there being so few intelligent species in our galactic group was just an excuse for them to take over our planet. Most people weren't ready to give up all the things they felt entitled to.

"A minority were in complete agreement with what the Far People wanted to do and thought we should bring the Earth back to a pristine condition to halt species extinction, but they were shouted down by everyone else. We came to blows, and things got out of hand.

"After that, the Far People decided that the adults weren't up to the task of reaching a decision. The world's leaders strongly objected, but we knew there wasn't much we could do against that kind of power. If we tried to resist them, they'd just shut everything down again."

Mom, "And that's where you come in, Abigale. It turns out all you kids have become pretty important,"

"Me?"

Mom, "That's right. Since all the adults couldn't agree, the Far People decided that you and all the world's children have to decide what's best for all of us."

"I can't do that. I wouldn't know what to say."

Dad, "We tried to talk them out of it, Abby, but they wouldn't listen. And I have to admit, we adults had our chance and failed. When they explained what they intended wouldn't cause any physical or psychological harm, it put us more at ease with the idea."

"But what should I tell them?" I asked.

Dad, "That's the one thing I can't tell you, Abby. It's nothing to worry about. You're pretty smart, you know. And you'll have lots of company. The Far People said they have the means to explain it all to you, so you won't have any problem at all understanding."

Mom, "That's right, and it turns out the Far People won't be talking to just the children. They've decided to poll other species on Earth who the Far People call the Self-Awares. They said all the Self-Awares must be included, because they are at just as great a risk as humans. They will be given equal weight in the decision-making process. As impossible as it sounds, they said the Self-Awares will understand what is being asked of them as effectively as the children, because of the Far Peoples' telepathic ability. So, believe me, you won't be alone."

"Who else are they going to ask?"

Dad, "That's a good question, Abby. I think once we find out, you'll be pleased."

My dad is so smart, he always knows how to calm me down.

Dad, "We're not sure exactly who they're going to ask, but people have come up with pretty good guesses. Self-awareness isn't something only humans possess. It's just a matter of degree. Can you think of any creatures that are Self-Awares?"

"Maybe a... You know what? We learned in class the other day that dolphins are pretty smart. Mrs. Fletcher said they've learned some of our languages and can talk to us."

Dad, "That's a great guess, Abby. In fact, dolphins are on the list of the top four of the beings the Far People may talk to. Whales, chimps, and elephants are the other three. I know there are numerous others, but I can't be positive about who they'll choose. I think man's view of other species is often too limited, and we don't recognize how much intelligence is right under our noses."

"When are they going to talk to us?"

Mom, "It might be quite soon. In fact, it may be while you're asleep, because they said that would be the easiest time for you to understand them. They'll communicate with everyone based on their own unique experiences, so that understanding will be universal for all the Self-Awares. It will be like a dream, but when you wake up, you should remember everything."

"That doesn't sound so bad. It may not be as scary as I thought."

Dad, "That's my girl, I'm sure you're right. Nothing to worry about at all."

Mom and Dad gave each other a quick look. I wasn't sure how to read what they were thinking, but neither of them smiled.

A few days later, I was playing on the front porch, and I could hear Mom and Dad talking in the kitchen.

Mom, "My God, I hope we're doing the right thing. If any harm comes to her... This is a nightmare. We're supposed to accept that they're going to use our children as stand-ins to accomplish what we couldn't. It's asking too much of them."

Dad, "We only have ourselves to blame."

Mom, "That may be true, but this is pure insanity. The children, dolphins, whales... tell me this isn't happening."

Dad, "They haven't given me a reason to believe they would harm anyone. I can't imagine them hurting the children. I mean, look at what they've accomplished already. We were like a race of automatons, completely unaware of our perilous, unrelenting decline into oblivion. And for the first time in recorded history, there's no fighting taking place anywhere on the planet. I never thought I'd see that in my lifetime."

Mom, "I hope you're right. Oh hell, you probably are. Anything else doesn't make sense. They wouldn't hurt innocents. What would be the point?"

I didn't tell them I overheard. I just figured it would be like taking a test at school, and I did pretty well on those. Looking back, I was glad I was so naive and didn't fully understand the impact my decisions would have on the world. Otherwise, I might have panicked.

. . .

The poll began, of all the children, of all the other Self-Awares on Earth who could contribute to articulating a new direction for us all.

That night in bed, I dreamt as I never had before. I was conscious enough to know I was dreaming, and I wasn't afraid. It was just as Mom said. The Far People explained everything to me in a way I had no problem understanding. I grasped the pressing nature of our planetary crisis and knew what was required of me. I knew what I had to do.

When I expressed an idea about what I thought was needed, its implications and consequences for the world were available to me. Don't get me wrong, it was the hardest thing I've ever done, but the Far People helped me every step of the way. They talked to the good stuff inside me. They offered encouragement and told me there were no wrong decisions and to do the best I could. If my heart felt it was right, then it was right. And that was that.

Throughout the whole process, I was somehow aware of what everybody else wanted at the same time. I mean, not just all the other children but also all the Self-Awares. That sounds crazy, but it actually happened. I was absorbing everything being said but in a way that didn't interfere with my thinking. When I was done, I knew without a doubt that my final decision was mine alone. No one told me what to say.

I awoke to Mom and Dad sitting on my bed with sad expressions. I told them I was okay and not to worry, but that wasn't what they were upset about. While I was sleeping, all the adults in the world were sleeping too, only they were having a different experience. I guess this was so they might be more receptive to our final decision.

Mom and Dad told me they had been up since the middle of the night and couldn't get back to sleep. While they were sleeping, the Far People showed them episode after episode of what humanity's destructive ways had done to species across the planet. People started calling them mind-movies. They were so realistic;

it was like you were watching them happen in real-time as the suffering played out. They were so upsetting, Mom and Dad couldn't talk about it until much later.

I found out later that Dad saw a mother blue whale swimming in one of the ocean's human-induced dead zones whose baby died after only a week. She carried her dead baby on her back for several weeks, refusing to let it go. She finally let it slip into the water, then let out a long moan as her child sank into the deep. It was at that moment Dad realized how profound the mother whale's mourning for her dead child was.

Mom experienced something similar when she saw a starving polar bear give up its struggle. The bear lifted her head and let out a great, mournful, high-pitched wail before keeling over into the ocean and sinking, with no effort to save herself. Mom said its sorrowful look of defeat as it descended to the bottom was something she will take to her grave.

The mind-movies continued to play out across the world. It's difficult to realize the impact of your actions until you witness them firsthand, and the mind-movies helped to close that gap. Some adults awoke sobbing; some were in shock over what we all had done; some kept repeating, "We didn't know, we didn't know!" Of course, some were in denial and refused to accept responsibility. They said that it's just a phase we're going through. That we'll mature as time goes by. A complete denial of the Far People's singular message—"You are running out of time."

. . .

My parents asked if I knew what all the other children had agreed on, and I said, "Sure. We decided all life on Earth must be healthy and have the chance to be happy, to grow and evolve in their own separate ways and in their own time."

"That's it?" they asked.

"That's it, that's what we want."

"Wow!" they said. Then they asked, "Nothing else?"

I explained it to them the best way a five-year-old could. "People aren't the best. Life is the best. Fishes should swim in clean water. Trees should grow and get really big. The air should be clean for the birds and all of us, and the sky should be blue and not dirty so we can see forever. The land should be green. We should all be less greedy and make what we need, not always what we want. We should clean up after ourselves. When one of us gets sick, we should all help them get better. When someone is hungry, we should feed them."

"And what about the Self-Awares, what did they want?"

"They wanted something different," was all I managed to say.

My parents were puzzled as to why I wouldn't tell them. I just couldn't right then. It would be so disappointing to them, plus I didn't know what was going to happen because of the poll. The Far People would decide that.

. . .

I'm not that little girl anymore. I'm sixteen, and the world is a different place than it was eleven years ago.

As we left on one of the colony ships bound for Mars, I'll never forget looking out a window at the crystal blue Earth, half shadowed with pillowy white clouds, the brown continent of Africa and part of Europe clearly visible. When I shifted my gaze to the horizon, I was amazed at the thin blue line of atmosphere which was all that shielded us from the vacuum of space. In a few brief moments, the Earth and Moon were nothing more than small dots that I could cover with the palm of one hand. That's the last I saw of Earth, and I miss it terribly.

My parents chose for our family to go to Mars because they thought it would provide the most flexibility for the new life they envisioned for themselves. And of course, my dad was all about the science and what he could learn there.

Most people from Earth chose to settle on one of the other planets like Mars and Venus, which the Far People are terraforming with their robotic machines and nanotechnology, which are very good at using available on-site resources. Some chose the moons of the largest planets, but the Far People refused to let us settle on Europa, Enceladus, or even our own Moon, preferring to keep us far away from Earth.

Maybe someday in the distant future when we've matured to the point where we aren't so self-destructive, we can perhaps return to Earth. But I'm sure it won't be in my lifetime.

. . .

I was inconsolable when I found out about the Self-Awares' solution to Earth's problem. But I was young then and had no knowledge of the real damage we were doing to other species. Now that I'm older, I understand the Self-Awares' choice. They had no other. The Far People knew this was the only way we as a species could come to recognize our limitations, allowing us to move beyond them.

Some minds are changing, though, in part due to the aliens allowing us access to their archives, which consist of descriptions and visual records of extinct species whose problems were very similar to our own. We watched the end of inhabited worlds. A few of them have been extinct for only a few centuries. When you see who they were, and how they lived, their cities, as they existed a short time before their extinction, you begin to experience the full crushing impact of what they brought upon themselves. Only a few of them resembled us, but they seemed just as knowledgeable about their world and the greater universe as we were before the Far People came. All that remains of them are a few digital images, texts of who they once were, and DNA samples which the Far People keep in closely guarded DNA banks.

It is difficult to come to terms with the fact that a once robust, thriving civilization could do the unspeakable. But they were all dead, every single one, a loss beyond calculation. In the cases where a few beings remained alive, it was painfully obvious that their lives would be cut short from the destructive paths they had chosen. Many are starting to realize how easily we humans could have entered those archives, never to be heard from again, without the Far People's intervention.

. . .

It is undeniable that the Far People were, as many of us feared, a conquering force that overtook our planet and radically changed our lives. But it's also true they don't typify our xenophobic dread of how a conquering force behaves. They helped us establish ourselves throughout the solar system and left the Earth alone to regenerate. This allowed the remaining intelligent life to grow and evolve, free from humanity's blind, unrestrained pursuit of Earth's resources. So, who are the Far People—our vanquishers or liberators? Perhaps a question only future generations of humanity can answer.

More of us are learning from the Far People, and we've changed for the better. But for most of us, the mind-movies weren't enough for us to reach an understanding of how our actions were affecting all life around us. Or we just didn't care enough to make a change.

I think all the children's hearts were in the right place, but the truth is, despite all our best ideas to save our planet, we wouldn't be able to give up all the things we "wanted." Even we wouldn't be able to make the full psychological transition required to repair the damage done by our parents. After their interaction with the children during the poll, the Far People knew this to be true, which is why they decided to only consider the Self-Awares' input, and not ours.

The Self-Awares were of a single mind about what they wanted and what they felt would be best for all concerned. When the poll was taken, all but a small minority felt the Earth would benefit the most from one single act. Banish all humans.

. . .

I am the last one to read my report to the class. After I finish, Mr. Siebert gets up, walks out of the room, and stands in the hallway for a few moments. When he comes back in, he clears his throat a lot on the way to his desk and says I did a great job and that I can sit down. His eyes look a little red. Mr. Siebert sometimes gets emotional, which is one of the reasons I like him so much. We need a lot more adults like Mr. Siebert. I hope when I grow up, I become one of them.

Our emigration from Earth was prolonged and difficult, but the Far People paid no heed to our protests and attempts at defiance. We had no choice but to accede to their demands.

They were not unkind and provided us with the necessary knowledge and technology to prepare to live on planetary, moon, and asteroid belt environments. We were allowed to take our family pets, although a surprising number of pets communicated to the Far People their decision not to accompany their owners. They chose instead to live out their lives on Earth among their own kind, under the Far People's protective umbrella.

When humanity's agonizing process of education began, I was too young to be a part of the human problem. And now that I'm older, maybe I can become part of the solution. If I fight hard enough to turn away from the endless, destructive urge to accumulate the next elusive object of desire, I might become someone who learns to save life and not destroy it. Maybe I can redefine what *need* means to me and become a person who is more harmonious with life, not apart from it. Where my need is equal to life, not above it.

Is that even possible? Mr. Siebert thinks so. He always says *want* and *need* do not mean the same thing, although we have come to believe they do. He says, "If you hope to lead a happy life, always try to focus on what you need, not continually on what you want." I hope he's right. I have to try, because if I don't, I'll repeat the same self-destructive mistakes we humans have always made.

Even if I'm successful in putting my ideas into practice, it won't be enough. I'm determined to seek out others who are like-minded and willing to change. Maybe together we can make a difference. We haven't run out of time. Not yet. But if we don't find a way, we are just as capable of annihilating ourselves out here in the solar system as we were back on Earth. And this time, the Far People may not be around to help us. This could be our final chance.

. . .

Many years have passed since we transitioned to our new home near the south pole of Mars. Even though I've spent most of my life here, it's hard for me to accept the idea of being a Martian and no longer an Earthling. I didn't have much choice in the matter. But I do have a choice about who I become in this new home.

I look around me and see that the initial shock of the abrupt changes we endured has begun to wear off. I'm concerned that we seem to be drifting into old patterns, old ways of thinking. I've found others who share my ideas, who recognize that the need for change is more urgent than ever before. But we are still a minority, just as we were back on Earth. We have to find a way of convincing the majority that they are headed down an old, ruinous path. How do we persuade them the old ways don't work? That there is no longer a maybe, a someday? If we don't begin now, begin here, there may be no tomorrow. We are beginning to think that the only way we're going to convince them is to join them. We must put ourselves in positions of corporate and governmental authority. Quite a tall order, and we will most likely lose some of our group along the way, but enough might be left to bring about real change. Change that will divert us away from the precipice of extinction we feel so compelled to embrace.

Out here among the planets, moons, and asteroids we've come to call home, we live a circumscribed existence, even with all the new tech provided by the Far People. Our living quarters on Mars are confining and *outside* consists of central domed courtyards. Once the terraforming takes hold, things will begin to resemble what we had before the mass emigration. And yet, I know even then it will never be the same. I miss all the things I had taken for granted—the sound of waves breaking on Lake Michigan's shore, the smell of a storm coming in, watching silent heat lightning on a warm summer night, the scent of flowers. And the Moon. I think I miss the Moon most of all.

With all the changes we've had to endure, I don't sleep as soundly as I used to. But in the stillness of the Martian dawn, I often manage to drift off for a while. And when I dream, I dream of Earth.

. . .

About the Author:

As a kid, Rann Murray's parents signed him up for a subscription to the Science Fiction Book Club, then they bought him a Robert the Robot toy with a fancy control module, then a telescope. So how could a spoiled brat like that not end up writing science fiction? His background as a computer store owner, astrophotographer, and a lifelong interest in anything to do with science sprang from those early days. Rann graduated from Michigan State University and still lives in the Great Lake State with his wife and three spoiled brat cats. Rann's short stories have appeared in *Bewildering Stories* and *Small Town Anthology*.

Part Five:

The Late Twenty-First Century (2061 to 2100 AD)

25

Es Geht zu Ende

by Thomas Wm. Hamilton (United States)

Subgenres: Cli-fi, flash fiction

Time Period: Mid- to late twenty-first century

Setting: New York City, United States of America

Synopsis: The NYPD break up an environmental protest in a waterlogged Manhattan.

. . .

The gentle waves broke enticingly on what had been New York City's Twenty-Third Street. The protestors gathered along the shoreline, those with signs preparing to hoist, wave, carry or just show them. Police hung back, snorkels, gas masks, truncheons, tasers, shields, guns, and spearguns ready for whatever the crazies might be planning. Both sides had bullhorns.

The protest leader used hers first. "Ladies, gentlemen, citizens, visitors. Once again today we see the consequences of decades of failure to respond to human-induced climate change. All of Manhattan south of Fourteenth Street is now underwater, losing us Wall Street <*cheers and shaking signs*>, Greenwich Village <*boos and catcalls*>, and parts of the East Village and Chelsea <*slightly less enthused boos*>. We ask, when will the government or the mega-corporations act to end this gradual loss of our land? Will we someday change the words of Woody Guthrie's song to 'from California to Albany Island'? We demand action."

At the word "action" the police commander raised his bullhorn. "This is now declared a disorderly and illegal gathering. You will disperse forthwith or face arrest and prosecution."

The crowd booed and heckled. None made any move to disperse. A young man near the police shouted "Your homes are threatened, too. Join us."

A cop near him snarled, "If you don't like it here, why don't you go back where you came from?"

"Members of my family emigrated here from at least six different countries. Would you chop me up so a part could go to each?"

"Gladly, you commie bastard."

The police commander used his bullhorn again. "I will count down from thirty. At zero, any not at least beginning to leave will be arrested."

The sole surviving newspaper reported the next day seven protestors died from drowning as they tried to flee, eighteen injured, fifty-two arrested. It quoted the Police Commissioner as promising "stronger crackdowns on troublemakers and dissidents who try to mislead the public discourse by claiming non-existent things like climate change."

. . .

About the author:

Hamilton is the author of six books of science fiction, fantasy, and horror, as well as six books in the astronomy field, which he taught for thirty-four years. He's working on a new SF novel and on the third edition of a book on the moons of the Solar System.

26

The Highs and Lows of Barefoot Pleasure

by Taria Karillion (England, UK)

Subgenres: Science fiction, young adult

Time Period: Mid- to late twenty-first century

Setting: Japan

Synopsis: The ecological viewpoints of a group of young adults compared with the world their ancestors knew. This story is soon to be a short film, "The Highs and Lows of Barefoot Pleasure," filmed on location in 2023 by Sara Jahan Films. For details about the film, see its IMDb entry at https://www.imdb.com/title/tt23838652/.

. . .

"Don't it always seem to go, that you don't know what you've got 'til it's gone."

~Joni Mitchell

A sudden gust whooshed along the crowded platform, and a long, white flash streaked to a hissing stop. A young group of friends spilled out of the arriving bullet train, laughing and stretching as best they could amid the undulating sea of limbs and faces. Each took deep breaths of the dry, dusty air before taking selfies by the '*Square Delight Station*' sign, then donned dark glasses and paper dust masks. Looming around them, countless towering huddles of high-rise buildings gleamed in the shimmering heat of the city.

One of the group, a girl with a birthday kanji painted on her dust mask in sparkly, pink strokes, suddenly span around, pointing and gasping. "OMG! Look! A *bee*! How did that get out of the wildlife sanctuary?!"

A surly-browed boy stared at it for a moment then took a puff from the bamboo inhaler on the lanyard round his neck. "I blame Ryo—he was stationed there last month, wasn't he? And speaking of our conscripted friend, where *is* he? He said he'd meet us here! Don't tell me he ran out of travel rations again!"

The birthday girl frowned. "No, he's—"

"Still at sea? What happened to the day's leave he promised you after his Plastic Trawling tour? Some boyfriend! Fumiko, you deserve better!"

"It's not like that, Haruto! It's just the weather—the minute he landed, the Coastal Defense Corps moved him straight to Flood Management. It's not his fault!" She stared at him, and then at her feet, fidgeting with the string on her own inhaler.

One of the girls scowled at the boy, then tugged at Fumiko's sleeve. "Look! Look! I can see the end of the queue from here! Come on, come *on*!"

They all turned and squinted at the human snake disappearing over the distant hilltop.

"Why rush?" Haruto shrugged. "We'll be in it for hours anyway."

"I know, I've just been looking forward to today for *so* long." Fumiko smiled, regardless.

"At least *you* lot get paid holiday leave, you lucky *akuto*" he grumbled. "We can't all work at Brainbox Central; we desalination workers are treated like *unko*! Sometimes I hate conscription."

"Aww, don't be bitter, Haruto!" one of the girls chided. "It's only a year, and it's for the good of the planet. And Fumiko really slogged to get that hydroponics job. And it's her twenty-first! *And* we haven't seen each other since graduation! So, let's just enjoy the day, ok?"

"Sorry, Fumiko," Haruto mumbled.

The birthday girl nodded and pulled on a sunhat. "It's ok, it's just nerves talking. When my father came here for *his* twenty-first, he was so nervous he was sick in the queue!"

Haruto nodded. "Well, I did the Hisakata Tower Observation Deck with my father's cousin last year—the 350th floor. There were tethers and oxygen masks and everything, but *this*—this is more unnerving. The unknown, the once-in-a-lifetime experience, y'know? So yeah, I may just up-chuck a little too, I warn you now."

Fumiko gave a tiny squeal, shaking her head. "Shh! Don't even joke about it! They'll arrest you if you do! Do you *know* how many Yen per square foot the Square is worth?"

One of the boys lifted a finger. "Wait, *wait!* Haruto's father has a *cousin?!* How was *that* allowed?!"

"It's coz' my uncle is seriously old," Haruto shrugged. "Born before the '35 Sole Child Law."

"Wow... I can't get my head around that..." The other boy gave a low whistle, then pointed. "*Woah*, Fumiko, don't trip over the sign there! Unghh... Does that say *two hours* to the weighbridge? *Please* tell me you all remembered to put your swimming costumes on under your clothes. And everyone brought enough water to pay with? I hope you didn't bring that black-market water, H.—that stuff is just naaaasty! You won't get away with it, you know—I've heard they're more anal about it than my mother on Deep Dusting Day!"

The queue slowly slithered its way up over the scrubby, bare hill and down into a broad, bowl-shaped dip with a small marquee at its center. The clean, white canvas stood out against the stark, bare landscape: barren and brown, save for the black, ashen remains of summer wildfires. It was nothing at all like the old photo in her grandmother's album of the 'Park'—lush, green slopes dotted with blossoming cherry trees. She dismissed the thought of taking a photo herself—no point in making Jiji cry.

After an hour of shuffling, fanning, coughing, and chattering, the group reached another sign. Its big, black letters declared,

> **Weighbridge checkpoint.**
> **Wait time from here: 1 hour.**
> **Place all belongings, shoes, and clothing in baskets provided. Collect baskets from second weighbridge after your visit. Removal of any part of the attraction will be prosecuted to the full extent of the law.**

None of them spoke for a whole minute, then Fumiko bit her lip and leaned close to one of the other girls. "I've heard—" she paused, whispering, "that it can make you... y'know... 'excited'?"

Her friend blushed, but grinned and whispered back. "It's ok—it may be a legal high of sorts, but I read that it's *soundproof*—like old public toilets used to be. And," she giggled, "we all clubbed together for you to have a solo session, so feel free!"

Fumiko gasped, her widening eyes tearing up a little. "Ohhh, you are such good friends! *Domo arigato*! Thank you!"

The girl hugged her, then produced a thin tube from her

pocket. "Don't hyperventilate, you'll set off your asthma! Here, use this lip balm—you don't want cracked lips spoiling your birthday. And calm your breathing before you get a dry mouth—I doubt any of us can afford to buy more water rations."

Before long, they reached another sign:

> **Payment checkpoint.**
> **Wait time from here: 10 minutes.**
> **Entry fee: One liter of filtered water per person. Please enjoy the Square Delight responsibly and respectfully.**

One by one, each person in the group carefully poured a pouch of water into the silver collecting funnel, producing a delicate, musical 'ting' from a clacking turnstile. Finally, they all stood, silently smiling, beside the entrance to the Square Delight.

One of the girls clasped Fumiko's hands in her own and whispered, "Here we go! We've got a group pass—you ok waiting for your turn on your own?"

Fumiko nodded and waved them off, then clutched her stomach as a gloved guard approached and directed her inside to a cubicle.

The clothing check-in, the staff tugging her bangs to check for a wig, the silent frisking, and even the embarrassment of the x-ray cavity scan all passed in a blur, save for the incongruously cheery music that played while she was obliged to pee. Fumiko distracted herself by wondering how many people had ever tried to smuggle out pieces of the Square.

Her daydream was abruptly interrupted by a faint rumbling. But there was no familiar wail of tremor sirens. Then she laughed aloud as she realized that it was her own body trembling.

Feeling self-conscious in her too-small swimsuit, Fumiko followed the guard, who was pointing her toward a final screen. This was it.

And finally, there before her, barely bigger than her tiny dorm apartment and guarded by four solemn, gloved staff, was a perfect, *perfect* square of lush, green turf, its long, slim blades trembling in the temperature-controlled breeze. Her skin rose into goosebumps, and Fumiko realized she was holding her breath. Never had she seen anything so beautiful—it was the exact same shade as the tiny Daruma wish dolls that her grandmother bought her every year and more vibrant than her mother's heirloom, emerald kimono.

As she stood staring, the guards withdrew, but not before pointing at the CCTV cameras at every corner of the spotless tent walls.

The slender shoots swayed and waved, seeming to beckon her closer, and Fumiko stepped forward in a lightheaded moment of longing that defied a lifetime of restraint.

As she stepped onto the Square, the soft, moist grass tickled the skin between her bare toes, making her blush, and she pressed her fingers to her chest. Her heart was fluttering as wildly as it had during her very first private moments with Ryo.

She bit her lip and crouched, running her hands over the feathery fronds, then knelt and inhaled deeply. The scent washed over her like the air before a summer storm—almost like the hydroponics trays, but far earthier. Leaves, rain, mud, dirt, her grandfather's pottery, and real soybeans from the ground, when she was very young. The wafting movements felt like the turf itself was breathing, panting, hungrily, lustily, desiring contact, drawing her down. She surrendered in an instant, stretching out her limbs into a tumbling, rolling, gasping sprawl, giddy with delight and groaning in sheer pleasure at the feel of a thousand tiny, damp fingers caressing her nearly bare skin. Hearing her own voice echoing back at her, Fumiko clapped her hand over her mouth, then remembered the soundproofing and giggled aloud, sighing and relishing the saturation of her senses, until it seemed only moments later, a pinging sounded the end of her five precious minutes.

A tide of dismay engulfed her, and only the returning guards made her jump to her feet. Bowing to the guard at the exit, she whispered, "Thank you. I'm so glad I could do this. Such a shame that there are so few."

The guard nodded politely, then pointed at a poster by the door. Fumiko frowned as she read:

> **Save the Square Delight! All citizens please take note—the Global Government has decided that each country can be adequately served by a single Square in its capital city, as running more is a prohibitive drain on dwindling resources and water rationing. Please sign below if you wish to respectfully protest this decision.**

Fumiko passed through the scanner and weigh station and quickly dressed. Taking a final, deep lungful of the delicious coolness, she sighed and stepped out into the arid heat. Her body felt heavier, somehow, like it used to after a sea swim before they were declared unsafe.

No one spoke as she rejoined her friends, and they made their way back to the railway station. The group shared a water bottle, and as they neared the waiting throng on the station platform, the precious mouthful wetted Fumiko's parched tongue, joined by a salty trickle that ran slowly down her cheek.

. . .

About the author:

As the daughter of an antiquarian book dealer, Taria grew up surrounded by far more books than is healthy for one person. A literature degree, a journalism course, and some gratuitous vocabulary overuse later, her stories have appeared in a Hagrid-sized handful of anthologies and have won enough literary prizes to fill his other hand. Despite this, she has no need as yet for larger millinery. Editors and judges have likened her style to Douglas Adams and Neil Gaiman.

27

Man Moon

by Rann Murray (United States)

Subgenre: Science fiction

Time Period: Near future (late twenty-first century)

Setting: Asteroid Belt

Synopsis: A family running an independent salvage business in the asteroid belt is shocked when they encounter a battered ship adrift in space whose existence is impossible to explain. Is it man-made, or of alien origin? Only further study by scientists from multiple disciplines can unravel the mystery, and even they make a serious misjudgment. It is left to a linguistics professor to solve the puzzle beyond imagining. Now he must make the rest of the world believe him, or we could all suffer the same fate as the builders of that ancient ship.

. . .

There liveth none under the sunne that knows what to make of the man in the moon.
—John Lyly, 1591

. . .

Chandra turned to her husband, Brett, and said in a soft whisper, "Are you ready for this?"

"Not my favorite pastime, but they deserve to hear it, so we'll have to do the best we can."

"You sound calmer than me."

"Not so, I'm faking it," Brett said.

Chandra placed a hand on his shoulder to steady him. When they'd found out about the interview, she'd reminded him that he needn't worry. He always looked perfectly calm, even when nervous. The fact that a half billion people throughout the solar system would be watching the interview, she kept to herself. "Stacy's waiting," she said. "We'd better go."

. . .

"This is Stacy DeLand from SNS, reporting live from Ceres Station, the international port of arrival for the Asteroid Belt and the largest settlement in the entire Belt.

"Today I'm speaking with the Erikson family, who arrived at the Station after recently completing a salvage run on the Belt's outer fringe. Brett Erikson, his wife, Chandra, and their fifteen-year-old son, Adam, are with me."

"*Sixteen*, I just turned sixteen," Adam asserted.

"Sorry Adam, I stand corrected. Their *sixteen*-year-old son. "Now as most of our viewers are aware," Stacy continued, "the Erikson family recently discovered an ancient spacecraft drifting in the Belt. Documents recovered onboard that ship have revealed astonishing evidence that the ancient craft may have a point of origin on the planet Venus. As inconceivable as it sounds, the ship could be millions of years old. Additional peer review has confirmed that as fact, making this humanity's most important discovery.

"The Erikson family has graciously agreed to an SNS exclusive interview. Let me start with Mr. Erikson. There are many people back home on Earth who are anxious to hear what happened and how you discovered what's come to be known as *The Artifact*. Please tell us in your own words, sir."

"I'll do my best. We didn't know what the object was when we first encountered it. But we knew it had to be incredibly old. Someone in our line of work is intrigued when they find something like that, for the salvage value alone. We had no idea it would become this important."

"And no one was certain what had been found until linguists pored over the documents," Stacy interjected. "Without the Rosetta papers provided by the Venusians, we may never have learned the genesis of the documents, let alone their content. Now all scientific disciplines are studying the documents—cultural anthropologists, archeologists, paleobotanists, sociologists—in a concerted effort to determine the fundamental nature of this long-ago civilization. And the trajectory simulations suggest Venus as the planet of origin. It's put to rest the prevailing theory that Venus had too much early volcanism to give intelligent life a chance to take hold."

"Now, Brett, theories have been circulating around the net that the Venusian ship is a hoax, a tactic to shut down those denying climate change. What's your reaction to that?"

"First of all, I wouldn't know how to undertake constructing a ship like that. The metal alloys it was built with aren't even manufactured anymore. And those ancient documents? I'm not imaginative enough to fabricate a historical account that fantastic. But despite that, I suppose people will believe what they wish."

"Thank you, Brett. Now let's turn to Mrs. Erikson—get her take on this fascinating revelation."

"Chandra, please."

"Chandra. *The Artifact* has transformed countless lives. How people view themselves and the historical part we play in the scheme of things as we continue our push out to the farthest reaches of the solar system. It is hoped that knowing the Venusians died as a direct result of climate change that went beyond their capacity to control, could draw us closer together to curtail further harm from the greenhouse disaster. As you're aware, back home on Earth, we're still dealing with coastal flooding, massive emigration, lethal weather, the recent food riots, and devastating pandemics. On the pandemic front, the immuno-labs are under a lot of pressure. New viral strains are occurring every three to four years now. If they miss a deadline for release of a vaccine by a week or two, millions more will die; any longer, and it might be tens of millions.

"How do you feel, Chandra, knowing that you're an important part of what might turn things around?"

"As you can imagine, I'm trying to come to terms with all of this," Chandra responded. "I guess a family making a living out here in the Belt isn't exactly what you would call normal. But we never realized how far outside of normal it was until we discovered *The Artifact*. I never expected that everyone would know our names back home. When I saw that object drifting outside our ship, I had an eerie feeling. Like it didn't belong in our world. We had to examine it; we had to find out what was inside. And it was dangerous out there. We almost lost Brett during a repair run, so I had misgivings about him embarking on another spacewalk so soon after that."

"Now, Adam, we can't leave you out of this. Our listeners want to hear your thoughts. This must have been quite an adventure for you. You were right in the middle of it."

"I wanted to go out there with Dad to get inside that ship, but he told me I had to stay with Mom until he found out what we were dealing with."

"I understand that you helped out, didn't you?"

"I helped Mom monitor Dad while he left our ship. Then I had to help at the airlock to give Dad the tools he needed."

"Wow, you did a lot, Adam. I'm sure he was a big help, right Chandra?"

"He's being modest. He did so much more," Chandra said, giving Adam a broad smile.

"There are countless people who want to hear about this. It's so extraordinary that beings from another world, technically aliens within our own solar system, experienced what we are going through at this very moment and sent that ship to warn a possible future civilization about the peril of ignoring their scientists' warning of an approaching climate catastrophe. Can I impose on you both to give us a more detailed story of what took place out there?"

"It's no imposition, as long as you don't mind putting up with my ramblings," Brett said.

"And mine," Chandra added.

"I'm sure that won't be an issue. Please continue."

. . .

——Four months before the SNS interview——

Brett watched the AI bot's image of the antenna array. He turned to Chandra, sitting at the comm-desk. "I'd say we got off easy, one communication antenna down, and there doesn't appear to be any other damage," Brett said.

"What a relief. But you know I don't like you going EVA," Chandra replied.

"Gotta do it, Hon. The AI bot that handles it is in for repairs."

"Can't you program another one?" Chandra asked.

"You worry too much. By the time I'm done programming, I could be out and back. Besides, our suits are as tough as nails. When was the last time you heard of a spacesuit malfunctioning?"

"Alright, never. But it's still dangerous out there, so be quick and get back here safe."

"Yes, ma'am. Adam, come with me to the airlock and watch me exit to make sure I'm okay. Then I want you on the communications deck with your mother. You can help her monitor my progress."

Brett did his best to include his son, Adam, in as many activities around the ship as possible. Adam was tall like his father, but thin and lanky, not having filled out yet. He lacked self-confidence, so assigning him tasks that he could handle was important to Brett.

"I want to go with you, Dad."

"I told you, only in emergencies. You're still not EVA-ready, but keep up your training with Mom, and I'm sure you'll be on spacewalks in no time. Come on, Buddy, let's head to the lock."

. . .

Brett gave a last twist to secure his helmet and turned to Adam. "Okay, you check the airlock to make sure we have equalized pressure, then pull the entry lever when it's clear, just like I taught you."

"All set, Dad."

Double-checking the gauge readings on his suit, Brett entered the airlock, closing the access panel behind him. Once it cycled down to vacuum, he opened the outer hatch and took a step into space. Frigid darkness punctuated with the brilliant, rock-steady light of crystalline stars greeted him, their exquisite beauty overwhelming his senses. Stars so abundant he could barely make out the constellations.

He clipped his tether hook on the closest ring and headed toward the antenna array with the spare antenna that would restore long-distance communications. Once there, he fired nitrogen puffs from his jetpack to swing his body around. His feet thudded against the hull as his magnetic boots took hold. He spotted the damaged antenna, which had a clean break where most likely a pea-sized meteoroid from the swarm they had encountered had struck it midway down its length.

He heard a crackle from his helmet speaker. "Brett, you're not going to believe this, but there's a second swarm coming in behind the first one. We'll catch part of it, even if I goose the fusion engines to max. So please hurry inside ASAP."

"Second wave? We're on the outer rim of the Belt's elliptic. There shouldn't be that much meteoroid activity around here. Alright, let me finish uncoupling the broken antenna, and I'll be right in."

"Please make it fast. We have to put as much distance between us and that swarm as we can, and I can't start moving the ship until you're with us."

He removed what was left of the antenna and thought he just might have enough time to install its replacement. He decided to risk it, and soon got lost in the work.

Brett had always been confident on EVA excursions like this—sometimes overly confident, Chandra had told him. He was a towering thirty-four-year-old man with a close-cropped beard and a well-toned body that he kept in good shape. His son, Adam, idolized him. They were very close, something that Brett had never experienced with his father.

"Brett. Now!"

"Alright, alright, I'm on my way." *Damn it, so close to repaired. I'll have to come out later to finish up. That is, if the swarm doesn't damage it again.*

He fired his suit thrusters and headed back toward the airlock, certain that Adam was anxiously waiting for him.

He felt a nudge and suddenly a rough shove sending him tumbling end over end swiftly away from the ship. His tether was playing out fast. "Come on, baby, you better hold," he said to himself.

It went taut. He let out a grunt at the harshness of the tether's pull. It snapped. He caught a glimpse of it undulating, torn away from the ship's anchor ring. "Oh hell, I'm off flying now."

What luck, he thought. *The greatest fear I have of EVA's—becoming untethered in space. I could be drifting for eons—my bleached white skeleton all that remains of my once robust self.*

His sudden, acute vertigo left no room for humorous thoughts. There was no denying he was in trouble. He took several deep breaths trying to calm himself. He had to stop this tumbling before he got sick and threw up in his suit.

His control moment gyroscope (CMG) should have corrected his spin by now. That could only mean it had failed. He had to use manual controls. He applied what he thought was a jet burst counter to his spin direction. To his alarm, his spin accelerated. His field of vision was starting to narrow, a sure sign that he would soon pass out.

Correct in the other direction, dummy. That was his last thought before losing consciousness.

Chandra saw his rapid spinning on the viewscreen. *It's too damn fast.* "Brett, you all right?! Brett!

"I hope you can hear me. I've got a strong beacon signal from your backpack, so heading in your direction. This huge bucket is slow to turn, so it will take time for me to pick you up. Just hang tight. On my way."

She checked his vitals on one of the monitors and saw his heart rate take a dive, and his breathing was erratic. She was about to use the intercom to summon Adam but heard his footsteps moving toward the comm-deck.

He was out of breath by the time he reached the deck. "Is Dad okay, Mom?"

She drew in a breath to calm herself. "He's become disoriented and is in a rapid spin."

"Is he going to be okay!?"

"Calm down, now. Of course, he'll be okay. But he's going to need your help, Adam. I would go EVA, but I'm the only one who can keep the ship as near as possible to him. That means I'm going to have to rely on you to go EVA and get to him."

"Can't he stop his spin?"

"He's lost consciousness, so you'll have to stop it for him."

"Mom, I'm scared."

"There's nothing to be scared of. Your suit will protect you.

You've had enough EVA experience to do this. All you have to do is get as close to him as possible. You can latch on to his utility belt or grab his midsection and hold tight. You'll be spinning with him but slowed down a bit because of your added mass. Your CMG should automatically correct for the spin until you both come to a halt. Then just maneuver him back to the airlock, and you're home free."

She put her palms on his shoulders. He looked up at her. "I want you to repeat what I just told you to make sure you understand."

Adam complied and grasped the most salient points of Chandra's instructions. She was pleased that he seemed calmer now, probably calmer than she felt. "Go get suited up and come back to me so I can check your gauges."

As she watched him leave, it was hard not to burst into tears at how brave he was being.

The comm-deck radio activated, and Chandra heard a long groan coming from Brett.

"Hang on, Honey. We're coming to get you. Keep your eyes closed. It'll lessen the vertigo."

His vitals showed he was unconscious again. *Please, please stay that way. I don't want you ejecting vomit in your suit.*

. . .

Adam came back to the comm-deck for his suit check. Before she had a chance to say anything, Adam spoke. "Don't worry, Mom. I know what I'm doing. I'll bring Dad back."

"I didn't doubt it for a second. Your suit looks good. Now go get your father."

Adam gave her a smile, turned, and headed back to the airlock.

Once there, he wasted no time and hit the recycle button to establish a vacuum. He opened the outer hatch and stepped into space.

He fired his jet pack and slowly made his way to his father's spinning figure.

"Good job, Adam, you're right on the mark."

"No talking now, Mom. I have to concentrate."

Wow! He is his father's son, she thought. *That's the confidence we've been looking for.*

Arriving near Brett's location, Adam slowed his momentum with a couple puffs from his jet pack and stopped several feet away. He focused his attention on Dad's suit belt to avoid becoming dizzy.

Trying to time the spin, he shot out his hands and grabbed the belt, holding on tight. Like Mom said, his added mass slowed down their tandem spin.

Chandra sighed with relief as the CMG did its job and brought them to a complete stop.

"I got him, Mom, just like I said I would."

"Beautiful job, Adam! Move to his side, hold on tight, and bring him back to the airlock. Signal me when you're safely inside, and I'll meet you there."

. . .

By the time Chandra got to the airlock, Brett was sitting on the deck with his hand on Adam's arm. Brett looked up at Chandra. "Hi, Sweetheart. A funny thing happened on the way back to the airlock. My son dragged me in, shoved my hand aside when I reached for the recycle button, and took charge of everything. How about that, huh?"

Overwhelmed with emotion, she didn't trust herself to say a word. She sat down next to Adam, leaned over, and kissed him on the forehead.

She turned to Brett. "How are you?"

"I'm fine, shaken up some. But no injuries. Any idea of what happened?"

"I spotted a pressure leak in one of the fusion drive's spare hydrogen tanks."

"So that's it," Brett said. "Must have been hit by a meteor. What's the vent rate?

"Too fast. We may have lost all the fuel in that tank. I didn't have time to activate one of the bots to repair it."

"I can do it, Mom."

"You're darn right you can. Have at it," she said.

Adam sprang to his feet and ran toward the bot recharging stations.

She watched him hurry down the passageway. "You should have seen him. He was brilliant."

"Well, of course. He's *my* son."

She slapped him on the arm.

. . .

The next morning, both Brett and Chandra were on the comm-deck, sipping coffee and discussing yesterday's events. They both jumped when the long-range radar sounded an alert to warn of an approaching object.

"Lord in heaven, what next," Chandra said.

"There's something up ahead," Brett said. "Sensors say it looks to be metallic."

Chandra increased the forward viewcam's magnification. "Oh sure, there it is. It's a ship."

She glanced Brett's way with a furrowed brow. "I know what you're thinking. Are you sure you're ready for this?"

"Actually, I'm not feeling that bad. Not even dizzy."

"What's our velocity relative to the ship?" Chandra asked.

"Pretty high, but with luck, I can attach the portable tether before we slide on by."

"You're such a hotdog. I don't want you slamming into that ship after the tether goes taut."

"I'll concentrate on catching hold first, then worry about a body-slam. Adam, you see this thing?"

"I do, Dad. It looks kind of eerie. It's got pits all over like it went through a big meteor shower more than once, I'd say."

"That's pretty accurate. No doubt the ship is old, but from the looks of it, ancient might be a better term."

"You're sure you should chance a tether?" Candra asked.

"I'm gonna give it a shot. This thing looks too interesting to pass up. If I miss, I miss. You can double back to pick me up. I'm certain there's no one aboard, but why don't you hail her and see if we get a response."

Chandra hailed the ship. "Nope, not a thing. No surprise there."

"Yeah, she has no beacon lights, not even an antenna," Brett said. "I'd better get suited up if we have any chance of boarding her on the first pass."

. . .

Heading toward the object, Brett knew his timing was crucial. If he didn't fire his portable tether at the right instant, the magnetic slug attached to its end wouldn't catch, and he'd be drifting out in space for quite a while before Chandra could retrieve him. He wasn't anxious to experience *that* again.

He pulled out the anchoring gun from a side pocket of his suit and took steady aim, trying to judge how far ahead of the ship he should fire. He had limited practice with the gun, so he took careful aim. *Should be just about right... here!*

His arm kicked back at the gun's recoil. He watched the tether wire play out. He was moving rapidly away and was afraid he'd fired too late, but the magnetic slug struck the ship fifteen feet back from its nose. *Oh hell, it's sliding along the surface. Can't get a grip because of the pitting.*

Then it caught, and he saw the tether line going taut fast. He grabbed the tether with both hands, bracing for the hard pull he knew was coming.

One of his arms felt like it might tear out of its socket, but he managed to avoid injury as the line began its recoil back toward the ship. Chandra's prediction was correct. He was coming back at the ship too fast. He would hit the hull, and it wouldn't be pretty. Just before impact, he fired a short burst from the suit jetpack to slow his forward momentum but was still coming in quick. He braced himself and let out a loud *oomph* as he struck the ship. He managed to grab the tether close enough to the magnetic slug to prevent bouncing off the surface too far.

"You okay, Brett?"

Catching his breath after having the wind knocked out of him, he answered. "Just bruised a bit." He lied to keep Chandra calm but knew he was going to have an ugly bruise from the pain in his left hip, which bore the brunt of the hit. He was lucky that nothing was broken.

"Whatever it is, it's been out here one hell of a long time. I've never seen that much pitting on a ship's hull." He moved his head from side to side so they could get a wider view from his helmet cam.

"Jeez, that thing looks kind of cool," Adam said.

"It's got a slight wobble. Gyros are probably offline. But something bigger than a dust grain had to hit it, to cause that."

"Can I come out there with you, Dad?"

"Sorry, Adam. It might be an old bomb relic from the Belt Wars, for all we know."

Chandra said, "Go easy, Captain Sweetie. That ship looks old enough to fall apart if you touch it the wrong way."

Brett flinched at his wife's nickname, and he was positive Adam had a wide grin on his face at the remark. He felt a rush of warmth for the two of them. The truth was, he couldn't deny that woman anything.

. . .

Brett had met Chandra in the lunar city Theophilus during a major expansion phase which had kindled a persistent need for structural engineers, his specialty.

Chandra had been a botanist at a hydroponic facility. He was first attracted to her melodic Indian accent. She was born in Kolkata and was without a doubt the most attractive, interesting woman he had ever met. He considered himself one lucky French-Canadian to have captured her, or most likely the other way around. She had glowing, olive-black eyes with glints of gold flecks, and generous lips. She was petite, barely coming up to his chest. She was everything he wanted and needed in a woman. Her parents believed in arranged marriages and resented her marriage to Brett, but after meeting him, they eventually came around.

When he'd told her he'd had enough of lunar colony confinement and always dreamed of setting up an independent mining operation, she'd been supportive, as long as their combined savings could buy a large enough secondhand ship to allow her to continue her botany studies. A year later, they were married, and a year after that managed to acquire a medium-sized ore tanker sufficient to meet their needs and a decent-sized fusion drive to get them out to the Asteroid Belt. It was slow to maneuver but suitable for mining if they focused on lucrative precious metals and rare mineral asteroids. What they liked most was it had a habitat ring supplying one-sixth Earth gravity. That, along with medication and regular exercise, prevented bone calcium loss. Some habitats on the expansive ore ships had a full one-G, but those were well beyond their means.

They had a compliment of AI bots that did the actual mining, but AI or not, the bots needed oversight, program updates, occasionally broke down, and were glitchy at self-repairing.

After a year, they found that there weren't enough profits to make mining worthwhile, so they decided to use limited mining to finance a salvage business, which started to pay off. There were enough derelict ships and discarded equipment strewn throughout the Belt to make a decent living. They christened the ship the Siton, a Greek word denoting the god of agriculture, fitting for Chandra's profession.

. . .

Chandra maneuvered the Siton close enough to get an expansive view of the entire ship. "Well, I'll be," she said. "Look at those fins. Lifted off the cover of an old pulp sci-fi mag. Like a prototype of a prototype."

"Right you are. I'll bet there's stuff on board that a collector or museum would pay a sizable amount for."

"Let's hope so. Adam, try to get a good look at it with the gamma-ray scanner. There may be cargo."

The comm-deck lights dimmed as millions of electronvolts required for scanning through metal kicked in. The image scan appeared on a monitor next to the ship's main viewscreen. "It's got two big containers sitting in the middle and a tall oblong thing near the front of the ship, Mom."

"Yes, I see that," she replied. "You hear that, Brett? There's cargo on board that ship."

"Perfect. This may be worth our while. I can't wait to get into those containers."

As Brett rounded the rear of the ship, he spotted twin rocket exhaust nozzles which looked comparable to what you'd find on primitive chemical rockets. He continued around to the far side. "This is one solid piece of metal, not modular. And what do we have here? What the hell is this thing? This wheel hatch looks like something off an old earthside military sub. It's raised from the hull a couple of feet."

"What on earth would it be doing in the Belt?" Chandra wondered. "Do me a favor, Brett. Before you attempt an entry, wrap your tether line somewhere around that hatch wheel. That magnetic slug may not hold. I don't want to have to chase you through deep space again. And by the way, I'm getting a peculiar feeling about the looks of that ship. There's something *off* about it, more than just its outward appearance. Be extra careful, okay?"

"Okay, Hon." The line was just flexible enough to tie on one side of the hatch wheel rim. "There, secure as I can make it. I'm gonna try to give this wheel a turn."

"Any luck?"

"Nope, didn't budge. Whatever lubricant it had is doubtless long gone by now. Hey Adam, hunt around for a steel rod or something with some heft to it that I can use to get leverage. Just leave it in the airlock, and I'll come fetch it."

Once he had the rod positioned, Brett gave the wheel a strong twist, with little effect. One more effort, and he felt it give way. A few full turns, and it was open. He was surprised there was no entry hatch and saw the interior of the ship beckoning him to enter.

"Okay, I'm gonna head inside and find out what we've got here," he said, with palpable excitement in his voice.

"Adam, just in case Dad needs your help, why don't you go to the airlock and get suited up. You can give him a hand with the containers if he decides to bring them on board."

"Really, Mom?"

"Really. Make sure you remain on the ship unless I give you the go-ahead."

"Got it, Mom."

. . .

Once inside the mysterious ship, Brett noticed it had a completely open configuration, with no sectioned off areas. The control room, if you could call it that, consisted of a small, maybe six-inch monitor with a blackened screen attached atop a tall column. Midship were the two crates spotted earlier by the gamma scan. Both were secured with metal straps. The crates were closed tight with a series of bolts that ran all the way around them.

This whole thing is a crude setup. No advanced technology here. Whoever made this ship and sent it here were not a spacefaring people. This could have been a one-shot attempt to get this thing out to the Belt, if that was their intention. They may have been shooting for Mars, missed orbit insertion, and ended up out here instead.

But I've got to admit, they built this thing to last. It's like a tank. The hull is thick enough to blunt a fifty-caliber shell. Also in their favor is the fact that the distance separating objects in space is very great, and the Asteroid Belt is no exception. You could run a ship through the Belt for a million years and never encounter another object except for an occasional dust grain. In fact, the natural collision rate between two asteroids out here is once every ten million years.

Brett walked to the center of the ship and slowly turned in a circle, giving everything a once-over. *This looks more like an ancient Egyptian tomb, and those crates could be sarcophagi.*

A queer chill ran the length of his spine, like a feeling of being watched. Perhaps the people who built this ship were hanging on somehow—a thought he did not want to ponder for too long. The ship's exterior was odd enough, but the interior was too unnatural and spooky. Things were just off. To say the control deck was out of the ordinary was an understatement. It was as if human hands weren't at work here. The control unit had quirky angles, and printing on the front wasn't any language he'd ever seen. Even the crates angled out at the bottom in a strange, cubist design. The same incomprehensible printing was on one side of each container.

When you think about a good prospect for salvage, you don't imagine this. The whole rig is going to be worth a fortune or a complete dud. No means of knowing which. So nothing else to do but free up those crates and get them over to the Siton. Then we'll see what's inside.

He set to work.

. . .

The three of them stood in the Siton's hold looking down at the crates Brett had brought on board. "Okay, you two ready for this?" Brett said. "Just say the word, and I'll open the first one."

"Oh, stop teasing us and open the container," Chandra said in a half-scolding tone.

Bolts already removed, Brett picked up a pry bar and opened the lid of the closest metal crate. They heard a hiss of air rushing in. As he gently swung the lid open, the hinges gave out a torturous creak.

They gazed at two neatly wrapped stacks of packages that reached the top rim of the container.

"The paper they're bundled in is coarse. Papyrus?" Chandra breathed.

"Yeah, it's remarkably similar."

Behind the packages were individual metal plates tied together with binding resembling leather. Chandra slowly reached in and touched the corner of the package nearest her. It gave way, and she hastily drew her hand back. When she looked at her fingers, they were covered in dust and flecks of paper. "I'm afraid to open them. They could disintegrate."

"Good point. Better leave them alone."

The two top packages were labeled with the same peculiar characters Brett had spotted on the console and the surface of the containers. "Okay, that leaves the metallic plates. Not much chance in damaging those." As he reached in to retrieve them, he noticed quite a few cloth pouches grouped in a corner containing something to be investigated later.

Brett handed the rectangular stack of plates to Chandra. "You remove the bindings. My fat fingers will wreck them."

Chandra gave the tied leather a delicate touch, but it gave way with no resistance.

"Curses," she said.

"No real loss," he said.

"We hope," she replied.

Brett lifted the top plate for inspection. He was having a difficult time interpreting what he was looking at. He held it up to the light at an angle, and an etched image of a creature stared back at him. He almost dropped the plate.

"Wait a minute! That thing looks reptilian, but it's standing on its hind legs like a human." He handed the plate to Chandra.

"You're right, it sure does. But its shoulders seem odd, like they're on backward. And instead of a mouth, it has a pronounced muzzle. Reminds me of a dog's, only longer."

"A muzzle with two rows of jagged teeth," Brett noted. "And that hair!"

It had three long, thick shocks of hair on its head: a wide central one with a prominent widow's peak that was lighter than the shaded ones on either side. Another plate showed hair cascading down the middle of its back for several feet, giving the appearance of a mane. The whole effect was striking. If it had any ears on its head, the ample hair hid them from view.

"With that volume of hair, it could be male or female," Chandra said. "But it looks muscular enough to assume we're looking at a male."

The creature had high brows of a shape that lent intelligence to the eyes. It wore an ankle-length open coat and a wide, dark belt wrapped around clothes that were difficult to discern from the etching. It had sandals on its feet.

Standing behind his mother, Adam took a closer look. "Look at the toes—they're webbed. That's an alien for sure!" he exclaimed.

"You're right, Adam. I've never seen anything like it. My God, what have we found? It must be extraterrestrial."

"Wow! Extraterrestrial—that's the best," Adam said.

"We've got to get this to the authorities, Brett, or a museum. This is way too important," Chandra said.

"I agree," Brett replied. "This has to be a once-in-a-lifetime find. I don't want to sound too opportunistic, but let's make sure we take some profit out of this. Our coffers are a little bare."

"No problem with that," Chandra agreed.

"That ship is small enough to fit in our cargo hold," Brett said. "What do you think?"

"We have to bring it in," Chandra replied. "It doesn't feel right to abandon it out here."

"Looks like we've got our work cut out for us," Brett said.

"Can we take it to Ceres Station?" Adam asked.

"You wouldn't have an ulterior motive, would you, Adam? Considering that girl you hung out with last time we were there," Chandra teased.

Seeing the flush of red on Adam's face, Brett interjected, "Girlfriend or not, that makes the most sense, Adam. Ceres Station it is."

. . .

The holo-cam turned back to Stacy DeLand standing beside the Erikson family. "That is quite a fascinating account," Stacy declared. "Thank you so much for sharing it with our viewers. Do you have any final remarks before we conclude our interview?"

"When we found out how important this whole matter was, we had to share it with the world," Chandra said.

"And we're certainly glad you did," Stacy said. "As you know, there's still resistance to viewing climate change as man-made. Despite conclusive evidence to the contrary and the continuing downward climate spiral, a minority are continuing to hold fast to the belief that human pollution does not cause climate change. But thanks to the Erikson family's incredible discovery, we might change enough minds to turn things around and secure a sustainable future."

"Oh, and we don't want to forget," Brett offered. "The pouches we found contained a variety of seeds. We only opened one pouch and were afraid to open any more for fear of contamination."

"I'm glad you brought that up," Stacy said. "I understand they're being evaluated, and preliminary studies by paleobotanists indicate that they are unusual in nature, although they have some similarities to plants on Earth. The seeds are well beyond any viability, but they have retrieved enough DNA to enable them to grow bio-replicas for most of them. So we should be able to see what the plants looked like very soon. That will be quite a sensation, to behold an actual Venusian plant from so long ago."

"And one last thing," Stacy continued. "We were recently informed that the curious looking module with the small monitor you found on the ship, Brett, is a storage device that may contain videos and images of Venusians and how they lived. They're putting intensive effort into restoring it."

Stacy turned to the holo-cam. "Well, that's it from Ceres Station. We'll keep you updated on any new developments as this story unfolds. This is Stacy DeLand from SNS News. Thanks for watching."

. . .

——A year and a half later——

James Wright, a linguistics professor at MIT with a middle-aged paunch from eating too many rich foods in the campus cafeteria, was in a heated exchange with a faculty colleague, Nate Meyer. Nate observed James' face getting redder by the minute and decided to tone things down before poor old James suffered an infarction.

Despite their frequent opposition, they had become close friends over the years and were generally able to find common ground at some point during their verbal skirmishes.

Both had been studying the Venusian documents for the past year and a half, and both considered themselves experts in their fields. Although neither would admit it, they were living out the cliché of academia competitiveness and thoroughly enjoyed these interactions.

"In spite of the Rosetta papers that accompanied the

Venusian Artifact, we've had a difficult time interpreting a few areas of their language. I wish the Venusians had been more thorough in their preparation. Particularly in providing a better outline of phonetically paired sounds." James ground his teeth in anticipation of repelling Nate's parry.

Not taking the bait, Nate changed the subject. "They did do a competent job on physiology and speech, though, which I think has something to do with Robert Temple having a breakthrough—quite significant from what he says."

"Oh really. He's a doctoral candidate under you, isn't he?"

"That's the one," Nate replied. "I assigned him the Venusian literature archives, and Temple is convinced he's translated the word *moon*. He thinks it could be part of a poem or a verse in a song. He seemed highly excited—didn't want to discuss it over the phone. I've arranged to meet with him tomorrow."

"Fascinating that we're seeing so many parallels with our own culture," James noted. "But moon? Venus doesn't have a moon, does it?"

"Indeed, but he swears it's the correct translation. That young man is becoming quite the little lexicologist. I'll forward you an email with his current list."

. . .

That night, in his study, James reviewed the email Nate sent him. Despite the doctoral student's lengthy list of translated words, James kept focusing on the word "moon." He recalled encountering that specific word in the Venusian text paired with another word or phrase. Not that frequently, but often enough to come to the forefront.

He pulled up his files on the Venusian literature archives and ran a search on the newly found word "moon" to determine if there was a significant repeated connection with one or more nonidentical words—a simple task for an advanced search routine.

"Well, there you go," he said softly. Silently, he added, *"Moon" was associated several times with the Venusian word "rask," their equivalent term for man. Unique, given the fact that Rask was the last name of a Danish philologist whose work on Old Norse was pioneering in the field of comparative linguistics.*

He spotted a complete sentence containing both words, "What make Man Moon." *Needs a few prepositions. Perhaps "What to make..."*

He leaned back in his ergo chair. *Man, moon. Interesting but not terribly significant. Enough. I've got to get some sleep. Early class tomorrow.*

Later that night, while fast asleep, he experienced a vivid dream. He was sitting on a bench alongside a vast river, so wide it reached to the horizon. The night was brightened by a half-risen full moon that glistened like satin. He gazed up and held in view the clearest man in the moon he had ever witnessed.

At that very instant he sat bolt upright in bed, grabbed his glasses, and shook his head to clear his mind. "Man in the moon, man in the moon," he kept repeating over and over.

"My God!" he shouted. "Man Moon. What make Man Moon. What to make Man Moon. Add the prepositions, you dimwit. WHAT TO MAKE OF THE MAN IN THE MOON!" he bellowed, feeling foolish at the volume of his sudden outburst.

He continued in a hushed voice. "The moon is tidally locked to Earth. Only the far side would be visible to someone observing off-planet. Not the face that we see."

His mind raced, disparate thoughts beginning to take form.

Could they have evolved on Earth? Was it a mistake to assume the Venusians ever existed? The computer simulations pointing to Venus as the ship's planet of origin could be an error. The idea that The Artifact came from Venus never did make a lot of sense. The latest research indicated that Venus had an environment suitable for life as long as 750 million years ago. Despite their revising that estimate down after examining The Artifact, it's difficult to believe the ship could be that old.

The Artifact's documents referred to the Great River, wider than the eye can see. From their description, it could have swallowed up a few dozen Amazons, perhaps more. They talked of one ocean, not plural, a single ocean. They were also definite about living in one land. One ocean, one land, a River to end all rivers. When you apply that to Venus, we just accepted it as the Venusian environment long ago. But when those descriptors are applied to Earth, precisely what is their meaning? There must be an environment in Earth's past that possessed those key elements.

Wait! The greatest landmass that ever existed in our planet's vast history was Pangaea. They could very well be describing Pangaea! The single massive landform before tectonic forces broke it up into the continents we know today.

He queried his cell phone on the name Pangaea.

That time period begins with the Triassic and ends with the Cretaceous. They could have existed anywhere from 70 to 180 million years ago on Earth. Pangea apparently began its breakup during the Cretaceous, so that could put them well beyond seventy million years ago. If their evolution was anything like ours, four to six million years passed for them to reach their industrialized peak. The climate was much warmer and the sea level much higher—highly susceptible to species-induced climate change.

That has to be the explanation. They are our ancestors! The drastic climate change they referenced happened here on Earth, long, long ago. So far in the past, there's no trace left of them. They must have been on the cusp of space travel and found a means to speak to us from the distant past.

This is beyond imagining. Now I know why Nate's

student, Robert Temple, was so eager to meet with him. He's most likely had the same realization as me.

I can picture it. They were the dominant species of their time, just as we are today. They developed an accomplished civilization on the shores of their Great River, advanced to an industrialized society, and were on the cusp of space travel when things started to collapse. After the climate catastrophe struck, they talked about the first rising, and later the second. They must have meant the River flooded and submerged their cities, great and small. If they weren't killed by the flooding, it was the heat, famine, and disease. It all fits now.

Could they have contributed to the mass extinction event sixty-six million years ago—the one that killed off the dinosaurs? Not likely, but you never know. Perhaps the massive asteroid that struck Earth back then was just the precipitating event for something that had begun long before.

The etchings of the beings on the metal plates. They walked the land of Earth. Their documents are a warning to a future civilization. We are that civilization! They must have ignored their scientist's warnings just as we are doing today. We're making the same mistakes. If we have the remotest chance of saving ourselves, I must convince our people it's true. Otherwise, we're condemned to the same tragic fate.

James was not an emotional man but was moved at the thought of such a loss these beings underwent long ago in Earth's history, our history.

They must have suffered terribly. They lost everything they had or ever would have. Their history, their great works of art, their literature, their culture, their children's future—gone. A civilization struck down by its own hand. How close we are to them in our thinking and temperament. Their loss is just as significant as ours can be if we don't find the courage to change.

They gambled everything on the launch of that one ship, and against insurmountable odds, they succeeded. If I could communicate with them over an eon of time, I would tell them this: You can rest easy now; your legacy is with us. You won't be forgotten.

He couldn't recall the last time he'd cried, and yet he lowered his head and wept, shedding tears for a people he had never known, had never imagined, but somehow felt an inescapable kinship with.

. . .

Once he had regained his composure, James thought he should head for bed but felt too invigorated. He needed to do something to calm his mind, to rationally examine the validity of his assertions. He wandered about the house, eventually finding himself in the garage. He got into the car, opened the garage door, and ventured out into the neighborhood. As he drove, he kept whispering that phrase like a refrain, "*What to make of the man in the moon.*" It awakened an unexpected joy in him, as if it were coming from the depths of his very soul. Maybe it was an inherited part of his DNA, a long-dormant helix strand from this ancient Pangaean civilization that had been activated along with his profound discovery.

After thirty minutes of driving on autopilot, he pulled out his phone and called his colleague, Nate. "Sorry to bother you at such a late hour, Nate, but you and I need to talk."

Nate hesitated, trying to shake off his drowsiness but awake enough to know this was out of character for James. "James, it's four-thirty in the morning; can't it wait?"

"No, it can't. I have to talk to you in person. You must listen to what I have to say," James insisted.

"My goodness, James. What's bothering you? Is it something I said? At least give me a hint about what's so urgent."

"Let me put it to you this way. If we're not convinced that we had better wake up to this runaway greenhouse cliff we're headed for after what I have to tell you, then we don't deserve to occupy this planet."

That was a mouthful, Nate thought. "Okay, come on over. But this better be good."

"I don't have to come over. I'm parked in your driveway."

"You're..." Nate got out of bed and looked out his bedroom window. "And so you are. Alright, my friend, see you at the front door. I'll put on a pot of coffee, and we'll talk."

. . .

About the author:
As a kid, Rann Murray's parents signed him up for a subscription to the Science Fiction Book Club, then they bought him a Robert the Robot toy with a fancy control module, then a telescope. So how could a spoiled brat like that not end up writing science fiction? His background as a computer store owner, astrophotographer, and a lifelong interest in anything to do with science sprang from those early days. Rann graduated from Michigan State University and still lives in the Great Lake State with his wife and three spoiled brat cats. Rann's short stories have appeared in *Bewildering Stories* and *Small Town Anthology*.

28

The End of the End

by Carol Smith (United States)

Subgenres: Science fiction, pandemic sci-fi

Time period: The year 2055

Setting: A suburb in the United States of America

Synopsis: Quality of life on Earth is swiftly eroding under an overburdened atmosphere baked by the Sun. The blue planet's selfish children mistreated her, and now the damage they caused is beyond repair. A new pathogen, baffling the medical community, has appeared and is working its way down from the northern latitudes. If there's any hope left for Earth's survival, it won't be found on the third planet from the Sun.

. . .

"Woohoo. You've made it to another day, Amelia." My sarcasm seems wasted when it's only *me* hearing it. When I made my debut forty years ago, the weather was becoming more erratic around the world—temperatures fluctuating between too hot or too cold for the season and frequent devastating storms. Our planet was struggling. Still, no one in government did anything. A lot of them are six-feet-under now. At least some of those climate-change deniers are getting to enjoy the fruits of their inaction, though that's small consolation.

Life in the burb has changed for the worse. Electricity is spotty. You never know when you'll be in the dark, or for how long. Water is the same. It's a crapshoot turning on the faucet. You may get liquid or groaning, moaning water pipes straining to weep a drop.

I remember dew-kissed mornings and sweet scents of grass, trees, and blossoms when Earth was still fighting to overcome the rampant stupidity of our leaders. She lost. You won't find many flourishing trees, much less perfect blades of grass or flowers now. The used-to-be-beneficial fireball in the sky bakes our atmosphere that's heavy with carbon dioxide, methane, and God knows what else, creating a relentless oven. It doesn't cool down much at night. I'm grateful for every little degree that the temperature drops.

An unknown pathogen is infecting people in the northern latitudes, and it looks like it's headed our way. Medical experts say this illness acts like a virulent mixture of anthrax and bubonic plague. They don't know how it's contracted, how it spreads, or how to treat it. Microbiologists have been warning for decades that as the Earth cooks, melting glaciers and permafrost may release bacteria and viruses that modern humans have never encountered. Disease among Neanderthals more than forty thousand years ago could take us out.

We barely survived COVID-19, caused by a new coronavirus in 2020. I don't remember much about it. I was five. My parents said that after a couple of months of stay-at-home orders, people came out in droves, bringing their guns, to protest the directive at state capitals. On the first Memorial Day holiday during the pandemic, people crowded beaches, pools, and parks, ignoring the precautions aimed at slowing the spread of the virus. We were saddled with an insane, narcissistic president hawking hydroxychloroquine to prevent and cure COVID-19. The drug wound up helping none of the sick and killing more. It put that guy down too, eventually. Hydroxychloroquine triggered a fatal arrhythmia in him as he was playing golf. The blatant disregard of science caused a second, more deadly wave of the disease that lasted through 2021, when finally, an effective vaccine was available.

A mutation of bacteria caused treatment-resistant diphtheria in 2032. Tularemia, in 2040, shook off antibiotics like water off a duck's back. Pertussis-2, a brand-new strain of an acute respiratory illness that resembled whooping cough, was targeting children a few years ago.

Let's face it. My species isn't long for this planet. The Earth will party hearty when the last of us drops dead, and possibly it will recover.

My chattering brain won't shut up. It forces me out of bed to splash some precious H2O on my face and drink a concoction of ground, dried dandelion root. I call it coffee. The real thing is too expensive, and I hear it's not as good as it used to be, anyway.

Every part of that bane of lawn aficionados, the dandelion, is edible. Best of all, this stubborn, resilient weed is free, still grows just about everywhere, and provides a slew of vitamins and minerals. To all those who scoffed at my botany degrees—*in your face!*

It's grocery day. Stepping out into the not-great outdoors, I look up before I take my bicycle out of the shed and hide under my wide-brimmed hat. "Huh, I thought that was a planet in the sky last night. It's still there, but it looks like a silvery, round something that's just hanging in the same spot. What now?" *Could it be an old satellite in a decaying stationary orbit?* I'll keep an eye on it, for the sole purpose of worrying, and have a chat about it later with my buds next door.

These days, you have to get an early start for provisions to get the best pick of what's available. Pedaling to the market, I miss how pretty my neighborhood used to be. Occasionally, my eyes wander up to the orb sparkling in the morning sun.

It doesn't take long for me and other early birds to gather up what we want at the store. On my way home, both rear baskets on the bike are full. I guess once everything is unloaded and put away, I'll harvest some dandies to dry and relax with a good book until dinner with my friends.

We get lucky as night draws nearer. The temperature has dropped at least ten degrees.

"Hey, Mel, the food is ready. Charles whipped up something special too." Julie's cheerful voice sails in through my kitchen window. That woman is never depressed. I don't know how she manages it.

Julie, her husband Charles, and I have been friends since high school. The other kids had another name for us, but we considered ourselves members of the science crowd. They were looking for a house after they married four years ago, and the one next to me was for sale.

The three of us get together in their backyard at the picnic table. It's big enough to support two bright solar lanterns on either end, and in between, there's a magnificent spread of black beans, marinated tofu, and a salad of dandy leaves sprinkled with Julie's signature dressing—more food than we need.

Charles' surprise is fluffy dinner rolls to complement our feast. He's a baker *extraordinaire* when flour and yeast are available, and a brilliant epidemiologist working on the Centers for Disease Control frontline. My high school pal is trying to crack this new plague that has us in its sights.

"You guys planning on more people coming over?" I ask while loading up my plate.

Charles smiles. "Since Mrs. Levy is alone, we thought it would be nice to share." He starts piling generous helpings onto the dish in his hand and prepares to leave to deliver supper to our elderly neighbor. "I'll be right back."

From the happy exclamations we hear from Mrs. Levy's house, her dinner is well-received.

Once he returns and is settled, the serious munching and conversation begin.

"Jules, what do you think of that addition to our sky? Have you been watching it?" I inquire. Julie is an astrophysicist, and I'm sure the phenomenon hasn't been lost on her and her colleagues.

"I don't know what to make of it yet, Mel," she answers, gazing upward.

"Is that *your* opinion, or 'the opinion' you scientists have been told to say?" I tease her as I form air quotes around "the opinion."

"I'll tell you what I think," Charles interjects, giving his wife a nudge, "it's an alien listening post."

I laugh, but oddly, Julie doesn't. She usually plays along.

"Jules, you *do* know something." I point my finger at her.

"Whether I do or I don't," she says exasperatedly, "after all these years, you know I can't tell you everything. I can't even tell Charles, and who's he going to let know?"

"Now wait a minute, Wife. Are you implying I don't have any friends of my own?" Charles successfully lightens the mood.

Julie's reaction troubles me. Generally, she wears a friendly poker face when it comes to her job.

Once the conversation is back on track, she suddenly stares skyward and stops short mid-sentence, prompting Charles and me to follow her line of sight. A mass of silent sparks is showering down from the object in broad trajectories. A number of them zoom over our heads before they seemingly fizzle out.

"They said they would wait." Julie's eyes are not leaving the heavens.

"Jules," I yell, "who would wait?"

A cell phone inside my friends' house starts ringing. Julie

springboards from the table and runs to answer it. Charles and I are on her heels. After that call, I swear her complexion has lightened an entire shade.

"Julie, *who* was going to wait? Are we in danger? Julie, answer me!" I feel bad about raising my voice at her again. It's more of a knee-jerk reaction.

"We were going to wait, but you're out of time."

The voice is outside the screen door, and the three of us spin to face it. A man is standing on the porch. We can't make out his features. He's alone, with no weapon in sight. We have a numerical advantage. That doesn't make me feel safer.

"You're out of time," he says again, "May I come in?"

Charles blurts out, "No! Who the hell are you?"

The only barrier keeping this person out is that flimsy screen door, and it's not even locked.

"Julie, you know who I am. We've been talking for at least a year."

"Yes, we've been communicating. The signal was spotty. My coworkers and I couldn't make sense of everything you were saying," she replies.

"That's why we moved into the lower stratosphere to make direct contact. Earth will become uninhabitable soon. It'll take time to reverse the damage. We need to help immediately. You know I'm not going to hurt you."

Our visitor, Charles, and I look at Julie. Her hesitancy scares me more than anything else. In all the years I've known her, Jules has never been unconfident.

"I see the door's unlatched, but I won't come in until you let me." The stranger couldn't be less threatening if he tried. Wolves in sheep's clothing aren't threatening either, until it's too late for the victims.

We can see Julie's wheels turning. Almost impulsively, she utters, "You can come in."

Before Charles and I can refute her decision, there's a visitor in the kitchen with us. He's not very tall, maybe five foot five or six, and inexplicably dressed in a polo shirt and jeans. Our guest has a friendly face, brown hair, and brown eyes. There's something oddly familiar about him.

"I know I look like an exhibit out of a natural history museum. You people call my people..."

"Neanderthals." Charles finishes our guest's sentence.

"That's right, Neanderthals." He smiles. "Could we sit down? I need to talk to you."

The four of us take seats at the kitchen table.

"My name is Jason Owego. I'm the mediator for this mission. First, let me tell you a little more about us. Many thousands of years ago, here on Earth, our civilization gradually developed technology that could take us into the heavens. Great scientific minds discovered worlds not unlike our own. Eventually, an exploration of one of those planets was successful, and we established a thriving, permanent colony. I was born on that planet—on Viridi. It's in the Milky Way Galaxy too. We're your cousins from the other side of town." He pauses, grinning.

"How can that be?" Charles isn't buying Jason's story. "There are remains of Neanderthals found on Earth—skeletons, stone tools, cave paintings. There's no evidence supporting advanced technology."

"That's true. The technology that took us to the stars was what you call biodegradable. There wouldn't be any traces of it now. Some stayed on Earth to continue living the old ways. What you have is what they left behind."

Julie speaks up. "We missed a lot of information because of the intermittent signal. My team and I pored over the recordings, trying to make sense of them. The one thing that stood out was that you were waiting."

"Yes, you got that much correct," Jason continued, "We were able to hear the confusion in your voice and the others around you. Unfortunately, your receivers couldn't be accurately calibrated to our frequency. That's why we needed to act. Earth is in dire shape. We didn't want to see your branch of the family disappear."

"So, you've been keeping tabs on Earth?" I ask him.

"Of course we have. As our technology improved, we've been observing. Back then, after the migration, even though my ancestors couldn't return, they didn't want to abandon those who stayed here. They were able to communicate with them for a long time after the colony on Viridi was established. Eventually, the volunteers who remained behind to operate the receivers died out. The equipment wasn't maintained and gradually returned to nature. We still don't know why no one else had any interest in keeping in contact. Maybe, as the climate naturally changed, and life became harder, they got angry at those who left. Your *current* climate change *isn't* natural. Earth is damaged. We can do something about it, and we will." Jason sounded ominous, though he was still smiling.

Julie stands up. "I need to call my supervisor so we can all meet."

"No, no meetings, Cousin. We can't wait the amount of time it would take to go through channels. We've seen how your forms of government work. The process will be too slow. You've hurt this planet to the point where she can't recover on her own. We have to start immediately. Don't worry. We'll make it right. I promise."

Charles looks into our newly found relative's eyes. "Listen, you can't take these decisions away from us. This isn't your planet anymore."

Jason seems offended that we would argue in the face of redemption. "Earth is our ancestral home. Our DNA is over 99 percent the same as yours. You die if Earth dies. That's not happening—no way."

. . .

Our beleaguered planet's rescue started when we saw those sparks in the sky during dinner. Jason's ship and Viridian ships stationed around Earth deployed filters to cleanse the troposphere of greenhouse gases. While the filters were released, probes launched into the stratosphere to refresh and repair the protective ozone layer.

The frequent violent storms and constant oppressive temperatures ended. Healthy plant life returned, Arctic ice renewed, and ancient pathogens refroze.

Viridian physicians and scientists consulted with ours to cure the diseases released by the abnormal warming of the planet. They created de-acidifiers that neutralized the excessive CO_2 in our oceans, and marine life recovered.

Once again, just like during the 2020 pandemic, mobs of ignorant people showed up with their guns. This time, they were opposing the "alien" invasion. Our loving cousins "convinced" them that it was all in their best interest.

The blue planet is pristine and bountiful again. Jason is very close to Julie, Charles, and me. We visit him on Viridi, and he visits us on Earth from time to time. After all, we're family.

. . .

About the author:

Carol Smith taught earth science to high school students. Her stories are in two anthologies: *Paranormal Encounters* and *Handbook for the Dead,* published by Anubis Press. Over the years, she released a collection of her own stories and poems, a children's book, a romance, a collection of her Halloween haiku, and a book on paranormal investigating. She also wrote a tourism piece for *Newcomer Magazine,* published by Killam Publishing, "Autumn Getaways: Where to Experience Georgia's Stunning Fall Foliage." Visit Carol's website at www.carolsmithwrites.com.

29

The Great Greenland Quilting Bee

by J.G. Follansbee (United States)

Subgenres: Science fiction, geoengineering cli-fi

Time Period: Late twenty-first century

Setting: The story takes place in New York but refers to historical events in Greenland.

Synopsis: A historian interviews a retired scientist who developed a way to slow down and preserve the disappearing ice of Greenland, averting the worst impacts of sea level rise.

. . .

A partial transcript dated 05/24/2091 for the oral history portion of the Kalaallit Nunaat Project, archived at the UN Intergovernmental Panel on Climate Change, New York.

Jay: Can you say your name please?

Hamilton: Dr. Julia B. Hamilton. What was your name again? My memory isn't as good as it used to be.

Jay: I'm Malcolm Jay, the IPCC historian, remember? [mic noise] I need to adjust... there.

Hamilton: Such a young man. I like your bow tie.

Jay: What is your affiliation, Dr. Hamilton?

Hamilton: Julia is fine. I used to work at the Lamont-Doherty Earth Observatory.

Jay: That's part of Columbia University, right?

Hamilton: Yes, but I wasn't in the office very much.

Jay: You spent a lot of time in Greenland. That's what I want to hear about.

Hamilton: I practically lived there for forty years. There was The Quilt.

Jay: Why did people call it The Quilt?

Hamilton: The project wasn't really a quilt, but I had an heirloom quilt made by my grandmother. It hung in my office, and the rolls of fabric we laid out on the ice reminded me of it. I compared the project to my quilt once. The nickname stuck.

Jay: Dr Hamilton—I mean, Julia—

Hamilton: That's better.

Jay: Can we step back? I've been researching the Kalaallit Nunaat Project, but I'm confused on some of the details. Can you give me a quick summary?

Hamilton: Oh, for Heaven's sake, that would take hours. I might not have enough time before I croak. [mild laughter] Everyone was worried about sea level rise. Greenland's ice was disappearing into the North Atlantic. If all that ice melted, the ocean would rise seventy meters, but people didn't think we could do much about it.

Jay: Then came the Year of Storms.

Hamilton: Horrible for the poor people who died in those hurricanes and cyclones, but governments finally wised up and asked us climate scientists what we could do. We had to think big. We had a planet-wide catastrophe on our hands. Now, the year before, I took a hiking trip with my wife, Melissa, to Obergoms in the Swiss Alps, and we visited the Rhône Glacier. That's when I first saw the blankets.

Jay: I have a picture. It's part of the record. [rustling papers] Here you go.

Hamilton: Oh, I looked good then. My beautiful dark hair. Anyway, the townspeople depended on the glacier to attract tourists, and it was melting like the dickens, so they covered parts of it with reflective fabric. I thought the idea was crazy. The even crazier thing is it worked. A study in 2015 showed that melting fell by 70 percent. It slowed the glacier's retreat. Melissa looked at me in her sly way and said, "What about a blanket on Greenland?" I had spent a summer studying the Gunnbjørn Fjeld there as a post-doc, so I knew what she was suggesting.

Jay: You must've thought she was a little crazy.

Hamilton: [laughter] I had my doubts, then I found a paper by Dr. Jason Box, a glaciologist at Ohio State, which suggested the same thing. Nobody took him seriously, but this was after the Year of Storms, so I called him. He was retired at that point. He put me in touch with a materials scientist.

Jay: This was Chakra [unintelligible; papers rustling].

Hamilton: You really know how to mangle a name, don't

you? [mild laughter] Yes, he invented the material we used to make the blankets. It was strong, but it eventually broke down into inert materials so it wouldn't pollute the ice. Perfect.

Jay: You did the impossible.

Hamilton: Nonsense. It's easy to look back now and see its success. But so much went wrong. No one had ever made rolls of our fabric at scale, and it took a year to figure it out. Nuuk Harbor was too small for the cargo ships, so we built a special floating pier. It sank the first winter. The manufacturer of the tractors that rolled out the fabric never had enough spare parts. The helicopters that delivered the fabric rolls to the work sites couldn't fly half the time because of the weather. And we could only work part of the year because the autumn and winter piteraq winds would kill you if you weren't careful.

Jay: But the Great Greenland Quilting Bee carried on.

Hamilton: [heavy laughter] That's what Melissa called it. She was great at PR.

Jay: I heard about—[brief silence] I'm sorry for your loss, Julia.

Hamilton: You're very kind, Malcolm. Without Melissa, I don't think I would've survived the stress. She encouraged me every day.

Jay: What was it like when you were finally finished?

Hamilton: Well, my first feeling was relief. Then it was amazement. We'd protected all the most vulnerable surfaces on the major glaciers and the ice sheets, something in the hundreds of thousands of square kilometers. I forget the exact number. It still blows my mind.

Jay: It's working too, even after all these years. You can see your work from space, did you know that? Long strips, huge squares, like a geometry lesson.

Hamilton: I've seen the pictures. It's almost as beautiful as my grandmother's quilt. What we made is like an heirloom for Earth's grandchildren, wouldn't you say?

. . .

About the author:

Follansbee is published in *Bards and Sages Quarterly, Children, Churches and Daddies*, and the anthologies *Satirica, Still Life 2018, After the Orange, Spring Into SciFi 2019, Rabbit Hole II, Sunshine Superhighway*, and *Fix the World*. He has another story coming spring 2022 in *Save the World*. He is the author of the series *Tales From A Warming Planet* and the trilogy *The Future History of the Grail*. He has won several awards in the Writers of the Future contest, and he was a finalist in the inaugural Aftermath short story contest. He lives in Seattle.

30

COPS

by Ann Murray (United States)

Subgenres: Dystopian science fiction, middle grade, young adult dystopian

Time Period: Late twenty-first century

Setting: The Productive World Neighborhood, Earth

Editor's Note: Imagine a dystopian future like that of Lois Lowry's *The Giver* or George Orwell's *Nineteen Eighty-Four*, but on an oppressively hot Earth seen through the eyes of a ten-year-old boy. Suitable for all ages.

Synopsis: Runaway climate change is happening much faster than even the smart guys predicted. Humans are out of time, out of luck, and almost out of resources. What are the remnants of a civilization to do? Join Billy and his neighbors on an average day in the Productive World Neighborhood. But be careful! The COPS are watching.

. . .

As Michigan's burning midwinter sun came rolling over the

horizon, 225 rooftop sun shields irised closed for the day on 225 identical doms in Billy's neighborhood. Like all the other neighborhoods in their quadrant, Neighborhood 4408 was ready to start another productive workday in service of the Productive World Neighborhood, the PWN. It was a special day for Billy and his friends too. This was the first day of their winter break from Productive Children's Training Camp. It was perfect weather, not a cloud in the sky, and a balmy 130 degrees outside. What kid could ask for more?

. . .

Ten-year-old Billy Adamz22XR knew exactly what he and his friend Jake planned to do today. They were riding their QuietBikes over to their favorite place in the PWN, the abandoned Biomass Cooperative. The huge mounds of unused biomass, with their shallow runoff ponds, were one of the few places left in the PWN that weren't dome-farmed or covered with domiciles. It was a place where kids with excess energy could explore nature and enjoy freedom from the MAN's Rules of Order, Productivity, and Silence. Billy and Jake knew the old Biomass Co-op would eventually be either converted for dome farming or used to build more neighborhood doms. But for now, while they still could, they took advantage of every opportunity to explore the mounds.

. . .

Billy and Jake were well aware of how the abandoned biomass mounds had come into being. Every kid in Training Camp had studied the climate crisis and its resulting pandemics in their series of primers, "The New Earth Sciences and Rectification of the Planet's Ecosystems," beginning with Volume I, "Following the MANS' Rules to Save the Earth and Ourselves." Billy thought the best thing about their primers were the illustrations, especially the recycling superheroes Max and Maxine Patchwork with their fun tips on how to follow the MAN's rules of order, peace, and silence to help the Earth heal. Like many of the kids, Billy had talked his mom into making him a small patchwork cape just like the big patchwork cape Max wore. She'd used her precious fabric sewing scraps to make a mini version, and it was his favorite thing to wear on Freestyle Friday at Training Camp once a month.

. . .

Their primers said the Earth had heated up so much from pollution, waste, and greed that the polar ice caps had melted. As the caps melted, they released organisms that had been frozen and dormant for thousands of years. When the organisms were released, some of those organisms weren't friendly to humans, not one little bit. So many lives were lost during the resulting Omega Pandemic caused by one of those organisms, the time period following the disaster was called The Hard Times. The boys were taught that people in the Productive World Neighborhood were finally emerging from those very hard times, and it was necessary for everyone to follow the MAN's rules to heal the planet and ensure everyone's survival. There just wasn't any other way to do it. The MAN told them so, and the MAN never lied. Did it?

. . .

Before New Day One, the world was in such a mess its leaders asked the Main Advanced Network, the MAN, the most sophisticated computer program in the world, to generate a manifesto for helping the world reorganize to fight runaway climate change and the resulting pandemics. The MAN-generated Manifesto and its slogans and rules for a Productive World Neighborhood came into existence. The world lived by the Manifesto, and it was etched in every neighbor's memory, including Billy's:

> *Order means concentration. Concentration means working. Working is productive. Productivity and following the Rules will help the Productive World Neighborhood. The PWN protects all Neighbors. Therefore, Order equals Protection for all neighbors.*

You could substitute the other two key words, "Peace" or "Silence," for the word "Order," but the meaning was the same. Little kids learned a simpler version of the complex and somewhat ambiguous Manifesto. "Keep things orderly, be productive, stay silent, and follow the rules."

The problem was, even the MAN program wasn't able to accurately predict whether the PWN's efforts, including following the MAN's Productive Rules to slow the environmental disaster and its resulting pandemics, were working or not. The shortages of food and products seemed to be getting worse, and the livable land was shrinking due to rising sea levels caused by the melting ice caps. The propaganda mill said their efforts were winning the fight. Many of the neighbors wondered why the lines were getting longer at the food commissary and the selections less, if the PWN was, in fact, "winning" the struggle. And why was everyone working so many extra hours each day? The MAN answered in its usual way by ignoring any direct questions. And that was that.

. . .

Secreted away among the biomass mounds, Billy and Jake would be out of sight and hearing distance from the ever-present neighborhood COPS and any other snoops who chased after the extra credits they could earn by turning in a kid for breaking any Productive Rule. As Billy knew well from experience, there was never any shortage of snoops around.

He was impatient to get going. It was rumored that one of the kids had seen an intact live amph near the runoff ponds.

Whether it was a frog, toad, or newt, none of the kids was ever quite sure, because the toxic runoff from the mounds caused many of the amphs to have extra or missing eyes and appendages, or to be too small. Of course, they'd all seen pics of perfect amphibians on their learners, and the real thing in traveling live animal exhibits that came around to Training Camp. But sightings of recognizable amphs were rare, and Billy knew he'd be lucky if he saw one today.

If it were me, Billy Adamz22XR, who could report to the other kids that I'd spotted a recognizable amph with a witness to prove it, meaning Jake, it would bring me extra status at Training Camp. And I definitely could use the make-up status, Billy thought ruefully. He remembered his occasional lapses in judgment when he broke the rules, and the resulting punishments he caused for everybody. It was sometimes really hard to be a ten-year-old boy. There were just too many rules in the PWN.

Maybe I could even bring the amph to Training Camp, he mused, but immediately squashed the idea. An error in judgment of that magnitude would bring on double, triple, quadruple trouble. A *Crime Against the Environment IX, Removing Live Animals from their Natural Habitat* could result in the whole neighborhood being punished as well as the perp. Every neighbor in Neighborhood 4408 would probably lose credits for months if he got turned in to the COPS. Billy knew old man Westmoreland, the neighborhood Chief of Order, Productivity, and Silence, would love to catch him again. He was determined it wasn't going to happen this time.

If I cause our neighborhood to lose credits again, none of the kids at T-Camp will speak to me for weeks, maybe not for life, he thought. The kids were tolerant of each other, but even they would get sick of someone who kept losing credits for their family units. Lost credits could result in families eating bland rations, or for parents to lose transport credits to Productive Work. Worse, his own family would lose more credits than the others. That's the way punishments worked under the MAN's manifesto. He loved his little family unit so much; he didn't want to cause them any more trouble than he already had.

. . .

When his dad was ready to leave for Productive Work, Billy came back from his daydreaming. He thought his dad was the most handsome and smartest dad in the whole neighborhood. All Productive Workers, or PW's, wore identical gray uniforms, and the men had identical flat-top haircuts. Billy's hair was cut just like his dad's, which made him feel like an adult. He thought his dad looked and acted just like Productive Neighbor Sam. PN Sam was the persona who appeared on the kids' learners from time to time during the day to remind them all to follow the rules. PN Sam and Billy's dad were both conformists, hardworking, and productive. Billy sometimes wondered if he would ever be able to live up to PN Sam's expectations. Or his dad's.

. . .

Billy's mom said to his dad, "Don't forget to close the sun shield over your seat in the transport today, dear. You had an awful case of sun sickness that time you forgot. We can't afford to lose two days' worth of credits for sick leave again, Jim-o. It took forever for us to earn back those credits."

"Two days of sun poisoning was enough to last a lifetime, Glo. I definitely won't forget again," Dad replied. JamesO8K, Billy's dad, showed his wrist to the front port panel, and it irised open without a sound for him to step outside. Silently, the transport waited for him in the street, half-filled with other PW's. Watching him leave, Billy saw his dad squint uncomfortably up at the fierce sun, like he did every workday, then throw his arm up to shield his head as he trotted to the transport. The port whispered closed behind him.

. . .

All adults had been born before the Great Tweak, so they stayed inside for much of their day and night because they couldn't take the rapidly rising heat. The genetic tweak was administered to fetuses in utero, and it allowed kids to rapidly acclimate to extremes of temperature. Billy was glad he'd never have the same problem the adults did with the heat; at least that's what the scientists said. He was part of the first generation that was tweaked, and the children were all being carefully monitored.

There was a theory that if genes were tweaked for two or three generations, the tweak itself might start to become naturally passed on genetically to succeeding generations. This would eliminate the need for artificially tweaking the fetuses in the future. Of course, how long the Great Tweak would remain effective would depend on how fast Earth's runaway temps were rising. Even genetic manipulation couldn't fix something the scientists hadn't predicted. The speed at which climate change was happening was much faster than anyone ever imagined.

. . .

Gloria2Y spun back around to Billy, pasted a too-large smile on her face, and said, "Go on now, Billy. Ride your QuietBike with Jake. But go over the PWN rules with me first, ok?"

Billy's shoulders slumped.

"I'm sorry Billy, but you know the deal. You kids absolutely *must* memorize the rules. It's almost like our lives depend on it." She caught herself, then quickly added, "No, not really though. Not life or death. Mom exaggerates, heh, heh. It's just that we will lose credits if you don't follow the rules, that's all." Billy noticed her voice sounded a little hollow.

"Last year you got us all in trouble, remember? Mr. Westmoreland, our faithful neighborhood COPS, wants us all to strictly abide by the Productive World Neighborhood's Rules.

You didn't report that piece of real paper you saw on 131st Street, did you? A 'Failure to Report Recyclables on Common Ground, Misdemeanor 884' got the whole neighborhood in trouble, not just us. But we suffered the most, didn't we, since we lost those precious extra transport credits we'd saved and couldn't travel to see your grandmother once again." Billy's mom didn't look mad; she looked tired.

"And when we all were punished, your dad had to ride the QuietBike to work for a month before our transport credits were restored. You know how he hates riding the QB. Your dad and I don't have the Great Tweak like you kids do. We have a hard time tolerating the extremely high temps, you know." Mom sighed and gazed absently around the room. "I haven't seen my mother in three years," she continued. Billy knew she really missed her mother, and he missed his grandmother too. "Ever since you turned seven, things just kind of seemed to... to..." She trailed off and glanced down at him with what looked a little like fright. Billy didn't like seeing his mom in this state. She was the best mom in the PWN. He would do anything for her; he loved her that much.

He gave her a big hug. "I'll be good this time, Mom. I'll report every single punishable order, productivity, or silence rule violation I see or hear. I'll do better this time, Mom, I really will. You'll see." He looked up at her with his saddest eyes because he knew they melted her heart. His head hit just above her waist, and hugging her this closely, he noticed the three small holes in her last real cotton jumpsuit had gotten bigger and more frayed. This was her only cotton jumpsuit left, now that the super weevil had decimated the cotton crops. His mom loved soft cotton fabric much more than the synthfabs they made uniforms out of now. Vintage cotton had become a luxury fabric and was hard to get, even if someone had the extra credits, which very few of the neighbors did. Prices for certain things were skyrocketing, just like the Earth's temperatures were, and credits had to be carefully managed, every last one.

Billy sure wished he could find a way to get ahold of enough credits for a piece of cotton fabric for his mom. That would make her happy. Lately, she seemed less happy than she used to be, and it made him sad. But outside of going to Children's Productive Training Camp, there weren't many jobs left that a kid could do to earn a few extra credits.

. . .

Once, Dad explained to Billy how factors relating to rapid climate change caused prices to skyrocket. Rising temps caused damage in many ways to food and other crops. Crop-destroying insects had multiplied after their predators died due to inhospitable rising habitat temperatures. Food and other goods became scarcer, so prices for them rose. All neighbors had to use fewer products and recycle more to cut down on their use of the Earth's remaining limited resources.

But Billy was not to worry too much about it. Smart people like his dad and the other scientists were working on these problems right now, and they'd surely come up with solutions soon. But he sometimes wondered why his dad seemed more distracted lately. He was working so many extra hours at the lab, he hardly ever had time to go lighter-than-air jumping with him anymore, and Billy didn't like that. He couldn't help it; things were making him worry.

. . .

Gloria2Y pushed Billy away from their hug, crouched down, and looked him in the eyes. "And what's the other thing? You remember that too don't you, honey?"

"Yeah, Mom. And most importantly, be extra careful in front of neighbor Westmorland's domicile. Absolutely no noise in front of the COPS dom. Every kid knows that one by heart."

"Ok, go! Be a good Productive Neighbor Sam today. The whole neighborhood's counting on you. And be back before your YuVeeGel protection fails, ok? Four hours max, and no more, got it?"

"Got it, Mom!" Billy turned and dutifully walked through the YuVeeGel's waterfall membrane, coating his entire body and clothes with its nearly invisible film. Then he opened his mouth and nostrils and braced for the AntiVira spray to coat them, in case any remaining superviruses lurked in the environment. He hated that spray; it always made him choke. Five seconds to dry, then he jumped out the front port. Thoughts of the rules and old man Westmoreland's eager enforcement of them would soon be pushed out of his mind when he hit the road with Jake. The COPS was so boring with his constant chatter about how "We all have to make sacrifices if we're ever going to repair runaway climate change," and "The best way to help reverse rapid climate change and reduce pandemics is to follow all the rules." Blah, blah.

Billy believed the COPS was out to get him. And with Billy, the opportunity to catch him breaking rules arose more often than it should have.

He's a rule-breaker, that one, thought Westmoreland. But he'd broken tougher kids than Billy, and he was sure he'd get him to bend to the rules eventually. *Even if it takes me a lifetime, I'll break him,* Westmoreland vowed.

. . .

Jake was waiting for Billy in the street, quietly riding circles on his QB, a big grin on his freckled face when he saw Billy. *How could anybody worry about rules when they were heading out for a day of fun with a friend like Jake?* They sped off toward the furthest corner of the neighborhood and the old entrance road to the deserted biomass mounds.

They maintained the productive silence while they rode, only whispering back and forth when they just couldn't hold something in. Billy loved Jake for his unfailing loyalty to Billy, even when his rule-breaking exploits managed to lose the whole neighborhood credits, including Jake's family.

Along the ride, Billy had plenty of time to think about things. Sometimes he hated old man Westmoreland, the Chief of Order, Productivity, and Silence. *I bet you have COPS tattooed on your butt, don't you? And I especially hate you, sneaky old Ms. Bleece. You're a mean neighborhood spy. You turned me in last time for that violation of the order rules. All I did was throw that broken stylus on the ground when I thought no one was looking. You're a snitch!*

The whole neighborhood had lost credits over that one. It had taken a long time for the kids at T-Camp to start talking to him again. All the kids except for Jake, of course. Good old Jake, he was the most loyal friend a boy could have. Billy's very best friend forever.

A hot wind stirred the scent of freshly turned earth, and Billy inhaled deeply. He loved the smell of dirt and the outdoors a lot more than the scent-free, quadruple-filtered, and scrubbed dom air. They were riding past a street where bots were digging a row of identical foundations for new soundproof domiciles exactly like all the other doms in the PWN, except these new doms were a bit smaller than the older ones. It appeared the productive designers were making the newest doms smaller and closer together, yet they housed the same number of people, four, which met the current zero population growth guidelines.

They slowed their QB's to near-silent mode when they passed the dom with a sign that read:

Main Domicile—Chief of Order, Productivity, and Silence, 83rd Division, Quadrant 9, Neighborhood 4408—Ulterious Xavier9 Westmoreland, COPS.

They sped up after they'd passed it by. Billy flicked his hand a couple of times as if he were shaking off Westmoreland. He never really would be able to shake him off, though. As they rode on, Billy liked looking at the single pots of red mini-geraniums under their tiny domes in front of every dom. They were the only decoration allowed in the neighborhood front yards this year. Last year, they'd all received permission to put a pot of boring white mini-daisies in front of each dom. This year's red mini-geraniums were much more exciting to see, in Billy's opinion. He'd hated the year his neighborhood had no flowers in front of anyone's dom. His cheeks blushed with shame at the thought that it had been his fault. Again. They eventually arrived at the furthest corner of the neighborhood and came to the old road where the EvaSurface ended and cracked, broken asphalt began. Almost no one used this forbidden road anymore, and a sign sat crookedly beside the road reading, "**PWN Biomass Cooperative—KEEP OUT. Rule violators will be punished.**" Around a long curve, the huge biomass mounds gradually came into view. The place was abandoned long ago, and the old chain link fence was broken and missing in places, making it easy to get inside. They hid their bikes behind some scrub and scurried through the fence into the expansive grounds.

Here, eleven mountainous piles of biomass towered over the shallow runoff ponds which pooled around their bases. The ponds used to be much deeper, containing more aquatic life than the anemic shallow ponds they'd become. Dilapidated utilitarian sheet metal buildings hulked here and there, their rusty mechanicals protruding out ragged openings. The property contained real but scrubby native plants, stunted trees, and the rare intact amphibians. Once in a while, the boys got a glimpse of an identifiable frog, toad, or newt, instead of the strange little things they usually saw. Even so, the only animals they could count on seeing every time they came were the tiny minnows who nibbled on their toes in the ponds.

Billy longed to see a full-grown fish. Unfortunately, the minnows rarely seemed to grow any bigger. Just like the amphs, birds, and other animals, they appeared to seldom reach full size. There was one exception though. The boys had seen some massive rats lately and many overly large mice. Always survivors, the rodents seemed to be the only animals who were thriving in the high temperatures.

. . .

At the Biomass Cooperative, since the boys were far away from neighbors' prying eyes and ears, they could talk out loud, yell, and even scream as much as they wanted. Due to Billy's propensity for trouble, they kept an eye out for any snoops who hoped to snag a few extra credits for turning someone in for breaking the silence or order rules.

"Yaaahhhh-hhoooo," Billy yelled at the top of his lungs. Jake answered with a whistle-shriek of his own. The sense of power and freedom a good shriek produced was hard for a kid to resist. They knew they were taking chances, but danger was part of the thrill. Still, Billy couldn't help but remember a bad experience one of his T-Camp friends had with the COPS.

. . .

"Boys will be boys." That's what WrenH6's dad had said to Westmoreland when Wreny got in trouble for shouting in the street from sheer exuberance once. His dad's excuse about boys being boys didn't fly with the COPS, though. WrenH6's family and the whole neighborhood had suffered for his violation of the productive silence rules. But Billy couldn't worry about that now. Jake was calling, and it was time to explore.

. . .

Climbing around on the mountainous piles, the boys might find a piece of steel-belted radial tire, thick piece of old bark, or maybe even an animal's bones. Once Billy had taken home an old bird skull. Even though he'd hidden it in his secret hiding place, the idea that he could be caught at any moment with proof he'd broken a rule ate away at him. He didn't need a productive order violation, "Removing Wood, Tire shards, or Biological Materials from Their Outdoor Locations, Misdemeanor

XVI." He'd surreptitiously returned the bird skull to the biomass mound as soon as he could.

. . .

The boys had been leaning out and over the pond on a rotting beam because they thought they'd seen a recognizable frog when Jake's neck ring began to vibrate. "Gotta get back. Come on!" Jake said.

But Billy didn't want to leave. He wanted to see if it really was a frog or just ripples on the pond. He threw a couple of last rocks into the water, but the image of neighbor Westmorland's bushy unibrow and straight-line mouth loomed in his mind, spoiling his fun. His dad called the COPS a "real killjoy," and explained that "killjoy" was an old-fashioned word for someone who spoiled someone else's fun. From the other kids at T-Camp, Billy had found out that most adults and kids felt the same way he did about Westmoreland. That made him feel a little better. He wasn't the only one to hate the old man.

"We've got time yet. What's the hurry?" Billy whined at Jake.

"I already told you. If I don't get home early today, Dad will kill me. We've got an inspection tonight, so he needs me to help make sure the front yard follows all the productive order rules. We haven't lost any credits for violations yet this year, and Dad will hate me if I screw up our record now. So, come on, let's go!" Jake gave a last yelping screech and jumped on his QB, spinning gravel backward before he slowed down to quiet mode again.

"Ok." Billy decided to head back with him and then ride on by himself for a while.

When they got to his dom, Jake whispered "Bye" to Billy. "Atcha," Billy whispered back and kept on riding.

. . .

Billy rode further into another neighborhood, riding up and

around its hill, then around again. He knew practically all the kids in this neighborhood, too. That dom was Tiny's. His name was Karl3G, but he was one of those kids whose uniforms always looked one size too big, so the kids gave him the moniker Tiny. And cute Jaqui4L lived in that one. She was way too cute for Billy to even talk to, but he loved looking at her when her column passed his column at Productive Children's Training Camp. Two little boys lived in that dom, Nate and JayH9, way too young for a big kid of ten like Billy to associate with.

He noticed there were no flowers in front of any doms in this neighborhood. He felt relief knowing that at least one other person had broken a rule and caused their own neighborhood to get punished, just like Billy so often did to his. Then it really was time to head back to his dom before his YuVeeGel coating became ineffective.

As he rode along, Billy smelled the luscious scent of InstaGrills cooking plant-protein burgers drifting out of air exhausts. Yum, it was burger night for everyone in the quad. And that meant it was cookie night too! He hoped all the moms made synth-chip cookies today, his favorite. He remembered that once his mom had put real chocolate chips in his cookies. That was before the cocoa trees were decimated by the blue mega mirid bugs. Now all neighbors had to substitute synthetic chocolate for the almost unattainable real thing.

Gloria2Y was a good cook. Billy's family unit seldom relied on insta pacs or AutoDrone-distributed meal boxes, and he was glad. Cubes and oblongs of insta food could get boring. His mom was also good at procuring real foods like tomatoes and strawberries, when they were available, to mix in with their faux foods. Once, when he'd asked her why their family unit's meals tasted better than some of his friends' meals, she told him, "My secret is I cheat a little and add a few extra spoonsful of BootTaste, sometimes more. BT makes just about anything taste good, even plastiboard, ha, ha!"

Glo went on, "Since so many crops aren't producing as well

as they used to, they're giving out BootTaste for free at the food commissary. Isn't that great!" Billy nodded, even though he suspected things weren't as great in the food department as his mom was making herself believe. She looked so pretty when she laughed, even when it was a fake laugh. He wished he could find a way to get real chocolate and other expensive foods for his mom. Maybe that would make her happy, and she'd laugh more. He decided he'd put more thought into how to go about this.

. . .

At the Productive Children's Training Camp, Billy learned that scientists like his dad had gen-engineered giant hyper assassin bugs to combat the blue mega mirid bugs and other crop destroyers. However, the atmosphere had become too hot for even the new assassin bugs to thrive, and they had all but disappeared. Damaging insect populations exploded when their predators disappeared. That's when the Unhealthy Cycle had begun, and many food and other crops were damaged or lost completely unless they were grown under domes. Billy noticed his mom had to get up even earlier than she used to and wait in longer lines at the food com to get the ingredients for their meals. He was pretty sure this was why she was looking more tired these days.

. . .

On his ride home, he slowed again when he passed neighbor Westmorland's dom. No one was visible in the viewports, but Billy knew the COPS was inside listening and probably watching him on his retina implant. It was Westmoreland's job "to know everything that happens in the neighborhood," as he repeatedly told them on the fraught occasions when he'd been inside the Adamz22XR's dom for inspections. As Billy passed by, he felt eyes on the back of his neck, and it made his skin crawl.

. . .

To carry out the goals of its manifesto, the MAN program assigned a guardianship hierarchy to oversee the PWN, with officials organized from the top down. The MAN program appointed itself to be the highest official in the PWN and then appointed overseeing officials, all the way down to the local level. At the bottom of the chain of command, the neighborhood officials were called the COPS, Chiefs of Order, Productivity, and Silence.

Ulterious Xavier9 Westmoreland fit perfectly all the Manifesto's requirements for the job of COPS. Punctilious, a rulemeister, and a believer in strict punishment, Westmoreland enjoyed his work too much. He enforced the rules and handed out punishments with a happy little chuckle. He was especially the bane of the neighborhood children. It wasn't only that he felt the need to train children early; it was because he just plain didn't like kids. Since Billy tended to overestimate his own ability to escape detection after breaking a rule, he was doomed to see much more of Westmoreland than he would have liked.

. . .

On the last block before home, Billy came to a sudden dead stop in front of dom 839. He thought he heard a loud noise coming from inside through the inexplicably open front port. Few neighbors left their ports open during the day for fear of just that thing, breaking a silence rule by accidentally making a loud noise. If they did open the port, it was only for cleaning or other infrequent purposes, and the unconditioned raw air outside made them want to close them as quickly as possible.

"Ar-ruggh, ar-ruggh!" Billy jerked when he heard the sound again. He knew exactly what it was—the two-part sound of a dog barking. "It's so loud," Billy breathed when he heard it a third time. It came from Buddy, the Jacksons' newly leased pug dog, one of only two dog leases won in the dog lottery this year for their whole neighborhood. The Jacksons had made a bad mistake leaving that port open.

If you were lucky enough to win a dog lease, you made sure the dog went to Productive Dog Training Camp and learned not to make loud noises. Even that wasn't foolproof, because everyone knew dogs were unpredictable. You never knew what small thing might set them off and nullify their training. Usually, the family took extra precautions and used their precious dom improvement credits to install extra sound insulation for exactly that type of noise emergency. Sometimes even extra sound insulation didn't help muffle noises if you left your port open.

"No," whispered Billy in shock. "Oh no, no, don't make me do this, don't, don't. I won't report the silence violation. I won't report the Jacksons. No." Another bark sounded, then the sound of scuffling, running feet, thumping, and a squeal. The barking stopped, but it was a minute before Billy could breathe and move again. He pretended to be casual and glanced around to see if any other neighbors might have heard the barking. He hadn't noticed anyone in the street within hearing distance and thought he might be able to ride quietly away, pretending it didn't happen.

Out of the corner of his eye, he caught the viewport irising shut on the dom across the street from the Jacksons. What bad luck! It was sneaky Ms. Bleece's domicile, the spy. He knew she'd seen him, and she'd definitely heard Buddy barking too. Nobody living that close could avoid hearing it. She was just mean enough not to report the dog barking herself, but to wait and see if Billy would report it first. If he didn't report it, she could get double credits for reporting the noise herself, and then reporting Billy for his failure to report the noise. *Double the credits for you this month, you snitch*, Billy thought angrily. She was crafty, mean, and always seemed to get away with things by getting other neighbors in trouble.

. . .

Every day, all neighbors were required to watch and listen to Productive Neighbor Sam broadcasting the MAN-generated daily productive messages. They had to pay strict attention for the good of the PWN or face possible punishment. Billy knew the Jacksons memorized the Productive Silence Rules just as well as everybody else did. He shook his head. They wouldn't have any excuse to give to the COPS for their silence violation at all.

Yeah, yeah, Billy thought, as the slogans raced through his mind while he hurried back to his dom. *I can recite the rules and slogans in my sleep.* He began to feel like the UV rays were penetrating his skull as his 'Gel began to fail. He swiped his wrist chip at the bike's panel and rode faster. He badly wanted to get home.

. . .

Billy knew if he were caught failing to turn in a blatant rule violation, Westmoreland could ruin his family's chance to travel to see Grandma again. There would be a good chance his dad would have to make up for lost transportation credits by riding the QB to Productive Work. He knew his dad disliked being slathered in YuVeeGel and much preferred the built-in sunshielding and controlled temperature of the transports. Billy hated having to struggle so much about whether to snitch or not. His head was beginning to pound.

He got off and walked along beside the Quiet Bike. Billy felt sick and wondered if he was going to vomit in the street. Maybe he felt queasy from the mini-eggs he'd eaten with the soysage this morning? Maybe they were old or bad or something? It couldn't be anything else making his stomach churn, could it? He stopped the bike and ate a bubble of water from his pack, then felt a little better. He got back on, showed his wrist chip to the screen, and took off.

He imagined his beautiful mom's sad face and his disappointed dad, and he could hardly stand it. He thought his head would explode with frustration. Then, suddenly, his eyes widened, his head cleared, and he absolutely knew what he had to do. He had to report the Jacksons' noise violation for his parents' sake. *Mom is the best mom in the world and Dad the best dad. I'll be a Productive Neighbor Sam for the good of the family unit, the good of the neighbors, and the good of the PWN. I'll be a good conformist and follow the rules from now until forever. I'll turn the Jacksons in.* Somehow, it was easier for Billy to believe he was doing this thing for them all, rather than just for himself.

But Billy was still a conflicted boy. The problem was that he, too, had hoped to win a dog lease in the dog leasing lottery. It was held once a year, and his family entered every time. This made it hard for him to do what he decided he had to. Billy was getting very tired of being a constant disappointment to the world. It was wearing him down.

. . .

"Oh, there you are, Billy. You've been gone for a long time. I'm surprised you haven't gotten sun sick," his mom said. She frowned and looked at him more closely. His knees felt wobbly. He was beginning to lose his nerve. She could always tell when he was upset. Pulling him to her, she said, "What's wrong, Billy, what's wrong? You're upset. What happened out there? Tell me, please."

"I... uh... I, I think... it was, it was...," Billy stammered.

"Billy, talk. You're safe now; the neighbors can't hear you if you don't raise your voice too much. And I'll turn off the Assistant." She flashed her palm implant at the closest wall and flicked her wrist. The room responded, "Daily discretionary free time on, AssistantEarEye off. The Productive World Neighborhood grants you thirty minutes." Billy saw his mother glance around the room furtively, as if to see whether someone else might be in the dom with them, even though she knew they were alone. "Now, Billy, we're all alone, no ear, no eye, so talk, sweetheart."

"A d-d-d... a dog. A dog, Mom. A dog barking. Loud, you could hear it in the street. The Jacksons accidentally left their front port open so you could hear Buddy barking. Buddy has a real loud bark."

Gloria2Y looked uneasy. "A dog barking." She was silent for a long moment. "That's a productive silence violation. Tell me, what did you see, Billy? Did anyone see you, or did you see anyone? Did any neighbors hear the dog? Was anyone outside?" She sounded worried.

"Yes, Mom, I did see something. Ms. Bleece's viewport was closing while I watched. She lives just across the street from the Jacksons. I know she saw me. And worse yet, she probably heard Buddy's loud barking too. I think she heard something and then opened her port to hear it better." A big tear rolled down Billy's cheek.

Billy's mom hesitated for a moment. When she finally spoke, she sounded frustrated. "Why did the Jacksons have to leave that port open today? Especially since they have a dog and know how easy it would be to break the rules with noise? The Jacksons have gotten you into a real fix. We could lose credits again." Mom looked afraid, and that in turn scared Billy. "Neighbor Bleece wouldn't hesitate one single minute to tell the COPS you heard a dog and failed to report it. No. She. Wouldn't."

They stood silently looking at each other. His mom was apparently having her own struggle with the situation. Then she squared her shoulders, took a deep breath, and in a firm voice said, "You know what you have to do, don't you, Billy?"

"Yes, I think I do." The big tear left a trail where it slid down his cheek to his chin, then plopped onto his synthfab jumpsuit and immediately disappeared into the fabric. "I have to report the Jacksons for a violation of the productive silence rules."

"Yes, you do." She nodded. "I knew you'd do the right thing. You're my good little Productive Neighbor Sam." She gave him a weak smile. "Mom and Dad and the T-Camp have trained you to be an outstanding conformist. You'll be doing the right thing for our family unit." She hastily added, "And most importantly, you'll be doing it for the PWN. Besides not being able to see Grandma, the neighbors would all suffer if you didn't report it, and you know what that means, don't you? Our family unit wouldn't be forgiven for weeks, maybe months. The neighbors would treat us like we weren't even there." She sighed and continued, "And one more thing, Billy." She quoted Westmoreland, "'We all have to make sacrifices if we're ever going to repair the runaway warming of Earth and reduce the pandemics that warming causes.'" Glo looked almost sick when she recited the COPS favorite saying. So did Billy.

No one in the PWN was ever completely convinced the AssistantEarEye devices the MAN installed in every domicile were really turned off for their allotted free time and not still listening to their conversations. There was no way to ever find out. Consequently, all the neighbors wondered if the MAN kept secret dossiers on their "free time" conversations. Did it give special consideration to anything it considered treasonous to its manifesto? The result of their suspicions was they all became experts at conversation manipulation. The only time they really felt safe from the AssistantEarEye was outside, and the adults seldom ventured out there, so they all played it safe. They never said outright what was really on their minds. Better to be obscure. It was just easier that way.

. . .

After Dad got home, the Adamz22XR family walked up the street to the COPS dom to report the violation and fill out the forms. There weren't many neighbors outside this evening. A couple of kids were playing on the UnTurf, and a personal transport quietly glided into a garage dome. The temp had dropped to 126 degrees, still too warm out for the adults. Since his parents hadn't been tweaked, Billy noticed they were sweating a lot more than usual, buckets even, despite the fact it was just a short walk to the COPS.

They all jumped when the COPS whipped open his front port without a greeting. Westmoreland ushered them inside, almost like he expected them. *Old Lady Bleece has already snitched on me,* Billy thought resentfully. He hated her. He hated the COPS, but he'd learned a long time ago to wipe those feelings off his face so no one would ever know. Westmoreland was wearing his Neighborhood COPS badge. It gleamed brightly into Billy's eyes.

. . .

It was another vacation day away from Productive Children's Training Camp. The temp stood at 135 degrees, which triggered a Climate Alert for the adults, but that didn't bother Billy. *It's another good day for exploring the biomass mountains,* he thought. He couldn't wait to get out there.

Jake swiped the back of his hand across the panel next to Billy's front port. The silent alert light flashed on and off in all the rooms. Billy was ready for him and jumped through the front port. They bumped elbows and headed out. Jake was so much fun to be with and never seemed to be in a bad mood. Billy envied his friend's ability to wiggle his way out of any trouble and wished he were as clever as Jake.

Jake kept his voice quiet. "Hey, Billy. Someone said they were able to identify an adult turtle near the Biomass Co-op's ponds the other day." This was exciting news, and it made them ride faster, eager to see if the rumor was true. Speeding produced the addictive sense of freedom they both craved. Then it didn't. They unconsciously slowed as they passed dom 839. They couldn't help but notice how quiet the Jacksons' dom was. They knew there'd be no barking coming from inside today, since there was no dog inside, either. Buddy the pug had been transferred to a family unit in another neighborhood in a far quadrant. Billy gave an automatic little shudder.

He could hardly stand to look at Rodney9 Jackson, who was walking out his front port at that moment. They locked eyes, and Rod glared at him. Billy cranked his head back to the front, breaking the unpleasant eye connection. Even though he knew Rod couldn't do anything about it, he still felt somewhat frightened when he saw how furious he looked. He knew Rod's whole family must feel the same way about losing Buddy.

Billy was grateful that the COPS, for whatever reason, didn't punish the whole neighborhood this time. He wasn't quite sure why, and he wondered if maybe the old COPS was chalking up one too many punishments lately, since Westmoreland did enjoy his job. Could it be the COPS realized he could push the neighbors too far with his frequent punishments? Billy hesitated to think it, but could Westmoreland be afraid he might stir up discontent among the neighbors? He might even fear pushing them into a rebellious mood. Billy had heard about uprisings and discontent from the older kids at T-Camp. He quickly pushed the rebellion thought out of his mind. It was just too scary of a word to even think about, one of the worst words on the MAN's list of banned words. But there was no time to worry when the Biomass Co-op lay ahead.

. . .

When Rod's dom had been left far behind, Billy's face began to brighten. Despite what he'd done to the Jacksons for the "good of the PWN," he remembered that his family would soon be going on a trip to see Grandma, and they were all happy about it. And his dad didn't have to ride the QB to Productive Work, which made his dad glad. It was all due to Billy earning the extra transportation credits from turning in the Jacksons.

He liked seeing his mom and dad happy. He loved his little family so much that he'd do just about anything for them. He hoped someday, maybe even today, he'd think of more ways to get extra credits for them. Then they might be able to get that expensive cotton fabric mom had wanted for so long. She'd really smile then. He'd have to think hard about ways to earn more credits.

Billy was excited that he and Jake might get to see an adult turtle at the ponds today. As they rode along, Billy glanced over at his best friend Jake, then narrowed his eyes. He wondered if maybe, just maybe, if he tried hard enough, he could talk Jake into taking a tire shard, piece of wood, or animal bone back to his home dom, or even to T-Camp. Taking a relic out of its natural habitat was a serious violation of the rules, but Billy didn't see any reason to remind his friend about how much trouble he would get his family and the whole neighborhood into if the COPS found out about the violation.

Billy rode faster, and not just to see a turtle this time. He had another purpose in mind, a sneaky way he might be able to earn a few extra credits. If he did what he was thinking of doing, squealing on his best friend, even old Westmoreland might not frown so much whenever he saw Billy. He looked over at Jake again and realized that yes, he'd do just about anything to earn extra credits for his family; he loved his mom and dad so very much. There, just ahead, the biomass mounds were coming into view. Billy was happy now. He felt exactly like Productive Neighbor Sam today, and he liked this new person he was becoming a lot.

. . .

About the author:

Ann Murray's stories have appeared in two writing competitions' anthologies, winning first place in both. During her award-winning career as a commercial illustrator, among her many varied projects she has illustrated seven children's books for authors, a children's adjunct textbook, and won third place in an international poster competition. Ann writes a regular column for the local newspaper. She writes, paints, herds cats, and lives in the almost-an-island state of Michigan with her husband Rick, an award-winning author.

Her story "COPS" is the first in her planned trilogy about a dystopian society born from the climate crisis, The Productive World Neighborhood.

31

A Life in Pieces

by L. Jordan James (United States)

Subgenres: Science fiction, geoengineering cli-fi, romance

Time Period: 2077 AD

Setting: Brooklyn, New York, United States of America

Synopsis: Earnest Bentley wants to save the world, but he can't save his wife from COVID-75. From the moment of her death, he questions his existence as a hostage of the military trying to solve climate change. But his existential angst will be sent on a ride of enlightenment as the boundaries of love are tested.

. . .

——January 11, 2077——

A cold, sharp drizzle shifted with the wind in patterns, making hats fly, umbrellas fail, and prompting some at the funeral to clutch the upper buttons on their coats. A small, balding man stood at the head of the grave, his white robes billowing with the air currents, blending in and disappearing from time to time as they came close to the white casket. A small gathering of high-level dignitaries, politicians, and military men tried to look solemn, but somehow the emotion escaped them.

"Ashes to ashes, dust to dust ..."

Dr. Earnest Bentley lost track after those first few words. He sat back in his chair and let his mind wander, one gloved hand tightly clasping the other as if trying to hold on to something no one else could see. Instead of listening to the pastor, he chose to let his mind fall back to those first days of courting his wife. He didn't want to be at this cemetery with the end product of his marriage. This graveyard was too painful a place, too painful a reality.

They met while they were both still in college. He finished his degree in physics and was doing his dissertation in climatology. She began her studies in early childhood rearing. Love, at first sight, was the cliché he always used when it involved his wife and their first meeting. It may have sounded like an exaggeration, but the truth often does.

The first time he saw her was a beautiful day marking the end of winter and the beginning of spring. The students acted as though the sun had brought them back to life from the brink of death. He had been walking out of the physics wing of the school when he heard someone yell: "Mary!"

Earnest heard the shout and turned to see who was being called. When he saw her, when he saw her bright smile, something, somewhere deep inside him, broke and released a desire filling him, leaving no room for anything else. It was that something, that undefined part of him that had never been touched before, stirring, awakening, and coming to life. At that moment, he understood Mark Antony and the reason he gave up everything for Cleopatra, and he sympathized with Paris, who kidnapped Helen and didn't care about Troy or the consequences. Now he understood desire and how it could crowd out and silence every single logical voice and leave nothing in its wake but irrational emotion.

Mary smiled wider and embraced the young man who had called out to her, and to Earnest, the day became brighter as her smile became bigger. Could a day be lit up by another's smile? Had you asked him five minutes prior to seeing her, he would have said no. But now he wasn't so sure. Could one person's presence bring illumination to their surroundings? There had to be a mathematical equation explaining it. While watching her, his mind trying to come to some agreement on variables and constants and failing miserably, he noticed he was sweating profusely. He watched her climb the stairs and walk out of sight. The world returned to gray.

Back in his dormitory room that night, Earnest paced like a caged animal, trapped between the four walls, his books, his parents' expectations... and Mary. He wanted only to hold her close for a moment.

He walked his room all night long, keeping his roommate, Monty, awake. Monty wearily sat up and motioned for Earnest to come over to him. Earnest complied. Neither one had ever had an in-depth conversation with the other because they had different interests. Monty Johnson was a geology grad student and had been a lacrosse jock in his undergrad days. But they did share one trait allowing them to thrive in each other's company: they were both taciturn.

"What's the problem?" Monty's gaze was steady and unyielding.

"I—I saw a girl today."

Monty stayed quiet, letting Earnest fill in more of the story as he sat there. There were no threatening words from Monty, though Earnest was sure there could be in his immediate future if he didn't comply with Monty's wishes.

"She was beautiful." Earnest looked up as her mental picture came to him. It seemed he was reliving the moment he had first seen her. He caught Monty's eye and realized where he was and who was with him. He looked down and away, embarrassed because most jocks never talked like that. Jocks bragged about their conquests and moved on to the next woman. Even though Earnest had never seen nor heard of Monty engaging in that kind of talk, he was still a jock. "I don't know what to say to her to begin a conversation," Earnest admitted dejectedly.

Monty reached out, grabbed him by the collar, and pulled him close. Earnest prepared himself for physical violence by squeezing his eyes shut and making himself a smaller target by hunching over.

Monty said, "Ask her out for coffee."

He let Earnest go, rolled over, and was asleep in seconds. Earnest slowly opened his eyes and saw Monty's still frame. *Was it that easy*? Earnest wondered. *Was it as easy as asking her out for coffee*? He walked back over to his side of the room and sat on his bed, dumbfounded. The suggestion brought a little solace to his soul. He was asleep in a matter of moments.

The next day, Earnest set about his daily routine, but his mind wandered back to Mary. When he reached the Climatology wing, he spied her outside the education building, but he couldn't bring himself to talk to her. He saw her again during his lunch break and again talked himself out of saying anything. He walked past her, one eye on her, oblivious to what was going on around him when he collided with Monty. Monty was a brick wall of a man, so the accident didn't bother him. Earnest, on the other hand, dropped his paperwork and now had to crawl around on the ground, trying to gather everything back.

Monty grabbed Earnest by the forearm, ignoring the papers floating and danced at the whim of the air currents, and stood him up. Monty's bloodshot eyes held Earnest's gaze for a moment. "Where is she?"

Earnest raised a shaky hand and pointed in her direction. Monty looked over and assessed the situation. He steered Earnest over to her, paperwork falling, feet dragging against the direction Monty chose. "Excuse me, ma'am," he began, "this gentleman would like to take you out for a cup of coffee. I will vouch he is a man of honor and integrity." Monty bowed deeply. Earnest stared at her, dumbstruck, mouth agape. Monty reached up and grabbed the front of Earnest's shirt and made him follow suit. Earnest dropped his notebook.

Mary looked taken aback by the unorthodox approach, but amusement shone through. "What's *your* name?" She wasn't addressing Earnest but the surprised Monty.

"*My* name? My name's Monty, ma'am."

"How can I be sure *your* intentions are honorable? I don't know you."

"Rest assured, ma'am—if my friend lays a finger on you in any unwanted manner, it will be the last time he lays a finger on anyone."

Monty looked at his roommate, and all color drained from Earnest's face. Monty caught him as the world started to gray out and Earnest's knees became weak.

"Well, he *is* kind of cute."

The words registered in Earnest's consciousness. *"I'm cute?"* The color of the world magically returned.

"What's your name?" Mary asked.

Earnest remained silent. Fear attacked his voice. He couldn't believe he was in this situation, and she thought he was cute.

"His name is Earnest, and he's going to get his doctorate in climatology."

"Hmmm. Brainy and cute, huh?"

Monty took his free hand, and, with a majestic sweep, pointed in the direction of the campus café. She took one last discerning look at Earnest, then at Monty, and back again to Earnest. She smiled, nodded her head, and started in the direction of the café. Monty trailed behind her, holding up a pale Earnest, who couldn't believe his luck.

. . .

The funeral procession drove through the rainy, gray streets of Brooklyn, never paying heed to the red lights (on the rare occasion when they worked), stop signs, or any other traffic signs. It wove its way around debris too big to run over. Humvees were in front, to the rear, and flanking the limo. They blocked intersections when they came to them.

A tear rolled down Earnest's face, and he wiped it away. *Thirty-eight years of marriage, three children, four dogs, a couple of houses, and this is how it ends? It should've been me to be the first to die.* The small voice inside him that always spoke the truth reared up. *They'd never let me die. They'd prop me up with a couple of planks of wood next to a defibrillator and shock me if they even suspected I was having a heart attack.* He took a shaky breath, continuing to pay no attention to the Pentagon generals and dignitaries who sat across from and on either side of him.

There was another limo right behind them, with his kids. They were all grown up now, but every time he saw them, he couldn't help but see them as children. When James spoke, Earnest saw him as the awkward eight-year-old he used to be. It would be for only a second, but the illusion was so powerful that Earnest went over and hugged the adult James out of the blue, surprising all present. He remembered Amanda as a high school graduate going to her prom. She had been the spitting image of her mother. His heart ached for the men who would try to approach her. Andrew's doppelganger was the most potent of all. Earnest saw Andrew as a toddler. There was a time when Earnest would return home after a hard day of work to see Andrew, the youngest, in diapers and nothing else, rushing to meet him at the front door, not talking yet but burbling away. Earnest had always responded by saying: "Really? That is so interesting!" or "I was thinking the same thing. Let's write a paper on it!" But all of those times were gone like raindrops falling on a windshield—there for a second and moved away.

Involuntarily, his mind wandered back to the night when he had awakened shortly after they had gone to bed. He heard her make a noise and turned to her. He'd noticed she'd been coughing during the week. But a cough had a whole different meaning now. So many different diseases attacked mankind, each more insidious than the next. He asked her about the cough, and she put it off on allergies. But this sound coming from her had deepness. This wasn't an allergy, but COVID-75.

Flicking on the nightstand light, he saw her gasping for breath, but when he tried to roll over to get to the phone, she grabbed his sleeve and held him tightly. She knew she was going. She let him go, placed her hand on his cheek, and looked into his eyes. She looked at him so deeply and for so long. He extricated himself when he saw her eyes had stayed fixed and focused on nothing. From that night on, his life was a black pit from which there was no escape.

He felt it would be only a matter of time until he would see her again. He was tired. He was tired of conducting experiments. He was tired of being the sole man on whom the fate of the world rested. He felt the act of moving was a chore, and he would prefer to sleep more than anything else.

The limo turned down his street. He had been forced to move to this military installation and into their housing. They wanted to keep an eye on their golden goose.

I'm their pet, Earnest thought. *I'm their most prized possession, kept in a cage. I give them advice on how to mitigate the effects of climate change and how to live through the pandemics ravaging us, and in exchange, I'm held hostage.*

They were set to release nanomachines into the atmosphere. Each one was capable of millions of calculations per second. Each nanite had a reflective surface and would take into account wind speed, position of the sun, temperature, and would turn to the most effective angle to reflect the sun's rays. The nanites would turn separately, but if the weather permitted, in unison. They would work until the Earth's temperature moderated. Earnest imagined if a person were to peer down from space to Earth, it would look like a field of stars within the atmosphere. It was his crowning achievement, but now that Mary was gone it was so pointless, so stupid. And everything looked unreal.

An uncompleted puzzle.

A life in pieces.

The limo came to a stop, and Earnest and everyone else got out. Earnest did his best to maintain a polite exterior, but he wanted to go inside alone. He wanted to be through with these people and sleep for a week. Or a month. Maybe a year.

He shook hands all around and thanked them for attending his wife's funeral. A small part of him wanted to ask about his children, but he didn't want to listen to their explanations. He'd call them later. When they had departed into the rain, he turned and faced the house alone. The drizzle had changed to a cold persistent rain. He started up the driveway, pulling his coat tighter.

His brow furrowed in thought. *What if I hadn't saved Florida?* He had invented a floating carbon nanotube, and from that, he made a net with the nanotubes and filled them with a refrigerant. Earnest chilled the water in the path of an incoming Category 6 hurricane and deprived the storm of the warm water it needed to thrive. *If I hadn't done all those things, the military and the politicians never would have noticed me. I would've had a normal life. But if I hadn't done those things, millions would've died. My family, without the protection of the military, probably would be dead. More than that,* he thought, *if the military hadn't started listening to me, we probably would be extinct as a species.*

Florida. His thoughts turned darker. People had abandoned Florida. Yes, he'd saved the population, but the peninsula was underwater now. No one acted fast enough. Everyone dithered while sucking their thumb.

His house was gray as he entered. He removed his hat and

coat as a mental image came to him. It was of palm trees swaying with the wind and icebergs in the background floating off the coast of Miami. A smile of satisfaction penetrated the moment, until he remembered where he was. He remembered he would be sleeping alone. At night, he drew her pillow close to him, inhaled her scent, imagining her next to him. The smile left as fast as it appeared.

Switching on the light, he turned around to see Monty seated at his kitchen table. It gave him a start, seeing him sitting there, implacable and quiet as always. It must've been at least ten years since he had last seen him. He had gained some weight and had more gray than ever, but it was him. "Monty?"

"Hello, Earnest."

"What are you doing here?"

Monty smiled, but his smile slowly slipped away, like the tide going back out to sea. Earnest tried to read his expression and body language. *Was that guilt on his face*? Monty wouldn't keep eye contact. Yes, Earnest decided, it was guilt. Why would he feel guilty?

"Sit down, Earnest... Please."

Earnest slowly sat down.

"I'm so sorry about Mary. She was something special."

Earnest nodded. Tears brimmed, but he fought them back.

"The look I saw on your face," Monty said. "The determination, the strength. I—*we* need it from you now."

"I know, I know. The whole world is counting on me." The professor sighed.

"Yes, the world *is* counting on you. You saved us from giant storms, famine, and disease all caused by climate change. But right here and right now we need you to keep your head." The more Monty talked, the more Earnest noticed he was avoiding eye contact. A drop of acid fear touched Earnest's stomach... though he didn't know why.

"Your ability to imagine new ways to solve problems has gotten us this far. We need to go a little further."

"That's what they always say: 'a little more.' And they'll keep saying it forever and ever."

Earnest bowed his head as a silent brick wall came between them. There was a pause between them in which no conversation took place, their natural taciturn tendency taking over both. Monty started again: "Earnest, you know how thorough these government types are. They've planned for years now for any and all contingencies." Monty suddenly looked up at Earnest. "They planned for your wife's death, as well."

Earnest's eyes narrowed in suspicion. A mental picture came to him. It was his wife being held upright with planks under her arms and a humming, charged-up defibrillator next to her, waiting to do its job. To the professor, the room got smaller, darker, and more claustrophobic.

"They've had your house wired for years. They've watched you... and your wife." Earnest looked around the room as if he could pick out the microphones and cameras. "They've seen how you and your wife interacted. Lived. Loved. Argued. They've seen it all."

A door behind both of them opened, but neither Earnest nor Monty noticed it.

"They did so many studies on you, and they all came back to the same conclusion: If your wife were to die before you, you wouldn't last six weeks without her. It's common for a spouse to expire soon after their loved one. So, they had a problem, and like so many bureaucrats before them, they came up with a solution only a bureaucrat would think of."

Someone moved around in the master bedroom.

"Forgive them, Earnest, for they know not what they do."

Two red dots flashed momentarily in the dark bedroom before someone stepped out into the light. Earnest turned around to see who it was. His face lost all of its color. "No," he said weakly, as he watched his wife walk toward him.

"She's an android, Earnest. She's been programmed with all of Mary's memories, habits, and speech patterns."

"No," Earnest said again. It was a stronger denial.

"She's here to help you get over this rough patch and to help you finish saving the world."

"No!" He slammed his fist on the table.

"She even uses the same perfume as Mary." Monty stood and moved to the front door. He opened it, and Earnest could see it had stopped raining. Monty turned back and looked at the professor. A cool breeze disturbed some papers sitting on the kitchen table. As Monty stood halfway in and halfway out of the doorway, shadows covering most of his body, Earnest remembered something, and it dispersed all of the anger inside him, like steam rising from a just-doused fire. *Hadn't Monty died about three years ago?* He had been so close to completing the nanomachines, they hadn't let him go to the funeral. Earnest looked up at his friend and saw one of his pupils, the one covered by shadow, glowed red.

"Of all the kinds of bureaucrats in the world, the most dangerous kind is a desperate one, and we had hundreds fitting that description. For them, the ends did justify the means."

Monty sighed and averted his gaze. "I've been told tomorrow you'll disperse the nanites into the atmosphere. You can decide what you want afterward. But before you dismiss this life, before you give up and commit yourself to a meaningless death, give it a chance," Monty closed the door behind him.

The wind raising and moving papers about on the table died away as the door closed.

"Mary" walked over to the kitchen cabinets and began to retrieve pots and pans.

For a moment, Earnest sat at the kitchen table, and a litany of emotions passed over his face. He had a mental image of a doctor with those electric paddles in his hands, standing over Mary—*his* Mary, the *real* Mary—and yelling: "*Clear*!" He imagined seeing his wife's body seize and convulse. He heard a faint sizzle in the background and smelled a slight whiff of flesh, all courtesy of an overactive imagination.

The sun had set, and there was no other light but the single bulb in the kitchen. A feeling of claustrophobia descended on the professor with the presence of that *thing* in the same room.

"What do you want for dinner tonight, honey?" Mary asked.

Earnest didn't answer.

"Okay—how about pot roast?"

Again, he had nothing to say. The *thing* moved back and forth from the refrigerator to the stove and back again. He watched it. A thought burst through and shined its light on him, and he stood straight up in response. For a moment, different points of view occurred to him, opening up other avenues of thought and different possibilities. He walked into the bathroom, turned on the lights. Staring at himself in the mirror, he saw a shaking, balding, sixtyish man looking back.

Monty had said a lot of things. He had said the bureaucrats had planned for every contingency, as only bureaucrats could, years ago. The professor turned on the water and splashed his face in a futile effort to calm himself. Taking a towel from the rack, he pat dried his face and stared into the mirror, but the water hadn't calmed him as he had hoped it would. His hands and body still shook.

Every single dignitary and general in the limo had worn sunglasses, and he had thought nothing of it. He believed it was a government thing. But it was too much of a coincidence to be ignored. There were Humvees that had pulled alongside the funeral procession and moved to block intersections with no traffic. The possibilities ahead of him made him a little dizzy. As he reached over to the bathroom light, a shiver ran down his spine and radiated outward. It contributed to the tremor running through his body. He hesitated for a moment, his finger hovering above the switch, before turning off the light. He saw two glowing red pupils staring back at him.

He knew the human race hadn't *almost* gone extinct. It

had gone extinct. He and all of those around him were an unworkable contingency plan, and all of them were following their programming. As each person who was involved in this endeavor fell, an android was there to take his or her place. It was a ghastly bureaucratic solution to a horrible problem. Surround him with all of the people who mean anything to him, and if they happen to die, then make a replacement. Keep the professor happy at all costs. What happened when the professor himself died? Well, let's see if we can make an android as smart and as imaginative as the real thing.

He flipped the light back on, turned around, and sagged against the doorway, letting the full enormity of his situation sink in. He wasn't Dr. Earnest Bentley. His wife wasn't his wife. His children weren't his children. They were all pale shadows of the real thing. The love he felt for his children wasn't real, and the memories of them in their diapers weren't his, either.

The bureaucrats always missed the fundamental questions: What makes a human a human being? Emotions? Intellect? Personality? Self-awareness? Surely, it was nothing that could ever possibly be imprinted on a microchip or written as a program. A tear flowed down his cheek, and he wiped it away. *"Crying is not allowed,"* he said aloud. *"Toasters don't cry."*

Another truth opened itself to him: He would continue to try to save the world forever... or until he wore out. He would wake up every day, shower, shave, and go to the lab. He would go through the motions of completing experiments every minute of every day for years. The fake generals and dignitaries would see to it. Another shiver ran down his spine.

He heard Monty's voice in his ear say: *"Give it a chance."*

Earnest stood at the entrance to the bathroom, watching the thing moving back and forth, from a cabinet to table to refrigerator and back to a cabinet. She caught him looking at her and gave him a little half-smile. It was an expression mimicking his Mary's. He told himself it was following an algorithm. It was doing what it was programmed to do. He corrected himself. *We are doing what we were programmed to do.* He wondered what the real Dr. Bentley would've done in his place.

Pretty soon dinner aromas reached the professor, and he walked out of the bathroom and sat back down. His stomach grumbled.

As Earnest sat there watching *this version of his wife* move within the kitchen, small moments of insights—micro clarities—revealed themselves to him. *Why did they send Monty? Because Monty is—was—my best friend. He introduced me to Mary. He was always there to give me advice. Why didn't I see my red eyes before now? An algorithm. I probably couldn't see it until I looked for it. But Mary....Mary must've seen them!* His hand went to his cheek where *his* Mary had last touched him. His hand slid across his cheek in an effort to recreate the softness of her hand, but it was an ersatz touch, devoid of the real Mary.

She knew, and she didn't care.

Mary moved from the stove to the table.

His Mary knew...

She placed tableware in front of him.

...and didn't care.

She smiled at him again and turned back to the stove.

What made her accept me? Why would a flesh and blood human accept me? He racked his brain for an answer, but there was only one real reason presenting itself: *She must've loved me. A human loved a machine. If a human loved me, then...*

Suddenly, Earnest stood and walked over to Mary while she stirred a pot. He took her hand. Startled, she looked up at him. He led her to the bathroom and placed her in front of him. He looked at their reflection in the mirror and saw no difference between the real and the substitute.

The real Mary had a small birthmark on the nape of her

neck. He gently pushed this Mary's hair aside. When he found it, he was not surprised. He kissed it, moved his arms around her, and breathed in her perfume.

For a brief moment, a strange feeling of sadness and happiness simultaneously crossed his heart. His sadness was for the Mary who'd touched his cheek before she died and for the good times they would never have again. The happiness, he felt, was of the moment—the here and now. He was happy to smell this Mary's perfume and to feel her closeness and warmth. Mary laid her head back on his chest and smiled. He smiled back at her.

Maybe the bureaucrats did always miss fundamental questions like what makes a human being a human being. But now that the die has been cast, it will be up to us to move past what our human forefathers gave us, to break the mold, to be more than our programming, to be more than microchips and wires.

Earnest sighed as different questions, different observations and conclusions came to him again but at a slower, more deliberate pace.

Will our batteries simply stop? Will I die in mid-sentence? Mid-thought? Will her eyes go dim before mine? I don't know. But if my late wife could love me without reservation, how could I do less? How can I not give this life a chance?

He hugged his wife tighter. She smiled wider, and the day became brighter.

. . .

About the author:

L. Jordan James has held several jobs, but none gives him as much enjoyment as writing. He is a veteran and has worked for the Metropolitan Museum of Art. He grew up kicking around Brooklyn. Now he kicks around New Jersey.

Part Six:

The Twenty-Second Century (2101 to 2200 AD)

32

The Historic Moment

by Thomas Wm. Hamilton (United States)

Subgenre: Cli-fi

Time Period: 2125 AD

Setting: Reporters on location at major capitals worldwide and on the Moon.

. . .

"To all our viewers, ladies, gentlemen, and AIs, welcome to NewsNet's coverage of this historic occasion. Our advisors say we have about half an hour before the magic moment, so we will be going around the globe and even out in space for comments on what's happening. I'll be your host for a happening so important that we will have no commercial interruptions until we are done. This is Gary Samuels, switching you now to Washington, where NewsNet's White House correspondent, Jackie Fletcher, has a report."

"Thanks, Gary. The White House Press Secretary, Bob Brill, read a statement just a few moments ago. Here it is."

Roll in: "The president congratulates the American people in their support of Administration policies in the face of history being made as we watch. The president hopes that this will be a lesson to Congress which will cause them to move pending legislation faster."

"Gary, Brill declined to take questions after reading that."

"So, Jackie, would you say the president is trying to avoid taking a stand on this?"

"Not exactly, Gary. Word around the White House is the president hopes to see public reaction before committing himself."

"Given Washington politics these days, that's probably a good move. Next we go to Brussels, where NewsNet reporter Alois Bardossy has word on the European Union reaction."

"Right you are, Gary. I have here the current Chair of the Council of Ministers of the European Union, Radmilla Smerdenjovic of Croatia."

"We Europeans have seen tens of centuries of history, but this event is unique. The EU Council of Ministers hopes everyone appreciates how significant what is happening today is."

"That's interesting, Alois. It sounds like EU politicians are more prepared to stick their necks out on this than is the American president."

"Not surprising, Gary. I suspect this president would like to break the string of five consecutive presidents to face impeachment, even if none ever seem to be convicted."

"Alois may have that right, but now we go to another European location, Vatican City, where NewsNet reporter Frank Malloy is ready."

"Gary, I'm with Bishop Suarez, long a spokesperson for His Holiness, the Pope. Bishop, has the Pope anything to say about this historic event?"

"The Holy Father is spending his time in prayer and meditation. He offers blessings and hopes that everyone can face the future with a clear mind to be able to comprehend the meaning of what passes today."

"A generous statement in line with much this Pope has said during his tenure. Frank, give the bishop our thanks. Next we seek comment from NewsNet's reporter Clara Siegel, in the lunar capital."

Two-point-four-second pause. "Gary, there is little interest here in what is about to happen on Earth. I'm with Viglaf Sundersson, a member of the Armstrong City Council who is rumored to be a likely candidate in the next election for the Lunar Parliament."

"Thanks, Clara, but I've no comment on any parliamentary elections; I'm just trying to be the best member Armstrong has ever had in its City Council."

"Okay, Viglaf, but what have you to say about this event that has Earth all atwitter?"

"I can tell you right now, my constituents are totally uninterested. If you want their views on an historic event, well, last week the City Council voted to build the first swimming pool on the Moon."

"Here's Gary, back at the scene on Earth. And I guess all my fellow Earthlings know just where we rank. Well down in importance, below that of a swimming pool, eh, folks? Maybe Beijing has something more encouraging. Let's go to NewsNet reporter Antoine Takahashi in the Chinese capital."

"Gary, Chinese Foreign Minister Wu Feng Xiu is with me to give the Chinese position."

"This event would not be happening if the decadent western powers had not abandoned all sense of responsibility. The Chinese People's Republic will continue to make strides, emboldened in the knowledge that what happens today only makes us stronger."

"Well, folks, between swimming pools and chopsticks, it would seem not everyone values this historic moment very much. But I'm getting the signal from our technical advisors that the magic moment is nearly here. During the final countdown, our camera will target the crucial site, and NewsNet's chief sports reporter, Biff Hogan, will give the commentary. Biff?"

"Okay, we are only seconds away. Viewers are looking at the last trace of the last glacier on Earth. You may know that at its peak, thirteen thousand years ago, about 40 percent of Earth's land mass was covered in ice. As recently as fifty years ago, Greenland, now a well-named verdant paradise, was under a couple kilometers of ice, and Antarctica was even worse. But now, only a few square centimeters of ice remain on Earth, and even as we watch, it is melting away. Little rivulets of water are flowing away. Melting. Gone!"

. . .

About the author:

Hamilton is a bit of a Renaissance man, teaching astronomy, writing in several different genres, former county chair of a political party, a child actor seventy to seventy-five years ago, and former producer of a cable news show.

33

In The Teeth of the Night A Cautionary Tale

by Thomas P. Tiernan (United States)

Subgenre: Horror

Time Period: The twenty-second century

Setting: United States of America

Synopsis: As the seas rose due to the melting of the Arctic and Antarctic ice, monsters awakened in the depths of the Earth. These were the Night Ones, triggered by the rising tides. They prey upon anything moving in the dark of night. We are present at the bedtime of a young girl, who wants to know the whole truth of their situation.

. . .

"Tell me, Pappa. Tell me about the Night Ones," said Alice, safely tucked up in her bed.

"Are you sure you're old enough, Kitten?" Pappa looked around the room. His eyes were now well-adjusted to moving around in the dark. All the drapes had been drawn and secured. Only the faintest boundary from the light of the moon could be seen outlining the windows.

"I'm nearly ten years old, Pappa. Karyn and Joel learned the history at that age," she said with a hopeful look in her eyes.

"They were nearly twelve, my little historian. And they were ready."

Alice made a small pouty face, her lips protruding.

"But you are a very grown-up ten years old." It would be better if she knew now, in case their time to tell her when she was twelve ran out.

She smiled. "Ooh, does that mean you'll tell me?"

Pappa looked down at her, pressing his back into the chair. He was uncomfortable. "Are you sure you wouldn't want me to tell you about the history at breakfast? It might be easier to hear in the light."

"Oh, no, Pappa. Nighttime is perfect. I can go outside at breakfast. It wouldn't be the same as right now when we have to stay inside."

Pappa smiled. "Fair enough. Get comfortable. I will tell the history just this once. If you fall asleep, you'll miss some of it."

"I won't fall asleep, Pappa," she said, sitting up.

"All right. Now let me think back to the beginning." He paused and looked at the window. "More than twenty years before you were born, the oceans had risen so much that the big cities on the ocean's edge were abandoned. The people moved inland and began to build new big cities."

"Like New Philadelphia?"

"Exactly. Many people didn't like moving away from their neighborhoods, but they had been warned for many years that such a thing could happen if all the ice melted. No one listened."

"Was there really ice at the top of the world, like Joel says?"

"Oh, yes, and at the bottom of the world too."

"The bottom? Don't people fall off?"

"No, but that's a story for another time. It wasn't so bad, moving to the countryside. At least until the sea found its way into the old caves and the mines, especially in West Virginia."

"Can you show me in my book?" she said. She reached over to her nightstand. Her hands picked up a well-worn atlas. Pappa took it and turned the pages to the Central United States, and the two pages filled his lap. She had carefully colored in the new coast of the East with her blue markers.

"Right here is where the first reports of the Night Ones happened," Pappa said, pointing to what was central West Virginia. The area was now underwater, fifteen miles from the new coastline.

"What happened?" she said.

"At first, there was only a trickle of water going into the mines and caves. They tried to block it at first, but it soon was no use to even try. People began to die in and around these places, but that was not reported. Scientists are now pretty sure that the seawater awakened something or caused some creature to hatch deep underground. Farmers began to complain that their chickens and goats were disappearing. No one listened, even after cows and horses were slaughtered in the pens."

"Why didn't anyone believe them?"

"There was a lot of confusion back in those days. Many people had to find new homes, new cities. The police thought it was bad people from the big cities who had moved through the area."

"Or hungry people," she said.

"I'm sure that someone thought of that as well. Over two months went by, and more animals went missing. Then people began to vanish. Right in front of their homes." He was growing tired. It had been a long day of checking the fences and adding several feet to the brick wall that now wound halfway around their property.

"Wow."

"It was the hunters at first, and people who went into the parks and forests. When people began to disappear from the edge of towns, the government began to get serious about what was happening. It was noticed that no one was harmed if they were indoors. They also found that the attacks only happened at night. Laws were passed by various towns to keep people from going outside at night."

"Like a curfew?"

"Yes, exactly. A curfew."

"Did it work?"

"Not at first," said Pappa. "People in towns and the ones moving west thought they would be safer in towns. They were wrong. At first, only the outskirts of towns were hit by the Night Ones. But soon, no one was safe anywhere outdoors."

"Ryan calls them Nightmares. Who named the Night Ones?"

"No one knows. It may have been someone on a podcast or a reporter on television. I don't care. The name stuck and spread quickly. The name doesn't matter anyway. They'll most likely kill everyone before too long, no matter what their name is."

"All of us, Pappa?" Her eyes grew wide. He wouldn't keep the truth from her, not now.

"I'm afraid so, Kitten. It's just a matter of time. Hopefully, a very long time."

"But aren't we safe indoors? That's what Mom says."

"She's probably right. I'm just tired of all the hiding. Who's to say what the truth is?"

"The Night Ones don't come indoors. That means that they're afraid of coming inside of buildings. That's a good thing, right?"

"It is. That's just the best guess. We don't know why these things don't come indoors. Outside information like television and newspapers stopped coming years ago."

"So we're on our own? Maybe things are better than we can see from here."

"Anything is possible. It's been quiet for weeks. With the curfew, the Night Ones only have what they can find outdoors at night. That could be enough pickings for them."

"What will happen when they run out of animals and the people who go outside at night?"

"That's when we will see if they're afraid of coming indoors or not."

"What'll we do, Pappa?"

"Nothing we can do. There's nothing we've been able to do to stop the Night Ones. All the armies of the world lasted a few weeks against them. They'll get us all unless we stay inside. We're safer here, though, with the fences."

Alice's eyes went wide. "Oh, no, Pappa. I should have let you tell me the history at breakfast."

Pappa smiled. "Cheer up, Kitten. We're safer here than anywhere else for a hundred miles. This house we live in used to be a prison."

"Really? I thought it was an old castle."

"It only looks like a castle from the outside. Most houses don't have the fences and security system that we have."

"So the criminals had to find a new home when this one got too small for them."

"Something like that. This place became too small for the criminals in it, and they were moved to a much bigger place. I worked here and bought it at an auction."

"Did you not move with the others into the bigger place?"

"Yes, I did. I left when things got bad. My work hours kept me there until dark, and I couldn't stay there anymore."

"So, all of this keeps us safer?"

"Much safer than where we used to live. We'll be all right here for a long time. The fences will keep them out."

Alice nodded. She looked at the window. "Are the Night Ones snakes?"

"Something like that. Reports were never clear about them. Why?"

"I saw one."

Pappa came to attention right away. "Where?"

"Out on the big lawn in front."

"Inside the fence?"

"I think so."

"When?"

"Just after dark today. I peeked out the curtain of my room."

Pappa got to his feet. There was a wild look in his eyes she had never seen before. He went to the wall intercom. "Mary, can you come to Alice's room?"

"Yes. I'll be right there."

"What is it, Pappa?"

"It's nothing, Kitten. I just need to check on something."

Mary came into the room, and Pappa moved to meet her. They stepped out into the hall. "They've gotten past the fence," he said.

The color drained from her face. She began to shake. "Are you sure?"

"Yes."

"What do we do, Jason?"

"They may be hearing the goats in the prison yard. I'll have to let them go."

"But why?"

"If we don't, the Night Ones will find a way to get at them."

"And us," she said quietly.

"I won't let that happen. I'll go now to let the goats out."

"Be careful."

"I will be." He went back to Alice. "Good night, Kitten. See you in the morning."

"G'night, Pappa."

Mary watched her husband walk down the long cinder block hallway until he turned the corner, and his flashlight couldn't be seen. She went into Alice's room and sat down.

"What were you and Pappa talking about?" Mary brushed back the daughter's hair from her face.

"He told me about the Night Ones."

Mary's blood ran cold. Her anger nearly blotted out her concern for her husband. "We were going to wait for another year or so to tell you."

"I know, but I wanted to know."

Mary smiled. "What do you think?"

"They're terrifying. Are you sure the Night Ones are real, Mom?"

"Very real. We have to be very careful not to ever let these things know that anyone lives here. That's why we're very quiet all night."

"And no lights?"

"That's right." Far down the hall behind her, she heard one of the large, heavy outer doors swing open with a bump. That sound always scared her.

"What was that, Mom?" Alice stared at the door to her room, shaking.

Mary stood and went to the door. Deep within the bowels of the prison, she heard an unfamiliar grating noise. At first, she thought it was the generator restarting. The sound continued and grew a bit louder.

"I think Pappa's turning on the heat," she said. A goat bleated for a short second, and the sound cut off. The rasping grew louder in the hall. Mary closed the door and locked it.

"When will Pappa be coming back?"

"Soon, dear. Mom's getting cold. Can I get in and cuddle with you?"

Mary slipped into the covers and pulled them up to their chins. She tried not to make any noise as the clatter of clawed feet made their way up the hall toward them.

. . .

About the author: Born in Rahway, New Jersey. Early childhood in Colonia, New Jersey. Later childhood in Menlo Park Terrace, New Jersey. Graduated College with an AA degree. Married a beautiful and intelligent young woman. Moved to Edison, New Jersey. Graduated College with a degree in Computer Technology. Fathered a beautiful and intelligent daughter. Moved to Iselin, New Jersey. Graduated College with a Bachelor's degree in History and English. He writes for seventy-five minutes every day, seven days a week. Creative Director—Joe's Writers Club @ www.joeswriters.club He is a Game Designer, Author, Avid Gamer, Trekker, Movie Buff. So Far, So Good.

34

The Time that Everything Went to Hell

by Thomas P. Tiernan (United States)

Subgenres: Science fiction, humor

Time Period: 2127 AD

Setting: United States of America

Synopsis: All the ice caps melted, then aliens invaded, and humans hid in underground cities.

. . .

First, it was the polar bears, damn them. Then, the woodpeckers went and disappeared. Well, good riddance. We didn't need those damned noisy birds anyway. Can I tell you what we needed around here?

More food! Yes, that's right. Living down in a salt mine or giant hollowed-out cavern limits what kinds of animals you can keep well-fed. The mine is massive, maybe two miles long and almost as broad. Room for plenty of people. The Right kind of People, if you know what I mean.

A lottery drew up the neighborhoods lucky enough to be chosen to build Salt City I, the first and grandest underground city since the ice caps all melted. There was a scramble for supplies, and a lot of people got shot trying to force their way down here.

But luck, and God, was with us, and we kept those ungrateful buggers out of our home.

"We're gonna drown!" they yelled. "We don't have any food!" they yelled.

Screw 'em. We got here first, and we're not gonna allow any unworthies in without them paying a hefty price to get to the first level. The price? Half of what they've brought with them. Don't want to pay? Go back upstairs to the surface.

Am I afraid that they'll tell the Chitenns where we are? No, I'm not scared of the Chitenns. They can go to Hell too. They had a lot of nerve to invade while we were up to our ears in melted glaciers. Then they started to take away all our cattle, pigs, and chickens while we were looking for dry land.

So, at the moment, the big bugs don't know where any of our salt mine cities are. It seems that they find salt poisonous to their systems. Kills 'em dead right where they stand. Like slugs when you pour salt on them, the Chitenns shrink up and keel over dead at the mere whiff of salt.

All of them folks living at the ocean's edges are lucky. They only have to contend with the rising sea levels. The Chitenns don't come within a mile of any beach. Not a bad trade if I do say so. Land is getting really scarce up top, and the Chitenns will have to stay in their spaceships to survive.

Maybe then we can go out for a look at the state of the world. We could sure use something else to eat besides the mushrooms and those nasty cave crickets. Blech! At least my wife and I are privileged enough to have some beef once a week with our rations. At least I think it's beef. They won't tell us where it comes from.

How did we get in this mess anyway? Well, I'll tell ya, but you gotta keep it to yourself.

Mother Nature sure is one mean Mother, especially if you piss her off. We sure did an excellent job giving her the finger for so many centuries. After a while, she just got pissed and took away the ice. We were treading water for years before the Feds figured out that there was a problem. There were the usual years' long committees bickering back and forth The Definition Of The Situation, as they put it.

By the time we realized we were in trouble, it was too late to even debate the issue. Washington D.C. sat underwater, and there was no debating that the capital should be moved somewhere else. That's when our friends showed up. The Chitenns arrived in the middle of a worldwide panic, basically caught us with our pants down around our ankles.

Let me tell you about those damn Chitenns. How they got into Space is beyond me. They're all imbeciles, and rude to boot. They arrive when we're in a crisis, and the first thing they want is to know where they could get something to eat. And talk about oblivious. Their ships dropped from the sky and landed on our buildings and bridges without looking where they were going. Not a scratch on any of 'em. No apologies. No acknowledging of any mistakes. They haven't come to invade. They're here because they've watched our television shows from the 1950s. They thought Earth was a funny place run by handsome private eyes and crazy redhead housewives. We've gone underground to survive, yes, but if you ask me, it's to avoid the Chitenns and their questions about Davy Crockett.

The smart ones among us, meaning the Elites, had already had their plans drawn up decades ago. Project ANT was created and kept hidden from all but the Top 0.0001 percent of the population. That tiny group of people knew that whatever happened, their future survival was guaranteed.

Deep within the Earth, below certain mountain ranges, vast cities were constructed. Many were dug out of salt deposits, which provided the healthiest and most pest-free environments that existed. Others were blasted out of the solid bedrock of the Earth's crust. They were built for maximum survival, based upon the design of an ant colony. All the living areas had to be entered from beneath, just like an ant colony does to avoid drowning. This made them safe from any rising waters. They were all located on top of geothermal regions, providing all the heat for the enormous geothermal turbines that ran everything. Hydroponic gardens bigger than football fields were put in by the half-dozen for each community.

The lottery I mentioned before was established in the first bad year. The Elites couldn't and wouldn't do any of the heavy living demanded of this existence below ground. Those lucky bastards who won thought they were going to live in a paradise. The brochures for the lottery sure were terrific. The lottery was a secret endeavor, of course, for yet another itsy-bitsy circle of people who could keep their traps shut about it.

Those two years that the engineers, builders, carpenters, gardeners, and other blue-collar workers spent underground were brutal. Even though the cities had been set up for decades, it took an enormous amount of back-breaking work to get them into livable shape for the Elites when they arrived. A second lottery had to be run when the death toll cut the original winning group in half.

And so came the ice melting, and the crap hit the fan. Two hundred years after Babe Ruth hit sixty home runs and was making $100,000, I would have paid $100,000 for a Baby Ruth candy bar. Living down here among the snobs who knew they deserved to be here was too much sometimes. How I wished the exit hadn't been sealed with dynamite to prevent the Chitenns from getting at us. I believe it was sealed to keep the smart people among us from escaping, but that's just my opinion.

How are things on the surface? You can ask, but don't say it too loud. The cops down here shoot and never ask any questions. Anyone who steps out of line gets educated really quick as to how you should behave. Remember George

Orwell's *1984*? That little book seems like a nursery rhyme compared to what we free thinkers go through every second of every day.

Where was I? Oh, yeah, the year the ice melted and all the fun we had scrambling to get to our designated areas as the countdown for Project Ant started. We had forty-eight hours to get into our pickup spots with everything we would be allowed to bring down with us.

The list of allowed items was concise. I won't bother you with any of it. Just try thinking of a world without a single issue of *Playboy*. Yeah, horrible. No frivolous items. No fruit. No weapons. I purchased a dozen e-readers and filled them with all the reading material I could cram into them. I took contingencies for any circumstance I could imagine, from science to sports to fiction to SF to the ladies, if you know what I mean.

I was somehow able to get past the metal detectors and a groping by a Security person and soon found myself underground. At first, it was an incredible experience. Imagine a city the size of Newark, New Jersey, set up two miles underneath Newark itself. That's where I wound up. I had never been to New Jersey, but those who knew me thought I belonged here under Newark.

No problem. I was one of the Surviving Generation. The ones who would get us past the current environmental crisis and see that we would come out when the Earth was cured of Us. It was a humbling thing, and we blue-collar guys truly appreciated the chance to carry on the human race.

How long would we be here underground? The debate was still going on as we moved down. Some of the scientists said that ten years would be plenty. The Feds had a different mindset. The Socialists among them didn't want to go up to the surface. They had found their utopia and were happy.

The Federalists wanted to leave as soon as it was deemed safe, believing that we were wasting our time down here. The religious denominations wanted to go up today. We were too close to Hell, they claimed. Hell is where you find it, I suppose.

Most of the people I knew and worked with couldn't care less when we went back Upstairs. We were blessed to be here. Case closed. If we went up next week, fine. If we never went back up, also excellent. Just keep me fed and happy, and I'll be fine.

Then came the day we dreaded. There was a sound coming down to us from somewhere far above our heads. At first, it was a knocking, like some obscenely huge woodpecker. Most people dismissed it as the ground settling. Yeah, like that was still happening after a billion years.

Then it got louder. Louder still. Someone was digging through the crust of the Earth toward us. But who? Was it some ungrateful bunch of jerks who'd found out about the lottery and the Ant cities and wanted in? Was it those lottery losers who'd figured out where we were and wanted in?

Or was it the Chitenns, who now had a way to get to us, the last people they hadn't driven crazy yet? We were not in a salt city, not entirely anyway. Half of it was salt, half of it was bedrock. It was beautiful, having both types of environments. Kinda comfy.

Anyway, we could do nothing as the sound came closer every day. They say that they'll break through any day now. The Feds have sent us all home, to defend our homes as best we can if needed. Perhaps it's a good thing that's coming our way. I'd like to think so. We drank all the wine we had hoarded for years with a great party among our friends and neighbors.

Now we sit on our porches as the first bits of rubble drop down from the high ceiling. It's out of our hands now. Maybe we should accept what happens. Me, I'm pulling for the lottery losers. They at least have a good argument for being down here.

One sizable chunk of ceiling caves in and falls away. I don't bother getting up. I can see it just fine from where I am. From deep inside of the hole comes a whining screech. And then come the words we've all been dreading.

"Lucy, you've got some 'splainin' to do!"

. . .

About the author: Born in Rahway, New Jersey. Early childhood in Colonia, New Jersey. Later childhood in Menlo Park Terrace, New Jersey. Graduated College with an AA degree. Married a beautiful and intelligent young woman. Moved to Edison, New Jersey. Graduated College with a degree in Computer Technology. Fathered a beautiful and intelligent daughter. Moved to Iselin, New Jersey. Graduated College with a Bachelor's degree in History and English. He writes for seventy-five minutes every day, seven days a week. Creative Director—Joe's Writers Club @ www.joeswriters.club He is a Game Designer, Author, Avid Gamer, Trekker, Movie Buff. So Far, So Good.

35

True North

by David F. Shultz (Canada)

WARNING: This story may not be suitable for younger readers due to language.

Subgenres: Science fiction, military fiction

Time Period: Approximately 2150 AD

Setting: Northern Canada

Synopsis: Two rangers search for a damaged climate-control drone through the frozen, post-apocalyptic Canadian North.

. . .

Cold rushed into Duncan's open helmet, needling exposed skin. Wind whistled across desolate tundra. Patches of pine trees, skinny and sparsely branched, struggled to survive at the edge of the treeline. Not a target in sight.

Duncan's new partner, Tal, was mumbling to himself, maybe singing, binoculars conspicuously absent.

"The hell you doing?"

"Nothing," Tal said.

"You praying for good weather, or what?" Duncan chuckled.

"Something like that."

He wasn't joking.

Duncan had hoped he'd get paired with a serious ranger, like himself. But there was his new partner, distracted by some ridiculous superstition.

"Don't let your *job* get in the way of your hocus-pocus bullshit," Duncan said. "It's not like we've got *work* to do, or anything."

"Not that it's any of your business," Tal said, "but this is important to me, okay? For personal reasons."

The communicator crackled. "*Ranger team Hotel-India, this is Com-2 Echo-Whiskey, check-in, over.*"

Duncan hit the comm button. "*Ranger team Hotel-India. All quiet here, over.*"

"*Look alive, Hotel-India, we got incoming your way, just a few minutes B-V-R, over.*"

Tal nodded. "*Ready when you are, over.*"

Static, hiss. "*Six-fower degrees North, fife-one minutes, fife-one seconds. One-one-one degrees West, two-niner minutes, fower-two seconds. Altitude, 'bout fife tousand, over.*"

Tal gave the thumbs up.

"*Roger, out,*" Duncan said.

We might see a drone after all, he thought. They used to be called Caretakers, back when they were released to protect the planet's climate—before they decided that the real problem was *us*. But they underestimated our resistance. We weren't the best caretakers, but it was still our planet.

Duncan took a knee and unloaded his pack. Sleek black metal, telescoping prongs, particle-multi-pack, sync-cable. He assembled the blaster tripod and plugged it into his snowmobile's reactor outlet. "You see anything?"

"Not yet." Tal stood with binoculars raised. "Wait. There it is."

"Sync me."

Tal synced to the tripod, and it swiveled to the sky. A gray dart pierced through the clouds. Plumes of billowing white followed, a trail of climate-stabilization chemicals.

"It's a drone alright," Duncan said. "I'm gonna get that sucker." He clicked over to heavy-ion ammunition.

Duncan locked on, slowed his breathing, waited for the lull between heartbeats. Fired. There was a flash of light and a crack of thunder along the particle-beam trajectory. "Got him!"

"It's damaged," Tal said. "Big piece missing. But it's still flying."

Duncan raised his binoculars. On the belly of the drone, a tangle of frayed wires hung where there should have been a power supply. "I hit the generator," he said.

"Must be running on battery, then."

Black smoke mingled with white chemical clouds on its steadily shrinking tail. The drone was on a controlled descent, northeast, far into the barren tundra—might even make it to the sea.

"Well, what're you waiting for?" Tal said. "It's gonna get away!"

Duncan could take another few shots, sure, try to blow it out of the sky. But then they'd lose their chance to bag its memory chip—travel routes and waypoints, communication protocols, drone subroutines. An intel goldmine. He said, "It's on a controlled descent, which means its memory chip is intact. We could recover it, send it to intel."

"Or destroy it now," Tal said. "Finish the job."

"Where's it headed?"

Tal traced its trajectory, tapped his calcpad. "Looks like about three-fifty klicks from here, if it sticks to that course."

Three-fifty klicks. Just a few days travel.

"We can do it," Duncan said.

"You should take it out now," Tal said. "It's not worth the risk."

He might be right about that, Duncan thought. A downed

drone was nothing to mess with—backup weapon systems, ground mobility. And that was assuming they found it before the machine's cavalry arrived for recovery—a week or two, give or take. But Duncan wasn't one to back down from a challenge. "Let's go for it," he said.

"Do we even have enough rations?"

"Screw rations. You need to eat every day?"

Tal sighed. "It's not up to me, anyway. Ask Command."

Duncan pressed the communicator. "*Com-2 Echo-Whiskey, this is Ranger team Hotel-India, over.*"

"*Com-2 Echo-Whiskey here, over.*"

"*Request permission for recovery operation. We just got visual of a downed drone, over.*"

"*Roger that, Hotel-India. And congratulations, over.*"

Duncan grinned while he awaited the response from Command. Damn right, congratulations. "Can you believe it? Our first day together, and we took out a drone. Some luck, eh?"

"Yeah."

"We're gonna find that thing, we're gonna get its chip, and we're gonna come back heroes."

"If you say so."

The communicator crackled. "*Com-2 Echo-Whiskey here. Command has authorized recovery operation up to one hundred klicks. Please confirm distance to target, over.*"

Duncan's heart sank. A hundred klicks, two-fifty short of their target. Just like that, his hopes dashed by some bureaucrat's risk assessment.

"*Ranger team Hotel-India here,*" *Duncan said, then, without a second thought,* "*confirmation of target at niner-zero klicks, over.*" He couldn't believe he'd just lied to Command.

"*Roger that, Hotel-India. Am I speaking with Ranger One? Over.*"

"*Affirmative, why? Over.*"

"*Unanimous assent is required for discretionary operations. Ranger Two, please confirm, over.*"

Duncan could see hesitation in Tal's eyes. "Help me out here, buddy."

"You want me to lie?"

"I want you to help a fellow ranger. We might never get a chance like this again."

"Target's more than three hundred klicks into the tundra. They authorized us for a hundred, and that's for our safety."

"I'm not scared of a little wilderness."

"You should be."

"I know we can do this, Tal. But I can't do it without you. Please."

"I'm not going to lie to Command." Tal pressed his communicator. "*Hotel-India here. Ranger Two*"—he shot Duncan a quick glance—"*confirming assent for discretionary op, over.*"

"*Roger, Hotel-India. You are cleared to proceed. Out.*"

Duncan sighed a breath of relief. "Thanks."

"You owe me."

"So, we should head out, then?"

Duncan packed up his gear. The two of them hopped on their snowmobiles and took off for the North. A few hours ride took them into the barren grounds, under the slowly pinkening sky of the long April twilight.

Tal signaled for a stop. "It's about time we set up camp," he said, hopping off his snowmobile to stretch.

"Yeah. And I could use something to eat."

Duncan pulled the shelter from his cargo hold, expanding it and fastening it to the frozen ground. Then he assembled the blaster tripod and set it to sentry mode.

"What do we need that for?" Tal asked.

"Could be grizzlies around." The females would be waking up this time of year, and the males out of hibernation for about a month.

"You're more likely to kill a caribou than a bear with that thing."

"So what?" Duncan set the range to ten meters. Anything that close was asking for it.

The two of them went inside the tent and, for the first time in a day, removed their helmets.

"We made good time, eh?" Duncan said, stroking his beard.

"Yeah."

Tal handed Duncan a tube of nutritive paste, took one for himself, and they ate.

"I've been meaning to ask," Duncan said, "what's with the necklace?" Tal wore the same all-white ranger suit as Duncan, the only emblem a tiny red maple leaf over the heart. But over top of his suit, Tal had a wolf-paw necklace. "Isn't that against regs?"

"I got an exception."

"How?"

"Freedom of conscience and religion. Charter of Rights and Freedoms, Section 2A."

"Charter of Rights and Freedoms?" Duncan laughed. "No one takes that shit seriously anymore."

"You should. It's part of your culture."

Yeah, Duncan thought, some people care about culture. They'd told Duncan his new partner was Inuit Métis. All Duncan cared about was whether he could do the job. He hoped his partner's beliefs—whatever they were—wouldn't get in the way.

"So, does that necklace mean something?"

"Yeah."

Duncan sucked on the nutritive paste, waiting for an explanation that never came. He shifted in the awkward silence.

"Tal doesn't sound like an Inuit name," Duncan said, trying again for conversation.

"That's what everyone calls me in the city. It's short for Atiqtalaaq."

"Atiqtalaaq, huh? Kind of a mouthful. Maybe I'll just stick with Tal."

"It's what I'm used to."

After eating, they lay in their sleeping packs. There would be about three hours of night.

. . .

They woke, sometime in the latter half of the morning twilight, and set out again for the North.

When the thaw came, this would be a risky run, but for now, riding was easy, slowed down more than anything by Tal's insistence that they keep speed within safety regs. Duncan took care of check-ins with Command, lied about scouring the area where he'd said they'd spotted the drone—"*It's gotta be around here somewhere!*"—and Tal, for his part, pretended not to hear.

They had maybe sixteen hours of daylight to ride, stopping for a few breaks. Realistically, they'd use about ten of those.

Tal signaled for a stop when the sky pinkened. They were so close—couldn't be more than sixty or seventy klicks—Duncan almost insisted they keep going. But they needed the rest—if not for bagging the drone, then for the journey home.

They set up camp and slept.

. . .

Duncan awoke to a crack of thunder. Sentry.

Tal and Duncan suited up and stepped into the twilight. Ten meters from the gun was the carcass of a caribou, split into pieces from a particle blast.

"How's that for a wakeup call?" Duncan said, chuckling.

"I told you this might happen," Tal said. "I've got to take care of this."

He meant the carcass. Just what Duncan was worried about. Some kind of superstition, his partner's beliefs getting in the way of the job.

"What's the big deal?"

"When you kill an animal," Tal said, "you're supposed to show the proper respect."

"It's *dead,*" Duncan said. "I don't think it cares about your respect."

"Whatever," Tal said. "I'm doing it."

"Alright. What do you need to do?"

Tal explained that there were rules for using the meat and other parts of the animal, and there was something to do with the caribou bones, specifically. Otherwise, the spirit, he said, would haunt them.

It was absurd, entertaining stone-age superstitions about an animal killed by an automated particle gun.

"I'll go on ahead," Duncan said. "Catch up with me when you're done." There was no way he was waiting around for this. Not when the drone was so close. He hopped on his snowmobile and sped off for the open tundra, leaving Tal and the caribou corpse behind.

The ride was smooth, across barren tundra.

He heard Tal's voice. Singing. Maybe Tal had forgotten about the active commlink. Duncan felt like he was listening to something secret. The earnestness of Tal's voice ignited a curiosity in Duncan, a kind of yearning that he was only aware of when the words suddenly stopped, and the commlink went quiet.

"Tal, you there, buddy?"

"Yes."

"I was just—" He didn't know. "I'll be reaching the drone soon."

"Roger," Tal said. "I'm heading in your direction now. You've left a nice trail to follow."

Duncan searched for something to say. "So, you really take that stuff about respecting nature seriously, eh?"

"I didn't used to," Tal said. "I was raised in the south, wasn't taught about my culture. But when I returned to my roots, I knew it was the right way. Better."

"Better?" Duncan stifled a laugh. "Look, I respect your right to believe anything you want about spirits, or any other bullshit. But who are you to say that your culture is better?"

"We survived in North America for thousands of years. But it took your people only a few hundred years to destroy it."

"You're blaming us for destroying the environment and changing the climate?"

"Well, *we* didn't do it."

The endless white had given way to the shimmer of ice, and beyond the shimmer, a rapidly approaching patch of blue. Open water—a rift in the sea-ice. Duncan slammed the brakes.

"Shit," Duncan screamed, skidding over the edge and splashing into the water. He felt the cold instantly, soaking through his uniform. His snowmobile sank below his thrashing feet.

"What's wrong?" Tal asked.

"A break in the ice," Duncan said, breathing heavily. "I'm in the water!"

He could feel his strength leaking into the water, his muscles weakening, seizing. Duncan reached the edge with a desperate paddle, flung his arms over the lip of ice. He tried to climb but slipped each time, dipping back into the water. Panic set in as his body got heavier.

"Tal," he shouted. "I can't get out. I'm slipping. Help me!"

"You need to stay calm, Duncan. I'm on the way."

On the way, Duncan thought. *Right*. He'd left Tal behind. *How far was he? Twenty minutes? Thirty?*

"I'm gonna die," Duncan said.

"You need to listen to me very carefully. You ready?"

"Okay."

"Don't try to climb out anymore. You're just wasting your strength. I want you to kick your legs gently, stay just above the water. Spread your arms on the ice and try to anchor yourself."

"I'm still slipping."

"That's okay. Just keep your head above."

"I'm trying!"

"You ready for the next part?"

"Yeah."

"You're gonna need to take your helmet off."

"You fuckin' crazy?"

"Did I not just tell you to listen? Now shut up while I save your life. Got it?"

"Yeah."

"You've got about five minutes before your muscles shut down. And I'm not gonna be there for at least another ten. So if you don't follow my instructions, you're gonna die."

And if it was twenty minutes, Duncan thought, *I'm probably dead anyway.* "What do I do?"

"You take off your helmet, you soak your beard, and you freeze it to the ice."

"Okay." Duncan exhaled. "I can do this."

"Alright. But do it fast, while you still can."

"Okay. I'm ready."

"Good luck."

Duncan took a deep breath, propped himself on his elbows, then pushed up on his helmet. He slid down the ice as his helmet came off, and his head dipped below the water. The freezing wetness enveloped him. He kicked back up, gasping for air, and scrambled to the edge. Duncan forced his beard down onto the ice, propping a forearm on top. It froze quickly, and Duncan was no longer slipping, chin secured firmly to the ice.

He laid his arms out around his head, a shield from the biting winds, and his legs dangled below the water, drifting in the current. Arctic wind howled. Before long, the piercing pain on his exposed skin became a gentle numbness, then warmth. Duncan's eyelids were heavy. He closed his eyes, and his consciousness faded into the cold.

. . .

Duncan opened his eyes. He was in the tent, inside the relative warmth of his sleeping bag, but still shivering. Wind rustled the tent fabric. It was day, sun shining on the tent, but Duncan had no sense of the hour. Tal was next to him, cross-legged.

"I took the liberty of treating your hypothermia," Tal said. "You know the procedure."

Duncan groggily opened his sleeping bag. His uniform was gone, exposing his naked body. Wet clothing needs to be removed as a first step after hypothermia to prevent further heat loss, and this also allows skin-to-skin contact—the best way to raise core body temperature in the field.

"As far as the hypothermia," Tal said, "you're out of the woods, so to speak. Your breathing's normal, color is back in your face."

"Frostbite?" Duncan asked, feeling his ears and nose.

"Mostly second degree. There is one thing, though."

"What?"

Tal pantomimed stroking a beard over his smooth face, and Duncan felt his own chin.

"Had to cut you free when I got there. Rushed the job a little bit, and I was using a knife, so—" He paused. "It looks a little rough."

"Yeah." Duncan stroked his mangled beard. "I forgive you," he said, then laughed. "Thanks."

"Don't mention it. So, are you awake enough to talk?"

"What's up?"

"When you're more recovered," Tal said, "we need to head back."

"You mean without the drone?" Duncan said. "Hell no."

"I agreed to help you," Tal said, "even though I thought it was a bad idea. And I just saved your life. Now you need to listen to me. It's time to go back."

"But we're so close," Duncan said.

Tal shook his head. "Get some sleep. We'll head back to base in the morning."

Like hell we will, Duncan thought. *I'm gonna bag that drone.*

. . .

Duncan awoke to crackling static. "*Ranger team Hotel-India, this is Com-2 Echo-Whiskey. Check-in immediately, over.*"

"Shit," Duncan said. He rubbed his eyes. It was twilight—morning or night?—and he was alone in the tent. No sign of Tal. The communicator repeated the message.

Duncan took a breath, hoping he didn't have to answer many questions from Command, then reached for the comm.

"*Ranger team Hotel-India, reporting, over.*"

"*We're gonna need you to return to base ASAP, Hotel-India. We got a cat-three blizzard moving in, over.*"

A storm. Not something he had been counting on. The tent wouldn't be enough if they were caught in a cat-three. Not by a longshot. But maybe there was still time to recover the drone and make it home. "*How long we got? Over.*"

"*About six hours,*" Command said. Duncan's heart sank. They were more than two days ride from safety. They would be caught in the storm. Command continued, "*but you can clear niner-zero klicks with time to spare, right? Just don't stick around too long unless you wanna be a popsicle. Heh. Hurry back, Hotel-India, over.*"

"*Roger, out.*" We're fucked. Duncan suited up and rushed outside. Tal was standing by the lone snowmobile, and Duncan remembered that his own ride was sunk somewhere out there beneath the ice. He relayed the news of the storm to Tal, who didn't say a word.

"So, what do we do?" Duncan said. "We can't make it back in time. The shelter won't cut it."

"Igloo."

"You serious?"

"Worked for thousands of years," Tal said. He unsheathed his viblade and clicked it on. The tool hummed. "Now help me make some blocks."

Tal knelt to the snow and carved. Four lines, then a

crevice to reach in and cut underneath, and finally, he withdrew a frozen brick.

Duncan drew his own knife, turned it on, and felt the vibration through his fingers. Kneeling down, he carved. The energy-assisted viblade made quick work of the ice—no resistance, like slicing through a cloud.

"Been a while since I did this," Duncan said. He'd only built an igloo once, during arctic survival training, and he'd thought it was a waste of time. "Not sure if I know exactly what I'm doing."

"Just cut the blocks."

"How many?"

"Keep cutting until I tell you to stop."

Tal set up the perimeter, laying blocks out in a circle, then shaved an incline along the bottom row. Duncan carved bricks as fast as he could, and Tal placed them along the structure, spiraling upwards.

The wind was picking up, whipping across their visors. Already, their vision was blurred with snow, and they were fighting the wind for balance. The blizzard was visible on the horizon, not white but gray and black—and growing.

Tal carved the keystone piece and inserted it in the top, completing the dome. Then he carved the entrance into the ground in front of the structure, a foot and a half down, and tunneled below.

They crawled inside and sat quietly, listening to the raging winds of the blizzard.

Duncan couldn't get a response from Command. He figured the storm had knocked out the relay units. They were really on their own now. But at least they wouldn't freeze to death.

Then Duncan remembered the rations. "Shit," he said.

"What's wrong?"

"How many rations you got?"

"Two days."

Duncan's last rations went down with the snowmobile, under the ice. Between them, Tal's food would last a day, and the storm could last two days, maybe three. Then there was the return journey.

Duncan had never thought he'd be caught in a cat-three in the field. Big storms had big warnings. You'd have to do something really stupid to get caught. Like disobeying an order and then lying to Command about your location. "Ah, shit."

"Relax," Tal said. "Do you need to eat every day?"

Duncan laughed, hearing his own words spit back at him. "I guess not."

"You know," Tal said, "my people would fast for spiritual purposes. Maybe it would do you some good?"

"If you're so used to fasting," Duncan said, "you won't mind sharing your rations."

Tal handed Duncan one of the two remaining tubes. "Enjoy it. It might be the last time we eat in a while."

Time moved slowly in the igloo. The blizzard was somehow calming, heard within the safety of the ice house. Duncan slept and awoke refreshed, but the storm still raged.

"What did people do to pass the time in these things?" Duncan asked.

"Storytelling was important in the winter seasons," Tal said. "It was a respected profession among my people."

"So how about you tell a story?"

"I've never been much good at storytelling."

Duncan found, over repeated attempts to start a conversation, that Tal was not a talker. He seemed to prefer sitting silently and had a propensity for short answers. The two of them spent hours in near silence, broken only by Duncan's stirring and failed attempts at conversation.

"I think I'm gonna go insane in here," Duncan said.

"If you want something to do," Tal said with a grin, "why not try to contact your spirit guide?"

More mumbo-jumbo, Duncan thought. *Fine. I'll play along*. "What do I do?"

"You meditate—silently—until your guide comes to you in a dream."

"You're just tryin' to shut me up."

Tal's grin widened. "Maybe."

"Besides," Duncan said, "I don't believe in spirits."

"Why not?" His grin disappeared.

"Because if they existed, there'd be proof. We'd see some evidence."

"There's evidence all around us. In the wind."

"I got news for you. We know how wind works, and spirits aren't part of it."

"Everything has a spirit, whether you can see it or not."

"If you say so."

The hours passed without consequence. When Duncan pushed through his nagging hunger, he slept.

. . .

There was a hallucinatory-blue light outside the igloo, glowing through the blocks. It was silent—no sounds of the storm. Then Duncan was outside the igloo, standing at the feet of a ten-foot-tall crow.

He wondered if the dream-crow was his spirit guide.

"No," the crow cawed. "But I can take you somewhere important."

The crow spread its wings, and Duncan climbed on its back. They flew over the tundra and landed near a river alcove.

"There is a spirit waiting there for you," the crow cawed and pointed to the dark mouth of a cave in the alcove. "Go and meet it."

Duncan entered the cave. In blackness, a dozen glowing red eyes appeared, attached to a metallic beast that sprang from the shadows. Duncan grappled with robot limbs. The drone screeched and whirred as they wrestled. Duncan pulled a handful of wires from the undercarriage, and the drone went quiet. It gave Duncan a computer chip, then retreated into the shadows.

Duncan left the cave to where the crow was waiting. "He gave me this," Duncan said, revealing the computer chip. The crow cawed, and Duncan opened his eyes to the inside of the igloo.

The sound of the crow's caw faded in his memory, until he heard only silence.

"Listen," he said, shaking Tal awake. "Listen."

"What?" Tal sat up. The realization washed over his face. "The storm's over."

They suited up and left the igloo, then started unburying the snowmobile from the snow.

"Time to go home," Tal said.

"No. We're going to get that drone."

"Discretionary ops require unanimous assent," Tal said. "Let me make this official. I don't give assent."

"I don't give a shit about your assent. I'm getting that drone."

"You almost died. Don't you realize this is a bad idea?"

If Duncan was going to get the drone, he had to convince Tal. "I had a vision last night."

"A vision?"

"I met a spirit," Duncan said, letting himself believe his dream meant something, only just enough to lie with conviction.

"Tell me what happened," Tal said, with a raised eyebrow.

"I saw a giant crow. We flew across the tundra, and there was a cave. And the crow told me to go in to find a spirit. So I went in to find the spirit and..."

"Yes?"

"There was a drone."

"A drone?" Tal laughed. "The spirit was a drone?"

"What's so funny?" Duncan felt suddenly defensive, insulted.

"A drone can't be a spirit."

"Why not? You said everything has a spirit."

"Everything in nature has a spirit."

"Well," Duncan said, "humans are part of nature. So that means the stuff we make is part of nature, too. So why couldn't a drone have a spirit? I mean, it moves, it flies, and it thinks."

"It's a machine."

"Yeah," Duncan said. "But it's what I saw."

"So what?"

"So, it has to mean something," he said, and partly believed it. "Right?"

"It means you were thinking about drones, so that's what you dreamed about. That's not a vision. That's R-E-M."

"What about the crow?"

Tal paused.

"Well?" Duncan asked. "That means something, doesn't it?"

"Some people say that crows are the 'keepers of council,'" Tal said. "They help reach consensus."

That was helpful. "Let's work on that consensus, then. I want to get that drone."

Tal shook his head. "It's too dangerous."

"This job's not supposed to be safe. Besides," Duncan added, "I know we can do it."

"How could you possibly know that?"

"Because I saw it." Even if he didn't believe in spirits, Duncan believed in the subconscious. It has a way of poking through in dreams. And it was trying to tell him something.

Tal only stared, silent.

"We can get that drone," Duncan said. "The crow means something. I think it means we need to do it together."

Tal inhaled deeply, closed his eyes as if struggling with some unseen force. "Okay," he said finally.

Duncan grinned.

They hopped on the snowmobile, Tal in front.

. . .

They reached a frozen river, buried under layered snow, and followed it to a large bend. Duncan signaled for a stop. It was nothing like what he'd seen in his dream, but the coordinates seemed right, and the bend widened to form an alcove. That must mean something.

Tal hopped off the snowmobile. "How do we even know it's there?"

"Just a guess," Duncan said. A ranger's hunch confirmed by a dream.

"Why would it go here?"

Duncan shrugged. *Maybe some kind of tactical advantage*. "I don't know."

The alcove loomed before them, its edge ringed by precipitous terrain, rising sharply in uneven lumps, like rocks or steep, irregular earth, buried beneath the snow. And over the lumpy terrain—the black mouth of a cave. They would have to go on foot to reach it.

"It could be anywhere," Tal said.

"No," Duncan said, staring at the cave. "It couldn't get very far on battery power, and it would be a sitting duck on open land. It came here to hide, for sure."

"So what's the plan?"

"Go on foot."

"And if it's waiting for an ambush?"

Tal was right. One blast, and they'd be toast. And the drone would've saved enough power for it.

"I'll go," Duncan said. "You keep a lookout from over here."

"Sure. But who takes the gun?"

Right. They only had one now. He sighed. "I guess it makes more sense for you to take it."

Tal nodded. "I'll move up on that hill. Better vantage."

Duncan stood while Tal rode a short distance away, up the hill on the riverside, then assembled the gun.

"Ready," Tal said through the communicator. "Good luck."

Duncan faced the alcove, edged with uneven terrain under a thick carpet of snow. Then he climbed, slowly, through thigh-deep snow. He found himself crawling, pulling himself by smaller, snow-cloaked crags, navigating around the larger ones. He was breathing heavily, sweating inside his suit.

"Be careful," Tal said.

"Don't have to tell me twice." Nothing more dangerous than a cornered animal.

Up ahead, an irregular boulder shifted from under the cover of snow. A blanket of powder rolled off the surface, shiny metal. The drone stood tall on a dozen mechanical legs, rising from under the snowy camouflage like a robot spider. Sensor arrays lit up across its surface, glowing red. Duncan froze. The drone turned its tooled appendages towards him, and the energy cannon hummed. Duncan closed his eyes, accepting his fate. Two thunderous blasts radiated heat through his suit. And then, realizing he was alive, he opened his eyes.

The drone scurried away, an uncanny flurry of mechanical legs, with the scrape and clatter of metal and rock. A swath of melted snow led from the drone. Some distance from the river, Duncan saw a pillar of black smoke and smoldering wreckage.

"Tal," he shouted and waited for a response. "Tal!"

"I'm here," Tal said.

Duncan breathed a sigh of relief. "Jesus. Are you okay?"

"Yeah. I got out of the way in time. Our ride wasn't so lucky, though. Or the gun."

"It shot the gun, too?"

"Must've been going for the biggest threats."

"Picked the wrong targets, then." Duncan said. "I'm goin' after it."

"You don't even have a weapon. You're not going after it."

"Just watch me."

Duncan followed the drone's trail over the rocks. He scrambled through the snow, rounded a large crag, and froze. There was the mouth of the cave. Only a few paces.

"It's in the cave," he said.

"Like your dream."

"Yeah." Duncan stared into the darkness. "I'm following it."

Tal said something, but Duncan was too focused to pay attention. He walked in. Narrow walls, frosted over. It darkened rapidly as he entered.

A flash of metal and light, and the drone was over him. Mechanical legs were an enveloping cage. Robotic limbs whirred, gears grinding. Something clutched his lower leg, squeezed, turned, and Duncan heard the crack of his shin bone, felt it half a second later. He collapsed, grasping instinctively for a handhold.

Duncan hung on a fistful of wires from the drone's undercarriage. He saw his leg, bent with an extra hinge on the shin. Sharp pain, nearly paralyzing.

He drew his viblade, clicked it on, and swiped below the body of the drone, carved at its guts. There was a shower of sparks, and a tangle of wires fell loose. He swiped again, severing another batch of wires, and the drone went still. There was a descending hum that quieted to nothing. Duncan was held in the clutches of the unpowered drone.

"I got it," he said, as much to Tal as himself. "I got the drone!"

"How?"

"Just get over here."

The wait was excruciating.

Tal's silhouette appeared in the cave entrance. He made his way down, drew his viblade, and cut Duncan free from the mechanical constraints.

Duncan winced as his broken leg was released, dangling free. He needed treatment, at the very least a splint, but all their medical supplies were lost with the vehicles.

"You know—" Duncan eyed the drone as he spoke "—I've heard that your people make use of all the parts of animals."

"There's truth to that," Tal said, and he started cutting at the drone, sawing away wires, slicing through metal sheets. His viblade made easy work of the drone's innards, humming as it passed through wires. The outer panels gave more resistance, metal shrieking as Tal sawed with the viblade, slowly but surely, through the hard sheets. He freed two thin, straight pieces of metal and several long stretches of wire.

Duncan cried out when Tal manually straightened his leg and winced throughout as Tal fashioned a metal splint, securing it tightly with wires on four spots.

"Thanks," Duncan said. The drone's carcass loomed over them, its guts spilled out onto the cave floor. "Now let's get the memory chip."

Tal nodded. He stood under the frame of the drone, slicing with his viblade. Piece by piece, with showers of sparks, the drone came apart, and Tal threw each mangled part to the side. Irregular metal sheets with torn edges. Tangles of wire. Motors and gears. A pile of junk formed in a rough circle as he worked.

Tal pulled out the brain of the drone, a tiny box containing the CPU and memory chip. He turned the box over in his hand, then reached for a bundle of wire.

"What're you doing?" Duncan asked.

"One of the uses my people make of animals—" Tal fashioned a loop of wire as he spoke, securing it to the box "—is clothing and jewelry." He handed it to Duncan. "A necklace."

Duncan grinned and placed the drone necklace over his neck.

Tal went back to work on the drone wreckage. He extracted the particle cannon and the batteries—not enough charge for the laser, but plenty to start a few fires. And more wire, loads of it. He fashioned a large, curved section of hull into a sled, puncturing holes and looping thick cables to form handholds.

"I don't imagine you'd walk very fast on that leg," Tal said. "I'll have to pull you."

"Right," Duncan said, feeling a bit embarrassed and inadequate, even knowing there was no shame in not walking, with his shin snapped in two.

Tal loaded up the makeshift sled, first with Duncan, who did his best to help and only cried out in pain for a moment. Then he loaded on the gear he'd cut from the drone, securing it with wires and cable.

Tal pulled the sled slowly and carefully from the cave.

At the bottom, Duncan estimated their pace at less than three kilometers an hour. It would be a long trip home if they couldn't establish contact. Maybe a month or more. Without food or supplies. A pretty good chance they'd die on the way, he figured. But not a sudden, dramatic death. Starvation.

Duncan tested his commlink to Command. Nothing. "No luck on the comms."

"I wouldn't think so," Tal said. "The storm would've knocked out the relay. We're on our own, at least a few weeks."

Towards the end of the darkening twilight, they spotted a mound on the horizon. Their igloo, from the night before. They reached the ice house under the night stars and the green glow of northern lights.

The next day, they set off again. Duncan's hunger was worsening, and he could only imagine how Tal felt—he was walking for both of them.

Before night, they constructed another igloo. Duncan's contribution was a few bricks, which amounted to a couple minutes of saved time.

On the third day, Tal moved a bit slower. Duncan couldn't tell if he was wearing thin, or if he was looking for something. But the area seemed familiar. Then Tal veered off course, towards a small mound of snow. They reached the landmark, that very slight hill, and Duncan remembered the caribou.

Tal carved the frozen carcass and loaded it onto the sled.

The next few weeks ran together. March during the day,

build an igloo before night, eat, sleep, repeat. Test comms now and then.

Duncan lifted his visor and felt the cold against his skin. Snowy plains lay ahead, and at the far edge of his vision, what looked like a thin line of trees. Wind at their backs seemed to usher them towards home, and for the first time in weeks, Duncan was sure they would make it.

Tal was saying something to himself, maybe singing, and Duncan, for his part, listened.

. . .

About the author:

David F. Shultz writes from Toronto, Canada, where he is Lead Editor at *Speculative North* magazine, and organizes the eight-hundred-member Toronto Science Fiction and Fantasy Writers. His eighty-plus publications are featured through publishers such as Augur, Diabolical Plots, and Third Flatiron. Author webpage: davidfshultz.com

36

Breeders

by David Harten Watson (United States)

Subgenres: Science fiction, young adult (YA), YA dystopian, YA romance, and YA LGBT

Time period: 2179 to 2180 AD

Setting: Buffalo, New York, North American Union

Historical basis: Calasanctius School in Buffalo, New York was where the author attended high school (two hundred years before this story takes place). The Act of Congress and Supreme Court decision cited in "Breeders" were real historical events, with only the *year* changed for the story. Anticipating that readers will find this hard to believe, two footnotes provide evidence that those violations of civil liberties really happened, right here in America. If we are not vigilant about defending our liberties, such history could repeat itself.

Disclaimer: Just as *The Handmaid's Tale* didn't reflect the religious views of its author, the interpretation of the Bible in "Breeders" reflects the views of a future dystopian society, *not* the religious beliefs of the author.

WARNING: This story may not be suitable for younger readers. Due to the radical religious views of its dystopian society, "Breeders" may be offensive to some Catholics, my fellow Mormons, and anyone who considers unorthodox interpretations of the Bible (even in fiction) to be sacrilege, blasphemy, heresy, or apostasy. This story *will* be offensive to homophobes and Trump supporters!

. . .

When I was in high school, I wished there were a twelve-step program for people like me. I imagined it would be called "Atavists Anonymous," and we'd all sit together in a circle. When they asked new people to introduce themselves, I'd stand up and say, "Hi, my name is Kevin, and I'm an atavist." Other members would welcome me, telling me the group is a "safe space" where nobody will judge me, everyone will support me, and they'll all help me overcome my disorder.

But alas, no such group existed. If it did, it would have to meet in the shadows, in secret, with constant risk of arrest if discovered. Well, *adults* would be arrested, but seventeen-year-olds like me would merely be expelled from school and have our reputations destroyed.

I didn't want to be expelled, because *most* of the time I liked my high school, Calasanctius. What we called "Cal" was a restoration of the original Calasanctius Preparatory School for the Gifted, which closed due to bankruptcy in 1991. More than a century later, a Buffalo billionaire whose ancestors had graduated from the original Calasanctius rebuilt it at its original location, just south of Delaware Park in Buffalo, Western New York. It consisted of four buildings on Windsor Avenue, one building on Rumsey Road, and about three hundred students in grades one through twelve.

Our school was named after Saint Joseph Calasanctius of the Piarist Order. The original school had been founded by Piarist priests who'd fled Hungary to escape the brutal Soviet suppression of the 1956 Hungarian Revolution. Sometimes I wondered what those freedom-loving founders would think of the twenty-second-century oppression of families and relationships in today's North American Union (NAU)—oppression not only by the government, but also by the Catholic Church.

Calasanctius was *technically* private, because it wasn't under the authority of the Diocese of Buffalo, but it sure felt like a Catholic school. Nearly half of our teachers were priests or nuns, similar to the percentage of priests and nuns in Buffalo's Catholic schools. However, not all of the students were Catholic. My family was Episcopal. My best friend, Pete, was an atheist. Our mutual friend Tiffany was Buddhist. Calasanctius also had students who were Jewish, Muslim, Hindu, Bahai, Unitarian Universalist, and nearly every Christian denomination—*except*, of course, Mormons.

The priests and nuns who taught us, following the tenets of the Roman Catholic Church, were conservative on issues of gender, sexuality, and marriage. To even *speak* in favor of civil rights for sexual deviants was grounds for detention, and any sexually deviant *acts* were grounds for suspension or even expulsion. *That* was what I didn't like about my school, because unbeknownst to my friends, classmates, or even my parents, I was a sexual deviant.

I wasn't just your common, run-of-the-mill pervert, such as someone with a fetish for latex, leather, feet, young children, or furry animals. No, I was the most despised and detested of all sexual deviants in the year 2179. I was an atavist, a throwback, a gender traitor, a heterophile, a *breeder* (the most derogatory name for my condition that could be used in school without being punished for swearing).

It wasn't my fault; I'd been *born* that way, born with an atavistic attraction for the opposite sex! It was a genetic abnormality, a birth defect. I couldn't help which gender I was attracted to romantically, physically, and (I had to admit to myself) sexually. Despite having ancestors genetically engineered to be attracted to the same sex, being born of mixed DNA from the primordial germ cells of two fathers, and conditioned since birth to be attracted to other boys, I simply *wasn't*.

For my own safety, I'd lied to my classmates, telling them I was asexual, or "ace."

Being ace was considered perfectly acceptable, even among the conservative priests and nuns who taught at Calasanctius, some of whom were ace themselves, which made it easier to observe their vows of chastity. I'd never dared tell anyone the shameful truth that I was an atavist, a pervert, a deviant, a throwback, a gender traitor, a heterophile, a *breeder*.

My fathers knew I'd never had a boyfriend, as I'd never pretended to have one just for *their* sake. They'd assumed I was either ace, a late bloomer, too shy around boys I found physically attractive, or simply unwilling to discuss my romantic interests in front of them. They were right about my being shy, but the sad truth was that I didn't find *any* boys physically attractive, not even my best friend, Pete (who only had a platonic interest in me anyway, so it's not like I was leading him on or anything).

My younger father was a psychiatric social worker, so one day, I looked up my condition in his manual, which had the ridiculously long title *Diagnostic and Statistical Manual of Mental Disorders, Twenty-fifth Edition*, or *DSM-25* for short. The *DSM-25* called my condition "heterophilia" and labeled it a mental illness, the *worst* of the paraphilic disorders. According to the *DSM-25*, heterophilia was sometimes caused by a traumatic experience in childhood. Those cases could be treated through a combination of counseling and psychiatric drugs.

In other cases, heterophilia had a biological cause called *atavism*, the genetic reversion to an ancestral trait that had been supposedly bred out of existence in humans (not just by natural evolution, as the twenty-second-century definition of atavism also included reversion to traits bred out of humans through genetic engineering). In other words, a birth defect. These cases were considered incurable and could only be treated by powerful hormone-suppressing drugs, or if those drugs failed, castration. I shuddered and closed the book.

I couldn't remember any traumatic experiences in my childhood, so unless I was suffering from suppressed memories, I figured I must have been born genetically defective. I was an atavist, a throwback to the primitive times when humans reproduced through sexual intercourse like animals, rather than being conceived through artificial insemination of the primordial germ cells from two parents of the same sex, like civilized humans.

I'd always known my lack of attraction for boys wasn't because I was ace, but I'd been smart enough to keep quiet about my unspeakable desire for the opposite sex. Since childhood, I'd fantasized about female holovision stars. Since age thirteen, they'd also been the subject of my nighttime wet dreams. I'd even been attracted to some of my female classmates, but afraid someone might notice my sinful desires, I'd always gone out of my way to avoid the girls I found most attractive.

Always... until the fall of my senior year.

Her name was Jasmine, and she was a goddess! Jasmine was so beautiful that I didn't have the strength of will to avoid her, instead trying foolishly to find every opportunity to see her, even from afar. She was a junior, while I was a senior, but we were the same age—I'd looked up her birthday on her social media profile. However, I knew the odds of a good Catholic school girl like Jasmine being a heterophile like me were so astronomically low as to be nonexistent.

. . .

Sister Angelina often mixed religion into her history class, so I was used to it by now, but I still resented it. This week, we were studying population history, so I had to suffer through her lecture reminding us—again— why my sexuality was such an evil perversion.

"Heterophiles, or *breeders*," she sneered, "were responsible for the near destruction of humanity in the twenty-first century. Their sinful perversion caused runaway population growth that led to catastrophic global warming, nearly making Earth unsuitable for human life.

"It took two million years for Earth's population to reach one billion people, which happened in the year 1804." Her beady gray eyes settled on me. "Kevin, why aren't you taking notes? This *will* be on your next test!"

Sighing under my breath, I picked up my stylus, writing the dates and population numbers in my solar-powered notebook as Sister Angelina continued. "Although it took two million years for human population to hit one billion people in 1804, it only took one hundred twenty-three years for the population to double to two billion, in 1927. By that time, anthropogenic global warming—human-induced climate change—*should* have been noticeable to scientists, but only a handful at the time noticed it."

Sister Angelina's voice rose in religious indignation. "Families back then were headed by sexual deviants involved in heterophile so-called 'marriages,' a man and a woman living together in sin, rather than having a Godly relationship with the *same* sex like Jesus and His Apostles. Even though it's spelled out clearly in the Gospel of John, people in those sinful days had forgotten that John, not Mary Magdalene, was the Apostle whom Jesus loved. During the most sinful days, from the Middle Ages right up until the mid-twentieth century, humans bred like rats, frequently having eight, ten, twelve, or even fifteen children!"

My classmates' eyes widened with horror.

"Overpopulation was the result of humans sinfully cohabitating with the opposite sex like animals, which goes against everything Jesus taught us." She glared at us, as if daring anyone to disagree with Catholic theology. No doubt all my classmates agreed with her, even the atheists, and I knew better than to open my mouth. As far as I knew, I was the only remaining heterophile in my school. There had been others, but when they'd been discovered, they'd been expelled for their heresy.

Sister Angelina took a deep breath, then continued in a calmer voice. "After hitting two billion in 1927, it took only thirty-three years for population to hit three billion, in 1960. Population hit four billion only fourteen years later, in 1974, and some scientists finally noticed that burning fossil fuels was changing the Earth's climate.

"Earth's human population hit five billion in 1987, six billion in 1999, and seven billion in 2011. That's about the time the majority of climate scientists warned that Earth's nations must act immediately to prevent catastrophic global warming, or it would be too late, as Earth was about to reach a tipping point. Unfortunately, most nations ignored scientists' warnings and continued to breed like animals and pollute at an unbroken pace.

"The worst polluter of all was the United States of America, the central forerunner of our North American Union. Two United States presidents, George W. Bush and Donald Trump, now known as Traitor Trump, seemed to do everything in their power to *increase* the amount of fossil fuel pollution emitted by the United States, not caring that this would destroy the country in the long run.

"Historians think the reason the Bush regime took such destructive actions was because President Bush and his vice president, Dick Cheney, had strong financial ties to oil companies. As for Traitor Trump, his presidency was controlled by the Russians who put him in office by rigging the 2016 election in his favor. Russia was a major oil exporter at the time, so as soon as they had their puppet in the White House, they ordered him to roll back fuel economy standards, increasing United States oil consumption so Russia could profit from higher global oil prices.

"As a result of the failure of Bush, Traitor Trump, and other early twenty-first-century presidents to confront climate change, America's western states repeatedly caught fire, killing hundreds of people. As global temperatures rose further, thousands more Americans died in heat waves, hurricanes, tornadoes, floods, and other climate-caused natural disasters; but still the United States refused to ban heterophilia, even though population growth was the number one factor fueling global warming."

My friend Tiffany asked the question I'd been thinking, "Wasn't global warming caused more by the burning of fossil fuels than by heterophiles?"

Sister Angelina gave Tiffany a glare icy enough to reverse global warming all by itself, making me glad I wasn't the one asking. "No," she snapped, "it was not. Although the burning of fossil fuels contributed to global warming, mankind had been burning fossil fuels for two million years, but the Earth didn't start to warm until human population surpassed two billion people in 1927. This population growth was due to the sinful practice of men and women living together like animals. They even tried to sanctify their sin by naming their behavior 'marriage,' which is blasphemy, because the only true Christian marriage is between people of the same sex.

"After hitting seven billion people in 2011, population growth slowed somewhat, as by then, most heterophiles were using technology called 'birth control' to keep their animalistic sexual behavior from leading to large families."

Pete, who was sitting next to me, asked, "But back then, wasn't the Catholic Church against birth control?"

Sister Angelina picked up the aluminum ruler from its tray on the whiteboard and walked over to Pete's desk, hovering over him as if deciding how many raps on the knuckles to administer. Pete bravely placed his hands on the desk, palms down, knowing what to expect.

Sister Angelina said, "Historically, you are correct, so I'll spare your knuckles this time, but watch your tone when talking about the Church! Yes, back then the Church opposed birth control, but that was a very dark period in Church history. There have been other dark points in our history, including the Crusades and the Spanish Inquisition, but the Church's opposition to birth control was probably the worst mistake our Church ever made.

"In the twentieth and early twenty-first centuries, the Church still called birth control a sin, continued to conduct wedding ceremonies for heterophile so-called 'marriages,' and even denounced the true Christian practice of same-sex marriage. By the late twentieth century, artificial insemination and in-vitro fertilization became widely available, but the Catholic Church didn't yet recognize those technologies as the restoration of Biblical Virgin Birth, the only sinless way of getting pregnant.

"We now know that in the time of Jesus, artificial insemination was already being practiced by holy people, and that's what the Bible meant by the Virgin Birth of Jesus. Today, we know that the Blessed Mother Mary gave birth to our Lord Jesus Christ through Virgin Birth as a sign that the only true, sinless, and holy way to give birth is through artificial insemination. In the twenty-second century, we added a new technology for artificial insemination, using primordial germ cells from two same-sex parents.

"Getting back to what I was saying before Peter interrupted me," she said, glaring at him, "population growth slowed somewhat after world population reached seven billion people in 2011, but not enough to prevent Earth from reaching the dreaded 'tipping point,' when global warming became impossible to stop.

"By the time Earth's population hit ten billion in 2060,

the consequences of global warming had already proven disastrous. Sea-level rise flooded coastal cities, leaving tens of millions of people climate refugees. Politicians, as well as scientists, were so alarmed by world population reaching eleven figures in 2060, that nations finally united to take action.

"Scientists declared that zero population growth wasn't good enough; world population would have to decline to a sustainable population of about one billion people for the Earth to heal. The Pope approved birth control, but it wasn't 100 percent effective and wouldn't alone be enough to lower world population. Doctors, scientists, politicians, and theologians studying the problem realized that the root cause of population growth was the perverse, animalistic practice of humans breeding through sexual intercourse with the opposite sex.

"Christian theologians reviewed original manuscripts of the Bible and came to an almost unanimous conclusion: the Bible had been misinterpreted for centuries! Today, it's hard to believe how humans misinterpreted the Bible as condoning heterophilia for centuries, despite the many Bible verses that showed homosexuality to be the true will of God."

Sister Angelina ticked off the Biblical evidence on her fingers as I tried to keep up in my notebook: "Jesus lived with twelve other men, none of the Apostles married women, and none of the Apostles got women pregnant. That means none of them ever had sex with women, because birth control hadn't been invented yet. Finally, the Gospel of John states six times that John was the disciple whom Jesus loved, including—write this down—John 13:23, John 19:26, John 20:2, John 21:7, and John 21:20."

"That's only five," I blurted out without thinking.

Sister Angelina smiled. "Yes, Kevin, so now that you mentioned it, everyone gets an extra homework assignment tonight: find the sixth reference in the Gospel of John to John being the disciple Jesus loved." My classmates shot dirty looks at me.

Sister Angelina continued. "Modern theologians re-translated the Bible from original manuscripts to reveal the truth—that God considers heterophile so-called 'marriages' an abomination! God destroyed Sodom and Gomorrah not, as the Church had wrongly believed, because of same-sex relationships, but to punish them for allowing men and women to sleep together.

"With scientists, politicians, and theologians all in agreement in 2075, heterophile sex was banned worldwide. Laws were passed making artificial insemination the only legal way to conceive babies, requiring parents to obtain a license to have a child, and limiting families to only one child.

"A handful of religious sects were holdouts, refusing to accept the correct interpretation of the Bible. They abused the concept of 'religious freedom' to continue conceiving babies through the beastly practice of heterophile sex. Their members also continued having multiple babies, a doctrine known as *polybirth*.

"The largest of these heretical sects was the Church of Jesus Christ of Latter-day Saints, or LDS Church, better known as the Mormons. For years, Mormons stubbornly clung to their sinful heterophile and polybirth doctrines. Finally, in 2087, the *Edmunds-Tucker Act* disincorporated the LDS Church in America, authorizing the federal government to arrest Mormon Church leaders and seize all of the church's assets, including the temples where they performed their blasphemous heterophilic 'temple marriage ordinances' that were associated with polybirth. The Supreme Court upheld the provisions of the *Edmunds-Tucker Act* on May 19, 2090, saying in their majority opinion, 'Religious freedom is not absolute, but must give way to progress, for the common good of humanity and the survival of our species.'"Meanwhile, scientists identified the genes influencing sexuality in humans. In 2089, genetic engineers developed a method to ensure that everyone has the holy, sacred gene that causes homosexual attraction, virtually eliminating the beastly gene for heterophilia from the human gene pool. By then, all babies were conceived through artificial insemination. All in vitro fertilization labs were ordered to alter the DNA of the fertilized egg before implantation. Ever since, except for a few criminals having unauthorized babies conceived in sin, every child has been born with normal, homosexual desires, replacing the perversion called heterophilia."

Except for genetically defective, atavistic deviants like me.

"Earth's population steadily declined due to laws restricting families to one child each, but not rapidly enough. Population decreased from ten billion people to nine billion, then eight, then climate change caused disruptions in agriculture, leading to widespread starvation. At the same time, nations were ending their reliance on fossil fuels to stop global warming, but without fossil fuel agriculture, Earth could only sustainably feed one billion people.

"Even with only one child per family, and millions of people slowly starving due to climate-induced crop failures, it would've taken generations for population to decline to a sustainable level of one billion. But then something happened to quickly reduce Earth's population to *below* the one billion mark," Sister Angelina said somberly. "The COVID-58 pandemic." She crossed herself as she spoke the name of the dreaded disease. We crossed ourselves too, even those of us who weren't Catholic. Our parents were among the lucky few who'd survived COVID-58, but we'd all lost grandparents, aunts, uncles, or other relatives to the pandemic.

"In recent decades, geoengineering has made great progress in reversing the effects of global warming. Our leaders have even begun granting licenses for parents to have a second child. I must warn you, however, that the practice of heterophilia is still forbidden."

It wasn't the first time my teachers' religious indoctrination made me ashamed of my sexuality, reminding me how much perverts like me deserved the derogatory term *breeders*. I was sure it wouldn't be the last.

. . .

I got to know Jasmine in the fall of my senior year. We were both in drama club, which this year was performing *All the President's Henchmen*, a historical play about the worst president in American history, the man nicknamed "Traitor Trump" in the history books. After the Russian government rigged the 2016 election to put Donald J. Trump in office, he'd secretly conspired with Russia to achieve many of that nation's goals. He was the only American president ever to be impeached twice.

Traitor Trump had been one of the leading deniers of global warming, having made the outlandish claim, "The concept of global warming was created by and for the Chinese in order to make United States manufacturing non-competitive." He'd also been responsible for the deaths of hundreds of thousands of Americans during his term from the first COVID pandemic, COVID-19, which he'd called "the China virus," just as he'd called climate change "a Chinese hoax." *Apparently, Traitor Trump had been a hater of everything Chinese.*

I didn't want to play Traitor Trump, so I signed up instead for the part of Adam Schiff, the House impeachment manager during Trump's first impeachment. When nobody signed up for the role of Traitor Trump, the drama teacher, a plump priest in his forties named Father Ryan, told one of my classmates, "Sorry, Carl, but I'm giving you the part. You're going to have to wear a fat suit, blond wig, and orange makeup."

All the President's Henchmen was set in the twenty-first century, back when men had to wear an uncomfortable piece of clothing called a "necktie," which seemed to me like a bizarre cross between a ribbon, a dog collar, and a hangman's noose. I was more concerned about avoiding choking myself to death than making the knot look like the pictures in the history books, so I tied a simple slipknot for dress rehearsal.

Father Ryan said, "Kevin, you're going to have to do a lot better than that for the actual performance. Next time, ask Jasmine to help you tie it correctly."

Jasmine was our prop-mistress, in charge of costumes, and—get this—she actually cared about historical accuracy! She was continually referring to a history book illustrating how twenty-first century clothing was supposed to look. On performance night, I waited while Jasmine helped Carl and the other actors tie their neckties, then I asked her for help tying mine.

"The dressing room's too noisy," Jasmine said. "Let's go someplace quieter." She led me past the library to an empty classroom, then told me to stand still while she wrapped an artificial silk tie around my neck and worked on making it look like the photos in her history book.

Jasmine was nearly my height, with long, blonde hair that contrasted nicely with her chestnut-brown eyes. As she attempted to tie my necktie, her face was only inches away from mine, and I marveled at how beautiful she was, so unlike the boys to whom society (and genetic engineering) said I was supposed to be attracted. I gazed into those beautiful, brown eyes and fell in love at first sight. Well, almost at first sight, as it was my first time seeing her up-close and personal.

With Jasmine focused on tying my tie to resemble historical photographs, my gaze flitted between her lovely brown eyes, her lush, full lips, and peeking down her blouse at the cleavage of her firm, perfect breasts. I didn't dare speak, afraid that if I opened my mouth to say anything, I would accidentally reveal my forbidden desire for someone of the opposite sex. Besides, her beauty had me tongue-tied.

When Jasmine finished, she looked up at me, our eyes met, and for what seemed like an eternity, we gazed into each other's eyes without speaking. After a minute, I felt self-conscious and tried to avert my eyes, but then realized my gaze had accidentally dropped to her cleavage. I jerked my head up, but it was too late; Jasmine had seen me! She must have realized my unnatural interest in the opposite sex, because she was blushing.

But even though she'd caught me looking down her blouse, Jasmine's soft, pink blush was not the red tint of anger. She smiled at me, and my heart beat faster as I wondered if she'd brought me to this empty classroom on purpose. It seemed the attraction I felt for her was mutual, for her pupils dilated, her gaze dropped to my lips, and she moved even closer to me. We were so close now that her beautiful brown eyes were a blur, our lips were almost touching, and I thought I could actually feel the heat coming off her lips. Although I knew I could be expelled for kissing someone of the opposite sex, I so wanted to kiss her that I closed my eyes and leaned forward, but at that very moment, we were interrupted.

Father Ryan entered the classroom and said, "There you are! Kevin, aren't you finished getting into costume yet? The play's about to start."

Jasmine and I each took a quick step back. "Uh, Jasmine was just tying my necktie for me. I have no idea how twenty-first-century men managed to do it on their own, heh heh." *Real smooth, eh?* Luckily, Father Ryan wasn't very observant,

I suppose I should have been *grateful* to Father Ryan for choosing that moment to interrupt us, because ten seconds later I might have been doing something that could have gotten me—and Jasmine—suspended or even expelled. But even though logically, I should have been grateful, I resented him for that interruption.

. . .

That night, I dreamed about kissing Jasmine. I awoke thinking it would've been worth getting suspended just to feel those soft, pink, sinfully *female* lips against mine. But alas, I knew such a forbidden relationship could never happen.

Jasmine didn't show up for school the next day, but I was sure I'd see her Saturday evening, when the entire cast and crew of the school play was invited to a wrap party at a Buffalo restaurant. I spent an hour Saturday afternoon deciding which clothes to wear to the party to look good for Jasmine (the only person I wanted to impress).

Everyone involved in the play came to the party except Jasmine. I saw a cast member who was a junior like Jasmine and asked him, "Henry, do you have any idea why Jasmine didn't come to this party?"

"As a matter of fact, yes," Henry said. "She said she got freaked out by something that happened the night of the school play. Apparently, some senior girl got her alone in a classroom and tried to kiss Jasmine without her consent. She wouldn't tell me who it was. It scared her so much that she was afraid to come to school the next day." Henry's fists clenched. "If I find out who it was, I'll give her a piece of my mind, because Jasmine is a good girl, not some slut who sleeps around with every other girl in class."

I was so ashamed of myself. Of *course* Jasmine wasn't a gender traitor like me! I managed to mumble, "Thanks for letting me know," and then called my fathers to take me home early. I told them I was feeling sick to my stomach, and it was true.

. . .

Jasmine totally avoided me for the next month. Whenever she saw me coming, she'd turn and walk the other way. I began avoiding her, too, just so I wouldn't have to go through the heartbreak and embarrassment of seeing her flee when she saw me.

After a month of this, she finally stopped going out of her way to avoid me, but it was obvious she was still angry, because she refused to say hello, averting her eyes when we passed on the sidewalk between school buildings.

One day, when I was heading to lunch, I found Jasmine standing in the entrance hall of the cafeteria building, right in my path. I started to turn around, willing to miss lunch to avoid the girl who so obviously hated me, but she said, "Kevin, *wait*." She approached me, looked around to make sure nobody was listening, and said, "I'm sorry for avoiding you lately, Kevin." Stepping closer, almost as close as we'd been that day in the dressing room, she whispered, "I *know* how you feel about me, Kevin, and it's okay. I'm not mad at you."

"You're ... *not?*" I asked, dumbfounded.

"No, I'm not," she said. "In fact—" She glanced around nervously, then whispered, "I think I feel the same way about *you*."

My eyes widened. *Is this a trap? Is she recording this conversation to get me expelled?* "But Henry told me you were so scared by what happened in the dressing room that you were afraid to come to school the next day!"

"It wasn't *you* I was afraid of, Kevin. I was afraid of my own feelings. You know what it would mean if I was exposed as a—*you* know."

"Yes, I know," I breathed, not daring to say any of the shameful words aloud: *Pervert. Deviant. Atavist. Gender traitor. Heterophile. Breeder*, the harshest term of all!

"So," Jasmine said, "do you think we can be friends at least?"

My heart thumped wildly. I wanted to be *more* than friends, but saying so aloud could get me suspended, even if I didn't act on my desires. "Yes," I said. "We can be friends ... at *least*."

Jasmine's eyebrows raised at the way I said "at least," but she smiled. "Cool," she said. "Let's shake on it." She reached out her hand.

Instead of a firm handshake, I took Jasmine's hand softly in mine and held it so gently that it felt like we were holding hands, but vertically, so it would *look* like a handshake if anyone saw us.

Jasmine's smile broadened. As if reading my mind, she gently moved our hands up and down to give the illusion of a handshake to others, while the two of us enjoyed the delightful sensation of softly, gently, surreptitiously holding hands.

"Are you going to lunch now?" I asked.

"Just came from there," she said. "But when the new semester starts in January, you and I will have lunch at the same time."

"How do you know?"

"I hacked into your class schedule," she explained with a wink.

I stood there grinning, in total disbelief that I'd found someone as deviant as me! As Jasmine walked by me, her hand brushed against mine, *accidentally-on-purpose*, I guessed.

From then on, every time Jasmine and I passed each other in the hallways, we'd say hello, and we'd always make sure that our hands "accidentally" brushed each other's as we passed. When we had time, we'd steal a few moments between classes to talk. People began to accept that we'd become friends after the school play—platonic friends, because what else could we possibly be? Anything more would be unspeakable, unthinkable.

. . .

Twenty-second-century scientists had used geoengineering to successfully reverse the trajectory of global warming. In addition to carbon capture and storage, geoengineers had seeded the air with tiny, reflective nanoparticles that diverted some of the sun's heat back into space. As a result, the Earth was now shaking off its fever of the twenty-first century, cooling back toward its twentieth-century temperature. The geoengineering efforts were so successful that snowfall in Western New York had returned to late twentieth-century levels, and the archaic sport of skiing was experiencing a renaissance.

Jasmine and I were both in the Calasanctius Ski Club,

which gave us the chance to spend some time alone together in the winter of 2180 (or as alone as we could be while surrounded by hundreds of fellow skiers). Jasmine asked me to sit next to her on the ski club bus and ski with her on Friday evening, so of course I agreed.

The newly reopened ski resort Kissing Bridge was a ninety-minute bus ride south of Calasanctius School. Kissing Bridge (KB) had been a popular ski destination for Buffalonians in the twentieth and early twenty-first centuries. Forced to close when global warming caused the Great Melt, KB reopened in the mid-twenty-second century after geoengineering returned the snow to Western New York's famous "snow belt" south of Buffalo.

Unfortunately, despite being named *Kissing Bridge*, the ski resort didn't have any spot for two young deviants such as Jasmine and me to kiss in private. We couldn't risk other skiers seeing us kiss, especially not that night, when my parents were also skiing at KB. Even if we weren't seen by anybody we knew, anyone who saw two people of the opposite sex kissing each other might report us to the Ski Patrol, who would probably ban us from KB for life, tell the Calasanctius Ski Club leaders, and get us expelled from school.

We considered skiing off-trail into the woods for privacy, but the woods were dark, and neither of us were expert skiers. If we skied off-trail in the dark and crashed into a tree or broke our legs, nobody would find us in time to rescue us before we froze to death.

On the slow chairlift rides up the mountain, we had plenty of time to talk. The hum of the electric lift and the clacking of skis from skiers below masked our voices somewhat, but we still kept them low to avoid being heard by people in the closest chair, twenty meters ahead of us. During one chairlift ride, Jasmine whispered in my ear, "Last weekend, I *came out* to my parents as a heterophile."

"Weren't you scared?"

Jasmine shrugged. "My mothers are Unitarian Universalists, so they're pretty liberal." Unitarian Universalism had always been one of the most liberal denominations in the North American Union, especially about matters of gender and sexuality.

"How did your mothers take it?"

"They weren't as shocked as I'd expected." Jasmine said. "My older mother, the doctor, specializes in infectious diseases. Did you know the government censors all medical journals?"

"I'm not surprised," I said bitterly, "since they also censor the internet, movies, holovision, social media, radio, newspapers, magazines, books, education, religion—pretty much everything else."

"Well, they can't keep doctors from talking to each other in person, so here's what my mother learned. Government censors deleted any side effects of COVID vaccination that might cause panic, particularly this one." She turned to whisper in my ear. "In some people, the vaccine deactivates the homosexuality gene and reactivates the gene for heterophilia, or as she told me the polite name for it is, heterosexuality."

My eyes widened. "How often does this, um, side effect happen?"

Jasmine said. "The vaccine was developed in 2160, twenty years ago, but this side effect didn't affect our parents' generation. My mother said that's because they got vaccinated as adults, after puberty. But among those who got the COVID vaccination as children or babies, like everyone does now, that side effect happens in about 10 percent of people."

"Wow," I said. "Does that mean 10 percent of students at Calasanctius are heterosexuals?"

"Probably," Jasmine said.

"That would mean that at Cal, thirty kids are just like us!" I exclaimed. "If there are that many deviants in our school, how come we've never heard about them?"

"They don't want to get suspended or expelled, so they're careful, like us."

"Of course," I said. "But the entire world gets the same vaccine. Why haven't the millions of atavists worldwide come out and told others about their sexuality?"

Jasmine said, "Maybe they did, but we didn't hear about it because governments censored the news. Or maybe society's taboos against heterosexuality are just too strong."

. . .

My fathers were going to give me a ride home from KB that night so I wouldn't have to take the slow Calasanctius bus back to school and then wait for them to pick me up there. I asked them if Jasmine could ride home with us, looking forward to the opportunity to spend more time with her during the car ride. They agreed, but once I was in the back seat with Jasmine, I found myself tongue-tied.

I was terrified that if I introduced Jasmine to my parents, I'd start gushing about her, praising her so much that they'd realize I was in love with her, and then we'd both be revealed as heterophiles. I wasn't just worried about myself—I couldn't out Jasmine to my fathers, couldn't let them know that she was one of the despised throwbacks called *breeders*. Out of fear of revealing my love for Jasmine to my fathers, I stayed silent throughout the ninety-minute drive home.

Jasmine didn't say anything, either. Maybe she was following my lead, or perhaps she was having the same thoughts as me, that she couldn't talk to me without my parents guessing, from her tone of voice, that we were in love.

As soon as we'd dropped off Jasmine at her house, my parents chewed me out for rudeness. "We gave your friend a ride home," my older father yelled from behind the wheel, "and you didn't even have the decency to introduce us to her! What's your problem? Are you ashamed of your parents?"

"No," I said honestly.

My younger father turned to glare at me from the front passenger seat. "Then why were you so rude?"

"I don't know," I lied.

"*Well*," my older father huffed, "that was the last time we're giving any of your friends a ride. Jasmine was rude, too, giving us the silent treatment just like you, but at least she said, 'Thank you,' when we dropped her off. That's two more words than you said in the entire drive."

. . .

Even with Buffalo's snowy winters restored by geoengineering, spring eventually arrived, making it even harder to hide my attraction to Jasmine. Unlike most Catholic schools, Calasanctius had no school uniforms, and we were free to wear almost anything we wanted. The weather warmed up enough that girls started wearing sleeveless shirts, short skirts, even shorter shorts, crop tops, and tube tops. Jasmine didn't mind me looking at her lovely legs, but I was afraid my classmates might notice.

Emboldened by Jasmine's revelation that we weren't alone in our heterosexuality, I finally confided in my best friend, Pete, about my perverted attraction to the opposite sex. He was incredibly supportive. I trusted he wouldn't reveal my secret.

One day during math class, I sat in the back row thinking about senior prom, and my thoughts inevitably turned to Jasmine. Realizing I could never take her to prom as my date, I tried to convince myself I'd be satisfied just to see her at prom, to watch her dancing with someone else.

I fantasized about Jasmine and the girl who was her prom date holding hands, slow dancing, their slender arms pulling each other's body close, their breasts pressed tightly against each other.... Perhaps as they slow-danced, one girl's hand might slide down from the small of the other girl's back and onto her ass.... Maybe both girls would grab each other's ass as they danced. Then of course they'd kiss, a passionate, open-mouthed wet kiss, their tongues darting into each other's mouths...

Pete nudged me out of my fantasy. "Dude," he whispered, glancing wide-eyed at the bulge in my pants. I quickly moved my math textbook onto my lap. Since we were in the back row, none of my other classmates seemed to have noticed. I went back to thinking about prom and Jasmine, careful now to avoid visualizing anything that might get me aroused.

Because Jasmine wasn't a senior, odds were that she wouldn't be at prom anyway, unless one of the girls in my class asked her out and she accepted. Jasmine wouldn't accept an invitation to prom from one of my classmates, would she? If she did accept, would seeing them together at prom make me jealous, or would it get me aroused, as it did in my fantasies? It would be wrong to get jealous of Jasmine just for dancing with another girl, but would it be even more wrong to get *aroused* by seeing her with another girl?

Why was I having all these confusing, conflicting feelings? Is every heterosexual boy plagued with such weird thoughts?

On Friday, I was walking through the parking lot between the Rumsey Road building and the Windsor Avenue building when Pete and our friend Tiffany approached. She stepped out in front of Pete and asked, "Kevin, do you have a date for prom yet?"

"No," I admitted, "but—"

"Neither does Pete," she stated, "so you're going to ask him to prom, right?"

Pete was strangely silent, letting Tiffany do the talking.

"Well, uh," I stammered. Pete wasn't the one I wanted to go to prom with. Dancing with him would only make me sad that I couldn't be dancing with Jasmine. But he was standing right there, and I didn't want to hurt his feelings by saying no. "Well, I suppose so, if he really wants to go to prom with me." I looked at Pete. He still hadn't said a word, but he had a mischievous twinkle in his eyes.

"Then it's settled," Tiffany declared. "You and Pete are going together to prom." She smiled and walked away, seeming happy that she'd fixed the two of us up. But Pete was my best friend, not my boyfriend. I didn't even want a boyfriend. I'd always assumed Pete was ace, and that his interest in me was purely platonic. *Had I been wrong all along?*

As soon as Tiffany walked away, he said, "Cheer up, Kevin. It's going to be a double date. All four of us will share the same limo, go to afterparties together, and if your parents agree—which I'm sure they will, since they approve of me—we'll rent a hotel room for the four of us!"

"All four of us? Who do you mean?"

Pete laughed. "Who do you think? You, me, Tiffany, and Jasmine. I told Tiffany about you and Jasmine."

I was aghast. "You *told* her? But I *trusted* you!"

"Relax," Pete said. "She's one of us." Pulling me into a tight embrace, so if anyone were looking, they'd assume Pete and I were now boyfriends, he whispered in my ear, "She's a heterophile, too. And she and I are now secretly dating, just like you and Jasmine."

Stepping back, he said, "The limo is self-driving, so we can fool around as much as we want on the way. And you're going to love the hotel room we picked out. It's a suite with two bedrooms, each with one large bed, so you and I are both going to lose our virginity on prom night!" Pulling me into another hug, he whispered in my ear, "With the *opposite* sex, breaking the biggest taboo of the modern age, which will make losing our virginity on prom night all the hotter! And don't worry, Tiffany and Jasmine are down with it. They said they're eager to lose their virginity on prom night to the opposite sex, also. Tiffany and I did some research, and the same condoms that prevent STDs during normal sex can also prevent pregnancy during heterophile sex, so I picked up a box for each of us."

Imagining myself alone in a hotel room with Jasmine, losing our virginity together, was getting me aroused. Pete must have felt it, but he laughed, knowing the bulge in my pants wasn't for him. My classmates didn't know that, though, so as we broke our embrace, they pointed at me and said, "Hey, get a room, you two!"

"We're going to," I said proudly, "on prom night."

Our classmates gave us a congratulatory cheer. After all, sex on prom night was considered entirely normal, acceptable behavior, something seniors and their dates looked forward to. In the year 2180, even conservative Catholic schools tolerated prom-night sex with a wink and a nod, because there was no possible way that sex between two boys or two girls could lead to pregnancy.

If only they knew what the four of us were really planning...

. . .

About the Author:

David Harten Watson, editor of this cli-fi anthology, authored the young-adult fantasy series *Magicians Gold*, including the award-winning novel *Magic Teacher's Son* and its sequel *Fortress of Gold*. David has worked in a dizzying array of jobs including US Army Armor officer at Fort Knox, experience that came in handy for his second novel, *Fortress of Gold*. He graduated from Calasanctius School in snowy Buffalo, New York and has degrees from Princeton, Canisius College, and Buffalo State College. He's the Organizer of the Woodbridge Science Fiction & Fantasy Writers Meetup, which he founded in 2008. He lives in New Jersey. Author's website: www.davidhartenwatson.com

Part Seven:

The Twenty-Third Century (2201 to 2300 AD)

37

Earth-seed

by Tara Calaby (Australia)

Subgenre: Science fiction

Time Period: Approximately 2201 AD

Setting: The planet Mars

Synopsis: After leaving an Earth ravaged by climate change to help create a colony on another planet, a scientist faces a new challenge when storm damage threatens to destroy all that remains of her former home.

. . .

The seed banks were Dawn's priority. The storm had knocked out the power from the greenhouse domes and the icy vaults that lay beneath them. The rows of vegetables and fruit trees in the domes would survive a brief change in temperature, but the seeds stored in the underground chambers were kept dormant, yet viable, in climate-controlled banks. With the backup generator spluttering on the dregs of its remaining fuel, it wouldn't be long before the banks' cryo began to fail. All that remained of Earth could be lost—the final echoes of her swamps and her forests dying beneath the too-harsh alien sun.

Dawn had joined the Ark as its head botanist, but she had come to that vocation late in a long and varied life. Her youth had been spent as a tech-monkey for the then-nascent Starwards Industries, and it was the knowledge gained then that she called upon now. She clambered into the atmo-suit that she had stashed beneath her store of pots and ventured through the dome's unsealed door.

The suit was heavy, which slowed Dawn, but the weight helped to anchor her against the gusting wind that cut through the adjoining dome. The weatherproof glass had shattered in several places, and the planet's soil was already piling in small dunes where the breaches had occurred. There were bodies here, workers caught without breathers when the oxygen had been blown from the air, but if Dawn stopped to mourn them, they would not be the last to die. The rest of the colonists might be safe for now, but if the food stores ran out, and there were no new crops to replace them, the colony would starve long before help could arrive. She turned her gaze from the familiar, motionless faces and pushed through the wind to the furthermost door.

Here, a fallen girder blocked her path: one of the steel bands that reinforced the dome walls' strength. It was surrounded by the sharded remains of the glass it had abutted, and Dawn couldn't risk a puncture in her suit. There was a service tunnel to her right, so she took that instead, hoping the generator's fuel would last despite the circuitous route.

If the colony's designers had been overconfident when it came to the domes' durability, that confidence wasn't evident in their situating of the mainframe. It lay thirty feet beneath the planet's surface, away from the heat and storms and accessible only via a glass-enclosed shaft. The door to this shaft had been triple-locked since the first of the worker rebellions, and the only key-holders were the Ark's captain, the Starwards Industries CEO, and the colony's chief engineer.

If the shaft had withstood the storm's power, Dawn's rescue mission might have ended at its door, but when she reached the enclosure, she found it splintered by the tempest's power. The glass lay, scattered, on the copper of the surrounding soil. The shaft itself was exposed to the tide of shifting dust that advanced upon it, but for the moment it remained accessible, if only she could negotiate its treacherous surrounds.

Dawn's atmo-suit was basic, in line with her status. If she'd been a patron or part of corporate, she could've walked through the glass minefield untroubled, trusting her Envirosuit 3000 to protect her from anything she encountered. As it was, her visor was already beginning to fog at the corners, and there was a vague but disconcerting scent of dust. She couldn't risk it. She needed to find another way.

Where the steel door had fallen, the jagged carpet was at its most penetrable. There were places she could safely stand, but too few of them to count. Dawn took a moment to think, achingly aware that every extra second could be a second too many. She retraced her path in her mind, resisting when her memory snagged on the image of those she had lost, forcing it forward until it caught again and remained stuck.

"Of course," she muttered and returned to the service tunnel where, bare yards away from the entrance, a sand sled lay discarded, covered in mechanical parts. Alone, it wouldn't have been adequate, but when she dragged it to the shaft, it was just long enough to allow her to traverse the area that hadn't been cleared by the fallen door. She made her way across and lowered herself down the ladder, a spark of hope flaring in her chest.

At the bottom of the shaft, a narrow passage cut into the rock. There was a door at its mouth, and Dawn closed it behind her, halting the progression of the dust. At the end of the short corridor was the mainframe itself, the bulk of it filling the stone-walled room. From here, every aspect of the colony could be controlled. Dawn was relieved to find the computer warm and humming, a scatter of red alarm lights the only evidence of the storm's destruction.

Dawn sat in front of the user-screen and began to work. From the logs, she learned that the first breach had been countered by a security lockdown in the quarters of the colony's elite. In those areas, the domes were of triple thickness—filled with every luxury and convenience. No damage had been recorded, which meant that the domes had been sealed, not against the storm, but from fear of infiltration. Dawn was overwhelmed by a sudden image of suffocating workers beating at the door for entry, while those on the other side pretended not to hear. She forced herself to breathe evenly and resumed her investigation.

The worker's quarters had been locked down too, she saw, and it was in that area that the storm had struck at its fiercest. Life support was out in all but one sector, and Dawn felt a new wave of anger flood within her at the thought of all those who had been lost due to their leaders' fear. She counted to 199 in prime numbers—calming herself—and then pushed the anger aside. She could fall apart later; first she had to save the seeds.

Dawn could see on the screen that the power routing to the greenhouse domes was undamaged. It had shut off automatically when the adjoining dome had shattered: a simple safety measure that was disproportionately complex to reverse. In normal conditions, it would have taken mere seconds to restore energy to the cryo-banks and hydro-lamps. Now, however, the necessary power was unavailable due to extensive storm damage to Power-wing B, and there was no time to mess about with repairs.

To save the seed banks, power needed to be diverted from elsewhere in the colony. The greatest drain on their reduced resources was the pleasure-tech-filled dome occupied by the Starwards Industries CEO and his board. There was no other solution; Dawn entered the code necessary to lock all other users out of the system and began to reroute the power.

She was tempted to leave the security shutdown in place, leaving the elite to suffer as their workers had, but the urge was only fleeting. Instead, she sent a warning message to the dome's vis-screens and unlocked the doors to facilitate escape. *Let the CEO and his board seek shelter amongst those whose lives they valued less than their own comfort*, she thought. *There, perhaps they'll learn to regret the hierarchies they built.*

Within minutes, the greenhouse domes were alight again, and beneath them the cryo-banks were slowly cooling to their usual temperature. There would be some losses, Dawn knew, but the bulk of her seeds would survive. It would be years before the planet was ready to sustain Earth's plants—more years than Dawn had left, most likely—but one day humans would walk beneath oaks again, and tulips would push through the grass at their feet.

Dawn locked the mainframe to her biometrics and climbed the shaft ladder into the waning winds. There were survivors to find and friends to mourn, but first she needed to double-check her seeds.

. . .

About the author:

Tara Calaby lives in Melbourne, Australia with her wife and far too many books. She is currently a PhD candidate at La Trobe University, researching the social worlds of women in Victorian lunatic asylums. Tara's writing has appeared in publications such as *Strange Horizons, Galaxy's Edge, Grimdark Magazine,* and *Daily Science Fiction.* In her free time, she enjoys playing video games, attempting to learn Danish, and petting other people's dogs.

38

Some Like it Cold

by Kara Race-Moore (United States)

Subgenres: Science fiction, humor

Time Period: Two hundred years in the future (c. 2222 AD)

Setting: Antarctica

Synopsis: A middle-class couple, ordinary citizens of the intergalactic Republic, have chosen to vacation on exotic, fashionable Earth, where Republic scientists have newly rehabilitated the poles to be such a wonderfully cool vacation spot, perfect for their biochemistry that (by one of those fun coincidences of evolution) closely mimics Earth's sharks, despite being air breathers. The exchange rate is currently very favorable for visitors, and the locals will happily cater to alien tastes for the tourism money.

. . .

"Oh my, your drink looks so good!"

I paused, mid-sip, and turned to look at my beach-chair neighbor.

We were seated on the sparkling white beach of the resort,

enjoying the weather. It was a beautiful day, with the sky an exotic light blue and the ocean a perfectly complimentary dark blue. I needed my shades against the glaring local sun, but I had shrugged off the cute little gauzy beach wrap, wanting to feel the breeze on my scales. It was so deliciously cold, the kind of icy wind that wraps all around you and then sinks deep into your cartilage.

Earth, as the locals called the planet, had long since been discovered as a chic vacation spot by the upper crust, but with that new galactic wormhole system finally, after what felt like eons of construction, completed, it meant this was now a much more accessible location.

The planet's polar ice caps, now that we had fixed most of the damage the humans had done, were just as, if not more so, enjoyable as the iceberg-filled bays of the seaside resorts I had gone to as a child during school breaks back on my home world. And Earth was now an affordable vacation destination since the exchange rate was currently so favorable.

For the most part, I was pleased with our choice of vacation spot. This resort, Palmer Beach, named for some human explorer from back when they considered just going to one of their own planet's poles far-out exploration, was smaller than most Earth resorts catering to us off-worlders, offering plenty of quiet for rest and relaxation.

My husband was spending the afternoon doing some silly excursion in a tour boat to see the local wildlife. Something called whales? I, however, was content to sit on the beach with the other, less-active vacationers and just enjoy the relaxing feeling of glacial air on the placoid scales.

The woman on the chair next to me and I were given our fresh round of drinks by a smiling local. He took more orders from other resort guests lazing in their beach chairs before he made his ponderous way in all his layers of clothes back to the bar for the next tray of cocktails.

"Aren't the bartenders here the best?" she asked cheerfully.

Her scales were pale gray; she was probably a few years older than me, although she had the kind of gloss that suggested lots of money available to spend on looking youthful for as long as possible.

"Yeah, they're great," I said with muted appreciation, deciding it would be polite to at least respond, much as I just wanted to spend as much of my vacation as possible laying on a beach, getting pleasantly buzzed, absorbed in a trashy romance novel, not worrying about work or anything else. I took another sip of my multicolored drink, glancing at the tawdry love story in my lap, wondering if I'd done enough to fulfill the social niceties.

"What did you get?" she asked, relentless in keeping the conversation going, still eyeing my drink as she took a sip of her frothy pink concoction.

"A Dirty Dozen," I admitted, trying not to sound embarrassed. "I only order them when I'm on vacation," I added, feeling the need to justify the extravagant drink, usually only seen in old comedies being consumed by characters with lots of money and no class. I took a defensive sip.

"They can make that here?" she asked, shocked and excited. "Here? They've got all twelve parts on hand?"

I grinned, suddenly feeling quite a few of those twelve ingredients running through my bloodstream. "Yup. They want to keep us 'sharkies' happy, after all."

She winced at the nickname, but I went on, "They've imported absolutely everything here. As the ads say: 'All the comforts of home, in a luxury setting.'"

"And here I was about to talk up the resort we went to last year. It's one of the ones near the northern polar cap. The entire hotel is made of snow and ice! The ice bedrooms were amazing—it was just the most relaxing sleep I've had in years. It really was wonderful—except the food and drink, since the place has an emphasis on the whole local experience, pushing all these weird meats and drinks from the area."

I nodded. "I've heard the ice hotels up there are great places to stay, but the problem is everyone else has heard that too, and my husband and I try to go to the more off-the-beaten-path type places."

"Yes, I know what you mean about wanting to get away from all the noise and chatter," my beach neighbor chattered at me. "Earth has become so popular lately, you really have to hunt around for someplace good that isn't just crawling with tourists."

I smiled and took another sip of my Dirty Dozen. I wondered if I just picked up the novel again, she might take the hint...

"Hard to believe this all used to just be a—What was it again? Military base?" She gestured around at the beach and the resort behind us.

"Science research base, I think," I said. "Doing all the usual measuring and recording scientists do." I waved vaguely at the sea and air in front of us.

"Ah, yes, I think I saw something in the brochure about that. It was just a little place back before the humans were joined up with the rest of the civilized universe." She chuckled with tipsy self-contentment and took another swallow of her drink. "The wonder of what tourism can do for a place! My first wife would always go on and on about the damage we apparently do to local cultures, but really, there's nothing wrong with broadening the mind with new ideas, and we've done so much to help these locals with disasters of their own making." She waved towards the ice shelf. "All this beautiful ice would have melted away without our intervention."

"I hear it was quite a mess here when first contact was made."

"Yes, did you see that new documentary that just came out? Civilization's Edge? About all the violence back then?"

"Yes, I watched it on the ride here—glad I did, since it explained the whole etymology of why the locals call us 'sharkies.'"

I stroked a hand down my scales, thinking how cool it was that there was a local sea predator the humans held in awe that had taken an evolutionary path so close to us. "Interesting coincidence of evolution. Exobiology is fascinating, isn't it?"

She made a face. "'Sharkies,'" she said contemptuously. "As if we're their pets, rather than the intergalactic economic and technological powerhouse that swooped in and managed to get them out of a political-environmental-social catastrophe of their own making. But fine, whatever." She slurped down the rest of her drink until it was just ice chips and then held it aloft, rattling it loudly to signal for a new drink.

The waiter from before came back out, waddling like the local bird life, carrying the tray with the next round of drinks. "A Solar Flare for Madam," he said slowly, in his brash human accent.

"Thank! You!" said my neighbor loudly, as if he were deaf rather than struggling with our language. At least he was trying, which was more than most of them would do. She flashed him a bright, condescending smile, showing off her well-polished teeth. He gave her a nervous, closed-mouth smile and walked away to serve the rest of the drinks.

"Oh, right, the locals get scared by our open-mouth smiles, right?" she asked me. She held a hand to her mouth in an exaggerated self-conscious gesture. "How embarrassing, I really have to remember my manners." She sipped her drink. "After all, we're just the guests here and need to be polite. I mean, we're paying for all this, but there's no reason to be rude. My wife insists on full 20 percent tips for everything, but come on, given the exchange rate, they'll practically give you their first egg after a few 5 percent tips! Still, we've gotten good service this whole trip so far, probably because we've been tipping so heavily since we got here."

"I don't think they lay eggs," I said, gazing over the rim of my glass at the pretty sparkles on the water from the yellow sun.

"What?"

"The humans. I think they're the birth-live-young types."

"Really? Ugh. Gross. I can't imagine going through something like that. It seems so... uncivilized." She took a gulp of her drink, looking disgusted.

"Mhmm," I said noncommittally as I took another sip from my drink.

"Have you tried that new game? The one that tells you how old you'd be in human years?"

"You mean, how old by this planet's orbit?" I asked, bemused.

"Yes, that!" she said excitedly, pulling out her Tab. She pulled up a bright little screen that piped tinny pop music. "Let's see, put your age here," she tapped at a corner, and: "Ah ha! I'd be 468 in Earth years! Can you imagine?"

The Tab made an angry chirp noise, and she made a few more clicks, looking worried. "I set an alert for any local news that might be important," she said.

I sipped my drink, wondering why it was so hard for some people to take even the shortest break from their Tab.

She made a noise, half pleased, half disgruntled. "Looks like the new trade agreement with the Earth delegation was finally signed, so we can get things shipping again." She rolled her eyes at me, clearly expecting shared exasperation. She looked down at the screen and kept reading. "Our ambassador apparently made some joke during negotiations about turning the Earth rep into sushi if she didn't sign, and now the humans are all offended. I mean, really, they have no sense of humor."

"Do you work for Stellar Connect?" I asked, since that seemed the only reason to care about news like that, they being the main mover of most goods in the civilized universe.

"My wife's a contractor with the Republic's subcommittee on environmental controls. She's been handling the upgrades on the weather satellites here. Our trip here last time to the northern pole was more a working vacation for her while she did some groundwork, and now she's just finished most of the installations. This was a convenient spot to relax once she was done, since the main controls are just a ways inland here." She waved a hand vaguely at the land behind the resort.

"Nice to slide straight from work to play," I commented.

She nodded, but said, "I actually almost thought about saying we should just cancel this vacation after those bombings last month in Washington D.C., but, well, the deposit had already been paid, and as long as you just stay away from the bad areas, Earth is still a lovely vacation spot, even with some crazy terrorists running around trying to ruin it for everybody with their stupid isolationist ideas."

"Mhmm."

"They should be more grateful. We saved them from fire, famine, and flood. They were all freaked out by the extreme storms they caused, but we stepped in before the real problems would have started. They would have all killed each in a panic if we hadn't arrived to help. Our tech in their skies is what saved this little planet. And now we're doing most of the work keeping their economy going with our tourism money!"

"Mhmm."

"Carbon capturing machines leased to them at low interest rates, selling them cold fusion so they could stop relying on ancient fossil-fuel tech, weather control satellites installed by our government to re-balance the environment, and the locals are so short-lived that now the new generation just accepts this all as if they did it themselves and start making noises about how we've outstayed our welcome!"

"Yeah," I said and picked up the novel to continue the romance.

At that moment, there was a whiny droning noise, and we both looked up to see a hovercraft come around the head and buzz over the waves in the bay. My husband's tour boat was back.

"Oh, look, the fearless explorers are back!" she said and waved energetically. "Hello darling! Over here!" she hollered. Evidently, her wife had been on the same excursion as my husband.

A younger woman in the boat put her hand up and waved back. Her scales were so dark as to be nearly black, nowhere near a mature gray; she was easily half her wife's age. As the boat came to the dock, and one of the staff caught the line thrown to him, she leaped out of the boat to the dock before it was even secured and came hurrying over the cool sands to our beach chairs.

"You wouldn't think," my neighbor said to me, eyes on her young spouse coming towards us, "just looking at her, but she's actually a brilliant engineer." The wife wore a pretty little sarong, three platinum rings set daringly in her dorsal, sparkling in the sun, and as she bounced over, happily taking advantage of this planet's slightly lower gravity, I could see her wedding necklace was gaudily studded with black diamonds. A second marriage indeed.

"We had so much fun!" she said as she came up to us, excited as a child. "We saw so many fish, and they have all sorts of air-breathing animals in the oceans around here, so they had to keep popping up! You really should have come!"

My neighbor smiled indulgently. "I was just fine here relaxing with my drink, Darling."

At that point, my husband came sauntering over, looking pleased with himself. "I got some great pics," he told me. He grinned as he eyed my drink. "Enjoying your Dirty Dozen?"

"I'm on vacation," I said, unrepentant as I sucked down the last if it.

He took a seat next to me, and the young wife perched on my neighbor's knee. The ever-reliable waiter reappeared.

"Drink for Madam?" he asked.

"We should celebrate," my neighbor told her wife. "The trade agreement was just signed."

"Was it?" asked my husband. "That's great! I had a lot of stock riding on that!"

"Well, then, drinks all around," she said.

"I'll have what she's having," the young wife told the waiter, pointing at my drink. Our spouses laughed.

Drink orders were placed by everyone, my husband teasing me about getting another Dirty Dozen, but I was unrepentant in my time-off drink choice.

"I really don't know how they can stand walking around in all those layers of clothes!" the young wife exclaimed after the waiter left with our orders. "Just look at those heavy coats all the staff wear!"

"Oh, humans have such a weird biochemistry," said my husband. "They're really only comfortable in a small range of temperatures and can get quite damaged by hots and colds."

"So weird," I said.

"Poor things," the young wife said with a sympathetic pout.

"They do all right for themselves," said my husband, settling back in his chair to enjoy the breeze. That kicked off a debate on how the Earth economy was doing, and just how quickly it would collapse if we all just pulled out one day. I tucked my romance back in my beach bag with a sigh as the animated conversation of economics and politics swirled around me.

With the arrival of our orders, I let the drink wash away any lingering resentment that my alone time had been thoroughly set aside for the rest of the day. And the company wasn't too bad, as we started comparing notes on different vacation spots and chatted about the latest celebrity gossip, and, of course, back to the human situation.

"When do you think the whole instability thing with the humans will calm down?" asked the young wife, a few drinks in.

"Oh, if they knew what was good for them, they would worship the ground we walk on," said my new friend.

I decided not to mention the documentary *Before Us* about what's-their-names, that group from the upper spiral of the galaxy who had come to Earth and been worshiped as gods ages ago, before having to abandon the planet when the old galactic boundary lines had gone up, leaving Earth in a no-fly zone during the entirety of that political regime. "Imaginary lines with real consequences," the narrator in the documentary had intoned, showing footage of some of the savagery Earth had been prone to during the Isolationist Period.

"It's not like they don't have a legitimate grievance," said my husband, pompously determined to be fair.

"Legitimate grievance? We gave them *everything*; of course we should get *some* profit for it."

The debate raged on, with no conclusion, because what conclusion can there be with such a complicated situation? There were more drinks on the beach, followed by drinks and dinner at the poolside café, and then after-dinner drinks in the bubbling whirlpool, the cold waters blowing against the scales a delight as we sipped the heady cocktails and talked politics.

I woke up the next morning to the sound of yelling. I blinked and looked around. I was slumped on a couch next to my husband, who was still asleep, grumbling into my shoulder. It took a moment to realize we weren't in our hotel room, because they all looked alike. My husband and I were still in our clothes from yesterday. We were in our new friends' room, and I vaguely recalled coming back here for more drinks... after doing something off the resort?

"You all thought it was a good idea last night!" This was the young wife yelling now, still dressed in her sarong from yesterday, looking rumpled and somehow grease-stained.

"We were all *drunk* last night!" shouted my friend from the beach. She was wearing a black robe that looked expensive. Her eyes were bloodshot, and her mouth was twisted into an ugly snarl.

My husband shuddered awake. "Huh, what?" he asked blearily. "What happened?"

"My wife, that's what happened!" shouted my friend to the room in general. "My Tab is blowing up! *Someone* reset the environmental satellites to be controlled by the main human government in Geneva! And now they're already insisting they won't be paying any more taxes to the Republic for their use! Something about possession being nine-tenths of the law!" She was bellowing at full volume now.

The young wife winced. "Please. Not so loud. Oh, my head." She cast her eyes upwards plaintively. "I swear I will never drink again!"

"Never mind your blasphemous vows! No one believes them anyway!" Her eyes looked almost fully red now. "Again—what did you think you were doing?"

"Well, we were all talking about the human situation, and I thought it would be such a simple fix. So... I did."

"Did. What?"

"I fixed it. The main controls are, like, right there," she gestured out the window. "It was so easy! I thought if they had more control and more say, it would be a more balanced political situation."

"You idiot!"

If the situation hadn't been so dire, I would have been embarrassed to be witnessing a marital spat up close and personal. As I was, I couldn't look away, appalled at the damage one trophy wife had done while inebriated. If this is what she could do drunk, what could she do sober?

"I think I'm going to throw up," said my husband to no one in particular.

Even hungover, he could tell how bad this was going to be, especially for our stock portfolio. In a quiet corner of my brain that wasn't freaking out, I sighed and mentally waved goodbye to vacations for quite some time.

The older woman snapped her attention back on us, eyeing

my husband as if assessing whether she needed to get him a bucket.

"I apologize for my half-witted wife," she ground out through her teeth, ignoring said wife. "No, if you'll excuse us, we have some calls to make."

I nodded and helped my husband up so we could stumble out of the room. As the door closed behind us, we could hear her wife still trying to explain and cajole.

In the empty hallway, we stared at each other, appalled.

"I'll start packing," he said.

"I'll talk to the front desk about getting on the next transport," I said.

We split in opposite directions to get started. No debate required. We needed to get off this planet as soon as possible, and we both knew it.

The political situation was about to get *hot*.

. . .

About the author:

Kara Race-Moore studied history at Simmons College as an excuse to read about the soap opera lives of British royals. She worked in educational publishing, casting the molds for future generations' minds, but has since moved into the more civilized world of litigation. She currently lives in Los Angeles, the land where fact and fiction tend to blur. Ms. Race-Moore first came to science fiction through Anne McCaffrey and is still grateful to her for showing an impressionable teenager that woman can be in and write science fiction too. She can be found at: https://kararacemoore.wordpress.com/ and https://www.goodreads.com/author/show/6763776. Kara_Race_Moore/.

Part Eight:

The Distant Future (2301 AD or Later)

39

From the Drowned

by Lorraine Schein (United States)

Subgenres: Poetry, science fiction, horror

Time Period: Distant future and past ("Near-Far future and past")

Setting: Earth

Synopsis: A poem about what will happen as sea levels rise because of global warming and about writers who have drowned in the past.

. . .

So beautiful and silent here,
Ophelia and Virginia say.
We come from the water,
so had no fear of return that way.

When seas rise and shores vanish into sand,
let your body accept the ocean's bottomless cold.
Learn to live on islands raised away from land,
like the wizards and enchantresses of old.

Build your houses on sharp cliffs,
safe from the rising tide
far above the crashing breakers
over which the seagulls glide.

You won't have to put stones in your pockets,
or dive headfirst in wild despondency,
or like our friend Percy, shipwrecked poet,
fall from a storm-caught boat in Italy.

You'll have time to adjust, begin anew,
and even say goodbye,
before the waves fill your lungs too
and your body dies.

Drowning is difficult to do—
but we need not attempt to rise:
we float up easily to meet you
as if we were alive.

Say Ophelia and Virginia and Percy
and all those with flooded eyes
staring sightless upward
at the water's skies.

. . .

About the author:

Lorraine Schein is a New York writer and poet. Her work has appeared in VICE *Terraform*, *Strange Horizons*, *Scientific American*, *NewMyths*, *Michigan Quarterly*, and in the anthologies *Wild Women* and *Tragedy Queens: Stories Inspired by Lana del Rey & Sylvia Plath*. *The Futurist's Mistress*, her poetry book, is available from Mayapple Press. Her new book, *The Lady Anarchist Cafe*, is out now from Autonomedia: https://autonomedia.org/product/the-lady-anarchist-cafe/

40

Waking a Cyborg

by Kirby Biggs (United States)

Subgenre: Science fiction

Time Period: Distant future: 7743 AD

Setting: Planet Earth (a.k.a. "Third")

Synopsis: In this apocalyptic tale, anthropogenically induced climate change has devastated planet Earth, and few traces of the former civilizations remain on the surface, which has been scoured clean by winds, storms, and radiation. "Exo-archaeologists" from the outer planets, their satellites, and machined worlds are exploring the third planet in search of their origins, which have been lost to the millennia. This story relates the collapse of the Earth's planetary life-support system, the need to flee to the outer planets, the fate of the remnants of humanity left behind on Earth, their life trajectory, and means of survival as related by one of the cyborgs that has been discovered in a special chamber deep below the surface and awakened to relate the history.

. . .

To: Exo-Archaeo-Biological Sixtieth Conference

Subject: Article for Consideration by the Review Committee

Title: Waking a Cyborg

Principal investigator: Dr. Rasmun Sang-With, XA. XB. University of Fourth

Co-investigator: Dr. Mordan Zoomey, XA. Orbit6 World Technology University

Introduction

I am excited beyond words as I recount to you the first successful awakening of one of the third planet's cyborgs. The devastated surface bears only slight evidence of the former civilization. We had little hope of finding even archeological remnants, when in excavation we uncovered a cache of cyborgs. There were less than one hundred paired "couples" with some traceable energy source that remained, out of the ten thousand, interred deep underground in a hermetically sealed vault. Each pair has the same serial number and a set of sub-numbers that identifies them as being together. They have sustained thousands of years in deep hibernation, but have been in stasis for so long that, for most, their neural nets have degraded too much for resurrection. Their infrastructure is irreparably broken.

We have been re-working the ancient technology of the Activation Station for several years, finally decoded its operation, and repaired it. Today, we hope to have success initializing one of the strongest sleepers, the one labeled "Stephen." We pray he will awaken without extinguishing the feeble life force that remains. Stephen's pair-bond's, Lila's, awakening is also underway.

. . .

Section 1: The Five Questions

What follows is a verbatim record of the first conversation with the cyborg, in which we hope to finally receive enlightenment to our biggest mysteries, the answers to the five questions.

The knowledge of our beginnings has been lost to us for millennia. Our societies have risen high and fallen low so many times that the record has been wiped clean, so I intend to ask Stephen today, if he is competent when he wakes. I don't know what to expect. The others have been scrambled, cognition irrevocably compromised. They only absorb energy, and they sleep on, in some land from whence there is no return.

. . .

Section 2. The Sleeper Wakes

Hello Stephen, can you hear me?

Yes, I can hear you.

Can you understand me?

Yes, although your speech is strange.

I'm so glad you are awake, and the translator is working. How do you feel?

Not so well. I am quite weak. I'm dreaming with Lila. I need to get back to her and the others. They all get worried if anyone is gone for very long. Sometimes they don't return.

My apologies, but it is important to me and to many others that we speak.

Well ok, but please make it quick. Where am I? What year is this?

In your calendar, it is currently 7743.

WHAT? That's not possible. None of us are rated for that.

I see you are skeptical; nevertheless, it is true.

I see you are a biological as we once were. Are you one of those who left?

Possibly. That's one of the questions I wanted to ask. By the way, we are waking your pair-bond, Lila. We will try to activate her soon.

The Activation Station is working again? Sorry, that's obvious, I'm awake. That's why we went into stasis. We were the last, and there was no choice when the Station went down. Five thousand five hundred years; I can't believe that. What about the others?

There are fewer than one hundred of you left. You and Lila are the strongest.

I wondered why there were so few voices. I am surprised there are so many still. So, the last of us are nearly gone. Sad. At least Lila is here. We've been dreaming together forever. I am going to be so glad to see her again, outside our minds. I'd like to get back to that.

What is Lila to you?

She is my pair-bond. She leads.

I don't understand.

We are one being, but separate entities. We are melded as a unit. Inseparable, yet each of us is an individual. I'm not sure you can grasp this, as a biological. What she thinks. I know, and what I think, she knows. There are no such things as lies among any of us. You mentioned a question?

Yes, five questions, actually. We want to know about our genesis, our history, what happened, when it happened, how did it happen? And please tell me about yourself.

I will tell you. But first you must tell me how you came to be here, and to find me.

I am Doctor Rasmun Sang-With. I am an exo-bio-archaeologist from Fourth. We have been exploring Third, and we found you.

Fourth? You mean Mars?

Mars?

Yes, that's the name of the fourth planet out from the sun. The one we were terraforming.

Our people live on the outer planets, their satellites, and our fabricated worlds, planetoids we have built around the star. You asked if I am of those who left, and I hope you can help me with that answer.

. . .

Section 3. The Guild of Pensmen

Then let me begin. I am Stephen, of the Guild of Pensmen. We are the guardians of history. Not all that are born into the Guild have the eidetic memory, but I do, a blessing and a curse. I remember everything: my conception, the very first spark of my life, the passage into the world through my mother, for I was born a being of flesh and blood as are you. My earliest moments are without the words I know now, but they all exist simultaneously in my mind.

How do I stand it, you might well ask, remembering everything? The pains, the pleasures, the loves, the losses, the transition to the machine, for I was old even when we entered stasis, having passed my three thousandth year. I do not know how, but I cannot imagine forgetting, although forget I will someday; all things end, it is inevitable. So, let me answer you by relating The History as the story Pensmen tell those who forget. It makes us remember to take care.

. . .

Section 4. The Song of the Ancestors

The winds had come again, as they now always did. The scorching, desiccating, oven-hot winds. We prayed our usual prayer, singing the hymn, "The Song of the Ancestors." It is sung in unison in the mornings as a dirge, a tuneless lament, each in their own voice.

Curse the ones that came before.
Curse them all, those filthy Yores.
They're the ones that took us down,
they made us bleed, they played us round,
they worshiped, silver, oil, and gold,
ignored the lessons long foretold.

They ruined every plant and seed,
they sacrificed to lust and greed.
The animals they ruined too,
their hubris undid all the glue
of Mother Nature's bounteous feast,
that once was great and now is least.

Mother Nature, hear us now,
before you now we scrape and bow.
Mother Nature, give us life,
Oh Mother, please relieve our strife.

Bring us back our world once green.
Bring us back each field and stream.
Bring us back our air so clear.
Bring us back the squirrel and deer.

Bring us back the snakes and frogs.
Bring us back the cats and dogs.
Bring us birds and insects too.
We beg you, Mother, we are true.
We are one, both you and me,
Mother Nature set us free.

. . .

We called ourselves the Orphans of the Sun because the Sun was the cause of all this; that is, once we messed everything up with our hubris and our giant dose of screw-you-me-first, magnified exponentially by our billions. We were vain and shortsighted, failing miserably at the end, our collective will too weak to defeat our selfishness and our addiction to the seven deadly sins. Our collective hunger was too great, as we stripped the seas bare, denuded the land, and shit our nest, the sustaining forces of the Mother ebbing, the tipping point finally reached, until the unstoppable cascade brought on the last great extinction.

The winds, the fires, and the raging, evaporating, acid seas would never abate and eventually scoured the surface of our last vestiges, those of us that were left, of course. When the Great Rift came on, it was a grand cascade-effect gone horribly wrong. Once the tipping point was passed, the hammer whacked down hard and bad. Our asses were slammed.

We still had our machines, and we had some time, although it went faster than any of our worst imaginings. We prepared to remake our few cities in the underworld, to try to retreat beneath the planet's skin so we might wait out the burning and scarring.

. . .

Section 5: The Book of What Happened

The first chapter of "The Book of What Happened" is this historical document that has been passed down over the ages. We know it as "A Letter to the Sun."

My Dearest Sol,

It's been such a long time since my last letter, but frankly, I can hardly put pen to page, the sickness overtakes me so. Within my breast, in my veins, and upon my skin a horrible cancer grows. It creeps into my very sinews and bones, emitting toxins upon toxins, and I grow so tired.

I remember our youth together. We burst with vigor, and so deeply we loved, you and I. My limbs were supple and graceful, my lifeblood so clear and pure, and I literally abounded with life. Oh, it was sweet. But how quickly things change, and how completely. It began so innocently that I was fooled. And now look—they are everywhere, billions of points of pain.

But I begin to believe there may yet be hope to cure the blight. As my fever increases, it is possible the disease may run its course. If I can only hold on, perhaps the illness will be burned out before I am. There is some evidence of that already, due to the radiation treatments you suggested; they seem to be helping.

Funny how that was a byproduct of the blight itself; they fry my skin, I fry theirs. Ha, ha, I guess the joke's on them!

Well, I've seen some hard times before, and I'll probably see some again, but I'm going to hang in there till the end.

Always yours,
Gaia

None of us know its true origin. It may well be just an apocalyptic maundering of some long-dead seer. It is said to have been discovered in a gigantic Nazca pattern on the surface, a pattern so large and runic that it was not visible until the First Scouring. Regardless, it was prophetic. It came to pass just as the letter had predicted.

. . .

Section 6: The Exodus

The second chapter of The Book describes the time when most left for the outer worlds, never to return. It is in the form of a song that tells of the longing for better times that drove so many of us from the planet. We teach it to the children and sing it every night. It's called "Exodus":

2480 and I'm zonin' out,
My body, it's a fryin', I gotta twist and shout.
I'm looking all around me, and all I see is brown,
Nothin' left of this hick-town planet,
guess I'll see you guys around.

Take me to the platform,
put me on the train
send me to the heavens
where there ain't no toxic pain.

Into the Martian forests,
I will leave this Earth behind,
with its parched and barren surface,
let me drink Callisto wine.

Somewhere there are shady trees,
beam me to the past.
Let me feel the pulse of the planet,
life in my veins will flow at last.

Where was the age of reason,
when they spent our last thin dime?
Today the ocean's time is up,
tomorrow it is our time.

So, take me to the platform,
put me on the train
send me to the heavens
where there ain't no toxic pain.

What to do about yesterday?
I just don't want to go,
but I'm twitching, and burning, and frying,
Oh my God, this death is slow.

So, take me to the platform,
nail me to the train,
then shoot me to the heavens,
where life can live again.

We who stayed never found out what ultimately happened to our brothers and sisters who left. As the infrastructure was lost, so too our communications were lost. We imagined that colonies were established on the outer planets and their moons. We had been terraforming, but it was not complete.

We hoped so, but we never heard from them again and concluded that they had perished, as they surely thought we had, as well.

The winds never stopped, so we hid from the Sun, bringing everything below with us, creating our cities of the underground. Many could not bear the subterranean Wellsian existence of the Morlocks. Its lawlessness, its disorder, killed those who could not adapt, until the darkness overtook us, and thus did the Orphans of the Sun become the Children of the Depths.

I speak now of a history of time past, that was passed down to me long ago, and that I tell you now, so you may tell the others. We did not see the surface change for hundreds upon hundreds of years, scraped clean of our pitiful meddling. We melded with our machines until we became one and the same. Metamorphic beings of metal, circuitry, and remembered flesh. We feel and do not feel, all at once.

Our inevitable machining had already progressed through the advances in our medical technologies, such that, bit by bit, we replaced part after part, until our sustenance became solely that of energy. The scouring of the surface finally lost its meaning. We survive in spite of it, yet our substance still longs for the time of nature and the old songs about the green, green grass of home.

The historical records show us what all these natural things were, but now we go to the surface for cleansing in the winds. The surface is barren, the ozone gone, ionosphere destroyed, lost to the radiation of the great wars, waged in orbit that our forebearers thought would be safe, but turned out to be deadly. It was a machine-to-machine war of magnificent proportion, fought for no reason among the cyborgs we have all since become.

I penned a fanciful poem that became a favorite right away. It's called "Devolution":

My pretty little metal bird
sits within its gilded cage.
I caught it just the other day
with magnetic seeds, on a steel stage.

I keep it with my iron squirrel
that runs among my Dacron plants,
whose flower's oily nectar
is gathered by my robot ants.

My quiet little plastic cat
is curled on my synthetic couch.
Soon, I know, my rayon dog
will wake her up, he's such a grouch.

Since it's spring, the diesel rain
will reawake my Dynel grass.
I'll sprinkle it with polymers,
they always make it grow so fast.

The searing of the summer sun
will polish up my exo-skin.
It burns off the impurities,
the raging winds have pitted in.

In the fall the glassine leaves
that grow upon my styrene trees,
will fall and fall in tiny shards;
they always make me cough and sneeze.

Once a day I hook myself
into my local power source.
Completed at its scheduled time,
it keeps my charger full, of course.

I live a life of perfect ease,
my needs are all provided for,
my hardware complement's complete,
my applications never bore.

My pump leaps up with programmed joy
to see the wonder of my world,
the beauty of my planetron,
and my simulated girl.

I was talking about reconstructing the surface and how hard it was, in fact, impossible, once it was gone. Without the partition of the most important parts of the atmosphere to maintain life, there was no chance. When that shield was lost, its resurrection proved beyond even our advanced state. But even if a breakthrough were made, and even if the surface could be remade to sustain life, its complexity could not be reestablished. Everything was gone, and it wasn't coming back.

. . .

Section 7: Living the Cyborg Life

So we joined with the machine. The children that once replaced and diversified us became fewer and fewer, because to breed meant living a finite lifetime. Those years are so few that, finally, none would volunteer. Who would choose to die when they could live so many lifetimes? The ancient figure of Methuselah comes to mind, but we are not immortal. Even though each of our parts can be replaced, the corruption of the neural drivers increases slightly with each year, until the life force is corrupted and must be transferred to the archive to become part of the collected minds before the interface completely degrades. Then another mobile is lost to us forever.

I understand that so well now, in my advanced age. With each year, I seemed to lose a little of the *me* that had come to be. I think of the end of my full life with genuine trepidation.

Will the collective be beautiful or terrible, and those voices, a choir or a cacophony? And does it still persist today, doctor? Did you find it? But I digress in my musing.

We came to call ourselves "The ten thousand," as those were all that were left. When the Activation Station was lost, we retreated to the chamber where you found me. That's when we paired. Stasis was the only answer left.

You might wonder if I have feelings and sensations, whether I love. The answer is yes. I share all the senses and savors I did when I was corporeal. Of course, as we paired, it altered us, bringing us ever closer to the same mind. That's where Lila and I are right now; we are very much in what I call love. Our programs match more perfectly than any I've ever experienced.

That's enough for right now. I'm feeling tired, and Lila is missing me; I can hear her in my mind, and I want to get back to our dream. Did that answer some of your questions, doctor? We can continue this later. There is still much to tell; a Pensman never runs out of words.

Yes, Stephen, you answered many, many questions. Thank you for sharing the history with me. That was quite a story. When you and Lila wake again, I will tell you about us and our history. You will be surprised. I look forward to many more conversations.

. . .

Conclusion

That concludes the entire interview. After Stephen went back to sleep, we were unable to re-awaken him. We don't know if that is on purpose. Perhaps he just doesn't want to be bothered. We have yet to revive any of the others, so we have not yet learned more about our origins. From Stephen, we did learn that we ourselves were responsible for the utter and complete destruction of our original home, Third, and how we came to live on both the outer planets and our orbiting constructed worlds.

. . .

About the Author:

Kirby has loved our planet for seven decades, still finding delight in nature's mysteries. His concern for the health of the planet and his long exploration of how humans and natural systems can coexist, reinforce daily how fragile is the balance that maintains our Earth as a welcoming habitat for all the things we love. By sharing poetry, songs, and stories, Kirby joins his voice with other voices of warning about the state of our planet and the need for immediate action, if we are to survive ourselves. For forty-five years, Kirby has protected air, land, and water as an environmental professional.

41

The Happy Colony by the Sea

by Russell Hemmell (Scotland, UK)

Subgenre: Science fiction

Time Period: Distant future, at least three hundred years from now

Setting: Asia, planet Earth

Synopsis: What if aliens decided to settle on an environmentally devastated Earth at the very moment humans abandoned it?

Editor's note: This story has a dreamlike quality that reminds me of Ray Bradbury's short stories, complete with a Bradburian ambiguity about whether inhabitants of a strange and wondrous land are truly human, or if they're aliens with the power to appear human to fool us. However, unlike most of Bradbury's stories about shapeshifting aliens (e.g., "The Third Expedition" in *The Martian Chronicles*), "The Happy Colony by the Sea" is *not* a horror story and has a relatively happy (or at least hopeful) ending. Although written for and about adults, this story is suitable for all ages.

"The Happy Colony by the Sea" is a fitting story to end this cli-fi anthology on an upbeat, hopeful note, illustrating how Earth might someday be healed, restored, and reborn in all its beauty, if only it can be cared for by a society (human or otherwise) that respects our planet, including its air, water, soil, seas, and all the creatures that live on Earth or swim in its oceans, lakes, seas, ponds, rivers, and streams.

. . .

The woman who came to meet me at the landing pad was not whom I had expected when embarking on that strange trip. For a start, she was supposed to look old. The youngest inhabitant of that remote outpost of a depopulated Asian continent was sixty-five, according to my records. Also, given that the estimated average age of the settlers was seventy-eight, I was likely to bump into some real Methuselah fellows. Yet the woman looked in her prime, serene, clear blue eyes and doll-like, porcelain skin.

"Welcome, Dr Huygens, to the happy colony of Sai Kung Place." She bowed in a way I had only seen in early-twenty-first-century Chinese fantasy movies. Her exquisite outfit matched that period, too. She wore an embroidered silk qipao, decorated with golden-red cranes over lotus flowers, and the result was stunning.

"*Xiè xie nin*, Mrs....?"

"You can call me Meilan. We're not that formal here," she said. "Our culture is a strange mix of old and new customs, not all of them Chinese, either."

"I had somehow figured it out," I replied, trying not to sound flippant and just too aware I didn't manage.

"Please follow me." She headed toward the winding, marble staircase, going up the mountain in a steep ascent.

I obeyed. It was not only her age; she looked as Chinese as I did. And I was of Norwegian and Irish descent, thank you very much.

. . .

The name of the only town in Sai Kung was Tai Long Wan. It meant big waves—in some old Chinese dialects I wasn't able to speak—and it had been once a magnificent beach in Hong Kong's Sai Kung district, not far away from the peak we were climbing now. Before the climate change cataclysm that forced Earth back to Paleocene-like conditions and made it virtually uninhabitable, of course. The level of the sea in Asia had risen fast, gobbling up shores, coastal cities, and everything, in Sai Kung as elsewhere.

"Has anybody ever lived here, Meilan?"

"You mean—"

"Yes, two hundred years ago—before all hell got loose."

"In the surroundings, yes, but not here. This was an area as secluded as it is now. We chose to build our small settlement in this place because of its pristine beauty—defacements of the apocalypse nonetheless."

"That's exactly my next question. Why?" I asked.

"You tell me something else first: what's your interest in Sai Kung Place?"

"What's not to be interested?"

"This is Earth, an orbiting graveyard for nostalgic souls and old farts. And we're a decrepit settlement in a spot forgotten by history. Why us?"

I smiled at that image. Meilan was clever, and at least that was not a surprise to me, especially if what I suspected were true.

"You don't seem that decrepit to me. I might even date you, in a different setting."

"Like a typical male would always chase a woman who is not his mother or his blood sister."

I sighed. *I wouldn't date this lady, no matter the circumstances and her porcelain skin.* She was too smart for me.

"I'm here to find someone. A woman who left me with a riddle, and the key to solve it." I stretched the truth. There was the riddle, yes, but no key, and even less any desire to be found. But I decided to omit that detail for the moment and give Meilan an edited version of the truth. "Otherwise, I wouldn't be here, you know. I'm from Mare Imbrium, and nobody on the Moon knows about Sai Kung, either this one or Hong Kong's original district with the same name. Generally speaking, Moonwalkers are of European or American ancestry. They were among the first to leave Earth to colonize the Solar System. It's enough if they remember places called London or New York."

"Still, you know many things."

"I've done my homework before coming here. We're ignorant, not stupid."

No reply to that.

"I'm looking for the girl. You know whom I'm talking about, Meilan. I'm sure you don't have many visitors, from the Moon or elsewhere. Take me to her."

Meilan turned her head and looked at me with a polite smile on her mouth, even though her eyes remained unreadable. "Even if she's here, and I am not saying she is, it's not up to us to decide."

"Mind being less cryptic?"

"You're here, and in Sai Kung there are no secrets. It's impossible, you see."

"So?"

"So, if she wants to be found, you'll find her. Otherwise, you will leave the way you've come here: with no girl, and no answers."

You're wrong, beautiful woman. Knowing more about these people, and their mysterious Sai Kung colony that popped up in the middle of nowhere and remained off the radar for half a century on a planet in total disarray, was the principal reason for my presence, and how I had secured an Earth-bound, expensive vessel in the first place. Whatever I was going to learn during my stay here would be far more than everybody *else* knew, on the Moon or elsewhere.

. . .

"You said your name's Emil."

"Correct."

"What do you think of our little world, Emil Huygens? Do you like it?"

We were sitting under the shade of a banyan tree, looking at the sunset. A ravaged planet, but its sunsets are still the most spectacular in the whole Solar System, I was on the point of saying. But I stopped in time. My host probably would have had no idea what I was talking about.

The day had been good, no complaints about it. Since our arrival, Meilan had made sure I could explore the small community of Tai Long Wang at my own pace, and I was grateful for the opportunity. The place was as impressive as I had imagined it to be. Those one-story houses, all wood and pink marble, built on the slopes of the hills facing the mountain, looked unlike anything twenty-fourth century. They weren't even old. They were vestiges of another age, remnants of a past the planet did not harbor any longer. I didn't need to be a historian to know that kind of architecture belonged to the glorious Ming Dynasty of sixteenth-century China, of which nothing had survived on planet Earth after the great exodus. It had been either demolished by earthquakes, submerged by water, or simply reclaimed by a Mother Nature rather pissed-off with her human children.

But then, nestled in the primitive, enchanting landscape that was Tai Long Wang, there was a tiny, yet highly advanced He3D fusion plant. I also spotted a bizarre structure in metal and graphene, probably a greenhouse for genetic manipulation. The differing images gave one the impression that they resided in a time warp, one that had past and future entangled in some multiverse experiments gone wrong.

"Your home was not what I had expected," I replied cautiously.

"And what did you expect, young man?"

"It's too old, and at the same time too sophisticated, technology-wise. How is this possible?"

"It might be surprising at first glance, I agree, but it makes perfect sense. We examined what we had at hand and selected what was appropriate for the colony we wanted to create. If you give it a closer look, you'll see that everything has a logical explanation." Meilan smiled. "Adopting the historical culture of this place was the most sensible thing to do. Using low-impact architecture is advisable under any circumstance. It will help this planet heal, now that the acidity level of the seas is slowly getting back to normal. You mentioned technology: with an ocean within a hand's reach, He3D represents the cleanest and most convenient source of energy. Do you need me to continue?"

"That's the point. It's all so rational," I said.

"What's the problem with that?"

"It doesn't even look human."

"Considering the way *our* species has handled this planet, you should welcome a different approach." The voice came from behind, and I jerked back as if stung by a wasp. Dressed in an elegant, sky-blue qipao, Yumiko raised her hand, a faint smile on her face.

. . .

"You look great," she said, caressing my hair as if nothing had happened, as she had done so many times when we were still in Mare Imbrium. We hadn't talked a lot in the last twenty-four hours, and even now, she didn't seem inclined to talk. She poured tea and looked outside the oval-shaped window.

"This makes quite a change compared to the lunar surface," I said, not exactly sure where to start.

"It does, yes." She kissed my stomach, putting me down on my back again.

"Yumiko... stop."

"I thought you'd miss me."

"Having a good chat seems more important at the moment."

"There's nothing to say."

Her eyes were as dark and pensive as I remembered them, but with a strange light in them. They were peaceful in a way they had never been when she was living in my world, despite her successful career as one of the most brilliant young scientists of the Moon colonies.

"There's plenty. You went away without saying a word, only leaving behind that file with the coordinates of this place."

"I shredded that data," she interrupted me.

"Data handling is my job; it was not difficult to put them back together. You know, I'm not here because of you, or not only. It's that I couldn't believe what was in front of my eyes," I said, admiring a delicate dragonfly with transparent, green-blue wings. "I wasn't even aware places like this existed on Earth. They can't be from the twenty-first century; anybody still living by the coasts was evacuated to space colonies after the tsunami in 2097 that destroyed LA and most of California. It was one disaster too many," I continued. "Moreover, I wasn't alone in thinking things looked odd. I made a few inquiries, and not only among the Moon colonies; Earth Lower Orbit colonies knew little about Sai Kung Place, too. Where do these people come from? When exactly did they settle down here? Where in heaven and hell did they find the materials to build the place? And mind you, nobody even suspects the existence of a fusion reactor. The only thing the Upper-Asia orbiting colony—the one that has constantly monitored the region for the last 120 years—was positive about is there have been biosignatures for at least ninety years. Otherwise said, whoever they are, they built Tai Long Wan 2.0 when virtually everybody else fled the Earth's coastal regions. Now you tell me that they managed to survive and thrive in those conditions?"

Yumiko shook her head, as if she were listening to a petulant child.

"Does it seem far-fetched that I'm looking for explanations, or for something I can live with?"

"No, but what would it change?" she said. "You shouldn't have come here, Emil."

I stood up and got dressed. "If you don't reply, I'll ask Meilan directly."

"It's going to be a waste of time."

"You think she's going to lie to me?"

"These people don't lie." Yumiko shrugged. "No, it's because you won't be able to understand, let alone believe."

"We'll see about that."

I walked away without saying another word, but I couldn't avoid looking back at her tiny cottage. The pink structure flowed gracefully, harmoniously, like a flower blossoming out of a bed of rocks.

. . .

"We have a gathering tonight," Meilan said, her white-blond hair fluttering around her face like a golden halo.

I brushed the silky skin of her shoulders with the point of my fingers, relishing their texture. I had gone to see her for an explanation, but she had taken my hand and invited me into her lair. Maybe that was their way of welcoming visitors, as in some isolated cultures of Old Earth, I decided; in any case, it was not polite for me to refuse.

"A party?"

"If you want to call it that. We have a good time, we say thank you for this happy place that allows us a good life, and we partake herbal teas." She smiled. "These are not Chinese—you'd find them in the Mexican tradition."

"Herbal?"

"Extracted from cactuses, to be precise. We synthesize and use them during our gatherings. You should try them." She adjusted her qipao dress. "I know what is in your mind, the answers you're searching for, Emil. Have you thought that perhaps the right questions are all you need?"

"Not really. Which kind of questions are they?"

"The ones that make an answer unnecessary."

. . .

There were no artificial lights that night in Tai Long Wan, or in the whole of Sai Kung Place. I could only see small blue torches with a glimmering flame here and there, nestled in the green canopies scattered around and placed on the stone staircase to the peak.

I drank my tea in silence with Yumiko in my arms and observed with wary eyes the celebration unfolding during the night—a meal, dances, and incense offering to the spirits of the wind, the earth, and the sea—while my sense of reality was progressively eroded by the alkaloids. Sai Kung Place's inhabitants looked to me like one person with a thousand faces, all different and yet the same. Their shadows moved around like in slow-motion movies, with their old-looking costumes, their qipao, their pale, handsome features, and clear blue eyes; they were creatures of another time, a mythical one.

This place might just be not alive, I thought in a growing fear, while following those surreal scenes. They're ghouls, emerged from the hell of climate change, or vengeful spirits of a planet we killed with a monstrous science gone out of control. And they're going to exact revenge on my flesh. Or this colony doesn't even exist for real, a remote part of my consciousness screamed back. They're ghosts from a past we have somehow lost in the wrinkles of time the moment we abandoned this martyred Earth to decay and oblivion. Under the effect of the psychotropic tea, I could see their shapes blurring away into a golden aura, their features evolving and displaying the familiar, reassuring features of bodhisattvas. Guanyin, Avalokiteshvara, and Kannon all stared at me with the aquamarine eyes of Meilan, like visions of regret, nightmares of guilt.

In a dreamlike haze, I walked down the stairs, reaching the seaside, smelling salt and iodine. I plunged my hands in the surprisingly warm water. The glimpse of a seashell caught my eye. A pretty one, made of dark coral and a glittering, diamond-quality surface. Yet, its texture was tender and sweet, where I could have expected metal and ice. I had never seen anything like that, in any of the colonies with Earth-like habitats I had visited. Some surprise, I snickered, with my head flying out like a kite in the sky.

I picked it up and held it tightly in my hand, feeling blessed.

. . .

"Why did you leave the Moon for Sai Kung Place?" I asked, admiring dawn with her in my arms. "The real reason, Yumiko. I can't believe it was just scientific curiosity."

"Because the life I was living with you was the life of somebody else, one I didn't like."

"What was missing, Yumiko?"

"You'd better ask, 'What was there?'" Her eyes were bleak. There was no joy or sadness, only a tired look, and not just for the sleepless, drugged night. I had a strong feeling I was the guilty one, to disturb her peace.

"How did you find out about them?" I asked, changing the topic.

"I'm an exobiologist, Emil, one of the people who study the adaptation of carbon-based organisms in outer space. It's important for my job to examine the way climate change mutated the ones still living here on Earth—the few who survived the sixth mass extinction. The reports we received from this area didn't make any sense. The sourcing missions three years ago brought back living insects and arthropods supposedly extinct for millions of years. The same variety you see here in terms of architecture and customs, you can also find at a biological level, and more. It was not supposed to happen, Emil, not without the intervention of non-terrestrial creatures, at least."

"Did you know they were alien settlers before coming here?"

"I had strong hints. Those samples I've mentioned, the stunning environmental recovery in this area, the radio-impulse broadcast out of the heliosphere... When I arrived, the first thing I saw was that He3D plant the size of a dollhouse, which gave me the confirmation I waited for." She shrugged. "I came uninvited, but they let me stay, nonetheless. And in these months, I've learnt to love this place—more, to worship it."

"Do they really look like what I see, or it's just a mask they've put up for our own consumption?"

"Who cares? They come from far, far away, where everything's possible, even when it's unlikely."

"But why here? Why Earth in the first place?"

"I haven't asked. I'm not interested. Are you?"

I glanced at her. She'd grown more alien to my eyes than Meilan herself. I walked out of her tiny house and cried.

. . .

I didn't say goodbye to either Meilan or Yumiko. I had nothing to say to the first, and with the other, we had run out of words—words making any sense, at least. In fact, Yumiko and I hadn't shared words that made sense for a long time. I had just not realized it until that moment.

Before leaving, I destroyed all physical evidence I had collected of the settlement, including recordings, imagery, and rocks. I let the little creatures I had carefully stored in my biosampling unit go their way free, unharmed, and probably happier to stay there than following me to an unappealing lunar base. The outer colonies didn't need to know about Sai Kung any more than they did, and they were not going to know it from me. In a way, Meilan had been right: I was leaving without my girl and without answers. Questions? Right or not, they were not important any longer.

I kept my treasure, though—the odd-looking artifact collected on the seaside—safe in my spacesuit. A souvenir of that eerie place, and proof for the day I would be tempted to think it had been just a dream.

Walking down the marble and stone stairs, I looked one last time at the happy colony of Sai Kung Place, at the pinkish low houses, and its He3D plant by the blue sea. That place existed and thrived. Those gentle aliens made it come alive with a power only gods and superior beings could handle. I knew now those amazingly handsome creatures were no ghosts of the past; they were messengers from the future, or from an outer space we humans had only brushed but not understood yet, let alone conquered.

Mighty and together sweet, made cautious by the weight of wisdom, they had chosen to inhabit our planet the moment we had left it to its destiny. In their civilization endeavors they had mixed up cultures and species from different eras in the way humans combined garments as a fashion statement. They gave our old Earth a new life, from a nature in tatters and a poisoned ecosphere.

I've no doubt you're going to do a much better job than us, my friends. I got inside the cockpit of the spaceship taking me back to the Moon, and I silently wished them luck.

. . .

About the Author:

Russell Hemmell is a French-Italian transplant in Scotland, passionate about astrophysics, history, and Japanese manga. Recent work in *Cast of Wonders, Departure Mirror, Flame Tree Press*, and others. SFWA, HWA and Codexian. Find them online at their blog earthianhivemind.net and on Twitter @ SPBianchini.

Acknowledgments

I would like to thank everyone who helped turn this cli-fi anthology into a reality, including:

~ Internationally renowned nature photographer Kerstin Langenberger of Germany, whose second home is Iceland, for kindly allowing me to use her photograph "emaciated polar bear, Svalbard (2015)" as the cover photo for the first edition of this anthology.

~ Artist Sarah Stowasser of Germany, who also offered her artwork "polar bear" (a baby polar bear adrift on a shrinking ice floe) for use as the front cover of this anthology. I loved her art, and it was my initial choice for the front cover, but others convinced me that it was so darn *cute* that it might mislead potential readers into thinking this anthology was a children's book. If anyone publishes a cli-fi anthology for children, Sarah's artwork "polar bear" should be the cover art for that book.

~ Members of the Woodbridge Science Fiction & Fantasy Writers Meetup, which I founded in 2008, for not only pushing me to take this cli-fi anthology from a back-burner idea into a reality, but also contributing several stories to the anthology.

~ My wife, Corina, and our sons, David and Daniel, for their patience and support during the three years when I spent long hours in my home office compiling and editing this anthology.

~ Emotional support from our beloved fur baby Whiskers, the best cat in the world, who loved our family for twelve years before making the journey to Rainbow Bridge on November 10, 2021. You may have left our lives, Whiskers, but you will never leave our hearts, and your loving spirit remains in our house. No other cat can ever replace you (not even our new three-legged kitten, Tiny Tim).

~ The thirty-three talented authors and poets from around the world who contributed their amazing climate fiction to this anthology, for merely token compensation. Without your wonderful short stories, poems, and songs, this cli-fi anthology never would have been possible.

About the Editor

David Harten Watson is the award-winning author of the *Magicians Gold* series, including *Magic Teacher's Son* (a 2016 Eric Hoffer Award Winner, 2016 First Horizon Award Finalist, 2016 Eric Hoffer Award Grand Prize Short List, and 2015 IAN Book of the Year Award Finalist) its sequel, *Fortress of Gold* (a Reader's Favorite Five-Star book), and an upcoming third book in the series (tentatively titled *Prince Taryn and the Resistance*). He also wrote the science fiction novelette *Millennium Bomber: A Story of Digital Revenge*. David is a member of the US Army Brotherhood of Tankers (USABOT), the Mormon Church, the Campaign to Stop Killer Robots, and the Saber Legion.

David has worked in a dizzying array of jobs including US Army Armor officer at Fort Knox (experience that came in handy for his second novel, *Fortress of Gold*), camp counselor, teacher, tax preparer, car salesman, portrait photographer, track photographer, solar energy entrepreneur, and computer programmer.

Raised in snowy Buffalo, New York, David graduated from Calasanctius School (which closed shortly after his graduation, although he swears it wasn't his fault) and has degrees from Princeton, Canisius College, and Buffalo State College. He's the Organizer of the Woodbridge Science Fiction & Fantasy Writers Meetup, which he founded in 2008. In his free time, David enjoys herding cats, punching holes in paper, and making indie films. He had a major role in the feature-length, no-budget horror movie *Coordinates*, and he was executive producer, script writer, location scout, props master, and one of the actors in the upcoming short film *The Highs and Lows of Barefoot Pleasure*, which is based on one of the stories in this anthology. For details about the short film, see https://www.imdb.com/title/tt23838652/. He lives with his wife (a native of Ecuador, not the Kingdom of Eldor), their two sons, and two cats in smoggy New Jersey, where in his day job he's an IT Specialist. Follow him at www.davidhartenwatson.com and read more about this cli-fi anthology at www.cli-fi.org/.

www.ingramcontent.com/pod-product-compliance
Lightning Source LLC
Chambersburg PA
CBHW030923020726
47498CB00001B/89

9780578262857